HORNED MOONS & SAVAGE SANTAS

HORNED MOONS & SAVAGE SANTAS

Edited by CHUCK WECHSLER

Illustrations by DAN METZ

Published by LIVEOAK PRESS, Inc., Columbia, SC

Horned Moons & Savage Santas is published by LiveOak Press, Inc.

Editor & Publisher: Chuck Wechsler
Designer: Ryan Stalvey

Publisher's Note: Every effort has been made to find the copyright holder for each story.

Printed in the United States.

First Edition
Library of Congress Control Number 2005932988
ISBN 0-9660212-5-8

When you have loved three things all your life, from the earliest you can remember: to fish, to shoot and later to read; and when, all your life, the necessity to write has been your master, you learn to remember more fishing and shooting and reading than anything else and that is a pleasure.
Ernest Hemingway, "Remembering Shooting-Flying," 1935

V

INTRODUCTION

by Chuck Wechsler

As the publisher of *Sporting Classics*, I've been blessed with a number of perks, such as trips to the world's best hunting and fishing destinations, the opportunity to try out the latest and finest sporting equipment, and on a daily basis, being able to work with a lot of terrific people in our industry. But after twenty years of editing the magazine, I know that nothing surpasses the joy I derive from discovering a good story.

I was in my early teens when I stumbled upon the treasure-trove of great hunting and fishing stories in the leading outdoor magazines. Many of those articles were ultimately published in books that we now regard as the classics in outdoor literature. Robert Ruark's *The Old Man and the Boy*, Gordon MacQuarrie's *Old Duck Hunters and Other Drivel*, Howard Walden's *Big Stony* – all were printed years ago, but their stories are as wonderful to read today as when they were written. Each of these books is well represented in this anthology.

Over the years, many other stories have been brought to my attention by *Sporting Classics* readers. "Savage Santa," by legendary western artist Charles M. Russell, is a good example. One of our loyal subscribers shared Russell's delightful, off-beat tale with us. Other pass-alongs in this collection include "The Christmas Rifle" (we still don't know the author's name) and Beryl Markham's "I Don't Want to Shoot an Elephant," a chapter from *West With the Night*, which Ernest Hemingway praised as one of the best books ever written about Africa.

Then there is the thrill of finding a gem among the manuscripts sent in by freelance writers. Most of these submittals never make it onto the pages of *Sporting Classics*, but occasionally there's a story of compelling literary merit. "Something Special" by Peter Wood and "Rogue Male" by Kenneth Cameron were both unsolicited articles that quickly found a home in the magazine and now in this anthology.

And finally there are the writings of *Sporting Classics'* longtime contributing and senior editors, including Tom Davis, Michael McIntosh, Mike Gaddis, Todd Tanner and Ken Kirkeby. All are talented, established authors, whose stories are always engaging and enjoyable to read.

This volume, which commemorates *Sporting Classics'* twenty-fifth anniversary, includes forty-five of our favorite magazine features from the past dozen years. It comes in the wake of two previous anthologies, *River Gods & Spotted Devils* (1988) and *Last Casts & Stolen Hunts* (1993).

All three books and their stories are centered around hunting and fishing and the places we treasure so passionately – wilderness streams and windswept marshes, piney woodlands and high mountain meadows. But what makes these stories truly endearing are the characters. Ordinary people. Fascinating, complex people. People who share strong convictions and deep passions, and each one eminently likable. On these pages you'll meet a British brigadier general hooked on fishing . . . A crusty old-timer who finds himself guiding a liberated young miss . . . A night cook at a sleazy cafe who becomes one of the greatest duck hunters on the Eastern Shore. And for a truly unusual perspective, there's a savvy old trout who can stretch the truth better than the anglers who pursue him.

While compiling these stories, I was continually reminded of my long-held opinion that the ability to write – to write *really well* – is the most impressive of man's skills. Painters, sculptors and baseball players are admittedly born with certain gifts, and with practice, can attain a high degree of competence and success. Writers likewise can improve on their craft, but only a fortunate few have that rare combination of intelligence and imagination to build a simple thought or idea into an entertaining story.

This book, then, is a celebration – a tribute to all of these writers who over the past twenty-five years have helped make *Sporting Classics* one of America's most respected outdoor magazines. Some of these selections are pure fiction, like Michael McIntosh's "Troll," a fanciful meeting of two worlds on a secluded trout stream, and Corey Ford's "The Road to Tinkhamtown," regarded by many as the best outdoor story ever written. This original, unedited version of "Tinkhamtown," incidentally, has never appeared in any book – until now.

Mixed throughout this treasury are several deeply personal essays – introspective, thought-provoking pieces that explore our passions for sport, such as Gene Hill's "The Gift" and Hemingway's "Remembering Shooting-Flying." You'll also find in-depth, meticulously researched articles, such as Tom Davis' "The Day the Duck Hunters Died" and Ken Kirkeby's "Congo Bongo," the story behind the most difficult and dangerous hunt ever made.

As you journey through this book, I hope you will come to share my thrill of discovery for each and every story. There is a timeless quality to these tales, and it is my fervent wish that you will come to treasure them as I have – as cherished legacies to pass along for generations to come. – *Chuck Wechsler*

CONTENTS

REMEMBERING SHOOTING-FLYING

What is it about the sound of whirring wings that moves us more than any love of country? In this 1935 classic from Esquire, *the legendary author shares his lifelong fascination with bird hunting the world over.*

By Ernest Hemingway

There is a heavy norther blowing; the gulf is too rough to fish and there is no shooting now. When you are through work it is nearly dark and you can ride out on the boulevard by the sea and throw clay targets with a hand trap against this gale and they will dip and jump and rise into strange angles like a jacksnipe in the wind. Or you can throw them out with the gale behind them and they will go like a teal over the water. Or you can get down below the sea wall and have someone throw them out high over your head riding the wind, but if you puff one into black dust you cannot pretend it was an old cock pheasant unless you are a better pretender than I am. The trouble is there isn't any thud, nor is there the line of bare trees, nor are you standing on a wet, leaf-strewn road, nor do you hear the beaters, nor the racket when a cock gets up and, as he tops the trees, you are on him, then ahead of him, and at the shot he turns over and there is that thump when he lands. Shooting driven pheasants is worth whatever you pay for it.

But when you cannot shoot you can remember shooting and I would rather stay home, now, this afternoon and write about it than go out and sail clay saucers in the wind, trying to break them and wishing they were what they're not.

When you have been lucky in your life you find that just about the time the best of the books run out (and I would rather read again for the first time *Anna Karenina, Far Away and Long Ago, Buddenbrooks, Wuthering Heights, Madame Bovary, War and Peace, A Sportsman's Sketches, The Brothers Karamazov, Hail and Farewell, Huckleberry Finn, Winesburg, Ohio, La Reine Margot, La Maison Tellier, Le Rouge et le Noire, La Chartreuse de Parme, Dubliners, Yeat's Autobiographies* and a few others than have an assured income of a million dollars a year), you have a lot of damned fine things that you can remember. Then when the time is over in which you have done the things that you can now remember, and while you are doing other things, you find that you can read the books again and, always, there are a few, a very few, good new ones. Last year there was *La Condition Humaine* by André Malraux. It was translated, I do not know how well, as *Man's Fate*, and sometimes it is as good as Stendhal and that is something no prose writer has been in France for over fifty years.

But this is supposed to be about shooting, not about books, although some of the best shooting I remember was in Tolstoi and I have often wondered how the snipe fly in Russia now and whether shooting pheasants is counter-revolutionary. When you have loved three things all your life, from the earliest you can remember: to fish, to shoot and later to read; and when, all your life, the necessity to write has been your master, you learn to remember more fishing and shooting and reading than anything else and that is a pleasure.

You can remember the first snipe you ever hit walking on the prairie with your father. How the jacksnipe rose with a jump and you hit him on the second swerve and had to wade out into a slough after him and brought him in wet, holding him by the bill, as proud as a bird dog, and you can remember all the snipe since in many places. You can remember the miracle it seemed when you hit your first pheasant when he roared up from under your feet to top a sweet briar thicket and fell with his wings pounding and you had to wait till after dark to bring him into town because they were protected, and you can feel the bulk of him still inside your shirt with his long tail up under your armpit, walking into town in the dark along the dirt road that is now North Avenue where the gypsy wagons used to camp when there was prairie out to the Des Plaines River where Wallace Evans had a game farm and the big woods ran along the river where the Indian mounds were.

I came by there five years ago and where I shot that pheasant there was a hotdog place and filling station and the north prairie, where we hunted snipe in the spring and skated on the sloughs when they froze in the

2

winter, was all a subdivision of mean houses, and in the town, the house where I was born was gone and they had cut down the oak trees and built an apartment house close out against the street. So I was glad I went away from there as soon as I did. Because when you like to shoot and fish you have to move often and always farther out and it doesn't make any difference what they do when you are gone.

The first covey of partridges I ever saw, they were ruffed grouse but we called them partridges up there, was with my father and an Indian named Simon Green and we came on them dusting and feeding in the sun beside the grist mill on Horton's Creek in Michigan. They looked as big as turkeys to me and I was so excited with the whirr of the wings that I missed both shots I had, while my father, shooting an old lever action Winchester pump, killed five out of the covey and I can remember the Indian picking them up and laughing. He was an old fat Indian, a great admirer of my father, and when I look back at that shooting I am a great admirer of my father too. He was a beautiful shot, one of the fastest I have ever seen; but he was too nervous to be a great money shot.

Then I remember shooting quail with him when I do not think I could have been more than ten years old, and he was showing me off, having me shoot pigeons that were flying around a barn, and some way I broke the hammer spring in my single barrel 20 gauge and the only gun down there at my uncle's place in Southern Illinois that no one was shooting was a big old L.C. Smith double that weighed, probably, nine pounds. I could not hit anything with it and it kicked me so it made my nose bleed. I was afraid to shoot it and I got awfully tired carrying it and my father had left me standing in a thickety patch of timber while he was working out the singles from a covey we had scattered. There was a red bird up in a tree and then I looked down and under the tree was a quail, freshly dead. I picked it up and it was still warm. My father had evidently hit it when the covey went up with a stray pellet and it had flown this far and dropped. I looked around to see nobody was in sight and then, laying the quail down by my feet, shut both my eyes and pulled the trigger on that old double barrel. It kicked me against the tree and when I opened it up I found it had doubled and fired both barrels at once and my ears were ringing and my nose was bleeding. But I picked the quail up, reloaded the gun, wiped my nose and set out to find my father. I was sick of not hitting any.

"Did you get one, Ernie?"

I held it up.

"It's a cock," he said. "See his white throat? It's a beauty."

But I had a lump in my stomach that felt like a baseball from lying to him and that night I remember crying with my head under the patchwork quilt after he was asleep because I had lied to him. If he would have waked up I would have told him, I think. But he was tired and sleeping heavily. I never told him.

So I won't think any more about that but I remember now how I broke the spring in the 20 gauge. It was from snapping the hammer on an empty chamber practicing swinging on the pigeons after they wouldn't let me shoot any more. And some older boys came along the road when I was carrying the pigeons from the barn to the house and one of them said I didn't shoot those pigeons. I called him a liar and the smaller of the two whipped hell out of me. That was an unlucky trip.

On a day as cold as this you can remember duck shooting in the blind, hearing their wings go *whichy-chu-chu-chu* in the dark before daylight. That is the first thing I remember of ducks; the whistly, silk tearing sound the fast wingbeats make; just as what you remember first of geese is how slow they seem to go when they are traveling, and yet they are moving so fast that the first one you ever killed was two behind the one you shot at, and all that night you kept waking up and remembering how he folded up and fell. While the woodcock is an easy bird to hit, with a soft flight like an owl, and if you do miss him he will probably pitch down and give you another shot. But what a bird to eat flambé with armagnac cooked in his own juice and butter, a little mustard added to make a sauce, with two strips of bacon and pommes soufflé and Corton, Pommard, Beaune or Chambertin to drink.

Now it is colder still and we found ptarmigan in the rocks on a high plain above and to the left of the glacier by the Madelener-haus in the Vorarlberg with it blowing a blizzard and the next day we followed a fox track all day on skis and saw where he had caught a ptarmigan underneath the snow. We never saw the fox.

There were chamois up in that country too and blackcock in the woods below the timberline and big hares that you found sometimes at night when we were coming home along the road. We ate them jugged and drank Tyroler wine. And why, today, remember misses?

There were lots of partridges outside of Constantinople and we used to have them roasted and start the meal with a bowl of caviar, the kind you never will be able to afford again, pale grey, the grains as big as buckshot and a little vodka with it, and then the partridges, not overdone, so that when you cut them there was the juice, drinking Caucasus burgundy, and serving French fried potatoes with them and then a salad with roquefort dressing and another bottle of what was the number of that wine? They all had numbers. Sixty-one, I think it was.

And did you ever see the quick, smooth-lifting, reaching flight the lesser bustard has, or make a double on them, right and left, or shoot at flighting sand grouse coming to water early in the morning and see the great variety of shots they give and hear the cackling sound they make

4

when flighting, a little like the noise of prairie chickens on the plains when they go off with fast beat of wings and soar stiff-winged, and see a coyote watching you a long way out of range and see an antelope turn and stare and lift his head when he hears the shotgun thud? Sand grouse, of course, fly nothing like a prairie chicken. They have a cutting, swooping flight like pigeons but they make that grouse-like cackle, and with the lesser bustard and the teal, there is no bird to beat them for the pan, the griddle or the oven.

So you recall a curlew that came in along the beach one time in a storm when you were shooting plover, and jumping teal along a water-course that cut a plain on a different continent, and having a hyena come out of the grass when you were trying to stalk up on a pool and see him turn and look at ten yards and let him have it with the shotgun in his ugly face, and standing, to your waist in water, whistling a flock of golden plover back, and then, back in the winter woods, shooting ruffed grouse along a trout stream where only an otter fished now, and all the places and the different flights of birds, jumping three mallards now, down where the beavers cut away the cottonwoods, and seeing the drake tower, white-breasted, green-headed, climbing and get above him and splash him in the old Clark's Fork, walking along the bank watching him until he floated onto a pebbly bar.

Then there are sage hens, wild as hawks that time, the biggest grouse of all, getting up out of range, and out of range, until you came around an alfalfa stack and four whirred up one after the other at your feet almost and, later walking home in your hunting coat they seemed to weigh a ton.

I think they all were made to shoot because if they were not why did they give them that whirr of wings that moves you suddenly more than any love of country? Why did they make them all so good to eat and why did they make the ones with silent flight like woodcock, snipe and lesser bustard, better eating even than the rest?

Why does the curlew have that voice, and who thought up the plover's call, which takes the place of noise of wings, to give us that catharsis wingshooting has given to men since they stopped flying hawks and took to fowling pieces? I think that they were made to shoot and some of us were made to shoot them and if that is not so well, never say we did not tell you that we liked it.

Reprinted with permission of Scribner, an imprint of Simon & Schuster Adult Publishing Group, from BY-LINE: ERNEST HEMINGWAY by William White. Copyright ©1935 by Ernest Hemingway. Copyright© renewed 1963 by Mary Hemingway and By-Line Ernest Hemingway, Inc. Originally published in Esquire *magazine.*

HORNED MOONS & SAVAGE SANTAS

HORNED MOON

His old friend had been driven to track one more lion, and now as they watched the ghost cat, they reveled in the knowledge they were sharing a truly incredible moment.

By C. S. Cushing

Somewhere in the forest came the warbling song of a night bird. Melodic, sweet sounds, but urgent and unanswered. It was quiet after that, except for the gentle breeze that played among the trees, mingling with the sound of water. Leaf greens of aspens and lodge-pole pines in the October dawn seemed to drip colors into clear pools along the Gallatin River in Montana.

Trailing moss beneath the water's surface played among ancient rocks, and fluttered above pebbles and sand in the gentle current, hiding native trout. Mist rose off treetops from the rain that had fallen during the night, like smoke from a hundred campfires. An aroma lifted off the streambank – eternal and remembered, nature's gifts, delicate scenes and scenes that men seek and understand, and find only in wilderness.

Willard looked across the creek to where he knew Nils sat silent, finding it difficult to pick him out amidst the foliage. They had gone to the river just before midnight when wind and rain muffled their descent, washed away

7

tracks and drowned their scent. It had been two days since they'd spotted tracks where the mountain lion had come to drink, crossing over when she was done and disappearing into quaking aspens and mountain meadows.

They'd camped two miles from the spot and this was their second night's vigil for two men huddled in green ponchos, one bent on shooting a cougar, the other watchful, worried about his friend.

Nils sold a camera shop in Sacramento, California in 1950 at the age of sixty-five, and Willard, his next-door neighbor, writer for the *Sacramento Bulletin*, retired that same year at sixty-three.

After retirement, Willard saw his friend slowly disappear into himself and then reemerge, and knew that Nils was driven by something. The note came in May of 1955, mailed and delivered by a post office letter carrier one address away.

Willard, it's time. I want to track one more mountain lion, maybe kill it. I've got this feeling! Nils

Willard slipped the worn sheet of paper from his pocket and read the words again without seeing them, for he knew them by heart. He felt a cold in his belly that no fall morning mist could settle there. He thought about their thirty-year friendship, the delivered note and Nils Walker's unwillingness or inability to speak words of explanation, that one time.

The cougar appeared without sound or warning. One minute the creek's bank was void of any living thing, and then she was there. Willard guessed her to be between four and six years old. Big, fluid and in her prime as she stood upwind from them not fifty feet away. One ear was split. Dark scars on her shoulder and head. She looked directly at Willard for a time not seeing him, then lowered her body on spring-steel legs, bent her head toward cold water and drank, her red tongue lapping up the life-giving liquid in noisy slurps.

The sights of Willard's Winchester rifle settled on the cougar, his finger curled at the trigger, waiting. When the sound came, it was unexpected, out of character, but accepted.

Bang!

The mountain lion exploded up away from the river in a blur of tawny brown motion, leaving behind a cascade of water droplets suspended in midair after her passing. An eye blink's span was all the time it took for her to disappear among aspens, tail high, shifting as she changed direction, shoulder and hip muscles driving her in thirty-foot bounds.

Neither man moved for a long time, satisfied to remain silent – each lost in his own thoughts and feelings. Willard felt tears trickle down his cheeks into hair by his upper lip and was unashamed at their coming. He tasted salty wetness and finally moved a gloved hand up to wipe them away. He eased himself up off the ground by degrees to a chorus of creaking bones and low

8

moans. Nils was standing too, gently stretching cramped muscles, unaccustomed to such long absence of motion.

"You get buck fever?" Willard asked, his voice soft but carrying far.

Nils took his time. "She didn't even know we were here. God! *Ain't that something?*"

"Thought you wanted to shoot a lion?"

"Did, but couldn't. Not that one, probably never again," Nils said, as he moved toward the water.

Willard waded into the river and felt the pull of the current against his legs. He felt a boy's joy as he moved, watching Nils' face, feeling the movement of the earth in the river, the current unique, complicated and urgent in its journey, and felt something else.

They were standing close then, and could read each other's eyes. Knowing glances between old friends satisfied with their lives, and thankful in the knowledge that the moment had been shared – each seeing and feeling it differently, but sure and confident in the moist-eyed looks passed back and forth.

"I suppose you'll be wanting to travel to Africa, hunt a rhino and not shoot that either," Willard said.

Nils smiled. "If I do, you'll be there, too."

Willard nodded, grinned. "We hunt rhino, one of us better shoot. We need to toast that cougar."

"Tomorrow, after we've had sleep." Nils stared at the spot where the mountain lion had vanished, nodded and turned toward camp.

Willard got up shortly after sunrise, broke his tent down and packed his gear. Cowboy coffee boiled in a blackened pot over the fire as Willard waited for Nils. After a while he went over and kicked at the side of his friend's tent. "Old man, it's time to go."

There was no answer. He kicked again, harder. Nothing stirred inside the tent. Willard bent down and unzipped the tent door. There lay his friend in that peaceful sleep he would not wake from.

"Damn," Willard said, softly. "You had a feeling about dying, didn't you."

He knew Nils would want it that way, out in the back country, someplace where he could feel wind in his hair. They had talked about dying a few times long ago. before retirement, but it didn't make the pain any easier. Had the trip been worth it? *Yeah*, he thought. *Yeah!*

I t was after dark when a gray-bearded, long-haired old man entered the Cattleman's Bar in Livingston, and quietly ordered a round of drinks from the bartender's best bottle.

"Leave it on the bar, I might want another."

Willard walked toward five men sitting on barstools in scuffed boots, Levi's, colorful western shirts, long black dusters and tall, sweat-stained hats on their heads.

"A seventy-year old man died in his sleep this morning on the Gallatin. His name was Nils Walker, my friend. We'd planned on standing here drinking a toast. I'd be obliged if you'd share that toast with me."

The oldest of the men spoke. "Old-timer, you say the words and we'll do the honors."

Willard's eyes grew shiny bright as tears welled and ran down his cheeks. He didn't look away from the hard-eyed men staring at him. His voice came soft, but clear. "To Nils, and to the spirit of the mountain . . . the ghost cat . . . the cougar."

Glasses touched sudden and final as each man downed his shot glass of raw whiskey. The cowboy who'd spoken reached for the bottle and filled the glasses full again. "Mister, if you don't mind, I'd like to do that one more time."

"No sir, I don't mind," Willard said.

Glasses were raised again as the square-jawed cowman spoke. "And to the *Hombre* who rode the trail with him."

They took their whiskey straight up and neat that night in a frontier cattle and rail town. Outside, a horned moon hung above the Beartooth and Crazy mountains, and wind-swept stars danced like fireflies across the black hearth of the Montana sky.

Along the Gallatin River, there remained what had always been – the sound of water and the gentle rustling of wind in trees in a land filled with earthly splendor.

And one other sound, faint as the fall of a feather, as the ghost cat inspected the sites where two men had hidden, then left her mark and moved to the river. With delicate nostrils flared, she sampled the tainted wind, lowered herself . . . and drank.

BIRTHDAY ON THE MANITOU

In this essay from The Singing Wilderness, his first book published in 1945, Sigurd Olson relives an encounter with another fisherman on the Manitou River, one of the many picturesque trout streams flowing into Lake Superior. Anyone who enjoys the solitude of angling, who returns time after time to a favorite fishing hole, will relate to this intimate tale.

By Sigurd F. Olson

While casting the long riffle below the pool, I became aware that I was not alone, that someone was there on the river with me. It wasn't that I actually heard anything, just a vague realization. I stopped and listened, but could hear nothing – only the plaintive calling of a whitethroat and the gurgling of the current beneath the alders.

I began to cast again and hooked a ten-incher from behind a boulder in midstream. Then I heard the soft unmistakable swish of a rod. It came from upstream, at the head of the big pool. There was no doubt now: *swish, swish, swish,* the sound of a man getting out his line. I waded out of the river and moved up toward the sound, and suddenly the joy of the morning was gone.

For years I had been coming to the headwaters of the Manitou over as rough and rugged a trail as there is along the North Shore of Lake Superior, windfalls and tangled jungles of hazel brush, rocks and muskeg, black flies and mosquitoes. But because the river was mine alone when I got there, it

11

had always been worth the effort. But now the sparkle was gone. I knew I was selfish to feel as I did about the Manitou. It was not mine any more than anyone else's, but I had always felt a certain kind of ownership there based on the fact that I had earned the right to enjoy it.

I climbed a little knoll above the big pool where I could watch without being detected. A stranger was casting a rise toward the far end. He was a small man, a spare little figure standing knee deep exactly where I used to stand at the point where the upstream riffle enters the pool. He was working the bank as though he had been there many times before and knew where to place his fly. His legs were braced and he made each cast as if afraid the force of it might throw him off balance. He was old. I could see that, far too old to be fighting fast, treacherous waters and slippery boulders of the Manitou. I saw him take a little trout and tremble with the effort of landing it, then a larger one. He waded cautiously back toward the shallows, slipped and almost fell when he stopped to use his net.

As yet he had not seen me and I had made no sound. A trout was rising again in the far end of the pool and he was trying hard to reach it. And then I began to wonder how he had come in and what it must have taken for the old man to negotiate that long trail.

As I watched, my resentment began to leave and I knew that, whatever the reason for his coming in, it must have been very important. Far better to share the river with someone who felt as I did, and I began to look with a certain approval at the way he blended into his background, at his weather-beaten coat, the ancient, patched-up creel, the torn hat band with its fringe of flies. He was part of the rocks and trees and the music of running water.

He was casting carefully once more, and so absorbed was he that he never once looked up toward where I stood. The fine leader soared above the pool, and each time it unfurled, a trout at the far end would break water and slap the fly with its tail. For a few moments he studied the surface, then reached down and picked up a fly eddying near him. After examining it intently, he thumbed slowly through his book. Selecting a new fly, he tied it on and began casting once more. This time the trout arched above it and the old man struck. The fish was on – not a large one, but he played it as carefully as though it weighed three pounds. Never wasting a motion, he anticipated every rush. At last the trout circled slowly at his feet. As he reached with his net, he looked up and saw me.

There was no surprise, just a smile and a nod as though he had known I was there all the time. There were fine wrinkles at the corners of his eyes, and in them was the happy look of a man who was doing something he wanted to do more than anything else in the world. Wading slowly out of the stream he came over to where I sat.

12

"Hello," he said, breathing hard. "You know the Manitou, too."

"Been here many times," I answered. "Nice trout in that pool."

He opened up his creel and showed me the three he had just taken, turning them over so I could see the flame along the undersides, the crimson spots and the mottling of the brown and green.

"Pretty," he said. "Worth hiking in here just to see them again."

He took off the old creel. It was laced with rawhide where the willow withes were pulling apart, was dark as willow gets through many years of use. He placed it in the shade of a mossy boulder just above the water, hung his net in a bush alongside, and stood his rod against a tree. Then he sat down on the bank beside me.

"Today is my birthday," he volunteered. "Eighty years old, and this little trip is a sort of celebration. Used to make it every year in the old days, but now it's been a long time since I came in."

He pulled out his pipe, tamped it full of tobacco, drew long and luxuriously as he settled back against a pine stump.

"Had to see the old river once more, take a crack at the old pool. Came in here the first time when I was cruising timber for one of the outfits along the North Shore. You should have seen the river then, all big pine and the water so dark you couldn't see the bottom anywhere. Trout in here then, big ones, three- and four-pounders lying in all the pools and the rapids fairly alive with their jumping."

"Still some nice ones if you hit it right," I said. "Always a big one waiting in the deep end of the big pool, and when there is a hatch on, most anything can happen."

"Yes, I know," he answered, "and the river is still mighty pretty, but mostly I wanted to come in here just to remember."

A trout was rising again, a good one, and the ripples circled grandly until they hit the bank.

"Just before dusk he'll take a gray hackle, perhaps a gray with a yellow body."

But the old man wasn't listening, nor was he watching the rise. He was seeing the river as it used to be.

"Where we're sitting right now, there was a stand of pine four feet through at the butt, so thick you could barely see the sky through the tops. No brush then, not a bit of popple or hazel except in the gullies, no windfalls or blackberries either – just a smooth brown carpet of needles as far as you could see. Could drive a two-horse team anywhere through these woods."

His face was alight with his memories, and his blue eyes looked past me down the river, took in the pool, the riffles below, and the whole series of little pools for a mile downstream. I followed his gaze and for a moment it seemed as though I had never seen the Manitou before. The old stumps blackened and broken by fire and decay became great pines, and the brush-choked banks were clean and deep with centuries of duff. The water before us disappeared in perennial shadows and the stream was full to overflowing once more. Rocks that now protruded were hidden beneath the surface, and from their tops floated long streams of waving moss. The water eddied and swirled around them, and trout lay in the wakes waiting for a fly.

Then while I watched, the vision seemed to fade and I saw again the poplar-covered banks, the bright sunlight on the water, and the old man dozing quietly beside me. He must have heard me stir, for he opened his eyes wide, smiled and rose painfully to his feet.

"Must have been dreaming a bit," he said. "I've a feeling there's another big one waiting in that pool. Better work in there, son, and take him."

I told him that I had a partner waiting for me downstream and that I'd have to hurry or I'd miss him. As I started to leave, he strapped on his battle-worn creel and picked his way once more down to the water's edge.

"Happy Birthday!" I yelled.

He waved his rod in salute, and I left him there casting quietly, hiked clear around the pool so I wouldn't spoil his chances with the big one at the far end. The whitethroats were singing again and high up in the sky the nighthawks were beginning to zoom. There was no wind – a perfect night for a May-fly hatch on the big pool.

From The Singing Wilderness *by Sigurd F. Olson, copyright© 1956 by Sigurd F. Olson. Used by permission of Alfred A. Knopf, a division of Random House, Inc.*

THE BIG BUCK OF DEEP CANYON

Old Hoodoo had outwitted and outmaneuvered every hunter in the county, and it would take a plan that was truly out-of-the-ordinary to get him.

By Jack O'Connor

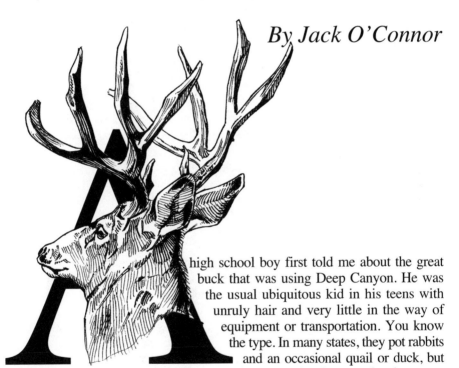

high school boy first told me about the great buck that was using Deep Canyon. He was the usual ubiquitous kid in his teens with unruly hair and very little in the way of equipment or transportation. You know the type. In many states, they pot rabbits and an occasional quail or duck, but in some parts of the country where big game is present, they become deer hunters.

"You ought to of seen him!" he told me. I was mooching along, hoping for a shot at some little ole forkhorn, when up pops this big buck on the other side of the canyon, about 150 yards away. Gee, he had a rack of horns on his head you could hang out a washing on!

"Well, I up and cut loose at him with Pa's old .30-30, but the barrell's kind of o' rusty and it don't shoot very strong any more. Anyway, I never touched him. He ran into the brush, but pretty soon he popped up on a ridge above me and about four hundred yards away. He stopped then and looked at me for a minute before he went down on the other side. Gee, if I'd of had one of them Springfields like

15

yours with a telescope sight on it, I'd of killed him sure!"

"So he was really big, was he?" I asked.

"Big? Say, you ought to of seen him! He was a whopper! They don't make 'em much bigger mister."

I was just a bit skeptical about that big fellow. Deep Canyon was pretty deer country, but most of the deer there were does, fawns and young bucks. Sunday hunters and boys like this one kept the buck population pretty well thinned out there. Most of them were knocked off before they matured. I had hunted there occasionally, but though I usually saw bucks, I had never seen any such monster as this lad described.

Yet the Deep Canyon country was a pretty place – no doubt of that. An old road to an abandoned corral and ranchhouse ran through three or four miles of rolling country wooded with pinon and cedar and buck-brush – all stuff that furnishes deer food when the snows come. Beyond the ranch the hills became mountains, so rough that for ten miles no road had ever been built and no automobile could travel.

It was back beyond the ranch that most of the Sunday hunters killed their bucks, in or near Deep Canyon, which was striped with gray limestone and orange sandstone and wooded, down where it was deep and cool, with yellow pines and a few spruce and fir. There were always food and water there; the lions had been pretty well thinned out, and if it hadn't been so thoroughly hunted it would have teemed with deer.

I next heard about the big buck from my barber. "Say, you should have been with me Sunday," he greeted me when I went in for a haircut. "I saw the doggondest big buck I've ever seen!"

"Where did you see him?" I asked.

"Deep Canyon."

"So he really was a whopper?"

"I'll say he was! He got up at around three hundred steps, but even at that distance I could tell he had an awful head of horns." He held up a brawny arm. "Shucks, those horns of his must be as thick through at the base as my arm!"

"Did you shoot at him?"

"I'll say I did! I cut loose at him with a whole magazine full of .30-30s. I could see the dust kicking up all around him, but I never touched him."

By the end of the week I had had three more reports on the big buck. He was very large and very wide, they all said. Still a bit skeptical, for I had seen many "whoppers" turn out to be very ordinary deer, I decided to see what could be done.

That first day I saw him, but I didn't even get a shot. I had topped the first ridge and was in a maze of draws and canyons that all fed into Deep Canyon. Suddenly I saw an enormous buck running up a ridge almost five hundred yards away. He was much too far away to shoot at, so I sat down and used the glasses. He was big, and his antlers had an extraordinary spread.

Just as he got on top, he stopped against the skyline and watched me for a moment. I could see those massive antlers in sharp relief against the pale sky.

16

They were impressive, no doubt of it, and for a moment I was tempted to try a shot. But I didn't. At that distance I had a very slim chance of hitting him, and he had been shot at plenty and was wild enough as it was.

I saw the big fellow twice again that season. Another time he stood against the skyline and allowed me to feast my eyes on those glorious horns. The third time he was less than three hundred yards from me, running though thick cedar like a fleeing ghost – head thrown back, great antlers lying along his powerful shoulders.

Through the scope he was a picture of power, speed and wildness incarnate – the very spirit of that wild rugged country.

I shot four times, but didn't hit him. That's easy enough to explain. I nearly always shoot behind running game in timber. Nevertheless, many claimed no one could hit him. A couple of hundred shots must have been fired at him that first season, yet not one connected. About that time he began to be called the hoodooed buck.

Later he came to be known as Old Hoodoo.

Shortly after the season closed, a wandering cowboy, unarmed and looking for some strays, invaded the Deep Canyon country. He claimed to have got so close to the big buck that he could count the points on his antlers. The story spread far and wide and grew in the telling. Presently it was accepted on all sides that the big buck was a ten-pointer, which in the West means ten points *to a side*.

When the next season came around, I hunted Old Hoodoo long and faithfully. I saw him several times, and shot at him twice, but in the end I had to go elsewhere to get my buck. Several hundred cartridges must have been fired at him that year, but he stayed in a relatively limited area. Why, I do not know. Perhaps the wisdom and instincts of animals go farther than we think and he knew there were many does, but no big bucks in that particular area. Perhaps he wanted to set up his practice where competition would be less keen.

After the deer season closed that year and a fairly high percentage of all the hunters in town had either seen him or shot at him, he was still at his old stand. Many a tale was told of his wisdom, his sagacity, his almost incredible wariness.

Late November was exceptionally mild. There had been almost no snow even in that high altitude, and though the nights were cold, the days were warm and balmy. So one Saturday my wife and I decided to picnic near the abandoned ranch and to hike back to the canyon and see some deer. It was a fine day. The weather was unseasonably warm and the sky was very blue except for a few misty streamers of clouds scudding along under the impetus of some lofty wind – snow clouds, they proved later. After we had eaten, we picked up glasses and camera and started up the first draw for the top.

We had hardly entered when my wife pointed above us and called out, "Look, Jack! Deer!"

They had been lying down at the head of the draw and they had moved as soon as the rising air had carried our scent to them. Among them was the big buck. The rutting season was at its peak then, and he had collected his harem – quite a harem at that, as there were fourteen of them and I think every one was a mature doe.

My great buck was extremely ungallant that afternoon. Instead of guarding his girl friends, he took a quick, lowheaded sneak off to the left while they jittered around on the ridge, looked us over, then finally went down on the other side. The man-smell in his nostrils had probably scared the love-lust out of him for the time being. He may have recognized my own individual smell for all I know – surely he had smelled me enough.

But I cut around to the left to see if I could spot him again. He was a grand fellow, and the sight of him always thrilled and elated me and made me feel ten years younger. And, curiously enough, I saw him!

On top a strong wind was blowing, and I eased along, alert for the flash of gray that would mean his presence. Then suddenly I heard rocks rolling, and he materialized before me, not more than thirty feet away, like a genie out of a bottle. For several long seconds – it seemed like five minutes – he stood there, looking me in the eye as if to read my very soul.

I like to think now that this wise old buck realized the deer season was over and, furthermore, knew I didn't have a rifle. Probably that is romanticizing. Since the wind was blowing so strongly directly from him that I could actually smell the heavy musk of that rutting buck, he could not get my scent. Then, too, he couldn't see me very well as I stood very still and was partially screened by a scrubby cedar. Apparently deer have rather short memories; so he may have forgotten the panic that sent him flying from his harem. For all I know, he may have taken me for a doe.

But I was close enough to see every point on his massive antlers. I could even see the whites of those wild, half-crazy eyes. As the rutting season was then about three weeks old, he was very gaunt. I could see a couple of scars on his neck and knew he had been fighting off the impudent young bucks that wanted to make love to his does. He wasn't a ten-pointer, but from a hasty count I decided he had about seven to a side, perhaps eight.

Then he snorted and was away. Three long, high bounds took him over a little point and out of sight. My favorite memory of him is as he stood there that day – free, majestic and beautifully alive. I'll never forget the picture he presented.

ext season, three hunters reported shooting at the big fellow on opening day. One of them claimed to have knocked him down, but that he got up almost immediately and ran as if uninjured. For a time I feared he was gut-shot and would go off to die miserably and become coyote meat. But after I had hunted for him two or three times, I saw him at long range as vigorous as ever.

About this time I decided that ordinary tactics would never get him. Nearly always he bedded down close to the top of a high ridge where he could see anyone coming toward him from the abandoned ranch and smell anyone below.

So I began to evolve a plan. The cowboy who had been up so close to him had ridden in from the other direction. It was ten miles across very rough country from Deep Canyon to the next ranch, but one could cover it on a horse in three or four hours. I decided to try it. Even if I didn't see the Hoodoo Buck, I would probably get a crack at another buck. I'd be riding through good deer country which was little hunted except on the side toward the road and close to town, where the big fellow ranged and the Sunday hunters tramped hopefully over the hills and through the draws.

I occupied a bunk at the ranch house one Friday night, and early the next morning I was up and eating. When I got my boot strapped on the saddle and the rifle stowed away, the stars were dimming and the sky to the east was just beginning to silver. It was cold, with that intense and bitter cold which comes just before dawn. Even with my flannel shirt, sweater and leather windbreaker, I shook and shivered.

The horse picked his way over a cow trail leading into the high country for the first mile or so. It was so dark that I could hardly see. Three miles from the house, I was on top. The sun was out bright, and almost warm after the bitter cold on the lowlands and the darkness. I was in rolling hills, carpeted with yellow grama-grass and spotted with dark cedars and occasional prickly pear. It was not a very difficult country to get over except for steep-walled canyons where the vegetation grew thick and dark and little intermittent streams left silver pools in the rocks.

I saw a good many deer – mostly does browsing on southern exposures to warm the chill of the night out of their bones. The few bucks I saw were mainly little fellows. I did not fire a shot.

Around nine o'clock I was approaching the Deep Canyon country and the ridge which seemed to be the Hoodoo Buck's favorite bedding ground. I decided to hunt on horseback, because if I killed him I'd have a horse to pack him in and, anyway, I could cover more ground.

I saw his big tracks several times, but they were always old. Once I was tempted to take a crack at a nice fat three-pointer that bounced out of a little clump of cedars across the canyon and ran up the slope. I followed him along through the sights, but I had come for the big fellow and decided not to shoot.

Since Old Hoodoo could be anywhere in about twenty-five square miles of territory, I hunted hard. At noon I still hadn't seen him; so I found a pot-hole for my horse to water in, took his bridle off to let him browse in comfort, and ate lunch. I dozed a little while in the warm sunshine behind a rock and out of the wind. At two I was riding again.

An hour later I topped a big ridge about three miles from the abandoned ranch, got off and used the glasses. The country was quite open, but there were little cedars here and there, and I had often known big bucks to bed down in country just like that. I saw nothing. Then, just as I mounted, I saw him! Perhaps he thought I was headed toward him – I do not know. If he had only lain quiet a few minutes longer, I never would have seen him, as I had planned to hunt down the ridge, cross, and go up the opposite slope.

It was Old Hoodoo, and no one else. He had been lying on the other side of a lone cedar, facing the ranch, the direction from which his enemies usually came. And he tore out in a hurry, traveling downhill and angling slightly to the right in the long swift bounds which mule deer usually use when traveling downhill.

I jerked my rifle out of the boot, sat down, and shot. My first two were misses, as I was pretty nervous. Curiously, though, I knew I had him. The country was so open that no matter where he ran, I would have him in sight for three hundred yards or more. I had the tactical advantage, and it looked as though his number was up.

The third shot stopped him in full flight. I have the impression that he wilted right in the middle of a jump and fairly slid along the ground, disappearing in foot-high sage.

I sat there on the ridge for several minutes. My horse, which had snorted and pricked up his ears when I began shooting, quieted down now and commenced to graze. I kept my eye on the spot where the buck had disappeared and calmed my jumpy nerves. I could not see movement.

Presently, I reloaded and started down the hill, my rifle ready in case he was only wounded and would jump up. Forty yards from where I had marked him down I still couldn't see him. And then I saw an antler sticking up above the sage! There he lay, as fine a mule deer buck as you'd see in many a blue moon of hunting. The shot had hit him high in the shoulder in the large nerve area just below the spine. I doubt if he even twitched when he hit the ground.

His head was a very good one, but not a record by any means. It measured thirty-four inches in spread and twenty-eight in main beam, and although it was irregular, it was very handsome with its seven points on one side and eight on the other. I dressed him and went for the horse. In a half-hour I had him tied on securely and was headed back for the ranch.

Yet I was not elated. Strangely enough, I was gloomy and depressed. Old Hoodoo was dead, and I had killed him. In doing so I had taken half the beauty and magic and mystery away from the Deep Canyon country. I have never been back. Without the mystery of his presence it wouldn't be the same. When I got back to the ranch where I had borrowed the horse and listened to the congratulations of the owner, I felt ashamed rather than proud.

A couple of years later I saw a drawing by a keen-eyed Western artist. It showed a big buck down, with a dude and a cowboy sitting beside it. The cowboy was sad, almost to the point of tears.

"Well," said the dude, "If you've been hunting him so long, it looks like you'd be tickled to death."

"No, I ain't." The cowboy answered. "Now I cain't hunt him no more."

The Big Buck of Deep Canyon originally appeared in the May, 1943 issue of Field & Stream. *Reprinted by permission of Time4Media.*

FISH ARE SUCH LIARS

In this classic from the pages of The Saturday Evening Post, *you'll be surprised to learn that fishermen aren't the only ones inclined to stretch the truth.*

By Roland Pertwee

There had been a fuss in the pool beneath the alders, and the small rainbow trout, with a skitter of his tail, flashed upstream, a hurt and angry fish. For three consecutive mornings he had taken the rise in that pool, and it injured his pride to be jostled from his drift just when the May fly was coming up in numbers. If his opponent had been a half-pounder like himself, he would have stayed and fought, but when an old hen fish, weighing fully three pounds, with a mouth like a rat hole and a carnivorous, cannibalistic eye rises from the reed beds and occupies the place, flight is the only effective argument.

But Rainbow was very much provoked. He had chosen his place with care. Now the May fly was up, the little French chalk stream was full of rising fish, and he knew by experience that strangers are unpopular in that season. To do one's self justice during a hatch, one must find a place where the fly drifts nicely overhead with the run of the stream, and natural drifts are scarce even in a chalk stream. He was not content to leap at the fly like a hysterical youngster who measured his weight in ounces and his wits in milligrams. He had reached that time of life

21

which demanded that he should feed off the surface by suction rather than exertion. No living thing is more particular about his table manners than a trout, and Rainbow was no exception.

"It's a sickening thing," he said to himself, "and a hard shame." He added: "Get out of my way," to a couple of fat young chub who were bubbling the surface in the silly, senseless fashion of their kind.

"Chub indeed!"

But even the chub had a home and he had none – and the life of a homeless river dweller is precarious.

"I will not and shall not be forced back to midstream," he said.

For, save at eventide or in very special circumstances, trout of personality do not frequent open water where they must compete for every insect with the wind, the lightning-swift sweep of swallows and martins, and even the laborious pursuit of predatory dragonflies with their bronze wings and bodies like rods of colored glass. Even as he spoke he saw a three-ouncer leap at a dapping May fly which was scooped out of his jaws by a passing swallow. Rainbow heard the tiny click as the May fly's body cracked against the bird's beak. A single wing of yellowy gossamer floated downward and settled upon the water. Under the shelving banks to right and left, where the fly, discarding its nymph and still too damp for its virgin flight, drifted downstream, a dozen heavy trout were feeding thoughtfully and selectively.

"If some angler would catch one of them, I might slip in and occupy the place before it gets known there's a vacancy."

But this uncharitable hope was not fulfilled, and with another whisk of his tail he propelled himself into the unknown waters upstream. A couple of strands of rusty barbed wire, relic of the war, spanned the shallows from bank to bank. Passing beneath them he came to a narrow reach shaded by willows, to the first of which was nailed a board bearing the words Pêche Réservée. He had passed out of the communal into private water – water running languidly over manes of emerald weed between clumps of alder, willow herb, tall crimson sorrel and masses of yellow iris. Ahead, like an apple-green rampart, rose the wooded heights of a forest; on either side were flat meadows of yellowing hay. Overhead, the vast expanse of blue June sky was tufted with rambling clouds. "My scales!" said Rainbow. "Here's water!"

But it was vain to expect any of the best places in such a reach would be vacant, and to avoid a recurrence of his unhappy encounter earlier in the morning. Rainbow continued his journey until he came to a spot where the river took one of those unaccountable right-angle bends which result in a pool, shallow on the one side, but slanting into deeps on the other. Above it was a water break, a swirl, smoothing, as it reached the pool, into a sleek, swift run, with an eddy which bore all the lighter floating things of the river over the calm surface of the little backwater, sheltered from above by a high shelving bank and a tangle of bramble and herb. Here in this backwater the twig, the broken reed, the leaf, the cork, the fly floated in suspended activity for a few instants until drawn back by invisible magnetism to the main current.

Rainbow paused in admiration. At the tail of the pool, two sound fish were rising with regularity, but in the backwater beyond the eddy the surface was still and unbroken. Watching open-eyed, Rainbow saw not one but a dozen May flies, fat, juicy, and damp from the nymph, drift in, pause and drift away untouched. It was beyond the bounds of possibility that such a place could be vacant, but there was the evidence of his eyes to prove it; and nothing if not a tryer, Rainbow darted across the stream and parked himself six inches below the water to await events.

I t so happened that at the time of his arrival the hatch of fly was temporarily suspended, which gave Rainbow leisure to make a survey of his new abode. Beyond the eddy was a submerged snag – the branch of an apple tree borne there by heavy rains, water-logged, anchored and intricate – an excellent place to break an angler's line. The river bank on his right was riddled under water with old rat holes, than which there is no better sanctuary. Below him and to the left was a dense bed of weeds brushed flat by the flow of the stream.

"If it comes to the worst," said Rainbow, "a smart fish could do a get-away here with very little ingenuity, even from a cannibalistic old hen like – hullo!"

The exclamation was excited by the apparition of a gauzy shadow on the water, which is what a May fly seen from below looks like. Resisting a vulgar inclination to leap at it with the violence of a youngster, Rainbow backed into the correct position which would allow the stream to present the morsel, so to speak, upon a tray. Which it did – and scarcely a dimple on the surface to tell what had happened.

"Very nicely taken, if you will accept the praise of a complete stranger," said a low, soft voice, one inch behind his line of sight.

Without turning to see by whom he had been addressed, Rainbow flicked a yard upstream and came back with the current four feet away. In the spot he had occupied an instant before lay a great old trout of the most benign aspect, who could not have weighed less than four pounds.

"I beg your pardon," said Rainbow, "but I had no idea that anyone – that is, I just dropped in *en passant*, and finding an empty house, I made so bold . . ."

"There is no occasion to apologize," said Old Trout seductively. "I did not come up from the bottom as early today as is my usual habit at this season. Yesterday's hatch was singularly bountiful and it is possible I did myself too liberally."

"Yes, but a gentleman of your weight and seniority can hardly fail to be offended at finding . . ."

"Not at all," Old Trout broke in. "I perceive you are a well-conducted fish who does not advertise his appetite in a loud and splashing fashion."

Overcome by the charm of old Trout's manner and address, Rainbow reduced the distance separating them to a matter of inches.

"Then you do not want me to go?" he asked.

"On the contrary, dear young sir, stay by all means and take the rise. You are,

I perceive, of the rainbow or, as they say here in France, of the Arc-en-ciel family. As a youngster I had the impression that I should turn out a rainbow, but events proved it was no more than the bloom, the natural sheen of youth."

"To speak the truth, sir," said Rainbow, "unless you had told me to the contrary, I would surely had thought you one of us."

Old Trout shook his tail. "You are wrong," he said. "I am from Dulverton, an English trout farm on the Exe, of which you will have heard. You are doubtless surprised to find an English fish in French waters."

"I am indeed," Rainbow replied, sucking in a passing May fly with such excellent good manners that it was hard to believe he was feeding. "Then you, sir," he added, "must know all about the habits of men."

"I may justly admit that I do," Old Trout agreed. "Apart from being hand-reared, I have in my twelve years of life studied the species in moods of activity, passivity, duplicity and violence."

Rainbow remarked that such must doubtless have proved of invaluable service. It did not, however, explain the mystery of his presence on a French river.

"For, sir," he added, "Dulverton, as once I heard while chatting with a much-traveled sea trout, is situated in the west of England, and without crossing the Channel, how could you have arrived here? Had you belonged to the salmon family, with which, sir, it is evident you have no connection, the explanation would be simple, but in the circumstances it baffles my understanding."

Old Trout waved one of his fins airily. "Yet cross the Channel I certainly did," said he, "and at a period in history which I venture to state will not readily be forgotten. It was during the war, my dear young friend, and I was brought in a can, in company with a hundred yearlings, to this river, or rather the upper reaches of this river, by a young officer, who wished to further an entente between English and French fish even as the war was doing with the mankind of these two nations."

Old Trout sighed a couple of bubbles and arched his body this way and that.

"There was a gentleman and a sportsman," he said. "A man who was acquainted with our people as I dare to say very few are acquainted. Had it ever been my lot to fall victim to a lover of the rod, I could have done so without regret to his. If you will take a look at my tail, you will observe that the letter W is perforated on the upper side. He presented me with this distinguishing mark before committing me, with his blessing, to the water."

"I have seldom seen a tail more becomingly decorated," said Rainbow. "But what happened to your benefactor?"

Old Trout's expression became infinitely sad. "If I could answer that," said he, "I were indeed a happy trout. For many weeks after he put me into the river I used to watch him in what little spare time he was able to obtain, casting a dry fly with the exquisite precision and likeness to nature in all the likely pools and runs and eddies near his battery position. Oh, minnows! It was a pleasure to watch that man, even as it was his pleasure to watch us. His bravery too! I call to mind a dozen times when he fished unmoved and unstartled while bullets from machine guns were pecking at the water like herons and thudding into the mud banks upon which he stood."

"An angler!" remarked Rainbow. "It would be no lie to say I like him the less on that account."

Old Trout became unexpectedly stern.

"Why so?" he retorted severely. "Have I not said he was also a gentleman and a sportsman? My officer was neither a pot-hunter nor a beast of prey. He was a purist – a man who took delight in pitting his knowledge of nature against the subtlest and most suspicious intellectual forces of the wild. Are you so young as not yet to have learned the exquisite enjoyment of escaping disaster and avoiding error by the exercise of personal ingenuity? Pray, do not reply, for I would hate to think so hard a thing of any trout. We as a race exist by virtue of our brilliant intellectuality and hypersensitive selectivity. In waters where there are no pike and only an occasional otter, but for the machinations of men, where should we turn to school our wits? Danger is our mainstay, for I tell you, Rainbow, that trout are composed of two senses – appetite, which makes of us fools, and suspicion, which teaches us to be wise."

Greatly chastened not alone by what Old Trout had said but by the forensic quality of his speech, Rainbow rose short and put a promising May fly onto the wing.

"I am glad to observe," said Old Trout, "that you are not without conscience."

"To tell the truth, sir," Rainbow replied apologetically, "my nerve this morning has been rudely shaken, but for which I should not have shown such want of good sportsmanship."

And with becoming brevity he told the tale of his eviction from the pool downstream. Old Trout listened gravely, only once moving, and that to absorb a small blue dun, an insect which he keenly relished.

"A regrettable affair," he admitted, "but as I have often observed, women, who are the gentlest creatures under water in adversity, are a thought lacking in moderation in times of abundance. They are apt to snatch."

"But for a turn of speed, she would certainly have snatched me," said Rainbow.

"Very shocking," said Old Trout. "Cannibals are disgusting. They destroy the social amenities of the river. We fish have but little family life and should therefore aim to cultivate a freemasonry of good-fellowship among ourselves. For my part, I am happy to line up with other well-conducted trout and content myself with what happens along with my own particular drift. Pardon me!" he added, breasting Rainbow to one side. "I invited you to take the rise of May fly, but I must ask you to leave the duns alone." Then, fearing this remark might be construed to reflect adversely upon his hospitality, he proceeded: "I have a reason which I will explain later. For the moment we are discussing the circumstances that led to my presence in this river."

"To be sure – your officer. He never succeeded in deluding you with his skill?"

"That would have been impossible," said Old Trout, "for I had taken up a position under the far bank where he could only have reached me with a fly by wading in a part of the river which was in view of a German sniper?"

"Wily!" Rainbow chuckled. "Cunning work, sir."

"Perhaps," Old Trout admitted, "although I have since reproached myself with cowardice. However, I was at the time a very small fish and a certain amount of nervousness is forgivable in the young."

At this gracious acknowledgement the rose-colored hue in Rainbow's rainbow increased noticeably – in short, he blushed.

"From where I lay," Old Trout went on, "I was able to observe the maneuvers of my officer and greatly profit thereby."

"But excuse me, sir," said Rainbow, "I have heard it said that an angler of the first class is invisible from the river."

"He is invisible to the fish he is trying to catch," Old Trout admitted, "but it must be obvious that he is not invisible to the fish who lie beside or below him. I would also remind you that during the war every tree, every scrap of vegetation, and every vestige of natural cover had been torn up, trampled down, razed. The river banks were as smooth as the top of your head."

"It would seem," said Rainbow, "that this war had its merits."

"My young friend," said Old Trout, "you never made a greater mistake. A desire on the part of our soldiery to vary a monotonous diet of bully beef and biscuit often drove them to resort to villainous methods of assault against our kind."

"Nets?" gasped Rainbow in horror.

"Worse than nets – bombs," Old Trout replied. "A small oval black thing called a Mills bomb, which the shameless fellows flung into deep pools."

"But surely the chances of being hit by such a –"

"You reveal a pathetic ignorance," said Old Trout. "There is no question of being hit. The wretched machine exploded under water and burst our people's insides or stunned us so that we floated dead to the surface. I well remember my officer coming upon such a group of marauders one evening – yes, and laying about him with his fists in defiance of King's Regulations and the Manual of Military Law. Two of them he seized by the collar and the pants and flung into the river. Spinning minnows, that was a sight worth seeing! 'You low swine,' I heard him say; 'you trash, you muck! Isn't there enough carnage without this sort of thing?' Afterward he sat on the bank with the two dripping men and talked to them for their souls' sake.

" 'Look ahead, boys. Ask yourselves what are we fighting for? Decent homes to live in at peace with one another, fields to till and forests and rivers to give us a day's sport and fun. It's our rotten job to massacre each other, but, by gosh, don't let's massacre the harmless rest of nature as well. At least, let's give 'em a running chance. Boys, in the years ahead, when all the mess is cleared up, I look forward to coming back to this old spot, when there is alder growing by the banks, and willow herb and tall reeds and the drone of insects instead of the rumble of those guns. I don't want to come back to a dead river that I helped to kill, but to a river ringed with rising fish – some of whom were old comrades of the war.' He went on to tell of us hundred Dulverton trout that he had marked with the letter W. 'Give 'em their chance,' he said, 'and in the years to come those beggars will reward us a hundred times over. They'll give us a finer thrill and put up a cleaner fight than old Jerry ever contrived.' " Those were emotional times, and though you may be reluctant to believe me, one of those two very wet men dripped water from his eyes as well as his clothing.

" 'Many's the 'appy afternoon I've 'ad with a roach pole on Brentford canal,' he sniffed, 'though I've never yet tried m'hand against a trout. You shall do it now,' said my officer, and during the half-hour that was left of daylight, that dripping soldier had his first lesson in the most delicate art in the world. I can see them now – the clumsy, wet fellow and my officer timing him, timing him – "one and two, and one and two, and –' The action of my officer's wrist with its persuasive flick was the prettiest thing I have ever seen."

"Did he carry out his intention and come back after the war?" Rainbow asked. "I shall never know," Old Trout replied. "I do not even know if he survived it. There was a great battle – a German drive. For hours they shelled the river front, and many falling short exploded in our midst with terrible results. My own bank was torn to shreds and our people suffered. How they suffered! About noon the infantry came over – hordes in field gray. There were pontoons, rope bridges and hand-to-hand fights on both banks and even in the stream itself."

"And your officer?"

"I saw him once, before the water was stamped dense into liquid mud and dyed by the blood of men. He was in the thick of it, unarmed, and a German officer called on him to surrender. For answer he struck him in the face with a light cane. Ah, that wrist action! Then a shell burst, smothering the water with clods of fallen earth and other things."

"Then you never knew?"

"I never knew, although that night I searched among the dead. Next day I went downstream, for the water in that place was polluted with death. The bottom of the pool in which I had my place was choked with strange and mangled tenants that were not good to look upon. We trout are a clean people that will not readily abide in dirty houses. I am a Dulverton trout, where the water is filtered by the hills and runs cool over stones."

"And you have stayed here ever since?"

Old Trout shrugged a fin. "I have moved with the times. Choosing a place according to the needs of my weight."

"And you have never been caught, sir, by any other angler?"

"Am I not here?" Old Trout answered with dignity.

"Oh, quite, sir. I had only thought, perhaps, as a younger fish enthusiasm might have resulted to your disadvantage, but that, nevertheless, you had been returned."

"Returned! Returned!" echoed Old Trout. "Returned to the frying-pan! Where on earth did you pick up that expression? We are in France, my young friend; we are not on the Test, the Itchen or the Kennet. In this country it is not the practice of anglers to return anything, however miserable in size."

"But nowadays," Rainbow protested, "there are Englishmen and Americans on the river who show us more consideration."

"They may show you consideration," said Old Trout, "but I am of an importance that neither asks for nor expects it. Oblige me by being a little more discreet with your plurals. In the impossible event of my being deceived and caught, I should be introduced to a glass case with an appropriate background of rocks and reeds."

"But, sir, with respect, how can you be so confident of your unassailability?" Rainbow demanded, edging into position to accept an attractive May fly with yellow wings that was drifting downstream toward him.

"How?" Old Trout responded. "Because –" Then suddenly: "Leave it, you fool!"

Rainbow had just broken the surface when the warning came. The yellow-winged May fly was wrenched off the water with a wet squeak. A tangle of limp cast lapped itself round the upper branches of a willow far upstream and a raw voice exclaimed something venomous in French. By common consent the two fish went down.

"Well, really," expostulated Old Trout. "I hoped you were above that kind of thing! Nearly to fall victim to a downstream angler. It's a little too much! And think of the effect it will have on my prestige. Why, that incompetent fool will go about boasting that he rose me. Me!

"A trout of my intelligence would never put myself in some place where I would be exposed to the vulgar assaults of every amateur upon the bank?" Old Trout declared. I invite attention from none but the best people – the expert, the purist."

"I understood you to say that there were none such in these parts," grumbled Rainbow.

"There are none who have succeeded in deceiving me," was the answer. "As a fact, for the last few days I have been vastly entranced by an angler who, by any standard, is deserving of praise. His presentation is flawless and the only fault I detect in him is a tendency to overlook piscine psychology. He will be with us in a few minutes, since he knows it is my habit to lunch at noon."

"Pardon the interruption," said Rainbow, "but there is a gallant hatch of fly going down. I can hear your two neighbors at the tail of the pool rising steadily."

Old Trout assumed an indulgent air. "We will go up if you wish," said he, "but you will be well advised to observe my counsel before taking the rise, because if my angler keeps his appointment you will most assuredly be *meuniéred* before nightfall."

At this unpleasant prophecy Rainbow shivered. "Let us keep to weed," he suggested.

But Old Trout only laughed, so that bubbles from the river bed rose and burst upon the surface.

"Courage," said he; "it will be an opportunity for you to learn the finer points of the game. If you are nervous, lie nearer to the bank. The natural fly does not drift there so abundantly, but you will be secure from the artificial. Presently I will treat you to an exhibition of playing with death you will not fail to appreciate. He broke off and pointed with his eyes. "Over you and to the left."

Rainbow made a neat double rise and drifted back into line. "Very mellow," he said – "very mellow and choice. Never tasted better. May I ask, sir, what you meant by piscine psychology?"

"I imply that my angler does not appreciate the subtle possibilities of our intellect. Now, my officer concerned himself as vitally with what we were thinking as with what we were feeding upon. This fellow, secure in the knowledge that his presentation is well-nigh perfect, is content to offer me the same variety of flies day after day, irrespective of the fact that I have learned them all by heart. I have, however, adopted the practice of rising every now and then to encourage him."

"Rising? At an artificial fly? I never heard such temerity in all my life," gasped Rainbow.

Old Trout moved his body luxuriously. "I should have said, *appearing* to rise," he amended. "You may have noticed that I have exhibited a predilection for small duns in preference to the larger *Ephemeridae*. My procedure is as follows: I wait until a natural dun and his artificial May fly are drifting downstream with the smallest possible distance separating them. Then I rise and take the dun. Assuming I have risen to him, he strikes, misses, and is at once greatly flattered and greatly provoked. By this device I sometimes occupy his attention for over an hour and thus render a substantial service to others of my kind who would certainly have fallen victim to his skill."

"The river is greatly in your debt, sir," said Young Rainbow, with deliberate satire.

He knew by experience that fish as well as anglers are notorious liars, but the exploit his host recounted was a trifle too strong. Taking a sidelong glance, he was surprised to see that Old Trout did not appear to have appreciated the subtle ridicule of his remark. The long, lithe body had become almost rigid and the great round eyes were focused upon the surface with an expression of fixed concentration.

Looking up, Rainbow saw a small white-winged May fly with red legs and a body the color of straw swing out from the main stream and describe a slow circle over the calm surface above Old Trout's head. Scarcely an inch away a tiny blue dun, its wings folded as closely as the pages of a book, floated attendant. An upward rush, a sucking *kerr-rop*, and when the broken water had calmed, the dun had disappeared and the May fly was dancing away downstream.

"Well," said Old Trout, "how's that, my youthful skeptic? Pretty work, eh?"

"I saw nothing in it," was the impertinent reply. "There is not a trout on the river who could not have done likewise."

"Even when one of those two flies was artificial?" Old Trout queried tolerantly.

"But neither of them was artificial," Rainbow retorted. Had it been so, the angler would have struck. They always do."

"Of course he struck," Old Trout replied.

"But he didn't," Rainbow protested. "I saw the May fly go down with the current."

"My poor fish!" Old Trout replied. "Do you presume to suggest that I am unable to distinguish an artificial from a natural fly? Are you so blind that you failed to see the prismatic colors in the water from the paraffin in which the fly had been dipped? Here you are! Here it is again!"

Once more the white-winged insect drifted across the backwater, but this time there was no attendant dun.

"If that's a fake I'll eat my tail," said Rainbow.

"If you question my judgment," Old Trout answered, "you are at liberty to rise. I dare say, in spite of a shortage of brain, that you would eat comparatively well."

But Rainbow, in common with his kind, was not disposed to take chances.

"We may expect two or three more casts from this fly and then he will change it for a bigger. It is the same programme every day without a variation. How differently my officer would have acted. By now he would have discovered my little joke and turned the tables against me. Aye me, but some men will never learn! Your mental outfit, dear Rainbow, is singularly like a man's," he added. "It lacks elasticity."

Rainbow made no retort and was glad of his forbearance, for every word Old Trout had spoken was borne out by subsequent events. Four times the white-winged May fly described an arc over the backwater, but in the absence of duns, Old Trout did not rise again. Then came a pause, during which, through a lull in the hatch, even the natural insect was absent from the river.

"He is changing his fly," said Old Trout, "but he will not float it until the hatch starts again. He is casting beautifully this morning and I hope circumstances will permit me to give him another rise."

"But suppose," said Rainbow breathlessly, "you played this game once too often and were foul hooked as a result?"

Old Trout expanded his gills broadly. "Why, then," he replied, "I should break him. Once round a limb of that submerged apple bough and the thing would be done. I should never allow myself to be caught and no angler could gather up the slack and haul me into midstream in time to prevent me reaching the bough. Stand by."

The shadow of a large, dark May fly floated cockily over the backwater and had almost returned to the main stream when a small iron-blue dun settled like a puff of thistledown in its wake.

The two insects were a foot nearer the fast water than the spot where Old Trout was accustomed to take the rise. But for the presence of a spectator, it is doubtful whether he would have done so, but young Rainbow's want of appreciation had excited his vanity, and with a rolling swoop Old Trout swallowed the dun and bore it downward.

And then an amazing thing happened. Instead of drifting back to his place as expected, Old Trout was jerked sideways by an invisible force. A thin translucent thread upcut the water's surface and tightened irresistibly. A second later Old Trout was fighting, fighting, fighting to reach the submerged apple bough with the full weight of the running water and the full strength of the finest Japanese gut strained against him.

Watching, wide-eyed and aghast, from one of the underwater rat holes into which he had hastily withdrawn, Rainbow saw the figure of a man rise out of a bed of irises downstream and scramble upon the bank. In his right hand, with the wrist well back, he held a light split-cane rod whose upper joint was curved to a half-circle. The man's left hand was detaching a collapsible landing net from the ring of his belt. Every attitude and movement was expressive of perfectly organized activity. His mouth was shut as tightly as a steel trap, but a light of happy excitement danced in his eyes.

"No, you don't my fellar," Rainbow heard him say. "No, you don't. I knew all about that apple bough before ever I put a fly over your pool. And the weed bed on the right," he added, as Old Trout made a sudden swerve half down and half across stream.

Tucking the net under his arm, the man whipped up the slack with a lightning-like action. The maneuver cost Old Trout dear, for when, despairing of reaching the weed and burrowing into it, he tried to regain his old position, he found himself six feet farther away from the apple bough than when the battle began.

Instinctively, Old Trout knew it was useless to dash downstream, for a man who could take up slack with the speed his adversary had shown would profit by the expedient to come more quickly to terms with him. Besides, lower down there was broken water to knock the breath out of his lungs. Even where he lay straining and slugging this way and that, the water was pouring so fast into his open mouth as nearly to drown him. His only chance was a series of jumps, followed by quick dives. Once before Old Trout had saved his life by resorting to this expedient. It takes the strain off the line and returns it so quickly that even the finest gut is apt to sunder.

Meanwhile, the man was slowly approaching, winding up as he came. Old Trout, boring in the depths, could hear the click of the check reel with increasing distinctness. The tension was appalling, for ever since the fight began his adversary had given him the butt unremittingly. Aware of his own weight and power, Old Trout was amazed that any tackle could stand the strain.

"Now's my time," he thought, and jumped.

It was no ordinary jump, but an aerial rush three feet out of the water, with a twist at its apex and a cutting lash of the rail designed to break the cast. But his adversary was no ordinary angler, and at the first hint of what was happening, he dropped the point of the rod flush with the surface.

Once and once more Old Trout flung himself into the air, but after each attempt he found himself with diminishing strength and with less line to play with.

"It looks to me," said Rainbow mournfully, "as if my unhappy host will lose this battle and finish up in that glass case to which he was referring a few minutes ago." And greatly affected, he burrowed his nose in the mud and wondered, in the event of this dismal prophecy coming true, whether he would be able to take possession of the pool without molestation.

In consequence of these reflections he failed to witness the last phase of the battle, when, as will sometimes happen with big fish, all the fight went out of Old Trout, and rolling wearily over and over, he abandoned himself to the clinging embraces of the net. He never saw the big man proudly carry Old Trout back into the hayfield, where, before proceeding to remove the fly, he sat down beside a shallow dike and lit a cigarette and smiled largely. Then, with an affectionate and professional touch, he picked up Old Trout by the back of the neck, his forefinger and thumb sunk firmly in the gills.

"You're a fine fellar," he said, extracting the fly, "a good sportsman and a funny fish. You fooled me properly for three days, but I think you'll own I outwitted you in the end."

Rummaging in his creel for a small rod of hard wood that he carried for the purpose of administering the quietus, he became aware of something that arrested the action. Leaning forward, he stared with open eyes at a tiny perforated *W* in the upper part of Old Trout's tail.

"Shades of the war! Dulverton!" he exclaimed. Then with a sudden warmth: "Old chap, old chap, is it really you? This is red-letter stuff. If you're not too far gone to take another lease of life, have it with me."

And with the tenderness of a woman, he slipped Old Trout into the dike and in a tremble of excitement hurried off to the auberge where the fishermen lodged, to tell a tale no one even pretended to believe.

For the best part of an hour Old Trout lay in the shallow waters of the dike before slowly cruising back to his own place beneath the overhanging bank. The alarming experience through which he had passed had made him a shade forgetful, and he was not prepared for the sight of Young Rainbow rising steadily at the hatch of fly.

"Pardon me, but a little more to your right," he said, with heavy courtesy.

"Diving otters!" cried Young Rainbow, leaping a foot clear of the water. "You sir! You!"

"And why not? Old Trout replied. "Your memory must be short if you have already forgotten that this is my place."

"Yes, but –" Rainbow began and stopped.

"You are referring to that little circus of a few minutes ago," said Old Trout. "Is it possible you failed to appreciate the significance of the affair? I knew at once it was my dear officer when he dropped the artificial dun behind the natural May fly. In the circumstances, I could hardly do less than accept his invitation. Nothing is more delightful than a reunion of comrades of the war." He paused and added: "We had a charming talk, he and I, and I do not know which of us was the more affected. It is a tragedy that such friendship and such intellect as we share cannot exist in common element."

And so great was his emotion that Old Trout dived and buried his head in the weeds. Whereby Rainbow did uncommonly well during the midday hatch.

Reprinted from The Saturday Evening Post, ©*1927.*

AIM OF THE HUNTERMAN

Pitted with rust and powder-scalds, the old musket would explode with a roar that sounded like the crack of doom. And now, in the dusky hands of the Hunterman, it was all that stood between life and a terrible death.

By Archibald Rutledge

The negroes in the golden-wide ricefield, as they reaped rhythmically, were singing melodiously; there was the glamour of autumn and harvest-time. It was cool for September in South Carolina, and there were hints of fall in the air; though that radiant, reddening, ripening time had as yet been stayed from the heavy-foliaged trees that fringed the ricefield. Toward Ned Alston, the planter, who was watching the happy workers with delight, there now advanced the smiling Scipio, the grandson of the old professional slave hunter of Eldorado; and, much to the pride of this unique character Alston always addressed him as "My Hunterman."

Scipio well deserved the title. No Cherokee Indian who ever ranged the pine forests and the cypress swamps of the South had understood them better than he. He possessed a certain untamed element in his nature which served to ally him to all wild things and their ways. His occupation was never fixed, unless roaming can be considered an occupation; real work he

33

disdained. But Scipio was full of picturesque accomplishments. He could pick the guitar, pray with much emotion at revival meetings, arbitrate differences among the negroes, and prescribe medicines in cases of sickness; and these remedies, being gathered from plantation woods and fields, could be recommended in that they were without money and without price. But by birth and breeding Scipio was a hunter. He alone could, after nightfall, make a direct road home out of the most desolate and trackless swamp; he alone knew where the wariest old buck of the branches would lie, and at just what point in the vast level pinewoods a running deer could be cut off. In all such matters, Alston had been accustomed to defer to him. The planter had to confess, however, that Scipio was hardly to be accounted an economic asset of Eldorado plantation; but he certainly made for sentiment and romance, and was as fine a figure of the black man as the Santee country had produced.

Tall and sparse, he had the power of endurance written in the movements of his limbs and in his easy attitudes of repose. All his actions appeared to be without effort, and he did things without appearing to strive. In feature, he was more like an Indian than a negro. His eyes were deep-set and keen, with a masked glitter of forest-wildness in them. The expression of his face was quiet but indescribably wary, while the gleam of his ready smile almost constantly lighted his cheerful countenance.

And now, as Scipio approached Alston, who stood under a gnarled live-oak on the ricefield-bank, the planter eyed the negro's musket with mock disapproval.

"Well, Hunterman," he said, "and what arc you loaded for this summer day?"

"Cap'n," the negro returned, "I come from Laurel Hill swamp. Two big bear done take up there, but I couldn't find them to-day. I hab a ball-bullet in my musket, sah," he went on, stroking the long barrel of his formidable weapon.

The eye of the planter rested with amusement yet with admiration on Scipio's gun.

This musket was of an age unknown and of a fashion long forgotten. Short in the stock but marvelously long in the barrel, it was throughout so pitted with rust-spots and powder-scalds that it frequently, when fired, emitted spurts of angry flame. The misshaped hammer looked ancestral, almost prehistoric, while the nipple was nothing but a worn stub. But in the hands of the redoubtable Hunterman, and charged with the double load which he was accustomed to using, it was a deadly weapon. The sound it made was unlike that produced by any other kind of gun. Scipio's musket blared, and it did so alarmingly. This fearsome roar was known to all dwellers in the Santee country, and what it meant filled everyone who heard it with deep pride in Scipio's daring and prowess.

On stormy twilights, when the wild-ducks would be pouring into the old ricefields, a sound like the crack of doom would crash the stillness of the plantation regions, and would reverberate for miles up and down the misty river. Then the negroes, hugging their cabin fires, would say, "Eh, brudder, what chance is a duck got 'gainst a noise like dat?" Again, when the roar of the musket would come from the pine woods, there would always be some who would hear it and would remark, "Deer can jump and run, but he can't jump powder and he can't outrun shot – not when brudder Scipio opens fire on him."

So now, when Scipio laid this extraordinary weapon down on the dewberry vines that had matted themselves on the slope of the ricefield bank, Alston eyed it with affectionate fun.

"Time you were getting a new gun, Hunterman," he said; "some day she's going to blow up and scatter you over a ten-acre field."

But Ned Alston's admiration for Scipio's skill as a woodsman now suffered a certain eclipse and depreciation, as, looking across the brown stiff stubble, over which the heat-waves shimmered and swam, he saw the Hunterman's wife toiling faithfully with the men and with the stronger women, though her own child was but a few weeks old. Yet it was hard to get angry with the picturesque Scipio; one might blame a domestic nature for such neglect, but not a nature which was essentially wild, restless, untamed. Yet the planter could not help saying:

"Scipio, you know this is no season for you to hunt bear. Why aren't you in that field reaping rice? You know Amy ought not work as she is working yonder, while her baby is so young. She had to bring him down here with her to-day; he's down the bank there, under the wahwoo bush. Amy ought to be at home with the child, and you ought to be in the field."

But the Hunterman ignored the planter's cogent reasoning.

"I done seen him yonder," he smilingly said, the light of a deep, shy, wild, woodland affection for his one baby coming into his eyes; "he done been asleep," he added softly, and still smiling, as if such a performance on the part of his baby was both wonderful and amusing.

The disagreeable subject of work was not again referred to; for Scipio, taking advantage of its temporary diversion, straightway began to tell Alston of a family of black fox-squirrels near the northern bound of the plantation that had been marked for the winter's pastime of the planter. The talk continued to be of things woodland until Alston moved out from under the little oak, thinking he would step down the bank to see what progress the harvesting would show from a different angle. Like every planter the world over, when he emerged from the shelter which had cut off his view of the sky, with its tokens of fair or stormy weather, he glanced upward. Scipio, equally solicitous about such matters, but from

35

far different reasons, also looked up. Both men saw at a glance the same dread apparition.

ith wide and powerful wings outspread in the heavens, in one of those last lowering circles ere he should fall, a great bald eagle was wheeling. Unconscious of the presence of the two men standing beneath the oak, he had been circling above them, they knew not for how long. And the moment they discerned him, certain at last of his reconnaissance and of the exact position of his prey, he eagerly arched his mighty wings and volplaned roaring out of the sky. His snowy head, with its cruel beak partly open in the heat of the hunt, was slightly outstretched. His stocky legs were letting down their talons to grip their prey. The fall of the eagle was terrible, a fearfully beautiful spectacle; impressive, but most sinister in its splendor.

Alston cried, "What an eagle, Scipio!"

But the dusky Hunterman, like lightning to think when wild life was in sight, had instantly discerned the goal of the great harrier's fall. He marked the tragedy in an instant.

"My lil' baby," he cried brokenly – "dat big eagle's gwine to get him!"

The negroes in the ricefield, who were working at a distance of some acres from the bank, were unaware of the impending disaster. They were reaping happily, laughing and singing. Even if they had seen and had realized what was taking place, they were far too distant to help. The eagle might have heard their shouts, but he would not have released his prey. Always bold, the bald eagle is amazingly so when a coveted victim, almost within his clutches, seems about to be taken from him. In the waving field, the little child's mother was singing with the rest, swinging the flashing sickle rhythmically and laying the golden reaped grain in rich windrows on the brown stubble.

At first, only the planter and Scipio were aware of the terrible scene now being enacted before their very eyes. If the child was to be saved, they alone must do it. Yet what hope had they of succeeding?

The plumed wahwoo bush beside which Amy had laid her child was more than a hundred yards from them down the grass-grown, briar-matted bank. It would take the men fifteen seconds to reach the place; and by then the eagle, bearing his prey, might be far beyond the cypress trees on the river-bank, or even beating his powerful way over the broad river itself. It was a desperate moment.

From his great height in the sky, the eagle had detected the movement of life near the bank; and the colorless cloth in which the baby was wrapped had not given him reason for any suspicions. He saw prey before him, far from the workers in the wide field.

36

He wheeled lower, gauging the distance and marking his victim with the piercing sight of fierce, clairvoyant eyes. Whether it was a fawn or the young of some other animal, he knew not; it mattered not to the great bird of prey. The little creature was alive and defenseless; therefore he would fall upon it. With his curved talons wide, he dropped like a black thunderbolt out of the blue sky. The wind roared through the hollow arches of his wings. His talons ached for the fatal grip. His steady eyes were aflame with cruel hunger and the anticipation of its instant satisfaction.

The moment that Ned Alston realized the terrible import of Scipio's words, he sprang forward with a shout, and would have raced down the bank, almost beside himself as he was with pity and horror. But the Hunterman, with a touch on his arm, stayed him.

"If you shout, Cap'n, he will fly faster," said Scipio. "We couldn't get him now no how. But wait a minute, please, suh."

The huge eagle, whose fall had been completed, and which had for a moment been buried in the grass beside the bush, now rose heavily above the bank. Gripped in his talons and held close to his great body was Scipio's baby.

But the Hunterman was going to have something to say in the matter. He was kneeling on the bank, his old musket at his shoulder.

"Scipio!" the planter cried out poignantly, "what are you going to do?"

"I'se gwine to shot him," the negro returned, in tones that betrayed not a tremor.

Alston suppressed a wild desire to protest against what he felt sure would be a peril as grave to the child as the eagle's attack. But instinct told him it was better not to speak. The Hunterman was taking aim. The shot would be most difficult as well as dangerous. It was at a small moving target, and the negro had told Alston that his musket was loaded with one ball – "a ball bullet," meant for bear in the Laurel Hill swamp.

In the fleeting second while the planter crouched breathless beside the kneeling negro, he caught the expression on Scipio's face. It was tense but not nervous, and flint-like in its determination. The eyes gleamed steadily. There was not a quiver in the statuesque black figure, immovable as marble.

The workers in the ricefield had heard Alston's first shout, and the nature of the tragedy was borne in on them by one of their number, who, being a hunter, cried out the danger. The big eagle caught their gaze at once. Now they could see the child, wrapped in the drab cloth, struggling feebly. They could not hear the pitiful little cry that came to the ears of Alston and Scipio. Amy, the mother, had begun to run wildly across the stubble, waving her arms, shouting, and weeping impotently. But the great eagle had nothing to fear from those far-away pursuers.

Then on the air the musket of Scipio blared. The giant marauding bird collapsed in his skyward flight and fell heavily in the marsh on the edge of the field. The aim of the Hunterman, even in such a crisis, had been true; and the ball-bullet of the Hunterman had gone home.

In a few moments, Amy had her child in her arms. And then something happened which pleased the planter even more than the wonderful shot Scipio had just made. "Give me yo' sickle, Amy," he said; "as long as we'se got a lil' baby, I will never let you wuk no mo'."

That eagle, the largest ever taken in the Santee country, now stuffed and mounted, is one of Ned Alston's treasured trophies. Though he cannot look at it without something akin to a shudder, yet it always vividly recalls one of the most thrilling moments of his life, when an innocent child was saved, without scathe, from a terrible death. When he and Scipio look at the eagle together, they understand each other with a perfect affection. And the planter is wont to say: "Scipio, to this day I don't know how you did it."

And Scipio answers, as if the feat had been simple enough:

"How, Cap'n, ain't I is yo' Hunterman?"

From Old Plantation Days, *1921*.

38

A PLACE IN THE WOODS

The little northwoods cabin is his anchor-hold, where time is measured in seasons and sunsets and where he can escape from the hurried, the hectic and mundane.

By Jack Kulpa

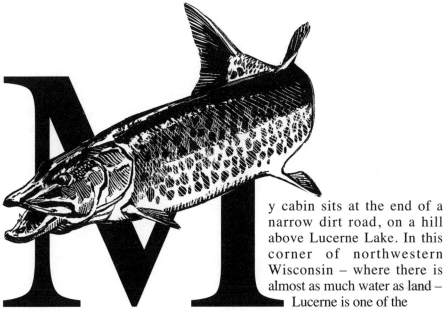

My cabin sits at the end of a narrow dirt road, on a hill above Lucerne Lake. In this corner of northwestern Wisconsin – where there is almost as much water as land – Lucerne is one of the many thousands of lakes that lie within the St. Croix River's watershed.

I built my cabin years ago, the way cabins used to be built: posts and beams; boards and battens; shakes and shims and stones. It stands among the jackpines as if it had always been there, as weathered and time-worn as a cedar. Just big enough for one or two friends and whatever gear we can carry, I built it as a getaway.

I live in a town not far from the cabin. The town is where I work, pay my bills, tend my family, help my neighbors, and try to contribute to the common good. But when the press of responsibilities is more than I can bear, I escape to the woods. The cabin is my anchor-hold – its changeless familiarity keeps me rooted against the currents of transilience. Here, where time is measured in seasons and sunsets, the past and its memories linger like echoes. Insulated by silence, the cabin's solitudes shelter me from the hurried, the hectic and mundane. The town is where I live, but the cabin is where I belong.

I n April, when the snow is all but gone and frozen lakes lie shattered with open leads of blue water, I return to the cabin to prepare for all that is to come. There are floors to sweep, mice to evict, a pump to prime, and tomorrows to dream about.

Days are growing longer as the sun climbs higher, and warm winds are flush with the scent of balsam and pine. The incessant patter of trickling snowmelt makes every brook roar like a torrent. Sunny cowslips are already blooming along muddy banks, and at night clamoring flocks of geese pass unseen through the dark. Killdeer are keening. Pike are spawning. And everywhere is a sense of quickening urgency. Winter is receding and life is unfolding as the advancing tide of spring returns.

April is the season of expectations. I spend its first days patching waders, repairing canoes and checking tackle. Alone at the cabin in April, I'm as free as a boy – and just as ready for adventure. I might decide to fish for crappies in a creek brimming with snowmelt; or maybe I'll try for steelhead in the rivers that tumble north to Lake Superior. Or I may go exploring to discover what the vanishing snow has revealed, and return with a pine-knot or deer skull – objects with a past as unfathomable to me as spring's resurrection. I watch seagulls cartwheel and eagles soar while splitting wood for the evening's fire. At night, when the fire burns brightly behind the glass door of the cabin's stove, I settle back and dream.

This will be the year I land "Big Bertha," the eight-pound bass that haunts the shadows under my dock; I've had that fish on twice before, and twice I've watched it spit my plug. This will also be the year I hit Popple Creek at the same time the woodcock do – and this year I'll remember my hip boots. This year I won't miss the salmon run on the Brule, and I'll wait for a trophy buck instead of bagging a spike-horn for the freezer.

In April, anything is possible.

Soon friends will gather at the cabin and in the days ahead we'll share trout streams, jon boats, duck blinds and deer stands – and then reality will intrude with empty creels and unused tags. But in April the cabin is my middle-aged version of a tree house where I'm free to be a boy again; a boy who – despite all the broken promises of the past – still believes in the dreams of spring.

40

Summer is the season of abundance, when life is easy and carefree. I live at the cabin from the time the loon chicks hatch until the teal flee south in late August.

This far north, summer is a long time in coming. It doesn't arrive until after Father's Day, when the bass move off their spawning beds. By then the air is thick with insects, and the bright blue flags of wild irises wave like showy emblems along lakeshores. The summer people have returned to their cabins and during the day the lake bustles with activity: kids dive from rafts or catch sunfish from docks; men in canoes hunt pike and perch.

By July my cabin has long been a base camp for friends. By then we've made dozens of fishing forays into the surrounding woods: rainbows on the Sioux, browns on the Clam, walleyes and pike on the Totogatic and Namekagon, smallmouths on the St. Croix, muskies on the Chippewa, and brookies in every beaver pond.

During the long and lush, green days of summer, it's easy to believe the freewheeling atmosphere will last forever. The woods teem with blueberries free for the picking; Juneberry trees sag with the weight of their fruit. Bluegills cluster around the ends of piers, and on the lake flocks of young ducks move about like armadas. The dusk is filled with the warbling of finches and after sunset flying squirrels glide through the trees. Through it all winds the trembling calls of the loons, a quavering cry that seems to ask: *Who are you?*

Most of the summer people give up on cabin life when August arrives: temperatures soar, the sun bakes exposed flesh, and lakes are thick with weeds and suspended matter. Biting flies and clouds of mosquitoes drive even the most resilient people off the water. But for me, the serious fishing is just beginning.

In August, when the sunset's afterglow has burned away and swarms of insects rattle the cabin's screens, I bathe in DEET, pull on sneakers and cut-off jeans, and go down to the lake with a Hula Popper. I wade the shallows up to my waist, testing each step with a toe, mindful of the submerged beaver slash and muskrat runs that make these shallows the kind of place where largemouths lurk on summer evenings.

At night the sound of bass feeding on the topwater is as noisy as a youngster slurping soup. When the fish jump they splash like otters. I cast to the edge of lilypads and pickerelweeds, letting the popper lie motionless while I watch shooting stars streak across the sky. At the north end of the lake, loons are yodeling. Bats dart over the water, so near I instinctively wave them away, a little concerned that their sonar might fail and I'll end up with a bat in my face.

These soft, summer nights are among my favorite at the cabin. Maybe it's because they remind me of other summer evenings, long ago. When I was a kid my father and I fished for walleyes on summer evenings during his annual, week-long vacation; on other nights I'd fish for bullheads and catfish with friends. We were kids, without worries or commitments, and sometimes we'd stay out until dawn, huddling around the light of a hissing Coleman lantern, occasionally dozing off on a bed of long grass and spruce boughs. Every one of those summers was a tintype copy of the last; it never occurred to us that things might ever be different.

These are the thoughts that keep me company as I prowl for bass on summer evenings. After the Hula Popper has laid at rest for a time, I begin its slow and sputtering retrieve. Almost before I complete a full turn of the reel, a largemouth bursts from under the lilypads and inhales the popper.

Most of the bass are decent size; one or two would look respectable on a wall – but all go back. I'm just getting the kinks out, I tell myself. My real quarry is "Big Bertha," the eight-pound monster under my dock.

I make my meandering way toward the dock and plant my sneakers in the lake's sandy bottom when I'm within two-dozen feet of the pier. At night I never risk long casts: there's too much out there to snag and entangle the evening in frustration. I cast the popper near the end of the dock; when I start my retrieve a bass as big as a small dog wallops the lure.

The fish jumps, twice, but I don't need to see it to know it's "Big Bertha." The drag of the spinning reel squeals. I keep the rod up, trying to turn the fish away from the weeds. Soon the bass is almost within reach, offering no more resistance than an anchor. And then suddenly, inexplicably and without any warning, the bass explodes like a bomb and spits the popper into the air. The fish is gone. "Big Bertha" has humbled me again.

But then, if I had caught her, summer would be over. And I'm in no hurry to say good-bye to the easy luxuriance and abundance that is summer.

"Take all the swift advantage of the hours," wrote Shakespeare, and that's what I do at the cabin during the few and fleeting days of summer. This far North summer arrives late and leaves early; almost before you know it is there, it is gone.

Autumn is the shortest season in the North. By Labor Day the teal are gone and rose-breasted grosbeaks have vanished. Wild rice beds grow sere and soundless while the woods burst into riotous color: flaming reds, tangerine-orange, lemon-yellows. Tamaracks smolder like smoky gold in the swamps and in the morning flocks of ringbills sail down into potholes. By noon the sun has burned away the frost and snipe break from the bulrushes. At dusk woodcock careen through the birches.

October used to drive me crazy when I was younger. There was too much to chase and never enough hours for pursuit. Until Columbus Day, there were too many leaves on the trees to hunt grouse; and then the leaves would drop, the steelhead would return, and bluebills came hurtling out of the sky. I wanted to do and have it all, but there was not enough time. Two weeks later snow would fall, lakes would freeze, and autumn was over.

Fifty years ago outdoor writer Gordon MacQuarrie had a cabin not far from mine and wrote about the dilemma: "How would you like to hole up in a country where you could choose, as you fell asleep, between duck hunting and partridge hunting, between small-mouths on a good river like the St. Croix or trout on another good one like the Brule, or between muskie fishing on the Chippewa flowage or cisco dipping in the dark for the fun of it?"

Not much has changed since MacQuarrie roamed these woods, except perhaps for my thinking. Like the dun-colored days and pewter skies of early November, a certain maturity has finally settled in.

In autumn at the cabin, I'm made keenly aware that life is not so much a journey as it is a pursuit. It begins as a search for who we are before the chase begins for the things we desire. The lucky few among us eventually learn that the real prize is not the quarry but the quest. The quest is life and living; everything else is straw.

Contentment is the most elusive of quarries. For me, it was as long in coming as the first flock of bluebills. It was always there, like birds in a thicket, but I never knew it until I discovered satisfaction in the small and trifling things I do at the cabin: chopping wood, watching the weather, going for long walks with the dog and a gun toward an end that cannot be known. I no longer need or want it all because – to my way of thinking – I already have a lot; and a lot is more than enough. And because I've come to understand this, I am the luckiest of men.

Autumn is the season of thanksgiving.

Winter arrives in November just before deer season. It begins as a hush, as if November were holding its breath, before a rustling sound stirs the brown and lifeless woods and the air becomes white with swirling flakes. The coarse, crystalline snow settles onto logs and leaves and frozen lakes, obliterating landmarks. Within an hour autumn is a memory. Now begins the long, inanimate and alabaster abeyance of winter, the season of resignation.

In late November friends and family gather at the cabin for deer camp: sons and fathers, brothers and uncles, nephews and cousins, old friends and new faces. A cabin that was meant to sleep three people is suddenly home to a dozen. After a week, it can get to be too much of a good thing. Yet, when the last deer is taken down from the meat pole, and the caravan of pickups winds its way back along the twin ruts of the snowy road away from the cabin, the solitude with which I'm left is not as companionable as I remember.

In winter I'm usually alone at the cabin except for the squirrels and mice and weasels. On warm days when sundogs play above the horizon, I'll set out tip-ups on the ice for pike, or take the snowshoes and shotgun in search of white rabbits – "varying hares," the Canadians call them.

Some nights I watch the northern lights blaze below Polaris, while the frozen lake booms and groans with the sound of expanding ice. At midnight aspens explode as if rent with dynamite as the temperature plunges to thirty-below. I feel alone in an arctic landscape where every element is extinguishing life. And then, from back in the dark timber, the night's wintry isolation is pierced by a mournful howl – a low, deep-throated tolling that makes the goose flesh swarm over my arms.

The timber wolves trot in a straight line down the center of the lake, their tails pointing straight out behind them. The snow reflects the light of the moon, and the scene is illuminated in shades of royal blue and ivory. I'm safe in my cabin, but the deer have no shelter; and in the morning the snow will tell a tale of death in the woods.

But for me, the lucky one, there will be another tomorrow, with wood to split, fish to catch, trails to tramp, and long nights in front of the fire for dreaming. And that, I suppose, is the reason for the cabin. I built it as a getaway, only to discover I wasn't fleeing anything at all. Instead, I was running toward something: toward mystery, beauty, joy and wonder – toward life, and the adventure it was meant to be.

A BEAR BEYOND REASON

Over the past thirty-seven years he'd guided more than a hundred different hunters for Alaskan brown bear and grizzlies. Every bear hunt was memorable, especially for the client, but some were infinitely more so than others. This was one of those hunts.

By Karl Braendel

avid Anderson of Montrose, Minnesota flew into my main camp near the south end of Kodiak Island in mid-April of 2003. We had fifteen days ahead of us to connect on a big Kodiak bear. David arrived in excellent physical condition and he was looking forward to our back-packing expedition. But as he would tell me later, "I got more than my wildest dreams."

The first three days of our hunt flew by, mixed with rain, snow, low clouds and cool temperatures. We saw a few bears, but nothing to get excited over. I was waiting for a favorable wind that would allow us to pack into a valley hemmed by tall, snow-covered peaks. Finally, on the fourth day an easterly wind developed, perfect for hunting the long, narrow valley. We loaded our packs with enough food, fuel and gear to stay the duration and headed back in.

Our campsite was one of those magical places, framed by majestic mountains and blessed with an abundance of game. Sitka blacktails watched our every move as we followed the receding snowline up the surrounding slopes. Mountain goats hung from cliffs above camp and often moved to within several hundred yards of our tents to dine on the first green shoots of spring. But more than anything, this was big bear country.

The first full day dawned clear and 20 degrees. Dave and I rubbed on sunscreen and climbed up a nearby ridge. Within a few hours the sun heated the land and it was pure pleasure to be sitting out there, and especially to be seeing bears. Over the course of the day we spotted fourteen, including one sow with three cubs. Most of the animals were passing through immense snowfields that loomed above the valley. One bear appeared to be in the ten-foot class, but it disappeared into a convoluted maze of meandering ridges and high basins. We also counted at least a dozen blacktails and forty-one mountain goats before the evening clouds tumbled over the mountains to the east, bringing change for tomorrow.

The next three days were dominated by intermittent rain, wind and fog. Low visibility kept us from seeing much – just six bears – but we did glimpse a huge boar backing down off a snowy peak. On steep, snow-covered slopes, brown bears back down in much the same way a man would, or should, first looking over one shoulder and then the other until they reach a safer angle. This bear left a wide trail, which was soon swept over by clouds into a gray oblivion.

In the days to come Dave proved to be not only a diligent glasser, but an effective one as well, spotting his share of bears. Many clients struggle with boredom as there are always long dry spells when nothing seems to be happening, but bear hunting is all about perseverance and patience, and Dave had plenty of both.

The ninth day dawned with clear skies and warmer temperatures, and we headed up to our glassing ridge with renewed enthusiasm. Despite the day's promise, spotting was slow. We observed two sows, each with two cubs, and a couple of medium-sized singles. Then, just before dark we spotted a bear in the ten-foot class. We watched him until it was too dark to see, leaving him bedded on an exposed patch of muskeg at the snowline.

Rain and wind returned in force the next day, and despite our best efforts, we were unable to locate the big boy from the night before. While I continued to glass for the bear, Dave scanned the mountains around us and soon spotted a big boar digging a hole in the snow just below a high cliff on Pelletier Peak.

The mountain fell away hard just below the bear, and he kept sliding downward as he dug his snow den. He completely disappeared into the hole six or eight times, only to reemerge and start digging again. The snow flew off his paws like it was blasting out of a big mechanical snowblower. When he disappeared for the last time, his hole resembled a twenty-foot trench that angled downslope from right to left. The den was soon shrouded in fog.

That afternoon Dave asked, "You ever go up into a place like that after one of these guys?"

As I studied the mountain, I determined that the only possible approach was from a high, snow-filled basin southwest of the den. The last part would be extremely steep. I caught Dave's eye and cautiously said, "It's doable with the right wind . . . which isn't what we have right now, judging by the direction the clouds are moving. It would take awhile."

The next day rain, clouds and fog persisted, along with the same wind direction. We glassed all around us, but continued to keep an eye on the snow den. Most of the time we couldn't see that high up and even our brief glimpses failed to reveal anything.

On day twelve we started early and headed up-valley to French Meadows, right below Pelletier Mountain. Through occasional breaks in the clouds and fog, we were able to observe the den site, but we couldn't detect any tracks leaving the area. Despite the murky conditions, change was in the air. The clouds no longer raced across the sky, but draped the mountains like blankets, and there was a glow up high that promised better weather ahead.

"Well," I told Dave, "I figure there's a 90 percent chance he's still in that hole. I don't really see how he could have left after the warm, rainy days and nights we've been having, without leaving tracks."

"I'm game," Dave volunteered. "If you think we have a chance."

e started up at 9:15. A little over two hours of hard climbing brought us to the edge of the second and highest bowl, where we confronted a solid curtain of fog. We hunkered down to wait. I could feel the sun's warmth as we watched rock ptarmigan clucking and buzzing and parading around us. They reminded me of fashion models strutting down a runway. Finally, about 1 p.m. the clouds raised up enough for us to see our destination, a rock outcrop that hopefully would be within good shooting distance of the den.

The sun broke out and we began dripping sweat as we post-holed up the sheer slope. After fifty minutes of slow, difficult climbing we reached the rock outcrop, only 170 yards from the den. Even though it had been two days since we last saw the bear, I knew that the absence of tracks meant he was still there.

"Dave, get into as good a shooting position as you can," I instructed. "Use your pack for a rest. This wind isn't perfect . . . if he gets a whiff of us he'll be smoking tracks.

"Another thing to be thinking about: Don't shoot until he's free of that hole. I don't want any part of him hanging over the den, 'cause if he were to die in there, hell, we'd probably lose him. He'd spoil before we could dig him out – *if* we could dig him out."

We weren't there fifteen minutes when the bear appeared about halfway out of his den.

"Ooooh, man," I hissed. "He does look big."

Slowly the bear swung his keg-sized head to survey the country below.

"He looks like Godzilla up there," I whispered. I could feel my heart pounding and knew that Dave's had to be doing the same. "If you feel nervous, like buck fever nervous, take two or three deep breaths," I said. "If that doesn't do it, take two or three more."

As we waited in our state of high anticipation, the bear decided to lay down, with his rear end extending down into the hole. Thirty minutes went by. We gradually lost our fiery edge as the bear became more and more relaxed in the afternoon heat. I knew he might sleep for quite a while, and after another fifteen minutes impatience got the better of me.

"Be ready to shoot," I warned. "I'm going to let him know we're humans, and he's gonna run, so be ready. And make sure he's away from that hole!"

I'll always remember the look on the bear's face when I shouted, "Hey bear! Hey bear!" Faster than you can blink his relaxed demeanor went rigid and he spun 180 degrees, diving out of sight into his den.

At first I could hardly believe what I had seen. Instead of running away as I had expected, he had done the one thing that could save his life. Like a trapped king in a chess game, he had countered us with a crafty move that, at the very least, resulted in a draw for the present and quite possibly paved the way for his eventual escape. As I contemplated this turn of events, I gradually came to the uneasy realization that what had appeared to be a sure thing was now anything but.

I looked over at Dave and shook my head. "I can't believe he did that. He's not coming out of there until tonight. I'll bet on it."

The sun glared down, its rays reflecting off the snow so brightly that I was almost blinded. Dave insisted that I wear his sunglasses – I'd left mine at the tent – so I could see what was going on at the den. While we waited an eight-foot Kodiak came around the corner of the mountain and passed only 150 yards below us.

In the afternoon heat, snowslides began crashing down from an overhanging cornice, dumping snow into the bear's den. It didn't seem to matter. At least we were safe from the slides on our rock outcrop. Later, in frustration, I fired two shots into the snow near the den entrance. Nothing. *Only three hunting days left*, I thought.

Toward evening, with the cooler air the snow-slides came to an end and I said, "I'm going up there. I'm gonna try to get him out."

"Jees," Dave said. "Okay. I'll be ready. Be careful."

Treacherous is the only word to describe what I was about to attempt. I stepped out onto the steep slope and began climbing toward the den. As I moved higher, the pitch increased ever more sharply until I was stomping in my footholds – ten, twenty times each – as though that extra effort could buy me some insurance. Below, black jagged rocks pierced the snow, and I knew if I slipped and went skidding, the result wouldn't be pretty. But each time I wrestled with turning around, I would think of the huge Kodiak hiding less than eighty feet away and refocus my resolve. So close.

I reached a rock ledge where I broke off several crumbling pieces and lobbed them into the hole. Nothing. I sang *So Lonesome I Could Cry* and *Kansas City* and got silence in return. Desperation drove me. In fits and starts I climbed higher and higher until I was perched twenty feet directly above the den. The hole extended down into the snow at least eight or ten feet, so from my angle I couldn't see or hear anything.

I said, "You better come out bear. It's time." As I stood there making the occasional inane statement, rational thought returned inch by agonizing inch. Looking down, it occurred to me that one slip and I'd fall right into the bear's den. I imagined his mood to be surly. Then I had the uneasy thought that should he come boiling out and I had to fire my .375, the recoil might jar me loose and I'd either tumble into the den or slide past it to be gutted on the sharp rocks below.

Oh, the possibilities!

When I looked back to where Dave was hunkered down behind his rifle, I noticed that I was uncomfortably close to his line of fire should the bear come out. That's when it finally dawned on me: *This has got to be one of the more idiotic decisions I've ever made.* Along with that came the realization the bear wasn't going to be panicked into making a dumb move.

Slowly, and with great care, I started back down my trail, thankful to be in one piece. Thirty minutes later, as I slipped back onto our rocky perch, Dave shook his head and said, "Man, you went way beyond the call of duty up there . . . *waaayyyy beyond.* I wanted to call out to you to come back."

"Yeah, I finally realized that I was playing the idiot. That dang bear . . . he ain't coming out of there until tonight."

We discussed what to do next. At this point no plan seemed appealing. Faced with so much uncertainty, we decided to "siwash" (an old mountain man term for a makeshift camp without bedding, food and, usually, sleep) in the faint hope that the bear would make his move before dark.

We situated ourselves about fifty feet apart, so we each had a slightly different view of the den. At 11 p.m. I looked through my scope to see if there was enough shooting light. It was dark down in the valley, but I could still see my crosshairs against the snow. I figured we had about twenty more minutes of shooting light.

Shivering from the night's cold, I had just dropped down to knock off some pushups when I heard the loud roar of Dave's .338 Winchester.

"Criminy!" I jumped up, heard a second shot and saw the bear sliding down the snow with his head up. Dave fired again as the bear passed out of my line of sight behind some boulders between us. I heard a fourth shot and then the mountain went dark and silent.

Quickly I came around to Dave's side of the outcrop. "I was doing pushups to get warm when I heard your rifle go off!"

"He came out fast . . . backing down," said Dave, his voice piercing the dark. "I got off four shots. He looked pretty limp when he slid out of sight."

49

"I can't believe we finally got him," I said. "I *hope* we got him, anyway. This is going to make our siwash a lot easier to take."

The next morning, after a long shivery night, we found the snow had frozen rock hard, making it too dangerous for us to cross the steep slope to where the bear had disappeared. Worse yet, I estimated that it would take much of the day for the snow to soften again. All we could do was retrace yesterday's footsteps down to an easier slope, then climb back up to where the bear had disappeared.

Before long we came upon bloody tracks leading down over cliffs on the north face, where it was impossible to follow. Once again we had to backtrack. The icy slope angled down in pitches that were either too steep or almost too steep. They would tease us until we'd find ourselves barely hanging on a slope we should never have attempted to cross. I was wearing Koflach mountaineering boots, which had a definite edge over Dave's boots. Several times Dave found himself caught between fear and sheer panic. Later he would tell me that getting down those icy slopes was the most frightening experience of his life.

Once we got below the snowline, we resumed our search for the bear's trail. We climbed in and out of dark gullies and over piles of moss-covered boulders, with alders and salmonberry thorns tearing at our packs and clothes. It was tiring, but a relief not to be worried about falling to our death. I had stopped to rest and was glassing the cliffs above us when Dave suddenly said, "Hey, isn't that blood? Right there, in front of you."

"Sure enough," I responded, walking over to look at a string of dark red splotches. We began glassing the dense cover and less than a minute later, we were able to make out the bear through a small window in the brush. It looked as if he had died going downhill, which seemed to square with the amount of blood we'd seen. After several minutes of watching, I couldn't detect any movement and his position looked unconventional, as if he had piled up in the brush.

"He looks dead to me," I observed. "You might as well stay here; you can see all around. I'll go down and make sure. Cover me."

The alders and salmonberry were thick and noisy as I banged my way down the slope. I felt so sure the bear was dead the noise didn't seem to matter. As I neared the bear's location the brush grew taller, canopying overhead and closing off the light. I could only see about eight yards ahead of me. Suddenly I heard a low growl, then saw the rising form and giant head of the wounded Kodiak.

I jerked up my rifle, wondering if I could plow a shot through all the brush when he spun out of sight down through the alders. I yelled at Dave, "He's still alive!"

Dave fired his .338 twice, while I clamored up some large rocks to see the bear 200 yards below, still on his feet. I fired my .375 and then heard Dave shoot again. Somehow the bear stayed up and raced into the alders. I could just glimpse him here and there – slashes of movement – as he charged hell-bent down the mountainside. Just before he disappeared for good I heard Dave's rifle one last time and moments later saw the bear's feet come up in the alders.

This time I was sure we had him. Dave and I met partway down and agreed that the bear had gone feet-up in a thick patch of brush. But even then we couldn't find him! I searched up and down that mountainside for an hour, and I didn't have a good feeling at the end of it. *Was this some kind of supernatural bear?* I thought. *Had he somehow gotten up again and slipped away?*

After everything we'd been through over the past twenty-four hours, my brain was frazzled. Tall alders, salmonberry and elderberry brush extended in every direction. We weren't likely to find him by chance. Despite my fatigue, I climbed back up, found the blood trail and followed it out to where I discovered the bear dead in an alder-tangled gully. Finally, we were able to get our hands on him. He was one heck of a bear, but more than that, we'd had one heck of an experience.

We staggered into our spike camp with the hide just before midnight, looking for food, sleeping bags and relief for our burning feet. We'd survived a harrowing but enormously rewarding ordeal over the past thirty-six hours, one that neither of us would ever forget.

BELLE'S ERA

The stranger's story had defied reason. But the years had imparted the wisdom to accept it for the simple blessing it was. Perhaps there truly are angels among us.

By Mike Gaddis

The journey to the mailbox should have been exciting. There was a flawless, expectant stillness to the air, as if the world held its breath in waiting. Dense, leaden clouds layered the bottom of an ashen sky, leaving the fields gaunt and drawn in the penetrating chill, the woods and thickets huddled and lonely. Sparrows and juncos anxiously worked the fencerows, bunching and foraging with frenzied urgency. Absent the usual malediction, a line of crows lugged slowly by. It was compelling, unmistakable . . . the promise of snowfall.

But the memory was too fresh. He would have loved this day, for there were only a few such in any year, even more rarely at the tag end of February. The birds would move. Always before snow or ice, the birds would move.

The mail was uninspiring. She turned and started for the house, undeterred from the mood of the moment. Uncle Murray had been intrinsic in her life. He and Mary had no natural children of their own, but the fascinations of their antiquated, country lifestyle were irresistible to two generations of nieces and nephews. Never beleaguered by social convention, the veneer of their existence betrayed the culture and fervor of their lives. The barn and outbuildings, ancient and drab, stood around doubtfully on splayed legs. The same turn-of-the-century farmhouse was their home for seventy-eight years. From the outside, it would have appeared plebeian, even unkept. For at least half that time, it had worn the tattered remnants of its maiden coat of paint. But inside was a wealth of period music, antiques, books and oils that would have been the obelisk of any elitist townhouse. And out back was a neatly kept kennel with running water and a sewage lagoon. It was a reflection of their simple creed . . . passion without pretense. The old house weathered the storms on its own terms, gracefully, as they did.

Murray Britt had made special of her from the beginning. From the time he took her and her third birthday frock into a barn-stall full of marauding, seven-week July pups, he had won her heart. It was her first lesson, of many, from him on what was most important in life. Forever an outdoorsman and dog man, he kept ranks of pointing dogs and legions of hounds. For all the years of her childhood and even after she was grown with family, he would show up on an anonymous impulse with a box-full of dogs and an invitation to go a-huntin', totally oblivious to the possibility that anything in life could be more important to the moment. More often than not, it wasn't. She could mark the memorable events of their relationship by epochs of dogs . . . by Jake, Sadie, Belle, Pat or Gabe. As he habitually remarked, "If it hadn' got a dog in it, I never cared much for it." Most of all he cared for pointing dogs and quail hunts.

She snugged her coat to her neck, taken with a sudden awareness that the chill was growing. It was then, also, that she became conscious of the crunch of gravel under tire rubber at the end of the drive. The car was unfamiliar, an older, generic sedan that had once been a more virtuous blue. It was proceeding up the drive and she stopped to wait, slightly ill at ease. As it neared, it appeared that the driver was the only passenger, an older man with white hair. She began to relax.

"Pardon me, miss, would you by chance be Nida Giddens?" he inquired, as he pulled alongside. His face was gentle, his countenance comforting.

"Yes . . ." she responded, cautiously intrigued at her spoken name, "can I help you?"

"Please forgive the imposition, but I wonder if we might talk for a few minutes."

He climbed out of the car, and steadied himself with the assistance of a cane. "Arthritis, the doctors say," he commented, answering the unspoken question, "an abomination of age, I'm afraid." He wore khaki trousers, a frayed-at-the-fringes, cinnamon sport coat of corduroy that contrasted pleasingly with the sterling tones of his hair and mustache, and lacerated hunting boots with leached toes. She liked him immediately.

"I'm Frank Gupton." He extended a hand, and an affable smile. She accepted both.

"I'm sure you don't know me, but I hope you will come to forgive my intrusion. We can sit in the car if you like," he gestured, "but it's all the same to you, I'd as soon sit by the fence and enjoy the day."

"Yes, thanks," she replied, "I would prefer that." She led the way to a nearby fence corner with a comfortable bench of earth, her curiosity rising.

54

"What would you like to talk with me about?" The stillness punctuated the question.

"Bird hunting, actually," he smiled.

"Bird hunting!??"

"Yes, I have gathered that subject is not unfamiliar to you. Do you mind if I call you Nida?"

"No . . . I mean yes, please." "Bird hunting!?," she was repeating to herself silently, incredulously.

"Do you know the significance of today," he asked.

"No." More than you know . . . she had started to say.

"It's the last day of the quail season. And could you ever find a better one?"

"No, it's virtually perfect," she agreed.

"As perfect as it is, there is another, even more special to me. Fifteen years ago. I was a bit younger and sprier then, still kicking up a little dust. Red was still here . . . a lifelong friend. We both kept dogs and bird-hunted. We loved it more than anything.

"Fifteen years ago almost to the day, the bird season had wound down to the last Saturday. We had about worn our local territory out by then, and were up for a change of scenery. Somebody had told Red about a laid-back crossroads two counties south that was thick with quail, so we loaded up the guns and the dogs and were on the way about 4:30 in the morning, excited as schoolboys with a substitute teacher.

"It was a beautiful day for February, which usually goes limp and balmy on its gasping breath. Different from today, but nice nonetheless. The morning dawned bright and yellow over a heavy frost, and when the first rays of the sun hit the tops of the pines the highlights in the ice looked like Christmas candles. The weatherman was promising light winds, and afternoon temperatures that would never get out of the forties. It was all ahead of us . . . bittersweet though, being the last day and all . . . and we were feeling mellow. Just as the sun climbed high enough to put a halo around the field edges, with the land still mostly in shadows, and all those fires in the frost, my old hunting buddy Red looked out the car window and said, 'Don't want anything more than this . . . never wanted anything more.' I'll never forget that. We never said a lot to each other. Wasn't necessary."

His tale was warming nicely. Yet, she fought the urge to ask him why on earth he had arrived out of nowhere to tell it. Why to *her*? But the lull and tenor of the old man's voice was captivating, and an interruption would have been unsouthern.

"The country turned out to be everything we had hoped for," he continued. "Very few houses. Laid-out beanfields everywhere, patches of scrub lespedeza . . . briery heads in old grown-up weed fields, broomsedge here and there. Now and then there was an old garden plot gone to seed, an abandoned hog lot, or a cast-off tobacco bed. You could read quail into every nook and cranny of it."

55

"It was like that everywhere when I was growing up," Nida observed spontaneously.

The old man paused and pulled two sticks of horehound candy from his coat pocket. She smiled. It had been a long time since she had seen horehound candy.

"Care for a piece," he offered.

"Yes, thanks."

They pulled silently on the candy for a minute or so. The chill was growing ever more convincing under the somber sky, the air dampening as the afternoon waned. It would start soon.

"Did it turn out as well as you hoped," she asked.

"Yes," he said gently.

"We rode around awhile admiring the territory until we found an inviting field with no poster signs. We weren't in the habit of hunting without permission, but there wasn't a house anywhere close to go ask, and we were so excited over the prospects, we decided to go ahead. It didn't sit well though and before we got halfway across the field, we decided to gather up the dogs and find somebody to ask. It wasn't easy; the dogs were full of vinegar and in no mood to get back in the box, but we finally rounded 'em up and leased 'em. We had almost made it back to our car when an old, beat-up, green pickup came by, slowed down like it was going to stop, and then went on. In a couple of minutes it came back.

" 'Red,' I said, 'we're in for a chewing,' as the old truck pulled up and stopped. It had gouges in every fender, the paint was flaking off in spots, hanging like loose bark on a sycamore tree, and it kept running for fifteen seconds after the switch was killed. Red looked at me wall-eyed.

"The driver got out and looked at us. He was middle-aged and in farming garb, two days' worth of stubble on his chin, obviously a local. 'Where you boys from?,' he asked. No show of emotion either way.

"Red took all kinds of pains telling him and begging the situation. I thought he was doing pretty good, so I just kept my mouth shut and tried to look genuinely pitiful and repentant. About halfway through Red's apologetic diatribe, the man's face began to lighten a bit around the corners, and Red, sensing progress, turned it on all the more.

"Finally, the guy interrupted. 'Listen,' he said, smiling for the first time, 'why don't you boys just load your dogs in the back and go hunting with me.'

"I looked at Red in complete disbelief. He had a strange grin on his face like he had one foot in Heaven and a promise for the other."

"I guess so," Nida said, laughing, now fully invested in the story. "You went, I guess?"

"Wasn't a minute's debate. We generally hung pretty tight to ourselves, but this man had a way, and no doubt knew the country and everybody in it. He introduced himself, we shook hands all around, and started loading guns and dogs into that old truck. We had three pointers, Pete, Bell, and Duke, pretty good dogs! But Bell hated to back, and would steal a point when you weren't watching. We didn't know what to expect dog-wise from our host,

56

but wanted to be on our best behavior, so we left Bell in the box. We climbed into what was left of the front seat, me in the middle with the floor shift and an old Fox Model B between my legs, and rode a mile or two down the road. Red was beside himself, talking more than he had for the past three years.

"When we got to the first field we were going to hunt and turned out, eight bird dogs got out of the box! Or seven anyway. One was a question mark. He had four of the biggest, raw-boned, double-nosed pointer dogs we had ever seen, a strapping lemon-and-white pup on a check cord, and one small bitch that could almost have passed for a rabbit or a deer hound. That little dog could cover more ground than any dog I have ever seen, before or since. In polite company, she would have been liver-and-white, but the liver was more of a washed-out brown and the white was a sort of tobacco-stain yellow. She blended with the cover so well you could barely see her, so he ran her with a bell around her neck.

"Oh, what a morning it was. Clear and still, with a bite in the air . . . patches of frost still splattered around. We hadn't been down twenty minutes, when the little bitch pointed. She was flying down a long edge when she smelled those birds and swapped ends like her nose was nailed to a wall. She took two mincing steps and snapped into a point . . . and left skid marks in the dirt where her toenails dug in. *God, it was nice.* The covey had fed about forty yards into beanfield stubble and she was reading them the bill of rights.

"I had followed bird dogs for thirty-eight years, but the next few moments were easily the most moving of my hunting life. The sun was hard in our back, nine-thirty high, in that forever blue, crystal sky, and the light reached over our shoulders and cut that little bitch out of her ground shadow like a carving relieved from a block of yellow fieldstone. Seven other dogs arrived on the scene from five different directions, all in turn, and caved at the withers like they had been cleaved, honoring the find. The pup was last up and a peaceable "whoa" was all it took. They ended up in a semi-circle, eight dogs! The intensity was electrifying. It was eloquent. Breathtakingly eloquent."

"I would loved to have seen it," Nida offered, tears welling. "Once, I hunted with my uncle and we had five dogs standing. It's mesmerizing. You want to lock the moment away and relish it forever. It's like a Christmas present in special paper with something wonderful inside, but too pretty to unwrap."

"We savored it for quite a while before we kicked the birds up. When they went out, Red killed two, I got one, and the fellow we were hunting with knocked down three! It went that way, more or less, most of the way. We called it quits about mid-afternoon with sixteen birds in the bag. We thanked our benefactor profusely, this man who had been a virtual stranger only a few hours before. Whatever we said, it was totally inadequate. The conversation home that night was the best Red and I ever had. For the first time we tried to tell each other how much the years between us had meant, to relive a lot of the wonderful times we had enjoyed outdoors."

For the second and last time, Frank Gupton paused in his account and looked away for long moments across the shadowy landscape. Waiting mutely, Nida Giddens respected his silence. His story was beautiful, but there remained a question in her mind. Finally, he turned and looked at her with softened eyes.

"Nida, we hunted that day near the little community of Turkey in Sampson County. The man we hunted with, who so generously gave us that exquisite, final day of the bird season fifteen years ago, was your uncle, Murray Britt. He was the finest hunter and quail shot I have ever had the privilege of associating with. Red felt the same way. To this day, when someone mentions sportsmanship, I tell them about that day, and Murray Britt.

"I read his obituary in the paper in December. He died just three months after Red. The family note mentioned a niece, Nida Giddens, of Creedmoor. I live in Oxford, near the Brasstown Road. When I saw it, I knew I had to come and see you. I don't know how much longer I'll be here; it was a way of thanking him again, one last time. I asked around and found out where you lived. I purposely waited until today to come, so it would be an anniversary of sorts. I thought you would want to hear it. I hope I haven't upset you too badly. I wish I could say I ordered the day; it seems made for the purpose. Makes you wonder."

Nida Giddens was struggling to compose herself, trying to speak through the constriction in her throat and the tears in her eyes, and the mixture of pain and gratitude in her heart. He took her hand. "Call me sometime," he said softly, as he rose to leave. She tightened her grip on his hand, speaking a profound "thank you" with her eyes. The gravel whispered under the tires again and he was gone.

For a long time, she sat and stared into the eternal gray of the sky, trying to comprehend the magnitude of the day. How could it have possibly happened as it had? It defied reason. But the years had imparted the wisdom to leave it be, to accept it for the simple blessing it was. Perhaps there truly are angels among us.

The little bitch would have been Belle. She became as much of a legend in her time as her uncle in his. She, herself, would have been thirty-something then, endeavoring to weave a teaching career between the assiduous threads of family responsibilities in a different corner of the world. Her uncle would have already been well into his fifties. She thought about the time which had transpired since, and his passing, reminded acutely of the irrevocable velocity of the years.

"The puppy on the check cord would have been Luke or maybe Joe," she thought, as she gathered herself and started for the house once more. It was his trademark, a puppy on a check cord. So it must always be with men who set their worth by the measure of their dogs, find a passageway to tomorrow in faithful, hazel eyes, and wrap their memories in eras that hasten by on canine feet.

Almost as an illusion, the first notion of snow was on the air . . . tiny, vagabond flakes faintly stealing by, caught against the cathedral green of the pines . . . their faint ticking against the tinder leaves a welcome intimation.

Dusk was near. She could hear the clamor of the dogs at the kennel. Jarrod must be feeding. He was fifteen now. Almost off the check cord.

58

THE CHRISTMAS RIFLE

*This poignant story by an unknown author reminds us that
sometimes the best gift of all is sharing with those in need.*

Pa never had much compassion for the lazy or for
those who squandered their means and then never had
enough for the necessities. But for those who were genuinely
in need, his heart was as big as all outdoors. It was from him
that I learned the greatest joy in life comes from giving, not
from receiving.

It was Christmas Eve 1881. I was fifteen years old and feeling
like the world had caved in on me, because there just hadn't been enough money
to buy me the rifle that I'd wanted so badly that year for Christmas.

We did the chores early that night for some reason. I just figured Pa wanted
a little extra time so we could read in the Bible. After supper was over, I took
my boots off and stretched out in front of the fireplace, waiting for Pa to get
down the old Bible. I was still feeling sorry for myself and to be honest, I
wasn't in much of a mood to read Scriptures. But Pa didn't get the Bible;
instead he bundled up again and went outside. I couldn't figure it out, because
we had already done all the chores.

I didn't worry about it long though; I was too busy wallowing in self-pity. Soon

Pa came back in. It was a cold clear night out and there was ice in his beard.

"Come on, Matt," he said. "Bundle up good, it's cold out tonight." I was really upset then. Not only was I not getting the rifle for Christmas, but now Pa was dragging me out in the cold, and for no earthly reason that I could see. We'd already done all the chores, and I couldn't think of anything else that needed doing, especially not on a night like this. But I knew Pa was not very patient at dragging one's feet when he'd told them to do something, so I got up, put my boots back on, and got my cap, coat and mittens.

Ma gave me a mysterious smile as I opened the door to leave the house. Something was up, but I didn't know what.

Outside, I became even more dismayed. There in front of the house was the work team, already hitched to the big sled. Whatever it was we were going to do wasn't going to be a short or quick. I could tell. We never hitched up the sled unless we were going to haul a big load. Pa was up on the seat, reins in hand. I reluctantly climbed up beside him. The cold was already biting at me, and I wasn't happy.

When I was on, Pa pulled the sled around the house and stopped in front of the woodshed. He got off and I followed. "I think we'll put on the high sideboards," he said. "Here, help me."

The high sideboards! It had been a bigger job than
I wanted to do with just the low sideboards on, but whatever it was we were going to do would be a lot bigger with the high sideboards on.

After we had exchanged the sideboards, Pa went into the woodshed and came out with an armload of wood – the wood I'd spent all summer hauling down from the mountain and all fall sawing into blocks and splitting. What was he doing? Finally I said something.

"Pa," I asked, "what are you doing?"

"You been by the Widow Jensen's lately?" he asked. The Widow Jensen lived about two miles down the road. Her husband had died a year or so before and left her with three children, the oldest being eight.

Sure I'd been by, but so what? "Yeah," I said, "why?"

I rode by just today," Pa said. "Little Jakey was out digging around in the woodpile trying to find a few chips. They're out of wood, Matt."

That was all he said. He then turned and went back into the woodshed for another armload of wood. I followed him. We loaded the sled so high that I began to wonder if the horses would be able to pull it.

Finally, Pa called a halt to our loading and went to the smokehouse where he took down a big ham and a side of bacon. He handed them to me and told me to put them in the sled and wait. When he returned he was carrying a sack of flour over his right shoulder and a smaller sack of something in his left hand.

"What's in the little sack?" I asked.

"Shoes. They're out of shoes. Little Jakey had gunnysacks wrapped around his feet when he was out in the woodpile this morning. I got the children a little candy too. It just wouldn't be Christmas without a little candy."

e rode the two miles to Widow Jensen's pretty much in silence. I tried to think through what Pa was doing. We didn't have much by worldly standards. Of course, we did have a big woodpile, though most of what was left now was still in the form of logs that I would have to saw into blocks and split before we could use it. We also had meat and flour, so we could spare that, but I knew we didn't have any money, so why was Pa buying them shoes and candy? Really, why was he doing any of this? Widow Jensen had closer neighbors than us; it shouldn't have been our concern.

We came in from the blind side of the Jensen house, unloaded the wood as quietly as possibly, and took the meat and flour and shoes around to the front door. We knocked. The door opened a crack and a timid voice said, "Who is it?"

"Lucas Miles, Ma'am, and my son, Matt. Could we come in for a bit?"

Widow Jensen opened the door and let us in. She had a blanket wrapped around her shoulders. The children were wrapped in another and were sitting in front of the fireplace by a very small fire that hardly gave off any heat at all. Widow Jensen fumbled with a match and finally lit the lamp.

"We brought you a few things, Ma'am," Pa said and set down the sack of flour. I put the meat on the table. Then Pa handed her the sack that had the shoes in it. She opened it hesitantly and took the shoes out one pair at a time. There was a pair for her and one for each of the children – sturdy shoes, the best, shoes that would last.

I watched her carefully. She bit her lower lip to keep it from trembling and then tears filled her eyes and started running down her cheeks. She looked up at Pa like she wanted to say something, but it wouldn't come out.

"We brought a load of wood too, Ma'am," Pa said. He turned to me and said, "Matt, go bring in enough to last awhile. Let's get that fire up to size and heat this place up."

I wasn't the same person when I went back out to bring in the wood. I had a big lump in my throat and, as much as I hate to admit it, there were tears in my eyes, too. In my mind, I kept seeing those three kids huddled around the fireplace and their mother standing there with tears running down her cheeks with so much gratitude in her heart that she couldn't speak. My heart swelled within me and a joy that I'd never known before filled my soul. I had given at Christmas many times before, but never when it had made so much difference. I could see we were literally saving the lives of these people.

I soon had the fire blazing and everyone's spirits soared. The kids started giggling when Pa handed them each a piece of candy, and Widow Jensen looked on with a smile that probably hadn't crossed her face in a long time.

She finally turned to us. "God bless you," she said. "I know the Lord has sent you. The children and I have been praying that he would send one of his angels to spare us."

In spite of myself, the lump returned to my throat and the tears welled up in my eyes again. I'd never thought of Pa in those exact terms before, but after Widow Jensen mentioned it, I could see that it was probably true.

I was sure that a better man than Pa had never walked the earth. I started remembering all the times he had gone out of his way for Ma and me, and many others. The list seemed endless as I thought on it. Pa insisted that everyone try on the shoes before we left. I was amazed when they all fit and I wondered how he had known what sizes to get. Then I guessed that if he was on an errand for the Lord, the Lord would make sure he got the right sizes.

Tears were running down Widow Jensen's face again when we stood up to leave.

Pa took each of the kids in his big arms and gave them a hug. They clung to him and didn't want us to go. I could see that they missed their pa, and I was glad that I still had mine.

At the door, Pa turned to Widow Jensen and said, "The Mrs. wanted me to invite you and the children over for Christmas dinner tomorrow. The turkey will be more than the three of us can eat, and a man can get cantankerous if he has to eat turkey for too many meals. We'll be by to get you about eleven. It'll be nice to have some little ones around again. Matt, here, hasn't been little for quite a spell."

Widow Jensen nodded and said, "Thank you, Brother Miles, May the Lord bless you. I know for certain that He will."

Out on the sled, I fell a warmth that came from deep within and I didn't even notice the cold. When we had gone a-ways, Pa turned to me and said, "Matt, I want you to know something. Your ma and me have been tucking a little money away here and there all year so we could buy that rifle for you, but we didn't have quite enough. Then yesterday, a man who owed me a little money from years back came by to make things square. Your ma and me were real excited, thinking that now we could get you that rifle, and I started into town this morning to do just that. But on the way I saw little Jakey out scratching in the woodpile with his feet wrapped in those gunnysacks and I knew what I had to do. Son, I spent the money for shoes and a little candy for those children. I hope you understand."

I understand and my eyes became wet with tears again. I understand very well, and I was so glad Pa had done it. Now the rifle seemed very low on my list of priorities. Pa had given me a lot more. He had given me the look on Widow Jensen's face and the radiant smiles of her three children. For the rest of my life, whenever I saw any of the Jensens, or split a block of wood, I remembered, and remembering brought back that same joy I felt riding home beside Pa that night. Pa had given me much more than a rifle that night, he had given me the best Christmas of my life.

THE LADY OR THE SALMON

Take care, dear reader, lest you judge this gentle man too severely. For there may come a point in life when not even the keenest sense of honour, the most chivalrous affection and devotion, can stop us from snapping like a salmon line under stress.

By Andrew Lang

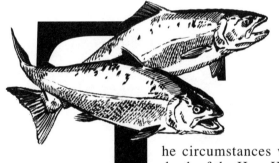

The circumstances which attended and caused the death of the Hon. Houghton Grannom have not long been known to me, and it is only now that, by the decease of his father, Lord Whitchurch, and the extinction of his noble family, I am permitted to divulge the facts. That the true tale of my unhappy friend will touch different chords in different breasts, I am well aware. The sportsman, I think, will hesitate to approve him; the fair, I hope, will absolve. Who are we to scrutinize human motives, and to award our blame to actions which, perhaps, might have been our own, had opportunity beset and temptation beguiled us? There is a certain point at which the keenest sense of honour, the most chivalrous affection and devotion, cannot bear the strain, but breaks like a salmon line under a masterful stress. That my friend succumbed, I admit; that he was his own judge, the severest, and passed and executed sentence on himself, I have now to show.

I shall never forget the shock with which I read in the *Scotsman*, under

"Angling," the following paragraph:

"Tweed – Strange Death of an Angler – An unfortunate event has cast a gloom over fishers in this district. As Mr. K–, the keeper on the B–water, was busy angling yesterday, his attention was caught by some object floating on the stream. He cast his flies over it, and landed a soft felt hat, the ribbon stuck full of salmon-flies. Mr. K– at once hurried upstream, filled with the most lively apprehensions. These were soon justified. In a shallow, below the narrow, deep and dangerous rapids called 'The Trows,' Mr. K– saw a salmon leaping in a very curious manner. On a closer examination, he found that the fish was attached to a line. About seventy yards higher he found, in shallow water, the body of a man, the hand still grasping in death the butt of the rod, to which the salmon was fast, all the line being run out. Mr. K– at once rushed into the stream, and dragged out the body, in which he recognized with horror the Hon. Houghton Grannom, to whom the water was lately let. Life had been for some minutes extinct, and though Mr. K– instantly hurried for Dr.–, that gentleman could only attest the melancholy fact. The wading in 'The Trows' is extremely dangerous and difficult, and Mr. Grannom, who was fond of fishing without an attendant, must have lost his balance, slipped, and been dragged down by the weight of his waders. The recent breaking off of the hon. gentleman's contemplated marriage on the very wedding-day will be fresh in the memory of our readers."

This was the story which I read in the newspaper during breakfast one morning in November. I was deeply grieved, rather than astonished, for I have often remonstrated with poor Grannom on the recklessness of his wading. It was with some surprise that I received, in the course of the day, a letter from him, in which he spoke only of indifferent matters, of the fishing which he had taken, and so forth. The letter was accompanied, however, by a parcel. Tearing off the outer cover, I found a sealed document addressed to me, with the superscription, "Not to be opened until after my father's decease." This injunction, of course, I have scrupulously obeyed. The death of Lord Whitchurch, the last of the Grannoms, now gives me liberty to publish my friend's *Apologia pro morte et vita sua*.

"Dear Smith" (the document begins), "Before you read this – long before, I hope – I shall have solved the great mystery – if, indeed, we solve it. If the water runs down to-morrow, and there is every prospect that it will do so, I must have the opportunity of making such an end as even malignity cannot suspect of being voluntary. There are plenty of fish in the water; if I hook one in 'The Trows,' I shall let myself go whither the current takes me. Life has for weeks been odious to me; for what is life without honour, without love, and coupled with shame and remorse?

Repentance I cannot call the emotion which gnaws me at the heart, for in similar circumstances (unlikely as these are to occur) I feel that I would do the same thing again.

"Are we but automata, worked by springs, moved by the stronger impulse, and unable to choose for ourselves which impulse that shall be? Even now, in decreeing my own destruction, do I exercise free-will, or am I the sport of hereditary tendencies, of mistaken views of honour, of a seeming self-sacrifice, which, perhaps, is but selfishness in disguise? I blight my unfortunate father's old age; I destroy the last of an ancient house; but I remove from the path of Olive Dunne the shadow that must rest upon the sunshine of what will eventually, I trust, be a happy life, unvexed by memories of one who loved her passionately.

Dear Olive! How pure, how ardent was my devotion to her none knows better than you. But Olive had, I will not say a fault, though I suffer from it, but a quality, or rather two qualities, which have completed my misery. Lightly as she floats on the stream of society, the most casual observer, and even the enamored beholder, can see that Olive Dunne has great pride, and no sense of humour. Her dignity is her idol. What makes her, even for a moment, the possible theme of ridicule is in her eyes an unpardonable sin. This sin, I must with penitence confess, I did indeed commit. Another woman might have forgiven me. I know not how that may be; I throw myself on the mercy of the court. But, if another could pity and pardon, to Olive this was impossible. I have never seen her since that fatal moment when, paler than her orange blossoms, she swept through the porch of the church, while I, dishevelled, mud-stained, half-drowned – ah! that memory will torture me if memory at all remains. And yet, fool, maniac, that I was, I could not resist the wild, mad impulse to laugh which shook the rustic spectators, and which in my case was due, I trust, to hysterical but not unmanly emotion.

If any woman, any bride, could forgive such an apparent but most unintentional insult, Olive Dunne, I knew, was not that woman. My abject letters of explanation, my appeals for mercy, were returned unopened. Her parents pitied me, perhaps had reasons for being on my side, but Olive was of marble. It is not only myself that she cannot pardon, she will never, I know, forgive herself while my existence reminds her of what she had to endure. When she receives the intelligence of my demise, no suspicion will occur to her; she will not say 'He is fitly punished; but her peace of mind will gradually return.

"It is for this, mainly, that I sacrifice myself, but also because I cannot endure the dishonour of a laggard in love and a recreant bridegroom.

"So much for my motives: now to my tale.

he day before our wedding-day had been the happiest in my life. Never had I felt so certain of Olive's affections, never so fortunate in my own. We parted in the soft moonlight; she no doubt, to finish her nuptial preparations; I, to seek my couch in the little rural inn above the roaring waters of the Budon.

Move eastward, happy earth, and leave
Yon orange sunset fading slow;
From fringes of the faded eve
Oh, happy planet, eastward go,

I murmured, though the atmospheric conditions were not really those described by the poet.

Ah, bear me with thee, smoothly borne,
Dip forward under starry light,
And move me to my marriage morn,
And round again to –

" 'River in grand order, sir,' said the voice of Robins, the keeper, who recognized me in the moonlight. 'There's a regular monster in the Ashweil,' he added, naming a favourite cast; 'never saw nor heard of such a fish in the water before.'

" 'Mr. Dick must catch him, Robins,' I answered; 'no fishing for me tomorrow.'

" 'No, sir,' said Robins, affably. 'Wish you joy, sir, and Miss Olive, too. It's a pity, though! Master Dick, he throws a fine fly, but he gets flurried with a big fish, being young. And this one is a topper.'

"With that he gave me good-night, and I went to bed, but not to sleep. I was fevered with happiness; the past and future reeled before my wakeful vision. I heard every clock strike; the sounds of morning were astir, and still I could not sleep. The ceremony, for reasons connected with our long journey to my father's place in Hampshire, was to be early – half-past ten was the hour. I looked at my watch; it was seven of the clock, and then I looked out of the window; it was a fine, soft, grey morning, with a south wind tossing the yellowing boughs. I got up, dressed in a hasty way, and thought I would just take a look at the river. It was, indeed, in glorious order, lapping over the top of the sharp stone which we regarded as a measure of the due size of water.

"The morning was young, sleep was out of the question; I could not settle my mind to read. Why should I not take a farewell cast, alone, of course? I always disliked the attendance of a gillie. I took my salmon rod out of its case, rigged it up, and started for the stream, which

66

flowed within a couple hundred yards of my quarters. There it raced under the ash tree, a pale delicate brown, perhaps a little thing too coloured. I therefore put on a large Silver Doctor, and began steadily fishing down the ash-tree cast.

"What if I should wipe Dick's eye, I thought, when, just where the rough and smooth water meet, there boiled up a head and shoulders such as I had never seen on any fish. My heart leaped and stood still, but there came no sensation from the rod, and I finished the cast, my knees actually trembling beneath me. Then I gently lifted the line, and very elaborately tested every link of the powerful casting-line. Then I gave him ten minutes by my watch; next, with unspeakable emotion, I stepped into the stream and repeated the cast.

"Just at the same spot he came up again; the huge rod bent like a switch, and the salmon rushed straight down the pool, as if he meant to make for the sea. I staggered on to dry land to follow him the easier, and dragged at my watch to time the fish; a quarter to eight. But the slim chain had broken, and the watch, as I hastily thrust it back, missed my pocket and fell into the water. There was no time to stoop for it; the fish started afresh, tore up the pool as fast as he had gone down it, and rushing behind the torrent, into the eddy at the top, leaped clean out of the water. He was seventy pounds if he was an ounce. Here he slackened a little, dropping back, and I got in some line.

"Now he sulked so intensely that I thought he had got the line round a rock. It might be broken, might be holding fast to a sunken stone, for aught that I could tell; and the time was passing, I knew not how rapidly. I tried all known methods, tugging at him, tapping the butt, and slackening line on him.

"At last the top of the rod was slightly agitated, and then, back flew the long line in my face. Gone! I reeled up with a sigh, but the line tightened again. He had made a sudden rush under my bank, but there he lay again like a stone. How long? Ah! I cannot tell how long! I heard the church clock strike, but missed the number of the strokes.

"Soon he started again downstream into the shallows, leaping at the end of his rush – the monster. Then he came slowly up, and 'jiggered' savagely at the line. It seemed impossible that any tackle could stand these short violent jerks. Soon he showed signs of weakening. Once his huge silver side appeared for a moment near the surface, but he retreated to his old fastness. I was in a tremor of delight and despair. I should have thrown down my rod, and flown on the wings of love to Olive and the altar. But I hoped that there was time still – that it was not so very late! At length he was failing. I heard ten o'clock strike. He came up and lumbered on the surface of the pool. Gradually I drew him, plunging ponderously, to the gravel beach, where I meant to 'tail' him. He yielded to the strain, he was in the shallows, the line was shortened. I stooped to seize him. The frayed and overworn gut broke at a knot, and with a loose roll he dropped back towards the deep. I sprang at him, stumbled, fell on him, struggled with him, but he slipped from my arms. In that moment I knew more than the anguish of Orpheus. Orpheus! Had I, too, lost my Eurydice? I rushed from the stream, up the steep bank, along to my rooms. I passed the church door. Olive, pale as her orange-blossoms, was issuing from the porch. The clock pointed to 10:45. I was ruined, I knew it, and I laughed. I laughed like a lost spirit. She swept past me, and, amidst the amazement of the gentle and simple, I sped wildly away. Ask me no more. The rest is silence."

Thus ends my hapless friend's narrative. I leave it to the judgment of women and of men. Ladies, would you have acted as Olive Dunne acted? Would pride, or pardon, or mirth have ridden sparkling in your eyes? Men, my brethren, would ye have deserted the salmon for the lady, or the lady for the salmon? I know what I would have done had I been fair Olive Dunne. What I would have done had I been Houghton Grannom I may not venture to divulge. For this narrative, then, as for another, "Let every man read it as he will, and every woman as the gods have given her wit."

"The Lady or the Salmon" is from Andrew Lang's 1891 classic, Angling Sketches.

I MAY HAVE TO SHOOT HIM

In this chapter from West with the Night, *which Ernest Hemingway once described as "a bloody wonderful book," the courageous aviatrix relives her hunting days with the Baron von Blixen and their terrifying encounter with a bull elephant.*

By Beryl Markham

I suppose, if there were a part of the world in which mastodon still lived, somebody would design a new gun, and men, in their eternal impudence, would hunt mastodon as they now hunt elephant. Impudence seems to be the word. At least David and Goliath were of the same species, but, to an elephant, a man can only be a midge with a deathly sting. It is absurd for a man to kill an elephant. It is not brutal, it is not heroic, and certainly it is not easy;
it is just one of those preposterous things that men do like putting a dam across a great river, one tenth of whose volume could engulf the whole of mankind without disturbing the domestic life of a single catfish.

Elephant, beyond the fact that their size and conformation are aesthetically more suited to the treading of this earth than our angular informity, have an average intelligence comparable to our own. Of course they are less agile and physically less adaptable than ourselves – Nature having developed their bodies in one direction and their brains in another, while human beings, on the other hand, drew from Mr. Darwin's lottery of evolution both the winning ticket and the stub to match it. This, I suppose, is why we are so wonderful and can make movies and electric razors and wireless sets – and guns with which to shoot the elephant, the hare, clay pigeons and each other.

The elephant is a rational animal. He thinks. Blix and I (also rational animals in our own right) have never quite agreed on the mental attributes of the elephant. I know Blix is not to be doubted because he has learned more about elephant than any other man I ever met, or even heard about, but he looks upon legend with a suspicious eye, and I do not.

There is a legend that elephant dispose of their dead in secret burial grounds and that none of these has ever been discovered. In support of this, there is only the fact that the body of an elephant, unless he had been trapped or shot in his tracks, has rarely been found. What happens to the old and diseased?

Not only natives, but many white settlers, have supported for years the legend (if it is legend) that elephant will carry their wounded and their sick hundreds of miles, if necessary, to keep them out of the hands of their enemies. And it is said that elephant never forget.

These are perhaps just stories born of imagination. Ivory was once almost as precious as gold, and wherever there is treasure, men mix it with mystery. But still, there is no mystery about the things you see yourself.

I think I am the first person ever to scout elephant by plane, and so it follows that the thousands of elephant I saw time and again from the air had never before been plagued by anything above their heads more ominous than tick-birds.

The reaction of a herd of elephant to my Avian was, in the initial instance, always the same – they left their feeding ground and tried to find cover, though often, before yielding, one or two of the bulls would prepare for battle and charge in the direction of the plane if it were low enough to be within their scope of vision. Once the futility of this was realized, the entire herd would be off into the deepest bush.

Checking again on the whereabouts of the same herd next day, I always found that a good deal of thinking had been going on amongst them during the night. On the basis of their reaction to my second intrusion, I judged that their thoughts had run somewhat like this: A: The thing that flew over us was no bird, since no bird would have to work so hard to stay in the air – and, anyway, we know all the birds. B: If it was no bird, it was very likely just another trick of those two-legged dwarfs against whom there ought to be a law. C: The two-legged dwarfs (both black and white) have, as long as our long memories go back, killed our bulls for their tusks. We know this because, in the case of the white dwarfs, at least, the tusks are the only part taken away.

The actions of the elephant, based upon this reasoning, were always sensible and practical. The second time they saw the Avian, they refused to hide; instead, the females, who bear only small, valueless tusks, simply

70

grouped themselves around their treasure-burdened bulls in such a way that no ivory could be seen from the air or from any other approach.

This can be maddening strategy to an elephant scout. I have spent the better part of an hour circling, criss-crossing, and diving low over some of the most inhospitable country in Africa in an effort to break such a stubborn huddle, sometimes successfully, sometimes not.

But the tactics vary. More than once I have come upon a large and solitary elephant standing with enticing disregard for safety, its massive bulk in clear view, but its head buried in a thicket. This was, on the part of the elephant, no effort to simulate the nonsensical habit attributed to the ostrich. It was, on the contrary, a cleverly devised trap into which I fell, every way except physically, at least a dozen times. The beast always proved to be a large cow rather than a bull, and I always found that by the time I had arrived at this brilliant if tardy deduction, the rest of the herd had got another ten miles away, and the decoy, leering up at me out of a small, triumphant eye, would amble into the open, wave her trunk with devastating nonchalance, and disappear.

This order of intelligence in a lesser animal can obviously give rise to exaggeration – some of it persistent enough to be crystallized into legend. But you cannot discredit truth merely because legend has grown out of it. The sometimes almost godlike achievements of our own species in ages past toddle through history supported more often than not on the twin crutches of fable and human credulity.

As to the brutality of elephant-hunting, I cannot see that it is any more brutal than ninety percent of all other human activities. I suppose there is nothing more tragic about the death of an elephant than there is about the death of a Hereford steer – certainly not in the eyes of the steer. The only difference is that the steer has neither the ability nor the chance to outwit the gentleman who wields the slaughter-house snickersnee, while the elephant has both of these to pit against the hunter.

The popular belief that only the so-called 'rogue' elephant is dangerous to men is quite wrong – so wrong that a considerable number of men who believed it have become one with the dust without even their just due of gradual disintegration. A normal bull elephant, aroused by the scent of man, will often attack at once – and his speed is as unbelievable as his mobility. His trunk and his feet are his weapons – at least in the distasteful business of exterminating a mere human; those resplendent sabres of ivory await resplendent foes.

Blix and I hardly came into this category at Kilamakoy – certainly not after we had run down the big bull, or, as it happened, the big bull had run down us. I can say, at once with gratification still genuine, that we were not trampled within that most durable of all inches – the last inch of our lives. We got out all right, but there are times when I still dream.

On arriving from Makindu, I landed my plane in the shallow box of a runway scooped out of the bush, unplugged wads of cotton wool from my ears, and climbed from the cockpit.

The aristocratically descended visage of the Baron von Blixen Finecke greeted me (as it always did) with the most delightful of smiles caught, like a strip of sunlight, on a familiar patch of leather – well-kept leather, free of wrinkles, but brown and saddle-tough.

Beyond this concession to the fictional idea of what a White Hunter ought to look like, Blix's face yields not a whit. He has gay, light blue eyes rather than sombre, steel-grey ones; his cheeks are well rounded rather than flat as an axe; his lips are full and generous and not pinched tight in grim realization of what the Wilderness Can Do. He talks. He is never significantly silent.

He wore then what I always remember him as wearing, a khaki bush shirt of 'solario' material, slacks of the same stuff, and a pair of low-cut moccasins with soles – or at least vestiges of soles. There were four pockets in his bush shirt, but I don't think he knew it; he never carried anything unless he was actually hunting – and then it was just a rifle and ammunition. He never went around hung with knives, revolvers, binoculars or even a watch. He could tell time by the sun, and if there were no sun, he could tell it, anyway. He wore over his closely cropped greying hair a terai hat, colourless and limp as a wilted frond.

He said, "Hullo, Beryl," and pointed to a man at his side – so angular as to give the impression of being constructed entirely of barrel staves.

"This," said Blix, with what could hardly be called Old World courtesy, "is Old Man Wicks."

"At last," said Old Man Wicks, "I have seen the Lady from the Skies."

Writing it now, that remark seems a little like a line from the best play chosen from those offered by the graduating class of Eton, possibly in the late twenties, or like the remark of a man up to his ears in his favourite anodyne. But, as a matter of fact, Old Man Wicks, who managed a piece of no-man's-land belonging to the Manoni Sugar Company, near Masongaleni, had seen only one white man in sixteen months and, I gathered, hadn't seen a white woman in as many years. At least he had never seen an aeroplane and a white woman at the same time, nor can I be sure that he regarded the spectacle as much of a Godsend. Old Man Wicks, oddly enough, wasn't very old – he was barely forty – and it may have been that his monkish life was the first choice of whatever other lives he could have led. He looked old, but that might have been protective colouration. He was a gentle, kindly man helping Blix with the safari until Winston Guest arrived.

It was a modest enough safari. There were three large tents – Winston's, Blix's, and my own – and then there were several pup tents for the native boys, gun-bearers, and trackers. Blix's boy Farah, Winston's boy, and of course my Arab Ruta (who was due via lorry from Nairobi) had pup tents to themselves. The others, as much out of choice as necessity, slept several in a tent. There was a hangar for the Avian, made out of a square of tarpaulin, and there was a baobab tree whose shade served as a veranda to everybody. The immediate country was endless and barren of hills.

Half an hour after I landed, Blix and I were up in the Avian, hoping, if possible, to spot a herd of elephant before Winston's arrival that night. If we could find a herd within two or three days' walking distance from the camp, it would be extraordinary luck – always provided that the herd contained a bull with respectable tusks.

It is not unusual for an elephant hunter to spend six months, or even a year, on the spoor of a single bull. Elephant go where men can't – or at least shouldn't.

Scouting by plane eliminates a good deal of the preliminary work, but when as upon occasion I did spot a herd not more than thirty or forty miles from camp, it still meant that those forty miles had to be walked, crawled or wriggled by the hunters – and that by the time this body and nerve-racking manoeuvre had been achieved, the elephant had pushed on another twenty miles or so into the bush. A man, it ought to be remembered, has to take several steps to each stride of an elephant, and, moreover, the man is somewhat less than resistant to thicket, thorn trees and heat. Also (particularly if he is white) he is vulnerable as a peeled egg to all things that sting – mosquitoes, scorpions, snakes and tsetse flies. The essence of elephant-hunting is discomfort in such lavish proportions that only the wealthy can afford it.

Blix and I were fortunate on our very first expedition out of Kilamakoy. The Wakamba scouts on our safari had reported a large herd of elephant containing several worthwhile bulls, not more than twenty air miles from camp. We circled the district indicated, passed over the herd perhaps a dozen times, but finally spotted it.

A herd of elephant, as seen from a plane, has a quality of an hallucination. The proportions are wrong – they are like those of a child's drawing of a field mouse in which the whole landscape, complete with barns and windmills, is dwarfed beneath the whiskers of the mighty rodent who looks both able and willing to devour everything, including the thumb-tack that holds the work against the schoolroom wall.

Peering down from the cockpit at grazing elephant, you have the feeling that what you are beholding is wonderful, but not authentic. It is not only incongruous in the sense that animals simply are not as big as trees, but also in the same sense that the twentieth century, tidy and svelte with stainless steel as it is, would not possibly permit such prehistoric monsters to wander in its garden. Even in Africa, the elephant is as anomalous as

73

the Cro-Magnon Man might be shooting a round of golf at Saint Andrews in Scotland.

But, with all this, elephant are seldom conspicuous from the air. If they were smaller, they might be. Big as they are, and coloured as they are, they blend with everything until the moment they catch your eye.

They caught Blix's eye and he scribbled me a frantic note; "Look! The big bull is enormous. Turn back. Doctor Turvy radios I should have some gin."

Well, we had no radio – and certainly no gin in my plane. But just as certainly, we had Doctor Turvy.

Doctor Turvy was an ethereal citizen of an ethereal world. In the beginning, he existed only for Blix, but long before the end, he existed for everybody who worked with Blix or knew him well.

Although Doctor Turvy's prescriptions indicated that he put his trust in a wine list rather than a pharmacopoeia, he had two qualities of special excellence in a physician; his diagnosis was always arrived at in a split second – and he held the complete confidence of his patient. Beyond that, his adeptness at mental telepathy (in which Blix himself was pretty well grounded) eliminated the expensive practice of calling round to feel the pulse or take a temperature. Nobody ever saw Doctor Turvy – and that fact, Blix insisted, was bedside manner carried to its final degree of perfection.

I banked the Avian and turned toward camp.

ithin three miles of our communal baobab tree, we saw four more elephant – three of them beautiful bulls. The thought passed through my head that the way to find a needle in a haystack is to sit down. Elephant are never within three miles of camp. It's hardly cricket that they should be. It doesn't make a hunter out of you to turn over on your canvas cot and realize that the thing you are hunting at such expense and physical tribulation is so contemptuous of your prowess as to be eating leaves right in front of your eyes.

But Blix is a practical man. As a White Hunter, his job was to produce the game desired and to point it out to his employer of the moment. Blix's work, and mine, was made much easier by finding the elephant so close. We could even land at the camp and then approach them on foot to judge more accurately their size, immediate intentions and strategic disposition.

Doctor Turvy's prescription had to be filled, and taken, of course, but even so, we would have time to reconnoitre.

We landed on the miserly runway, which had a lot in common with an extemporaneous badminton court, and, within twenty minutes, proceeded on foot toward those magnificent bulls.

Makula was with us. Neither the safari nor this book, for that matter, could be complete without Makula. Though there are a good many Wakamba trackers available in East Africa, it has become almost traditional in late years to mention Makula in every book that touches upon elephant-hunting, and I would not break with tradition.

Makula is a man in the peculiar position of having gained fame without being aware of it. He can neither read nor write; his first language is Wakamba, his second a halting Swahili. He is a smallish ebon-tinted Native with an inordinately wise eye, a penchant for black magic, and the instincts of a beagle hound. I think he could track a honeybee through a bamboo forest.

No matter how elaborate the safari on which Makula is engaged as tracker, he goes about naked from the waist up, carrying a long bow and a quiver full of poisoned arrows. He has seen the work of the best rifles white men have yet produced, but when Makula's nostrils distend after either a good or a bad shot, it is not the smell of gunpowder that distends them; it is a kind of restrained contempt for that noisy and unwieldly piece of machinery with its devilish tendency to knock the untutored huntsman flat on his buttocks every time he pulls the trigger.

Safaris come and safaris go, but Makula goes on forever. I suspect at times that he is one of the wisest men I have ever known – so wise that, realizing the scarcity of wisdom, he has never cast a scrap of it away, though I still remember a remark he made to an overzealous newcomer to his profession: "White men pay for danger – we poor ones cannot afford it. Find your elephant, then vanish, so that you may live to find another."

Makula always vanished. He went ahead in the bush with the silence of a shade, missing nothing, and the moment he had brought his hunters within sight of the elephant, he disappeared with the silence of a shade, missing everything.

Stalking just ahead of Blix through the tight bush, Makula signalled for a pause, shinnied up a convenient tree without noise, and then came down again. He pointed to a chink in the thicket, took Blix firmly by the arm, and pushed him ahead. Then Makula disappeared. Blix led, and I followed.

The ability to move soundlessly through a wall of bush as tightly woven as Nature can weave it is not an art that can be acquired much after childhood. I cannot explain it, nor could Arab Maina who taught me ever explain it. It is not a matter of watching where you step; it is rather a matter of keeping your eyes on the place where you want to be, while every nerve becomes another eye, every muscle develops reflex action. You do not guide your body, you trust it to be silent.

We were silent. The elephant we advanced upon heard nothing – even when the enormous hindquarters of two bulls loomed before us like grey rocks wedded to the earth.

Blix stopped. He whispered with his fingers and I read the whisper. "Watch the wind. Swing round them. I want to see their tusks."

Swing, indeed! It took us slightly over an hour to negotiate a semicircle of fifty yards. The bulls were big – with ivory enough – hundred-pounders at least, or better.

Nimrod was satisfied, wet with sweat, and on the verge, I sensed, of receiving a psychic message from Doctor Turvy. But this message was delayed in transit.

One bull raised his head, elevated his trunk, and moved to face us. His gargantuan ears began to spread as if to capture even the sound of our heart-beats. By chance, he had grazed over a spot we had lately left, and he had got our scent. It was all he needed.

I have rarely seen anything so calm as that bull elephant – or so casually determined upon destruction. It might be said that he shuffled to the kill. Being, like all elephant, almost blind, this one could not see us, but he was used to that. He would follow scent and sound until he could see us, which, I computed, would take about thirty seconds.

Blix wiggled his fingers earthward, and that meant, "Drop and crawl."

It is amazing what a lot of insect life goes on under your nose when you have got it an inch from the earth. I suppose it goes on in any case, but if you are proceeding on your stomach, dragging your body along by your fingernails, entomology presents itself very forcibly as a thoroughly justified science. The problem of classification alone must continue to be very discouraging.

By the time I had crawled three feet, I am sure that somewhere over fifty distinct species of insect life were individually and severally represented in my clothes, with Siafu ants conducting the congress.

Blix's feet were just ahead of my eyes – close enough so that I could contemplate the holes in his shoes, and wonder why he ever wore any at all, since he went through them almost in a matter of hours. I had ample time also to observe that he wore no socks. Practical, but not *comme il faut*. His legs moved through the underbrush like dead legs dragged by strings. There was no sound from the elephant.

I don't know how long we crawled like that, but the little shadows in the thicket were leaning toward the east when we stopped. Possibly we had gone a hundred yards. The insect bites had become just broad, burning patches.

We were breathing easier – or at least I was – when Blix's feet and legs went motionless. I could just see his head close against his shoulder, and watch him turn to peek upward into the bush. He gave no signal to continue. He only looked horribly embarrassed like a child caught stealing eggs.

But my own expression must have been a little more intense. The big bull was about ten feet away – and at that distance elephant are not blind.

Blix stood up and raised his rifle slowly, with an expression of ineffable sadness.

"That's for me," I thought. "He knows that even a shot in the brain won't stop that bull before we're crushed like mangos."

In an open place, it might have been possible to dodge to one side, but not here. I stood behind Blix with my hands on his waist according to his instructions. But I knew it wasn't any good. The body of the elephant was swaying. It was like watching a boulder, in whose path you were trapped, teeter on the edge of a cliff before plunging. The bull's ears were spread wide now, his trunk was up and extended toward us, and he began the elephant scream of anger which is so terrifying as to hold you silent where you stand, like fingers clamped upon your throat. It is a shrill scream, cold as winter wind.

It occurred to me that this was the instant to shoot.

Blix never moved. He held his rifle very steady and began to chant some of the most striking blasphemy I have ever heard. It was colourful, original, and delivered with finesse, but I felt that this was a badly chosen moment to test it on an elephant – and ungallant beyond belief if it was meant for me.

The elephant advanced, Blix unleashed more oaths (this time in Swedish), and I trembled. There was no rifle shot. A single biscuit tin, I judged, would do for both of us – cremation would be superfluous.

"I may have to shoot him," Blix announced, and the remark struck me as an understatement of classic magnificence. Bullets would sink into that monstrous hide like pebbles into a pond.

Somehow you never think of an elephant as having a mouth, because you never see it when his trunk is down, so that when the elephant is quite close and his trunk is up, the dark red-and-black slit is by way of being an almost shocking revelation. I was looking into our elephant's mouth with a kind of idiotic curiosity when he screamed again – and thereby, I am convinced, saved both Blix and me from a fate no more tragic than simple death, but infinitely less tidy.

The scream of that elephant was a strategic blunder, and it did him out of a wonderful bit of fun. It was such an authentic scream of such splendid resonance, that his cronies, still grazing in the bush, accepted it as legitimate warning, and left. We had known they were still there because the bowels of peacefully occupied elephant rumble continually like oncoming thunder – and we had heard thunder.

They left, and it seemed they tore the country from its roots in leaving. Everything went, bush, trees, san-sivera, clods of dirt – and the monster who confronted us. He paused, listened, and swung round with the slow irresistibility of a bank-vault door. And then he was off in a typhoon of crumbled vegetation and crashing trees.

For a long time there wasn't any silence, but when there was, Blix lowered his rifle – which had acquired, for me, all the death-dealing qualities of a feather duster.

I was limp, irritable, and full of maledictions for the insect kind. Blix and I hacked our way back to camp without the exchange of a word, but when I fell into a canvas chair in front of the tents, I forswore the historic propriety of my sex to ask a rude question.

"I think you're the best hunter in Africa, Blickie, but there are times when your humour is gruesome. Why in hell didn't you shoot?"

Blix extracted a bug from Doctor Turvy's elixir of life and shrugged.

"Don't be silly. You know as well as I do why I didn't shoot. Those elephant are for Winston."

"Of course I know – but what if that bull had charged?"

Farah the faithful produced another drink, and Blix produced a non sequitur. He stared upward into the leaves of the baobab tree and sighed like a poet in love.

"There's an old adage," he said, "translated from the ancient Coptic, that contains all the wisdom of the ages – 'Life is life and fun is fun, but it's all so quiet when the goldfish die.' "

FOR MY WIFE

Nothing, it seemed, would ever relieve the ache that he felt for his wife and quiet the furies in his soul. And then, at the edge of his beloved Solitude Pool, an old man appeared with a favor to ask.

By Todd Tanner

he river is bordered by oak. In truth, there are other trees on the surrounding hillsides – maple, birch, the occasional willow – but the oaks give the river its character, its flavor. As the vintner's barrel shapes the wine, so a hardwood defines this narrow New England valley and the river that shares its name.

There's a pull-off on the west end road, a narrow strip of dirt and gravel just big enough to hold two cars. It's bounded by asphalt on one side and an old, vine-laced stone wall on the other, and it's the last place to park before the country lane that follows the river turns and climbs the ridge toward the small town of Kent. Between the wall and the river are oaks, and the trail (six hundred and twenty-three paces, give or take a few) down to Solitude Pool.

Each and every night after work, John Morrison parked in that last small pull-off. He parked his pick-up dead center, so that not even a Volkswagen (or the Reverend Cunningham's tiny yellow Yugo) had room to squeeze in beside him, and then he walked down to the river in his waders and vest.

On occasion, he felt guilty about monopolizing his parking spot. Only on occasion, though. Most of the time, it didn't enter his mind. And never after he reached the river.

The fishing was that good.

On a warm Tuesday evening, with his windows rolled down so he could enjoy the scent of the newly budded leaves, John arrived at the pull-off – which, over the last few years, he had come to think of as *his* pull-off; almost as if he were the President and CEO of Solitude Pool and, as such, deserved his own named and numbered parking slot – only to find that a station wagon occupied his space. Or, to be accurate, one-half of his space; there was, curiously, just enough room for him to slip in alongside.

John grumbled a bit over the inconvenience of someone else taking his spot (and over the possibility of having to share his favorite stretch of river with a stranger) but it was, at most, a brief grumble. After all, he no more owned the river and the parking spot than he owned the air he breathed, and chances were that the station wagon belonged to either another flyfisherman or, perhaps, a couple walking their dog. How could he complain?

So, in a tradition that stretches back into the dim recess of angling history, he dressed and assembled his gear, then started down the trail. To the Solitude Pool.

It's an apt name, the Solitude Pool. The river's bend is gentle, like the flowing curve of a woman's calf, and the oaks that line both banks shield the view from above and below. The water, colder than you might think, spreads from shore to shore with hardly a ripple, and one lone boulder, the remnant of an earlier age, an age when fire and ice fought to shape the earth's surface, sits mid-stream. It is a place for dreamers, and for fishermen.

There was indeed a man there. He stood on the bank, looking out over the river, and though his back was to John, it was obvious he was older, perhaps twenty-five or thirty years older than John's own forty-two. He wore a sweater despite the evening's warmth, and a nondescript pair of oft-pressed pants and his hair, what was left of it, was past gray, yet not altogether white – salt and pewter instead of salt and pepper.

He turned as he heard John approach, surprised at the sound of another human being, and John was struck by the old man's eyes. They were clear and blue.

John nodded, the tip of his cap rising and then falling, and kept walking. The old man said nothing, but nodded back, the gesture of a man who understood where he was, and what type of response was appropriate. In rural New England, there's an art to speaking without words.

John moved past, thirty yards or so, then waded out into the river, taking his time as he made his way. On most nights, he sat on the bank for half-an-hour, even forty-five minutes, before slipping into the water, all the while watching the surface and getting a feel for what the evening might bring. Tonight, though, he wanted to be waist deep, immersed in the rhythm of the current and the complimentary rhythm of his casting; separated by distance and water and the keen edge of concentration from the world of people and distraction.

Later, when the sun had slipped down behind the western ridge, he looked over and noticed that the old man had gone, and that he was alone.

The next night, and the next, and also the night after were very much the same. John parked alongside the station wagon and walked down to the river, where the old man waited, blue eyes tinged with . . . with something John couldn't quite read. Perhaps, he thought, perhaps it was understanding.

Always they nodded, and always John walked by, and the old man watched him fish for a time before leaving. Briefly on the fourth night, before the passion took him, John wondered what it would be like to look through the old man's eyes.

Blue eyes.

John never fished on the weekends – there were too many people doing too many things; kayakers and canoeists and hikers and birders and a gaggle of other fishermen, all tripping over each other until the river took on the sunset summer buzz of a beehive. Monday came soon enough, though, as Monday's are wont to do, and once again John parked next to the station wagon.

As he anticipated, the old man was waiting at the Solitude Pool. John nodded and kept walking, but the old man cleared his throat, a prelude to speech, and John stopped.

It was cool in the shade of the oaks.

"Young fellow," the old man started, his voice soft, yet deep and resonant. "I have a favor to ask.

"I've noticed that you're an angler, and quite a good one. Like you, I used to fish with a flyrod. In fact I fished here for years . . ."

He paused, and his right hand motioned toward the river, sweeping around to take in the expanse of Solitude Pool.

John looked to the water, following the old man's gesture, and then his eyes sought the other's weathered face.

Understanding. Yes, he was sure it had been understanding.

"But I can't fish anymore."

To John's ears, that sentence, with its five simple words delivered in a level, even voice, was incomprehensible. He took a step back.

To stop fishing. To give up the river and its mysteries. To lose the soothing, hypnotic rhythm of those graceful metronome movements. What, he wondered, thinking of the darkness straining inside, what would quiet the furies in your soul?

The old man waited for a moment, giving John a chance to digest what he'd just said, and then went on.

81

"So, I was hoping that if you caught a few small trout tonight, you might keep one or two. For my wife."

Flustered, John looked down at the rod in his hand and then off toward the river.

"She loves trout. Brookies most of all, but a rainbow, even a brown trout, would be fine."

They both stood there in silence, John eyeing the water while the old man waited.

After a minute had stretched to two with no sound but the breeze, John finally answered.

"I'm sorry . . .," he said, his words coming slowly to start, then gathering speed as if they were birds in flight, "but I don't keep the fish I catch. I let them all go. It's called catch and release, and it's the reason the river's come back so well. In fact, it's . . ." His voice trailed off as he noticed the slump of the old man's shoulders and the way he'd dropped his eyes.

"I understand," the old man said. "I know about catch and release. It's all right. Thank you anyway."

As John walked past, strangely grateful their brief conversation was over, he heard the old man speak again.

"They were . . ." the old man paused, pride warring with the obvious need to make John understand. "They were for my wife."

Half-an-hour later, as he cradled a small brook trout with its glowing halo spots and fins all edged in white, John thought about the old man's request, and then about Mary, his own dear, sweet Mary, and the accident. If she had asked, if she had been there to ask, how could he have denied her? How could he ever deny her anything?

He slipped the trout back into the water, gentle as a father with a newborn babe, and turned his face from the watcher on the shore.

The next night John was on the water early, even before the shadows, and he fished hard and with a vengeance. Vengeance is no way to fish, however, and the still waters of Solitude Pool rebuked him. By dark he'd caught no trout, and if the old man waited on shore, John hadn't noticed. Finally, he walked out alone with the moon shining down through the trees.

The following day, a Wednesday, John arrived early once again. He fished differently, though, with a pace more befitting the long rod he plied, and when the old man trudged down the path a full hour later, slow and careful because of the exposed rocks and roots, John was already waiting on the bank.

The old man nodded, and John, realizing that the time had come, nodded back. He thought for a moment about what he'd done, examining the implications in his mind, rolling them around and around as if each thought was a smooth, gray pebble from the bottom of the river, and then he reached down into the water.

He felt the cold and wet on his hand, the pool's icy cool embrace, and his fingers closed around a stick he'd cut with his pocket knife twenty minutes earlier. A forked stick. When he pulled it out of the river, two brook trout dangled from the forked end, a nine-incher and an eight.

For a time the old man said nothing as he studied John and the trout. Then, in a voice that matched the gratitude in his eyes, he told John, "Thank you. Thank you very much."

The old man took John's offering, took the stick with the two dangling fish – their spots glowing fierce in the setting sun, luminous with the incandescence of distant stars, or an evening meadow alight with fireflies – and started up the trail.

After a few steps, though, he paused and turned back to where John was standing.

He smiled, then, for a moment, and said, "They're better fresh."

John nodded.

"I know."

Then he watched the old man walk away.

A few hours later, as the last vestiges of twilight gave way to full-blown darkness, John himself headed up the trail from Solitude Pool. Bats flitted through the trees around him, and crickets sang their nightly chorus. In his left hand he carried his rod, an old bamboo that had belonged to his father, and in his right he carried a forked stick of his own, with a lone brook trout hanging from the end. As he walked, he rubbed his thumb over the point of the stick, and thought back to all the things his father had taught him.

Afterwards, in his kitchen, he cleaned the fish, and cut off its head, and fried it in a cast iron skillet with butter and lemon. He boiled potatoes, and made a small salad with spinach, arugula, lemon and garlic, and then he sat down to eat. Before he did, though, he opened a beer and looked across the table at Mary's place, and he remembered her smile, and felt the ache that never really went away.

Later, when he was done and there was nothing left but thin white bones, he sat in his chair and thought about the first trout he'd kept in a dozen years, and the love of an old man for his wife, and about what it really meant to be alone. After a while he sighed, a low, soft sound like summer slipping into autumn.

On the next night, a Thursday night in the middle of the month of May, no one came to the Solitude Pool. It was quiet and peaceful, and the only sounds were from the river passing by and the evening breeze sliding through the oaks.

DUEL AT TURNER'S POOL

He learned a sacred lesson that day at Turner's Pool – that some things must never be compromised, not for glory, not to save face, not for friends or even for family.

By Cliff Hauptman

It happened just this way in the spring of 1962, thirty-five years ago almost to the day. I saw it with my own eyes.

The old guys, looking like a box full of White Wulffs, were all inside Putnam's Fly Shop, sitting on the chairs they had just dragged back in from the front porch where they had been sitting before the blackflies found them. Now they were back in their winter formation, occupying the corner opposite the counter where Putnam had the cash register and the dry fly display. I was over to the left of the counter, trying to put the wet flies and streamers back into some kind of order, this being just after opening day.

It had been a warm spring so far, things seeming to be happening a little ahead of the usual schedule – shadbush popping out by April Fool's Day and the maples in nearly full leaf soon after. Still, though, the mayflies were slow in coming and opening day anglers showed early success with many of the classic wets like Coachmen and Rube Woods. That caused a run on the shop by nearly everyone who came in the next wave and, now, eight days later, I was still trying to clean up the mess, picking #10 Gray Ghosts out of

85

the #10 Hornbergs, and #12 Black Gnats out of the #10s.

The old guys weren't fishing because it was Easter Sunday. All widowers, they shared a peculiar deference to their departed wives, whom they all felt would have looked badly upon their not spending the day in church. While none had the slightest inclination toward formalized prayer, they all, to a man, and without discussion, saw the hiatus from fishing as a judicious, if not mandatory compromise. Putnam, himself a widower, opened the shop so all the old guys could have a place to spend the day, halfway between God and the stream.

My Granddad, Max Craft, was one of the old guys. I always saw him as their undeclared leader of sorts, kind of a Royal Wulff among the Whites, the one to whom all eventually conceded in matters of fishing, if nothing else. That may have just been my own perspective, though, distorted by my juvenile love for the old man. He was in the process of teaching me everything he knew about flyfishing. I, as a fifteen-year-old, thought he already had. The culmination of his influence, it seemed to me, was when he had cajoled Putnam into hiring me as clerk in his flyshop. Putnam's acquiescence I took as proof that I was the *wunderkind* I thought I was.

When the stranger walked in, the shop fell so silent that I actually heard the #12 Micky Finn I had just dropped hit the floor with a whispered click. From my perspective opposite the newcomer, I could see the eyes of the old guys, scanning him from top to bottom, every face agape, as though a brand new creature had just introduced himself into the universe.

The stranger looked to be in his mid-thirties, a dapper little guy as well-coiffed and clean-shaven as a perfectly clipped Muddler Minnow. He wore wire-rimmed glasses and an expensive safari-style shirt with epaulets, which could be seen peeking above the top of his waders. Most obvious, though, was the stranger's stature. Barely five feet in height, the man was lost in his waders, which gathered bulkily at his knees and covered his trunk clear to his armpits.

The old guys all looked at each other with delight. The stranger noticed none of this, having marched straight into the shop, stood with his arms akimbo, back arched and took in the whole of the place with a look that expressed something like the pride of discovery. He completely ignored the old guys and me, looked over the general stock that included a rack of about two dozen bamboo rods; shelves piled high with boxes of reels, lines, tying vices and thread; a glass case of tying tools and flyfishing gizmos; a display of fly boxes; racks of flytying materials; and a bookcase full of some of the best flyfishing literature in the county. Then he walked right past Putnam over to the wall behind the counter, and studied the snapshots of anglers holding notable fish, all taken (with the shop as backdrop) by Putnam himself over the

86

past twenty-odd years that he had owned the place.

"Can I help you, friend?" asked Putnam from over the stranger's shoulder. The stranger spun around as if startled and seemed to notice Putnam and the old guys for the first time, as though he had perceived the shop as having been unoccupied.

"You the owner?" the stranger asked.

"Asher Putnam, at your service," answered Putnam with a nod.

"You the owner?" the stranger repeated, as though Putnam's reply had not sufficiently answered his question.

"Yes, I'm the owner," said Putnam, and I noticed just the tiniest edge in his voice, one that implied that the rest of the world would have been satisfied with his first reply. The stranger may have caught it, too, looking Putnam up and down with his own little edge.

"How old are these photos?" the stranger asked, poking his thumb at the wall and then bending in again to study a couple of them more closely, his nose about six inches from the emulsions.

"It varies," said Putnam. "This one here," he touched the one the stranger was studying, pushing his forefinger past the man's nose, "was taken a few years ago. About five, I'd say. When'd you catch that 22-incher, Max?" He turned to look at Granddad and moved his body aside a little so Granddad could see which picture he was pointing at. The stranger looked up, too, to see who Putnam was asking.

"Am I wearing that fore-and-aft kind of hat?" Granddad asked, straining to see the photo from his chair, ten feet away.

"No," said Putnam, squinting at the photo. "Looks like your grandfather's cap."

"I gave you that three summer ago," I said, referring to the dark blue baseball-type cap I'd found at a flea-market when I was twelve. Across the front were embroidered the words, "World's Best Grandfather" in gold. The stranger glanced my way when I spoke.

"Three years ago," said Putnam to the stranger, tapping the photo.

"Any of them newer, more recent?" asked the stranger, scanning the collection, trying to divine which ones might be more current.

"The 21-incher should be up there," said Granddad. "That's from last year."

"Yeah," said Putnam, leaning back in to find it. He tapped his finger on one of the photos and said to the stranger, "This one's from last fall."

The stranger studied the photo. Then he studied the rest of them again and looked over at Granddad. "You seem to show up in a lot of these," he said. "You some kind of local hero or something?" He said this without smiling. No one could have regarded the question as friendly banter, or even as rhetorical. The stranger, in fact, had yet to smile, or even to exhibit any of the subtle conventions that suggest cordiality. Neither, though, was he belligerent or threatening. He was simply serious, businesslike, self-absorbed. Granddad did not know what to say.

"I've been fishing here a long time," he finally answered.

The other old guys grunted and nodded. I could tell they had also been wondering how Granddad would respond. And I could tell the stranger had them all somewhat off guard. Normally, a question like the stranger's last would have come more like a wisecrack, a shot of male banter to break the ice, a tossed-out invitation to engage in some mildly opprobrious badinage that would lead to good feelings and camaraderie. The old guys would have been offering a blizzard of commentary to insure the diminution of any status as local hero Granddad might attempt to claim. But they had been silent. The stranger's question had not been delivered that way.

"So I guess you know the waters pretty well," the stranger said.

"*Very* well," Granddad said with justifiable pride. And the old guys, in a rare display of unanimity borne by their distaste for the stranger's style, all mumbled their agreement, united in support.

"Where did you catch that one last fall?" the stranger asked.

I could see that Granddad was wrestling with the answer. He had, of course, gone back and released the fish into Turner's Pool where he had caught it; all the old guys released their catches after having their picture taken. Granddad did not know whether this stranger would release such a fish, but it was not an easy matter to catch a fish like that one in the first place, especially one that had been caught and released. It took significant angling skill, and knowing where to fish was but a small part of being successful. I knew that because I had learned it from Granddad, and that is why I knew he would tell the stranger the truth.

"I caught that one down in Turner's Pool," he said. And the other old guys all quickly looked at each other and then nodded in exaggerated agreement, saying "Yep, Turner's Pool. That's right, Turner's Pool." They were clever old guys. They knew that would throw some doubt into the stranger's mind about the verity of Granddad's information, all these old guys so quick to support such a valuable exposé. Granddad got a kick out of that. His face broke out in a wide grin and his shoulders shook from chuckling. He looked at the stranger, and still smiling, held up his hand as though swearing to the truth of it.

"Turner's Pool," he repeated.

The stranger did not return the smile nor find the exchange amusing. There was no hint that he even understood the time-honored rivalry between strangers and locals in the search for fishing information and the proprietary claim upon it. It is similar to the understanding one brings to a flea-market; the seller will tell the buyer a price based on the expectation that he will haggle. The buyer, in turn, expects that the seller's announced price is negotiable. If either party fails to uphold his role in this drama – if either the buyer simply walks away without making a counter-offer or the seller displays inflexibility – the other feels somehow cheated. If the roles are upheld, though, both are satisfied, whether a deal is consummated or not. It is the same with fishing information; the stranger will accept a little imprecision in directions if the delivery is cordial, while the local becomes increasingly helpful as certain assurances become offered by the stranger. Like anything else, when decent people are involved, goodwill prevails.

"I know where that is," said the stranger. "How do I fish it?"

"Christ!" blurted one of the old guys in astonishment, "D'ya want us to go down there with ya and help ya cast?"

"I can do my own casting, thanks," the stranger said quickly to no one in particular. Something like a smile flitted momentarily across his lips, a sour, pinched smile, almost a grimace, that was gone as soon as it appeared. "How do I fish the pool?"

Granddad, I could see, had had about enough of this fellow. He had spent a full quarter of my life teaching me how to fish that pool, and he was not about to waste any time on a man who not only lacked the social graces to elicit friendly advice, but seemed insufficiently experienced to even narrow his inquiries to items that afforded feasible answers, should anyone care to provide them.

"You go down to the head of the pool," Granddad began, "and you wade out about balls-deep." The old guys all leaned forward in their seats. I could feel something electric happening, like when you know absolutely that the next twitch of your fly on still water will break all of hell loose.

"No offense meant, stranger, but you'll have to go out about tit-deep. Just keep your elbows high." The old guys broke up. Putnam looked embarrassed and stared at the floor, his hand on the back of his neck. Acting as though he was surprised by the ruckus, Granddad looked from the old guys to me to Putnam and back to the old guys. The stranger's face had turned the color of a Parmachene Belle.

"You think that's funny?" shouted the stranger, glaring at Granddad. "You think you're some kind of hotshot who can insult strangers just because you've been fishing around here your whole life? I'll bet you any amount you and the rest of these old farts are willing to put up that I can outfish you on your own damn stream."

"The hell you can!" shouted one of the old guys. And the rest crowded around Granddad, offering amounts of money they were willing to wager. Granddad looked a bit confused, but encouraged by the adulation and confidence of his cronies. Faster than I could see how it all came about, there was $200 put on the bets, details worked out on the time, place and nature of the duel, and the stranger had made a mad and hasty retreat.

Dead silence fell upon the interior of Putnam's Fly Shop. The old guys all looked at their shoes and listened to the uniquely comforting sound their fingers made when rubbed across the stubble on their chins. Some of them crossed their legs and looked at the ceiling. One of them, Arty Dubrowski, a man whose eyebrows met over his nose like the wings of a perfectly tied Hendrickson, was the first to speak.

"Kind of a funny way for a fella to react to a gibe," he said. The other old guys grunted in general agreement.

"Challenges you to a duel of all things," said Putnam to Granddad. "Kind of old-fashion, don't you think? Makes you kind of disappointed he didn't throw down a glove or something."

"Except it isn't exactly a duel; it's more of a bet," said Bill Page, an old guy whose mustache made him look as though he had an Elkhair Caddis stuck on his lip.

"I'll be damned!" roared Granddad suddenly, after another short spell of silence. "We're being hustled. The more I put everything all back together, the more certain I am that the fellow has set us up for a hustle. And although I've never before heard of such a thing, I do believe the man's a goddamn flyfishing hustler!"

I recall that moment as being the very first time I ever spoke off-color in front of Granddad. It just popped out, propelled by jubilation. "Beat his ass, Granddad."

The duel, or the bet, whatever it was, commenced at noon the following day. By then, nearly everyone in town had heard about it, and when lunchtime rolled around, the bridge above Turner's Pool was jammed with spectators munching sandwiches, hotdogs and slices of pizza. Those who could not get a favorable position on the bridge crowded the banks. It was a nearly perfect spring day.

Down below the bridge, halfway between the span and the head of the pool, the two contestants stood facing downstream, ten yards apart, Granddad off to the right of center, the stranger off to the left. The flow, for this time of year, was not particularly strong, and Granddad seemed to be having no trouble holding his position, the water pressing against the backs of his thighs and streaming through between. The stranger, though, looked as though he were standing in a hole, the full force of the water pushing against his back. He seemed on the verge of being swept away.

Finished tying on his fly of choice, the stranger bit off the tag end of line, placed his fly box back in a pocket of his vest, said something to Granddad, and began casting downstream. Granddad, meanwhile, had his fly box open in his hand, his rod tucked up under his arm, and seemed to be frozen in thought. His focus appeared to be centered on a point in the stream some twenty feet below him, and from my vantage point on the bridge, I wondered if the faint, liquid-gray shapes I imagined seeing undulating in the current at that point were real. If they were, they were the two largest trout I had yet seen in my relatively short life. I did not know then, but I do now, what Granddad was seeing.

He was watching the interplay of liquid light, shining water, dappled shadows on mottled stones, and exquisitely cryptic living creatures, patterns of form and movement so essentially interwoven and eternal that they forged a thing inseparable, no longer composed of individual elements, but an entity itself. It was a hallowed thing that dwelt on the very edge between reality and illusion, between consciousness and dream, slipping smoothly back and forth between the two, at once something that could be caught and something that could never be caught, that could be comprehended, yet never comprehended. It was intensely familiar, profoundly moving, piquant, alien, terribly far away. He felt an almost irresistible need to float a fly down to the thing and watch it react, to see it either haughtily refuse his entry into its realm, impassively ignore his nonexistence, or suddenly and emphatically connect, a supernova impact of two polar worlds colliding – the compacted event in which the real and the unreal are no longer two opposite things.

He stood staring for a long time, the fly box held open in his hand like a prayer book, its feathery verses shiver-ing in the vernal light and air. The stranger was fishing, the contest was underway, the crowd was becoming restless, wondering what was going on with their local entrant, my Granddad, my hero, the old guy who was going to blow this hustler away.

Granddad closed the box and put it in his pocket. He reached down into his waders, into the pocket of his trousers, and brought out a handful of green bills. Holding up his other hand and saying something to the stranger, he pushed through the current toward him, handed over the two-hundred dollars, continued around him to the bank, and climbed up out of the stream. I ran down off the bridge and met him coming up the grassy slope.

I wish I had known then what I know now. If I had, I would have taken his warm, papery hand and walked with him back to the house, basking in the furnace glow of love and pride and the gratitude I should have felt for that sacred and cherished lesson: that there are things that must never be compromised, not for glory, not to save face, not for friends, not for family, not even for the other things that must never be compromised.

No doubt, if I had continued fishing with Granddad, I would have known those things much sooner. Instead, I called him a coward and walked away.

God help me; I had not yet learned a thing.

CONGO BONGO

Charged by elephants, buffalo and hippo. Imperiled by snakes, crocs, pitfalls, cannibals and trigger-happy rebels – all in oppressive jungle heat. The amazing story of the single-most difficult hunt ever made.

By Ken Kirkeby

Most of us are familiar with the name Jack Atcheson. His company, Jack Atcheson & Sons, has served as consultant and booking agent to more than 15,000 sportsmen worldwide.

With a lifelong dedication to hunting that borders on fanaticism, Jack has pursued big game in some of the most remote corners of the earth. Many of his adventures have been truly remarkable, but the one he calls his wildest ever was his five-week safari for bongo and elephant in 1971.

Formerly the Belgian Congo, Zaire is one of Africa's largest countries, about one-fourth the size of the U.S. Back then, it would have been an understatement to say conditions in the central African nation were primitive. Even now, with new roads and oil exploration, many areas remain as they have for the past 200 years. During Jack's trip, the Congo was still in the wake of a bloody civil war. Leftover land mines dotted the

93

roads, tribal fighting continued, and deep in the bush, many natives practiced cannibalism.

J ack and fellow hunter Larry Hammer were met in Asiro by safari operator Arnold Callins, a former mercenary who a few years earlier had been wounded by four arrows and left for dead. Since the weather was hot and dry, Jack and Larry agreed to hunt elephants and buffalo while waiting for rain to improve tracking conditions. Bongo, their interpreter explained, are impossible to track in the dense forest except when the ground is damp.

They were also told that some excellent elephants had been taken by earlier clients, but to find a really big tusker, the safari would have to venture deep into largely unexplored forest along the border of the Central African Republic.

Crossing the Uele River on a pontoon raft of old canoes, the group arrived at a mission called Anvo, where twenty nuns and twenty-four priests had been hacked to death by local chieftains four years earlier. One of the survivors, a Catholic nun, described the horrifying incident and pointed out a few nearby men who had participated in the slaughter. The nun explained the men had only been acting on orders from the witch doctor and doing what seemed right to them. She assured the hunters that everything was quiet now, but from that day on Jack always kept his rifle loaded.

The next day the group visited Chief Suffa, who had actually helped stop the Anvo massacre. Hoping to get his permission to hunt, they found the chief holding court in a thatched hut, surrounded by nervous natives and the newest of his fifteen wives. The chief was busy settling some squabbles and meting out punishments to thieves. After obtaining his approval, Jack's group elected to depart before the sentences were administered (one man was scheduled to lose a hand for stealing).

In the weeks to come, the Americans would be continually amazed at how each village would already be anticipating their arrival. This was due to the system of drum communication between settlements. Wherever they traveled they could usually hear drums beating in the distance, day and night.

The only water available to the safari was in creeks, and while it appeared clear, it had to be boiled and purified. Dereck McCloud, Jack's PH, refused to drink boiled water and soon became ill (after the safari, doctors discovered the man's intestines were riddled with parasitic worms). Dereck's illness would result in Jack hunting alone much of the time, with only a tracker or two to assist him.

The group soon arrived at their hunting camp, a site Jack remembers as

94

one of the most beautiful he'd ever seen. The spot had been swept clean to deny cover to poisonous snakes and biting insects. While there were few mosquitoes, the hunters did encounter army ants, sometimes in columns ten feet wide. Large bats and snakes were also numerous; one native tried to sell the hunters a 28-foot python skin.

The trackers chose to hunt dense, streamside thickets where elephants and buffalo had ample amounts of food and cover. A number of women and children who had ventured too close to the rivers had turned up missing, so the men were constantly on the lookout for crocs and hippos.

This was uncharted wilderness – definitely not a good place to become sick or injured. There was no plane to call in and no radio to call on. The camp did have a snakebite kit, but if someone was struck, they would have to positively identify the reptile so the correct antidote – and the antidote for the antidote, if needed – could be administered. Jack and Larry agreed that if bitten, they would most likely die, so wherever they went they tried to follow in the footsteps of a tracker.

Although the trackers and local tribesmen appeared friendly, many still ate human flesh. Chief Suffa had joked that white flesh was probably as relished by local tribesmen as it would be to crocodiles. While everyone was laughing at the chief's comment, Jack casually buttoned up his shirt to hide his pale skin.

The hunters observed a variety of monkeys and smaller animals, but the natives had decimated the game close by the settlements. The group did find tracks of elephant and buffalo, but other big game was scarce, so they decided to venture farther afield.

The hunters visited another village to obtain permission and to hire guides, and after Jack took several Polaroid snapshots of the chief and his wife, everything was set. Once again pictures proved better than money.

The new area was just as thickly vegetated, but now the group had to watch out for game pits, each lined with sharp bamboo spikes. The trackers soon found fresh elephant sign leading into thick, jungle bottoms where the men followed tunnel-like runways formed by elephants and hippos. Tracks were everywhere, but the going was incredibly dangerous. In this dense growth they could not detect the big animals until they had virtually stumbled onto them. What made matters worse is that many of the elephants had been wounded in the past by muskets and arrows, and once they detected a human, they were more apt to charge than run away.

Hoping to drive a herd of elephants toward Larry, Jack and his PH were edging quietly through the bush when they heard deep stomach rumblings. A bull elephant stood less than ten feet ahead, testing the air with his trunk, his ears fanned. Suddenly, there was a great crashing as 30 or 40 of the huge animals stampeded away.

The tracker explained that the nearest bull's tusks were not very large, so they elected to follow a herd of red buffalo that had ran off with the elephants. The men trailed the buffalo, eventually catching up to them in heavy brush. Jack hit a good bull with his .458 Winchester, but was forced to abandon the blood trail at dark. The next day a tracker found the bull, completely devoured by hyenas and vultures. With no conception of trophy value, he had not bothered to recover the horns!

In the days to come new trackers and porters replaced those from other villages. Each native wore only a breechcloth made from pounded tree bark and carried several spears. All had elaborate tribal marks cut into their faces and bodies, and their teeth were filed to point. Some had never seen a white man.

Near the same area, Jack picked up the tracks of a large elephant and followed him into a dark creek bottom. A strange snake slid through the water only inches from Jack's leg. Drenched from the heat and humidity, his clothes clung to him and he drank continually, doubling the number of Halazone pills each time he filled his canteen with the yellowish water. Dereck's fever persisted, forcing the group to stop and rest often. The going was slow. The men had to place their feet carefully, stepping around or through a maze of long, clinging vines.

Jack's tracker stopped to squat and listen. In sign language he warned of many elephants only twenty-five feet away. At that instant a wall of small trees began snapping in front of them as the entire herd bore down on the hunters. Dereck and Jack dropped to the ground as the animals thundered past. The charge was over in seconds; luckily, none of the elephants stopped to look for the hunters. As he rose to his feet Jack heard laughter and looked up to see his tracker waving from the safety of a thirty-foot tree.

The hunters were also subjected to attacks by much smaller adversaries. Jack had heard stories of army ants eating livestock and even people, and one night he was awakened by a stream of ants crawling over his face and all across the tent floor. On another occasion, while reaching for his waterbag just outside the tent flap, he stepped barefoot into the middle of a column of army ants. The pain from their bites was excruciating.

The PHs suggested another area, so they visited yet another chief who after receiving gifts and having his picture taken, allowed them to hunt where no white men had ever been. Jack hired twenty porters for the forty-mile hike and promised each of them plenty of meat, including elephant meat and intestines, which the natives ate raw.

With no maps to guide them, the hunters thought their position to be in one of the drainages of the Gwanie River. Although they primarily wanted to hunt elephants and bongo, Jack and Larry had to spend more and more time hunting whatever they could find for camp meat. They killed buffalo, waterbuck, waterhogs and even a large hippo that charged to within five feet of Jack and Dereck before they stopped him with a volley of well-placed shots. Larry, meanwhile, had to kill a cow elephant that charged him in the thick brush.

Now with enough meat, the Americans had to deal with a new problem. Some of the porters wanted to bring the meat back to their villages to sell. Jack and the PHs insisted they stay and dry it into strips, called biltong. Through the night the Africans talked loudly and looked at the Americans with contempt. Jack slept with his back against a large tree and kept his rifle close. By morning five natives had left, taking much of the meat with them.

The days grew hotter, with the temperature climbing to 120 degrees. Still, they managed to cover about ten miles a day, stopping occasionally to sip water directly from elephant tracks. There were puff adders and other poisonous snakes along the way and crocodiles lurked at every waterhole. While crossing a narrow stream, Larry fell into a deep hole and disappeared from sight. The trackers thought he had been grabbed by a croc, but in seconds Larry popped to the surface and sputtering loudly, quickly swam to shore.

The rains finally arrived, making it easier to track bongo, but worrying the PHs that they would be unable to get the vehicles out. The decision was made to relocate once again. After several days of driving, without a map and in a truck with no brakes, the group reached Dungu where they were able to purchase badly needed supplies from a store owned by Greek merchants.

Here, too, the hunters found grim reminders of the savagery gripping the war-torn country. Just below the bridge into town they noticed several rows of freshly dug graves. An interpreter explained that the makeshift cemetery contained the bodies of twenty nurses who had been gang-raped and slain by rebel soldiers. Some of the same men who had raped the women had helped to bury them – or so they were told.

Two hours farther along brought them to the tiny village of Duro, where they stopped to repair the truck's brakes. The next day, after a late start, the safari set out on a rough, rain-soaked road and it was after midnight before they crossed the Nyeka River and reached their bongo camp.

Though it hadn't been used in a year, the camp was in surprisingly good condition and in a lovely setting. Still, the interpreters continually warned the Americans about hostile natives and to "sleep light." Jack slept on the ground in a corner of the tent with his rifle and pack full of escape gear.

97

Larry was equally watchful, and several times they woke to see a man standing outside their tent or staring at them from behind a tree.

Other problems plagued the safari. The trackers often lied about seeing bongo or tracks simply for the Americans' reward money. Jack suggested he hunt alone, with one good tracker. When he visited the local chief and met Bittee, he knew he had found his man. Friendly and powerfully built, the native had filed teeth and Jack was to learn later that Bittee had consumed human flesh on many occasions. Though he could not speak English, Bittee made himself understood through pantomime, often playing the role of the bongo. One fact was crystal clear, however; Bittee could track an ant across solid rock.

Jack and Bittee hunted the first few days without seeing anything. They followed countless tracks, but each time the bongo would disappear like ghosts. They made a number of game drives, but the animals would circle soundlessly behind them and escape. Once again the hunting was dangerous – snakes and capture pits were everywhere. Witch doctors would confront them and interrogate the trackers, and Jack had to use extreme care not to offend them, as doing so could be fatal.

The brush was thick, the strangulating air hot and humid. The bongo led the men into low, almost impenetrable jungle, where they would soon lose the trail. What made their pursuit even more difficult was Bittee's fear of getting too close to a bongo. The Azande people believe that the animals climb trees and then drop down onto their pursuers, impaling them with their horns. They also believe that bongo meat should never be touched or eaten because it carries leprosy and an evil animal known to pursue and rape women.

Once, while following the tracks of a big bull through a tangled creek bottom, Jack noticed an odd-looking stick only inches from his face. Bittee motioned him to slip off to the side and it was then Jack realized that the twig was actually a highly venomous stick snake.

On their fifth day of tracking bongo, the hunters were edging through the dense undergrowth when suddenly Jack felt a strange sensation, as if being watched. Through his binoculars he saw an eye, a bit of ear and some horn about thirty feet ahead. Jack pointed his rifle at where he thought the shoulder would be and fired a 500-grain solid from his .458. Hit, the bongo raced off through the forest. Jack fired again, with the bullet smashing into a small tree. The animal turned and ran toward the men. At fifteen feet, Jack shot a third time and the bongo crashed to the jungle floor. It was a cow, but with exceptionally massive horns and what Jack still calls his greatest trophy ever.

Although the pressure was finally off to take a bongo, Jack and his companions could not really relax or let down their guard around the natives. While returning to their hut, Larry reported that one of the crew had been strung up and beaten with sticks. They investigated the situation, but were warned by the interpreter not to get involved. The next day they were told the man had died, though they never saw his body. Jack still wonders if he was eaten by his killers.

Jack continued to hunt bongo, right up to the last afternoon of the safari when he shot a bull only twenty-feet away. The 500-grain bullet cut a noticeable tunnel through the leaves and branches, hitting the bull between the eyes. The bull had a much larger body than the cow Jack had killed, but its horns were somewhat smaller.

Now that their safari had come to a close, the Americans faced another series of difficult and frustrating moments in their attempts to get out of the country.

After a dangerous incident with some armed and drunken boatmen, the group arrived in Isiro to find their plane seats had been commandeered by the military. Most of the soldiers occupying the town carried automatic weapons and appeared to be drunk. Arnold Callins had already had several run-ins with the military and he was inclined to drive their gear and trophies to Kenya. However, he was hesitant to take Jack and Larry as the trip might involve shooting it out with local factions at the border. A Greek merchant put the hunters in touch with a man who operated a river boat traveling to and from Kinshasa. Problem was, the trip would take thirty-five days through malaria-infested jungles.

Refusing to spend another month in the country, Jack and Larry pooled their money, a total of $4,000, and bribed the airport manager to get on the plane, leaving their trophies with a Greek merchant. (Their trophies arrived in the U.S. about a year later.)

After landing in Kisangani, Jack was able to find an American "representative" of sorts, a Peace Corps hippie who was distributing communist literature. Reluctantly, the man helped the Americans arrange a flight to Kinshasa, the capital city. Hours later, en route to a hotel in the Kinshasa, the driver told the Americans to remain in their rooms because some rebels were scheduled to be executed that day. Sure enough, they were.

The next morning Jack and Larry were able to catch a flight to Spain, though their problems were still not over. Somewhere over North Africa the aircraft made an unscheduled landing at a remote airstrip where all male passengers were thoroughly searched at gunpoint. Finding nothing, the police officer apologized, shook hands with each passenger, then passed around free Cokes. Jack and Larry reboarded and were relieved to finally land in Madrid.

lthough Jack Atcheson would continue to make exploratory hunting trips around the globe, he remembers his Congo hunt as far-and-away his most difficult and dangerous adventure. For thirty-six days he hunted hard, enduring insufferable conditions, to take one of the world's great trophies. And, in Jack's words, he had seen the end of ancient Africa.

The complete story of Jack Atcheson's bongo safari has been published in Hunting Adventures Worldwide, *in which the author relives more than twenty-five expeditions around the world.*

THE PRESENT

*It was Christmas, forty-one years ago that grandmother
gave me the present. Her philosophy was simple: Take a
kid fishing and you had at least a few hours to work on
making something out of him.*

By G. Duncan Grant

t was the summer of 1956, and almost daybreak. The old
Plymouth rolled smoothly down Highway 601, its dim, yellow
headlights aimed toward Elloree, South Carolina. A batch of
cane fishing poles protruded from the car's right rear window.
Cans of pork 'n beans, slices of cheese, packages of saltines,
and peanut butter sandwiches wrapped in waxed paper were
packed in a brown grocery bag and stowed on the
package shelf beneath the back window.

In the trunk, earthworms squirmed in white cups, crickets and catalpa
worms crawled around in screen-wire cages, and two dozen minnows
circled the bottom of a galvanized steel bait bucket. Little bottles of Coca-
Cola lay buried under ice in an old Coleman cooler.

Two tow-headed boys, one eight and one seven, excited by the
prospects of catching huge stringers of big bream and even bigger bass,
stared wide-eyed out the Plymouth's side windows as fields, farms, forests
and swamps passed by in the early morning light. The small, white-haired
woman at the Mayflower-adorned steering wheel was 70. And she was

about as unusual as grandmothers get. At the time, my brother and I had no idea of how lucky we were.

It was this little woman who taught us how to swim and how to drive a car. She taught us where and how to fish, to paddle a boat and to run an outboard. She taught us to respect other people and to earn respect from them. And she taught us the difference between right and wrong. But all that was just the beginning.

She was 62 when I was born. And she died in 1989 at 102. We were best friends until the end.

Grandmother smoked Winstons until she was 98, dominated the family, and never lost her ability to debate politics or religion with great passion.

Besides the Winstons, there were several other things she loved: Her art (painting flowers and landscapes, mostly), fishing, God, Christmas and me. God and Christmas, of course, came first. Fishing second. I knew I was third, but I felt honored because she liked fishing *a lot*. Besides, according to my brother, everyone else in the family fell in behind me. I was one of those kids who never asked for much. But when I did, I could always count on her.

Even at eight, I knew she was different from other grandmothers. Though 70, she thought nothing of loading my brother, Ron, and me into her old Plymouth and driving the forty-five miles to Pack's, or one of the other muddy little landings along the Santee River. We'd rent a boat and motor, and fish all day, stopping only to eat the lunches she'd packed.

Grandmother was a confirmed cane pole and live bait fisherwoman. She had little use for rods and reels and no use for artificial lures. "Too much noise and too much jerking around," she'd say. "You boys need to be still in the boat. Fish can hear as good as you." She would, however, resort to rods and reels for stripers or fishing in the ocean. After having her cane poles destroyed by stripers on two occasions, she'd out-fitted herself with a sturdy open face reel mounted on a rod with a tip as thick as your thumb.

In addition to a constant barrage of warnings to be still and quiet, Ron and I got lessons on religion, discipline, manners, history, and the importance of going to college. Given enough fishing trips, you can learn a lot from a woman born in 1887. We'd head home when our stringers were heavy with bass and bream, or it started getting dark. Most times it was both.

We fished several times a month, on Saturdays or holidays (never on Sundays) from the end of February until the middle of November. After that, according to her, it was too cold. Besides, getting ready for Christmas was more important. There were gifts to buy, pecans to shell, decorations to put up.

Christmas at my grandparents' rambling old farmhouse was as good as it gets. And the Christmas of 1956 was no different. Turkey, ham, cookies, cobblers, cakes, pies and all sorts of other food covered the big table in the dining room and perfumed the home with smells of the season. She had my brothers, sister, cousins and me dress up and do a little play involving the three wise men, Joseph, Mary and the Christ Child. At the time I hated it. Today, forty-one years later, I wouldn't trade the photographs for a new car.

Spread out under the tinsel-covered cedar tree in the living room were dozens of colorfully wrapped presents. Some of them would be for me. And since, like my father, I had inherited my grandmother's love for fishing, I knew... I hoped... that at least one *wouldn't* be underwear, socks, shirts, or school supplies. I hoped one would be the new rod and reel that I'd seen advertised in *Field & Stream*.

After dinner and the traditional Christmas carols, grandfather summoned all the kids to the living room, where he would call out the names on the presents. As the pile shrank, it became obvious that all the remaining packages were too short to contain a fishing rod.

Though I never said a word, a dark cloud of disappointment descended on me. But I immediately felt ashamed of myself. While we had much more than many of our neighbors, we were a long way from wealthy. A rod and reel would have been a luxury, and I needed the school clothes more. Besides, as grandmother had reminded me so many times, Christmas wasn't supposed to be about what you got. So I cheered up and glanced around the room at all the happy faces, silently resigning myself to another year of cane poles.

She was sitting on the sofa near the Christmas tree. And when I noticed her, I had the feeling that she'd been watching me for some time. Her small, soft blue eyes were focused squarely on my freckled fore-head. An ever-so-slight smile appeared at the corners of her mouth and wrinkled the almost translucent skin around her eyes. Her right hand slid off the arm of the couch and down toward the floor. Slowly, without anyone else noticing, she pulled a long package out from under the couch and pushed it under the tree.

Grandfather eventually picked up the package and started to read my name, but I was already up and moving through the flood of torn wrapping paper on the floor. I was as happy as an eight-year-old can get.

It was a warm fall day, some thirty years later, that I took her fishing for the last time. She was 98. We visited a friend's pond that I knew to be well-stocked with bass and bream. Using minnows for bait, grandmother caught several nice bass from a chair that I'd placed on the weathered boards of an old dock.

A big straw hat shaded her face, but I could see her watching me as I fished along the edges using a spinning outfit. And for the first time that I could recall, I was actually catching more fish than her.

"You sure are catching a lot of bass with that thing. What kind of lure are you using?" she asked from the dock. "Plastic worms," I answered clearly, so she could hear me over the noise of the spillway.

"Wouldn't mind having an outfit like that myself..." she said. Then, thinking about her age and health, her voice trailed off, "...one day," she added quietly, almost as if she didn't want me to hear.

But I made a mental note. Christmas was just around the corner. And I'd never be able to give anyone a better gift.

FIVE-SHOT ADAM

He was an anemic, dreary-looking young man who toiled through the night in a cheap New York hashery. Who could have imagined that he would someday become one of the greatest wingshots on the Eastern Shore.

By Roland Clark

t is claimed by many that to acquire precision with gun or rifle, a man must grow up with firearms and burn a prodigious amount of powder before reaching the topmost rung.

I shan't dispute this in the main but I do say that there is, here and there, a marksman ready born, with leads and angles a matter of instinct.

One Adam Jones stands out in my memory as a typical case in point.

By no possible stretch of the imagination would one ever conceive of Adam Jones in the role of a mighty hunter. The field of his activities, as first observed by me, was as far removed from the sphere of ballistics as the sun is from the moon.

It happened some years ago that I was engaged in the newspaper business – more modestly stated, I was a reporter on one of the New York dailies, and not too good a reporter if I recall the judgment of my boss.

I early discovered that the rottenest jobs – late night and before dawn assignments – were reserved for the poor young cub who should have been garnering sleep. At all events, were it not for my unseasonable rambles during this period, I might never have met young Adam and this story would not have been told.

Just a short half block from the press rooms a cheap little "restaurant" crouched between the loftier buildings about it, only deserving the name by virtue of the fact that it did serve meals of a sort to the hardier of mankind. I don't think the Excelsior closed its doors from one year's end to another. The food was frightful; the coffee vile; but here at the midnight hour, or in the chill of a graying dawn, I would sometimes drag my weary legs. "A cup of coffee, Adam," and a drowsy youth would stumble forward, "Yes, sir, comin' up."

If there were other patrons who visited the place, I have no recollection of them. Adam and I, at such unseemly hours, were alone in a world of devastating silence and unappetizing smells.

I can only describe young Adam Jones as the dreariest, most anemic looking boy it has ever been my lot to meet in a semi-social way. For we were social, eventually confidential perhaps, our friendliness inspired no doubt by a fellow feeling of disillusionment with the work each had in hand.

Adam hailed from Maryland; a farm boy wafted by some ill wind to a sloppy hashery in the lower end of New York.

He often spoke of the "Eastern Sho,' " and "reckoned," maybe, he was happier hoin' corn and fightin' wire grass than he'd ever be again.

Uncongenial as his duties must have been, one great pleasure Adam did have, a pleasure furnished at no cost and ever close at hand.

Starting at the door and running the full length of one wall of the Excelsior Restaurant stretched a most astounding mural of aquatic birds in flight. It was garishly colored with every tint of the rainbow and the birds dipped and waved, darted and skimmed in joyous abandon across a purple sky.

To Adam the thing was sublime. He called it to my attention at our very first meeting and every time thereafter that I happened into the place.

"What you reckon kind of ducks they are?" he'd ask me. "Mallerts – or wild geese, maybe?"

It was a difficult question to answer.

"I should say, Adam, that they are of varied breed and species," I would answer. "They differ. Several have the plumage of the hoot owl and the conformation of the mackerel gull. That big chap in the middle of the string resembles a cormorant in spots, but it has the head of a merganser drake."

"Well, they're ducks, ain't they?"

"Perhaps," I replied guardedly. "It's anybody's guess."

"Gee! If I just had a mess o'fowl like that in front of me once and one of them ten-shot guns, couldn't I lace 'em! Um! Um!"

He snatched a broom from behind the counter and aimed it at the onrushing flock.

"Bing! Bing! Bing! Bing! Bing! Bing!"

106

"That's enough," I interposed. "There are no ten-shot guns manufactured. You'll have to be content with six."

"I found out about them ducks," he told me one day. "You must've been wrong. They're canvasbacks. Feller was in here the other night and he says he's seen a sight of 'em. They're the best duck there is. Gee! If I just had the chance . . ."

"Drop it, Adam," I moaned. "The coffee, please." I was gradually losing interest in Adam's ducks and his continual comment on them.

I n the course of time I severed my connection with the newspaper – or was severed – and my old haunts knew me no more.

Several years passed before I again thought of Adam Jones. Perhaps I went up or down the street of the Excelsior a dozen times or more without recalling the place at all. Then one day I hauled up short before its dingy doorway. There was the sign to assure me further, hanging just as it always had hung, a trifle out of plumb. I went in, feeling, I believe, a little guilty at having neglected Adam so long.

A beefy man in a dirty apron shambled behind the counter. The fresco, I noticed, was still intact. The smells were as of old.

"Adam Jones?" I asked. "Is he still connected here?"

"Who? Jones – Adam? Oh, hell, no! That guy! Been out o'here two year or more. Uncle died and left him a farm or somethin'. Acted always like he was crazy if you ask me."

So, I thought, there was an end of Adam and our talks of six- and ten-shot guns – of ducks and the havoc he would create in their ranks if "just he had the chanct."

But fate, after a pattern of her own, had arranged things otherwise. I had well nigh forgotten Adam, but the boy still remembered me.

Opening my mail one morning, I found a letter from Adam Jones. Though months old, forwarded from pillar to post, it had finally reached the newspaper office and was properly directed to me. Adam wrote from his farm on the "Eastern Shore," an odd, haphazard sort of letter, yet reflected in every passage a full enjoyment of life. He brushed lightly over the details of his windfall. The real meat of his epistle was a fervent invitation to visit him "when the ducks come down this fall." He went on to set the day and hour. Nothing must prevent my coming, short of sudden death. "I'll show you ducks, a mess of 'em," he wrote, "an' there'll be some canvasbacks among 'em like the Excelsior's, only different." I must bring warm clothes and high rubber boots. Adam had forgotten nothing in the matter of equipment. There followed advice on shells and loads, all set down with the intelligence of a gunner long in the game.

Would I go? It took me but a moment to decide that. If the invitation still held good, I would steal time for at least one day and visit Adam Jones. Only two days remained till the opening date in Maryland, but my wire brought a prompt reply. "You bet you come. Been countin' on it right along. Meet you Monday morning. Ducks ahead of you."

Then, in no time, I was getting my traps off the train at Stockton in the mist of a chilly dawn. Only two or three men were visible about the platform but none of these could be Adam Jones. At all events, this strapping fellow in flapping oilskins seemed to sense my difficulty and came quickly forward.

"Now," I said, "if you'll help me get these bags . . ."

"Gee! Will I? Man, it's good t'see you again!"

Adam! Poor pimply, scrawny Adam Jones? Now a big, broad-shouldered chap with the grip of a Goliath!

"Here. Gimme your gun and trappin's. Flivver's t'other end of the platform. Gee! Won't the wife – but that's a surprise. Come on."

From there on, for the next two hours, racing at breakneck speed over slippery pavement and through soggy clay, Adam turned loose a flood of duck talk that took my breath away.

"Happened funny, now, didn't it," he laughed, "my gettin' back here again? Ducks been usin' about the marsh a lot th' last few years and the redheads and canvasback out in Chincoteague like you couldn't hardly believe. Rain's been fine for marsh ducks. All the pond holes full o' water. I've corned a sight o' those holes."

I was still having trouble in associating this rugged disciple of Nimrod with the stoop-shouldered Adam of earlier days when, at last, we bumped through a grove of pines and into the clear again.

"That's my old shack yonder."

Adam pointed to a little building at the edge of a narrow creek. As we came to a halt before the door a chorus of strident honkings arose from the water's edge.

"Decoys," Adam said briefly. "They always welcome me when I've been away from home. Kinder nice, ain't it? Hey! Maggie! Bill! Bill!"

The door flew open and Maggie and Bill appeared as one. I was thrust forward by the ever-eager Adam. Introductions followed, and I had just begun to voice some compliment on Adam's choice of a wife when she dashed off with a word about "burning rolls" and a "ruined breakfast."

"Did you string those black-duck decoys, Bill? Bale out the punts? Good! That's fine."

Adam slapped the boy's back affectionately.

"Bill's learnin' fast; he's like his sister. Tell 'em once and the thing's good as done."

"Come on, yo' all," Maggie called at this point. "Breakfast! Ad! Bill! Coffee's gettin' cold. Come on."

Coffee – hot! Crisp rolls, pancakes done to a golden brown and an oyster

108

stew that put to shame all other oyster stews yet manufactured for the solace of a starving man. Fortified inwardly, re-clothed externally, I felt a different man when we pushed out toward the distant marsh.

"Yeah!" Adam agreed, when I touched on the theme gastronomic. "Mag's a danged fine cook."

Then a flock of widgeon swept past us, and all my thoughts were centered on ducks and anticipations of what the day might bring forth.

Happily, the rain had stopped by now and a broad band of amber sky showed above the rim of the ocean. Catspaws of wind crept across the bay. It was growing appreciably colder with every breath of air. And, oh, that sudden awakening of life spread out over Chincoteague Bay! Great rafts of ducks came into view – one moment clearly etched on the skyline, then lost again in the mist.

"Goin' to blow," Adam stated briefly. "I was aimin' to rig in an offshore blind, but I reckon we'll do better on black ducks an' sprig somewheres in th' marsh."

Still light in force, the westerly wind had started ducks moving everywhere. Over the marsh, now, but five or six hundred yards away, I could see many small bunches swing in from the bay, pitching at length to favored spots where I hoped Adam had lavished his corn. From time to time the r-r-rupp! r-r-rupp! of a distant gun told us that the business of the day was already under way.

"Better slip in a couple o' shells," Adam advised, "Them last sprig was temptin' close." He laid aside the pushpole and handed me the battle-scarred pumpgun I had seen him place in the boat.

"Here! Try 'em with Old Ironsides. It's like you said. I couldn't find a ten-shot gun nowheres, but this here does mighty well."

Bill was poling his decoy-laden skiff some hundred yards behind us, trying manfully to keep up with the rapid pace Adam had set from the start.

Soon we were threading our way through narrow channels in the heart of the far-flung marsh. Here was a stretch of broadening water with scattered islets of tumbled sedge, there some reed-bordered coves in the shallows where we continually stirred up ducks.

Guns were now barking from several points; long lines of widgeon and pintail trading over Chincoteague Bay. My impatience was mounting with each moment. Why the devil didn't Adam haul up at one or the other of the little coves where we'd found so many ducks? Then, just as I'd decided to say my word, we rounded a point in the stream and Adam waved back to the oncoming Bill.

"Look!" he said to me. "Yonder – to the left of the point. That body o' birds is mostly blacks, cleanin' up my corn."

Almost as he spoke, they rose in a cloud – black ducks, widgeon and scattered pintail – a tower of flashing wings. Adam's blind was practically invisible until we had run the skiffs ashore within ten feet of its base. Out went the decoys in record time. They conformed to no set pattern, taking impartially of the characteristics of different species. I thought of the Excelsior's "canvasbacks" and decided Adam had molded them all from a memory of that wall. What matter? We were set out; my spirits were high; ducks were moving on every side. Stragglers, returning to their interrupted feast, viewed the terrain below them with marked suspicion – high-flying scouts prepared, no doubt, to make a report of their findings.

A wise old "red-leg" circled us several times, measuring distance carefully, until one unwary sideslip brought him to the edge of the danger zone. My choke barrel dusted him thoroughly, but Adam sent him hurtling down some yards farther on.

We had broken the ice! And, as though it but needed this small beginning to properly open the ball, we soon were laying down a barrage that must have sounded like machine-gun fire to any who chanced to hear.

ow a stiff wind was blowing out of the northwest and the ducks, breasting in against it, made easy shooting, although I know I missed a good many with no excuse whatever.

Adam, on the contrary, was bringing down his birds with deadly consistency. Giving me the best of the breaks, he still had little difficulty in keeping the score well in his favor throughout. Did I miss a pair of green-wing – phantom shapes seesawing crazily past before the boosting wind?

"Well . . . they was summ' at too far for a little gun."

When Adam killed them after me it was just a "lucky shot." Kindly Adam! Chivalrous Adam! Would that there were more of your kind to leaven the world today!

One thinks of a marsh blind as more or less snug and comfortable – a cozy corner where the wind may blow to its heart's content without causing the slightest trouble. You welcome a blow if properly rigged. Ducks are prone to be less suspicious when weather conditions are at their worst and pitch to the decoys with a confidence that is lacking at other times. But there are, too, those occasions when the best-sheltered blind in the world becomes well nigh untenable; you wish you were anywhere else.

I believe Joe Ben's blind in the "Pocket" was, on that November afternoon, the bleakest, coldest patch of ground south of the Arctic Circle. A veritable gale had risen, dragging our decoys together in bunches, turning many bottom side up until they should have appeared unnatural to the stupidest duck alive. But they continued to come in, nevertheless: black ducks, widgeon, an occasional sprig and those maddening teal that invariably caught me off my guard and were past like a flash of light.

I had just dropped a pintail in the decoys and had dived down into my pocket for a couple of shells. My pocket was empty. My shell box was just beyond reach.

110

"Keep down!" Adam whispered. "Six widgeon right in the sun."

"Take them," I groaned. "No loads in the gun."

And then they shot into view – six feathered bullets, speeding on for parts unknown. Three of them just missed my head as Old Ironsides caught them full and fair and sent them hurtling into the marsh behind us. Quite leisurely, it seemed to me. Adam swung. For a split second I saw twin dots in the air, then the big gun roared above my head. Had my eardrums cracked? I thought so. Half deaf, I still heard Adam's voice as from a distant sphere.

"Missed him! Dang it! Missed him clean. That's for bein' too sure!"

Bill had stuck up his head from a nearby clump of grass.

"Pick up those five widgeon," Adam called, "before yo' all forget." Too plumb sure," he repeated. "I'd oughter got all six."

Twice again, that afternoon, five ducks fell stone dead at a volley from Adam's gun. Watching him, I knew that the score still failed to satisfy – I verily believe he considered himself a little disgraced in my eyes.

Daylight was fast fading when at last we picked up our decoys. Snow clouds, which had been gathering throughout the afternoon, now completely blanketed the sky; we were barely started on our long pull home when the whirling flakes swept down on us on the wings of the bitter wind. It was too much for young Bill and his heavy skiff. Halfway home, Adam came to his rescue. We left the boat and decoys at a point in the marsh and, with all hands taking a turn at the poles, made fairly good time on our return to Adam's house.

Sitting over the fire that night, I attempted to draw Adam out in the matter of his shooting which, measured by my standards, had been beyond compare. Apparently he saw nothing unusual in his manner of handling a gun. I referred to the three occasions when he had taken a toll of five separate ducks out of a possible six.

"Oh, that," he said. "Well, they was comin' in nice. I don't get 'em every time."

He looked slyly across at the buxom Maggie, now busily wiping dishes with the help of brother Bill.

"I'll tell him about Joe Ben's Pocket, eh Maggie? Joe Ben is Maggie's pappy," he whispered, "an the Pocket's where we all rigged today. Old Joe'd been gunning th' marsh for forty years, pretty well takin' all th' good spots till I come back to th' farm. He hated me like a rattlesnake 'count o' my lookin' at Mag here, an' when I begun to pot 'round the marsh he was madder'n hell-o-pete.

"Anyway, the Pocket was always reckoned one o' th' best holes in th' marsh. Every year, Joe Ben took up the same old blinds, patchin' 'em up in the early fall so's to hold 'em for himself. Well, when I started in I didn't know none o' th' rules on th' marsh an' I stuck out a blind on Rutter's Point, a gunshot from Joe Ben's. Gawd! What a time I had with that blind! Buildin' it over again, when the old man busted it down. O'course, all the while I was patchin' it up, I'd be flarin' the old man's ducks. Finally he let it be, figurin', I reckon, I was doin' more harm thrashin' around than I could be settin' still in th' blind an' killin' my share o' ducks.

"Sometimes they'd stool to Old Joe an' again, maybe, pass his by, an' swing in to my decoys. You can bet I wanted t' kill those ducks whenever they came my way. Joe Ben would be watchin' acrost th' cove an' whenever I missed one he'd rare up from his blind an' hoot an' laugh, wavin' his hat an' sayin' things that weren't too nice to hear. Trouble was, Joe Ben himself could shoot t' beat all hell. When he pulled down on a duck with Old Ironsides, you just counted one more in th' bag.

"Yeah, Old Ironsides." Adam threw an affectionate glance toward the corner. "That's what Joe Ben called it. Useter belong to him once on a time but . . ."

"Ad! Yo'all goin' t' wear folks out," Maggie called from the opposite room. "Ducks, ducks, guns an' ducks. Better get t' bed, I'd say, after the day you've had."

Bill had long since disappeared and in a moment Maggie picked up a lamp and followed in his wake.

"That old pump," Adam began, "but wait a minute." He went out to the kitchen cupboard and returned with a jug and glasses. "Maybe a drop or two won't hurt, if you're a-mind to try straight corn."

"But I started to tell you about Joe's gun an' how I come to have it. The gun I had was a mis'able, worn-out trap that I'd bought for a dollar or two. She'd fire a few times without jammin' an' then you'd have t' swill her with oil t'keep things workin' right.

"I knew dang well what Joe thought o' me, an' I was set on changin' his mind. Maybe if I got to shoot like him it would make some sorter difference. Maybe he wouldn't be so low-down mean when he caught me talkin' to Maggie back o' th' kitchen porch.

"I bought me a new gun then, an' I begun t'shoot right good. Sure enough, old Joe started to take notice after a coupler weeks. When I missed a duck now an' then, he didn't hoot an' holler at me like he useter do. Sometimes, when I'd get down four or five, Joe Ben would hail me, pleasant-like, an' kinder wave his hand.

"Then, one day, I pulled down six big greenheads. One of 'em towered a hundred feet straight in the air an' fell dead in the old man's stool. It was 'long about sundown an' we just ready to give up for the day.

"Joe Ben got in his decoys first and when he pushed past me he chucks the mallard into my punt. 'You're gettin' on good, sonny,' he says. 'Them mallards was pretty well timed.'

"I didn't say nothin' and he pushed on a ways. Then he calls back to me. 'Some o' th' young folks is stoppin' by tonight for cider an' a snack. Maybe you'd like t' drop 'round.'

"Well, that sorter greased the ways. You can't judge a hog by his bristles

112

nor his grunt. I'd played hell some days with the old man's shootin', an' sassed him a'plenty when I got th' chance. But it looked, on a sudden, like he'd forgotten all that. I reckon Maggie'd been workin' on him when I wasn't nowheres around. Anyway, he got to askin' me to gun with him after while, an' there's a lot Joe taught me before he quit th' marsh. That was only last winter, just when the gunnin' was gettin' best. We was rigged one day in Shadow Pond an' th' ducks hadn't started to move, when Joe Ben dropped his gun in th' blind an' keeled over like he was shot.

"Gawd! How gray the old man looked when I tried to raise him up. 'It's all right,' he says, after a minute or two. 'Just my arm. Gimme a lift, Adam, boy.'

"I got him on his feet, knowin' right away that it weren't only his arm. The whole right side of him was useless, an' his leg hung kinder limp.

"He leaned back against th' thatch of the blind an' I held him so for a while, him starin' out at Chincoteague like he was afraid he might forget it.

"A bunch o'mallard circled the stool an' went off without a sound. 'They've gone, Adam,' he says to me. 'Gone! I won't ever see 'em again. The marsh . . .' An' then a sorter surprised look came over his face, an' he slipped down again in th' blind.

I don't know rightly how I got him into th' skiff at last an' worked back through th' marsh. But, anyway, I made it, an' he seemed a little better when we'd brought him here to the house.

"Joe Ben's never spoke a word since that day at Shadow Pond, but just before they took him home he stretched his hands towards Old Ironsides an' made us understand he was givin' his gun to me."

"Five-Shot Adam" was among six waterfowling stories in Roland Clark's Pot Luck, *his third and last book. Totalling only 92 pages,* Pot Luck *was published in 1945 by Countryman Press, a subsidiary of A.S. Barnes and Company, New York, which during the latter stages of World War II produced a number of books by the great sporting writers of the day.*

HORNED MOONS & SAVAGE SANTAS

A JACKPOT DAY

Hunting quail in February is 'One way to separate the men from the boys,' the Old Man declared. If you can survive all that nasty cold and rain, you might just find some of the best shooting of the year.

By Robert Ruark

I don't know why they didn't take February right out of the calendar, instead of monkeying around with it and making leap years out of it, because it is the worst-weathered of all the months, being halfway between winter and spring, with all the bad habits of both. I mean cold and rain and a little snow and a lot of wind and just natural nasty.

The trouble with February is that January's gone and March is coming next, and March is the most useless month of all, since there is nothing you can do in March except sniffle and wish the wind would quit blowing. All the hunting's over and generally it's too early to fish. "There's ain't any wonder," the Old Man said, "that they told Caesar to beware the Ides of March." I didn't ask the Old Man what an Ide was. I was afraid he'd tell me.

But we aren't talking about March. The subject is February, and there's one thing you can do in February better than any other time of the year. That is shoot quail. For a long time I didn't believe it, but the Old Man always insisted that February was the best quail month of all.

I remember one day it was drizzling that slow, cold, nasty, steady sizzle-sozzle that is so cold it burns like fire and turns your ears into ice blocks and makes your nose run steady. The sky was a dark putty, and you could see the icicles hanging on the window frames and on the roof of the porch. The Old Man was sitting in front of a fire that was drawing so strong that she whistled as the flames sucked up the chimney, and occasionally he would cut loose and spit in the fire. It sounded like a blacksmith tempering a horseshoe. *Hissss!*

The Old Man stuck out his foot and nudged a log that had almost burned through. It dropped in a shower of red coal to the bottom of the hearth and shot fresh slashes of flame up through the topmost chunks. The Old Man looked at me.

"There is always one way to separate the men from the boys," he said. "That is to watch and see if a feller'll do a thing the hard way, when all the other fellers are sitting around grumbling and quarreling that it can't be done." He cut loose another amber stream at the fire and looked at me with his head cocked sidewise, like a smart old dog. "Most people quit doing things as soon as the wire edge has worn off and it ain't fashionable or comfortable any more. That makes it the beauty part for a few individualists. Soon as the clerks run to cover, the big people got the field to themselves."

I didn't say anything. I knew the old buzzard pretty well by now. He was as tricky as a pet coon. All I had to do was make one peep, and he'd have me hooked. It'd be something he wanted me to do that he didn't want to do himself. Such as going to the store in the rain for some new eating tobacco, or going out for more wood, or having to report on Shakespeare, or something.

"You take quail," the Old Man went on. "When the season opens around Thanksgiving, every dam fool and his brother is out in the woods, blam-blamming around and trampling all over each other. The birds are wild, and the dogs are nervous, and they crowd the birds and run over coveys they ought to sneak up on. The ground is dry, and the birds run instead of holding. There practically ain't no such thing as good single-bird shooting, because the bobwhites take off and land as a covey, instead of scattering.

"Then along comes Christmas and New Year's, and the part-time quail hunter is tired of bird shooting, and it's too cold and too rainy, and he has to clean his guns ever' time he comes in to keep the rust off; so he ties up the dogs and forgets hunting until next year. This leaves the woods free of the city slickers and the ribbon clerks and the fashionable shooters. By this time the birds are steadied down and the dogs have had a lot of practice, and they've steadied down too. The young birds have been shot over and have grown their heavy feathers, and the young dogs have figured out that if they find birds the man will shoot some and they will bring them to the man, and that everybody – the dogs, the man and the birds – is in business together. It ain't a game any more, like running rabbits. It's men's work."

I gave up. He had me nailed. "I'll go get my gun," I said. "You can drive me out and sit by the stove in Cox's Store while I catch pneumonia. That is, if the dogs will go out in this weather."

"They'll go out," the Old Man told me. "The dogs are professionals. They ain't part-time sports like some people I know. Go get 'em, and you better wear those oilskin pants and the oilskin jacket. The woods'll be sopping."

Man, I reckon I'm never going to forget that particular day. I sure was glad I wasn't a fish, because those woods were wetter than a well, with the little droplets clinging onto the low bush, the gallberries, and the broom grass, and the trees dripping steady. There wasn't a steady rain. It just sort of seeped down, half drizzle and half fog. My hands on the gun barrels were so cold that my fingers practically stuck to the steel. Rain collected on the gun sight and ran down the little streamway between the barrels. The dogs looked as miserable as any wet dog always looks, sort of like a land-borne otter.

Rain is miserable anywhere, but I expect there's nothing quite so cheerless as a wet wood in February. The sawdust piles have been soaked stiff and hard and dark brown. The green of the trees all turns black in the wet, so that you don't get any color contrasts, and the plowed ground is a dirty, ugly gray. The few shocks of corn that still stand are spotted and shriveled, and the sad little heads of cotton hanging on the dead stalks look like orphans lost in a big city. But the good Lord put feathers and fur on birds and animals to keep them dry and warm, and life goes right on. Except that the Old Man is right, as he nearly always is. Wet woods make birds a heap easier to find, because the birds don't move around very much, and you can spot exactly where they're apt to be. And a dog's nose works dandy in the wet, just as a car runs better on a rainy night, when you get richer combustion.

I hadn't been out of the Liz for five minutes when Sandy, the covey dog, disappeared into a little copse of pine saplings halfway between a peafield and a broom-grassed stretch that led to a big swamp. Old Frank, the single-bird expert, went to have a look and then came back to give me the word. He jerked his head in the direction of the pine trees, impatient as a traffic cop who wants a car to move on, and then he dived into the bush with his tail assembly shaking like a hula dancer.

Maybe I have mentioned that I don't shoot very well except when I'm by myself or with the Old Man, because I'm not self-conscious in front of him and don't have to worry about shooting too fast or competing for birds. But when I'm by myself it seems as if it's almost impossible to

117

shoot bad, because you shoot in any direction – backward, sideways or whatever – without worrying about blowing somebody's head off.

I knew what old Sandy would be doing when I stepped into the dark, dripping grove. He would have suggested to the birds that they move to the outer edge of the pine thicket, so that they would have a nice clear field of soggy broom grass to fly over on their way to the swamp. I was pretty well trained by now. The dogs had been working on me for a couple of years, and the Old Man said he was surprised, that sometimes I showed as much bird sense as a half-trained puppy, and there was hope that I might grow up to where the dogs needn't be ashamed of me.

Sandy had herded the covey to the edge of the thicket, sure enough, and old Frank had come up on his right flank, inside the thicket, and was protecting the right wing. All I had to do was show a little common intelligence and walk along the left wing, outside the thicket, and when I came abreast of Sandy's nose Frank would run in from the right and Sandy would charge straight ahead and the birds would flush, leaving both me and the birds in the open. Then all I had to do was shoot some.

It was an enormous, great covey – about twenty or twenty-five birds in it. Either it was two shot-over coveys that had got together, or one that had been missed entirely; I reckoned it was the latter. When Frank roared in from the right and old Sandy broke point and jumped into the birds, they got up in a cloud and fanned perfectly past me, giving me the best shot there is – a three-quarter straightaway where you lead just a little and let the shot string out behind your chosen bird.

This was jackpot day. Lots of times I had killed two birds with one shot, which is always an accident. You pick one out and aim at him, and the shot string knocks off another. I held on one of the front-flying cocks and pulled, and the whole doggone sky fell down. I stood there with my mouth open, just watching the rest of the birds sideslip into the edge of the swamp, and didn't bother to shoot the left barrel.

The dogs started to fetch – even Sandy, who doesn't care much about it as a steady job, because he reckons any damfool dog can pick up a dead bird and fill his mouth full of loose feathers. But they were interested in this job, because by the time they finished collecting the enemy I had six birds in my coat with one shot. The answer, of course, was very simple. Just as I pulled on the cock bird some of his relatives executed a cavalry maneuver and did a flank on him, and I simply fired right down the line, raking the face of the flank.

Sandy brought the last bird and spat him out on the ground and looked over at old Frank and sort of winked. *Lookit the kid*, Sandy was saying. *By the time he gets home, he'll think he did it on purpose. This time next year it'll be twelve birds when he tells it*. Frank laughed and nodded agreement.

118

e hunted through the sopping woods, and everywhere a covey of birds was supposed to be, a covey of birds was. I couldn't miss anything that day. I had to use two barrels on one single, was all, and I got that extra barrel back again a little later. It was just one of those days when all the birds got up right, pasted flat within an inch of the dog's nose before they rose. The singles clung to the ground like limpets, and you literally had to kick them up. Birds fly slower when they're water-logged, and it was pretty near murder.

The extra barrel I got back, to make the score perfect for the day, was a present from Frank. I shot into the last covey and had fourteen birds in the coat with a double on the rise. Frank fetched both birds and then disappeared into the big, spooky black swamp into which the rest of the covey had flown.

A year ago I would have thought he was acting like an idiot, but, as I said, the dogs had trained me pretty good, and Frank, of all dogs, was no covey chaser. I reckoned that I had hit another bird and wounded him without knowing it, and that Frank had seen a leg drop, or something. I sat down on a stump and let the rain punish my face, and old Sandy sat down by me and shrugged his shoulders as an adult will when he cannot control a child. *If that damfool dog wants to go drown himself in that swamp on a wildgoose chase,* Sandy said with his shrug, *let him. Not for me, bud. There are too many birds around.*

Frank was gone for nearly half an hour. When he came back, he was wetter than a drowned rat, but he had a live bird in his mouth. He had evidently chased the runner for half a mile. I cracked the fugitive's neck and shoved him in my coat and went back to the store to collect the Old Man. He laughed out loud when we came into the bright warmth of Mr. Cox's potbellied stove. We must have been a sight – wet dogs, wet boy, wet coat full of bedraggled birds.

The Old Man is real clever. "How many shells?" he asked.

"Nine."

"How many birds?"

"Fifteen," I said, with pardonable pride.

"Don't tell me how it happened right now," the Old Man said. "I want to get you out of those wet clothes, and I reckon I'll need a little spot of nerve medicine to make me strong enough to listen to the bragging. But tell me one thing: Was I right about February bird shooting?"

"Yessir," I said. "But then you ain't generally very wrong about anything in the woods."

"That," the Old Man declared, as we walked out into the rain and climbed into the Liz, "is a very sage observation from one so young, and I am highly flattered. If it'll make you feel any better, I made all my

119

mistakes when I was young, which is the difference today between an old man and a boy. Youth is for making mistakes, and old age is for impressing the young with your knowledge. My Lord, it's an awful day, isn't it?"

"It's a beautiful day," I said.

THE OLD MEN'S POOL

It's amazing what some men will do when anger clouds their thinking… like the time Joe Denny and Mr. Hamilton, two old and stubborn friends, caught up in a damfoolish fight, took on one of the most dangerous stretches of salmon water in Newfoundland, not saying a word all the harrowing way.

By Ben Ames Williams

he Newfoundland Railroad runs on a narrow gauge, and the seats are proportionately restricted, and the aisle is narrow too. Nevertheless, the trains are companionable and accommodating conveyances. Thrice each week, when the Caribou docks at Port-aux-Basques, the Express takes aboard travelers and mail and freight, and starts on a journey of something more than twenty-four hours, in a great half-circle clear across the island; and thrice each week another Express returns to deliver traffic to the steamer about to sail. These are the only passenger trains, but there are freights besides.

And all these trains are neighborly. The tale, perhaps apocryphal, is told of a lady passenger who asked the conductor: "Do you know what those flowers were beside the track a few minutes ago?" And he said: "No, but I'll have the engineer back up so you can pick some and see."

Certainly all these trains – even the Express – will stop anywhere for the fishermen; and there are many stations which are no more than signboards beside the track, with a meandering footpath leading across the barrens to some

121

spruce-clad slit in the mountains where a salmon river runs. When the train stops, everyone looks out of the window to see fishermen alight, cased rods in hands, their guides with corked gaffs and shoulder packs bulging with supplies and cooking dishes. Or it may be to see other fishermen come aboard, with great salmon heavy in a short sack that has been tied end to end for easier carrying. Sometimes horses pasturing at large wander onto the tracks and canter ahead of the train while the engineer proceeds cautiously, waiting for them to get off the right of way, or perhaps stops so the fireman can go forward and drive them to one side.

Once Frank and I were coming back to camp from Seven Mile Pool, and I heard the whistle sound, long, short, short; and I thought ignorantly that we would stop to pick up other fishermen. We did not, but a moment later I saw slide past our windows a faded sign-board lettered with the legend: *The Old Men's Pool*.

The path beyond, leading toward the river, was badly overgrown and almost invisible; it was obviously seldom used nowadays. I wondered why the whistle blew.

"I thought we were going to stop," I said to Frank. But he shook his head.

"No, that was a running blow!" he said... .

On another day I saw the Old Men's Pool itself. Down the river, when in spring the ice goes out, sweeps a battering ram, hundreds of tons of weight driven irresistibly on by the water banked behind. You may in summer see, twenty feet above the river's level, where from the trunks of trees ice has rasped the bark away; and the solid rock walls where the valley narrows to a gorge are planed by it and left smooth and bare, the naked rock veined with wandering lines of white where threads of marble run through the softer stuff.

And the scouring ice changes, from year to year, the contour of the river's bottom, scooping up boulders and gravel in one spot, only to deposit them farther downstream. At one such spot, upon a certain day, as the boat impelled by Frank's iron-shod pole bore us downstream, I caught a glimpse of a cabin all ruin and decay, on the lofty bank above the water; and Frank to my question said:

"Yes." The word hissed softly as his slow tongue lingered on the final consonant. And he said: "Joe Denny built that cabin for Mr. Hamilton, when there used to be a good pool here. The pool's filled up and made again and filled up again in my time."

But Joe Denny was only a name, and Mr. Hamilton was no better, and I did not at the moment connect this ruined pool with that faded signboard by the track, and the engineer who whistled the running blow. But I would remember them when presently the tale came to be told.

Fergus Hamilton was his name, a New York man of means and leisure, both earned by his own efforts; a man used to command, and used to having his opinions received with respect and used to a certain deference. He came to fish the Little River and the Grand, and Joe Denny was his chance-allotted guide. Joe was the older by half a dozen years, and it was said of him that he had guided on more rivers than any man hereabouts. He was a driver and a worker; and – unusual among Newfounderlanders, whose many rivers are more apt than not to have an icy bite borrowed from the snowbanks which even in July linger on the moun-tain flanks – he swam like an otter, as much at home under the water or in it as in his canoe upon its surface.

He taught Mr. Hamilton to cast a light and accurate fly, to fish the fly in many sweet, seductive ways, to see the shadow of a moving fish in time to anticipate and meet the strike, to play a salmon boldly at first and gently as the fish came near the gaff, to meet every wind condition – and winds forever scour these rivers – with an appropriate length and strength of cast, to roll his fly into an upstream wind so that it would point downstream on landing, to cast high with a following wind, so that the spent fly would settle lightly on. He taught him the whole lore and art of angling for salmon, which are the most mysterious and unpredictable of fish.

And between these two, not in one year but in many, a deep bond formed. Joe Denny was a widower, with one son named Mat who was an engineer on the railroad, and two others who were guides like their father; but Mr. Hamilton was a bachelor, a man alone. And year by year he returned to Newfoundland, and year by year Joe Denny was his guide. Sometimes they stayed in waters near at hand; sometimes, with an outfit assembled by Joe and financed by Mr. Hamilton, they went afield. Once they cruised along the south coast where small salmon are so plenty; and one mid-afternoon, Mr. Hamilton hooked a fish which did not break the surface, and they played it by turns for three long hours and lost it at last and had never a glimpse of it, so that Joe Denny opined it must have been a seal, but Mr. Hamilton clung always to the belief that it had been a gigantic salmon of a record-breaking immensity.

And they fished the Torrent, where salmon fought and scuffled to reach the fly, and the fruitful reaches of the Serpentine, and the great Humber from Deer Lake to the Falls, and many lesser and more easily accessible streams.

There was a pool on the Grand River which above all others Mr. Hamilton loved. Salmon came there fresh from the sea, bright as silver; and there Joe Denny built a cabin, and there year by year they made headquarters from mid-June till the last week in July. Fishing for the mornings; long drowsy afternoons when no rod crossed the pool; fishing again from sunset to early dark. The traffic on the river, moving up and down in boats, might see Mr. Hamilton sitting on the screened porch, or thigh deep in the pool; and Joe Denny leaning motionless upon his gaff near by, or busy by the cooking hearth ashore. They were both old men now. The water they had chosen was by other rods left courteously free; and it came to be called the Old Men's Pool.

"It's all filled up with gravel now," said Frank to me. "You saw one day where it used to be, and the old cabin on the bank. It filled up the spring after Mr. Hamilton died. Never been any good again."

And I thought of an ancient clock in an ancient song which "stopped short, never to run again, when the old man died."

And Frank said: "Sometimes in the afternoon Joe would swim in the dead water toward the foot of the pool, but Mr. Hamilton never did. He couldn't swim."

So, year by year, though for shorter and shorter periods each day, the two men fished the Old Men's Pool.

For the most part, they dwelt in harmony, but once or twice they disagreed. In fishing, as in other matters, times change and tackle too. Fergus Hamilton and Joe Denny were of that generation which believed that great fish must be taken with great rods, seventeen or eighteen feet long, fitted with leaders and flies to match. Such a rod, used all day in the wind, becomes a burden for strong young arms, and much more so for older thews.

Then someone discovered that a thirteen-foot rod with sufficient line, well handled, will kill any salmon; and Mr. Hamilton, persuaded against his prejudices by some New York acquaintance, brought one of these new rods to Newfoundland. Joe Denny looked at it with a malignant scorn, and for a fortnight refused even to set it up, and the two old men spent more time in argument than in fishing. But in the end Joe yielded, though grudgingly and the lighter rod had a trial.

"It's no more than a switch to tickle 'em," said Joe Denny in a deep hostility.

"Aye, but it's easy on an old man's arms," Mr. Hamilton urged, almost pleadingly.

"A man too lazy to handle a proper rod has no place on the river," Joe said. Nevertheless, he saw that the new rod laid a light fly and killed fish; and so was silenced.

Yet he never openly admitted his defeat; nor did Mr. Hamilton prod the raw wound to Joe's pride. Silence at the right time is good cement for the structure of a friendship and these two were friends.

The new rod had another virtue too. It tired Mr. Hamilton so little that he felt young again. A batsman swings two or three bats as he goes to the plate, so that a single bat may feel no heavier than a wand in his hand when he flings the others away. It was so with the old man now. He fished longer hours, caught more fish, went back to New York rejuvenated – and the delusion of youth persisted so long that in March he wrote Joe Denny a letter.

"I want to go up the Humber again this year," he said. "To the Great Falls. I'll be on the boat that gets in on the twenty-third of June."

Joe wrote back in protest that it was a hard trip, that there might be logs in the river, that Humber fishing was not particularly good, that they would have to tent, that the flies would be bad.

"If you don't feel equal to it," Mr. Hamilton replied, chuckling as he wrote, and meaning this for a jest which Joe would understand and appreciate, "get a younger man to take me in."

Now, it is possible to say a thing with a smile and give no offense or hurt, but you cannot smile in a letter. Mr. Hamilton knew this, but he had forgotten it. So

124

when he landed at Port-aux-Basques, he was surprised to see Joe Denny there to meet him in store clothes, wrinkled blue serge and a dusty derby hat.

And old Joe said, with a grim countenance to meet Mr. Hamilton's greeting:

"Your outfit's in the baggage car, sir, and here's my son Dan to take care of you." He added, with the hurt bitter in his throat: "He's a younger man!"

So Mr. Hamilton knew what he had done; but for some things there can be no sufficient apology. Yet also he knew that Joe Denny would commit a double murder with mayhem before he let Dan Denny or any other man take his place. Therefore, he said loudly:

"Don't be a blithering jackass, you cranky old fool! Take off that fireman's hat and that undertaker's suit and get on the train." And to Dan, standing grinning by: "Go on home, youngster, and wait till you're a man!"

Dan was no youngster. He would never see forty again. But he only chuckled and said: "Aye, sir. It was the old man's idee!"

"He's cracked in his head," said Mr. Hamilton. "But a blooding by the black flies will cure him."

So the two old men got aboard the train, and Mr. Hamilton put on an urgent good humor and a loquacity quite out of character; but Joe would not be mollified so easily. He spoke, it is true, but gloomily and shortly; and by and by Mr. Hamilton mopped his brow and was silent, and the train plodded on its neighborly way, stopping here and there. Joe Denny's son Mat was the engineer of this particular train; and when in due time they alighted at Deer Lake, Joe still grim in serge and derby, Mat got down to see their outfit unloaded, and he said with a dry grin:

"The old man decided to try it himself, did he, Mr. Hamilton?"

Joe merely sighed, but his silence had frayed Mr. Hamilton's temper, and the New York man flamed at the engineer in a low white wrath.

"Keep your tongue t' yourself, Mat!" he said forcibly, "or I'll stuff you into your own firebox."

And Mat chuckled and climbed back in his cab and left these two to finish their battle as they chose.

ou've not seen the Humber," Frank said to me, by way of parenthesis, as he told the tale. "But it's a bold river, and dangerous too. I went up once with a big party, and there was a New Brunswick guide along supposed to be the best canoeman in the province. His canoe got broadside on a rock in one of the little rapids and broke in two. Lost every piece of gear and had a time of it to save the men.

"And the Little Falls, the easy way is to carry around. There's a drop of as much as forty-fifty feet in not more than two hundred yards. Coming down, you'd lower the canoe with a rope, with someone holding back hard. You can't hold her with a pole. You come down a chute straight for a rock that looks as big as a house, and swing off at the last minute to go around it and then on down again, the water boiling like in a pot and rocks like teeth all around.

125

"Going up, it's pole most all the way; and coming down it's paddle and pole, pole and paddle. The hard places, you have to take the pole to hold her; and the Little Falls nobody ever runs and there's three or four other places you have to ease her down."

He filled his pipe again, and having thus set the scene resumed the tale.

Frank said that Joe Denny, old man though he may have been, took Mr. Hamilton up the Humber from Deer Lake to the Big Falls. Call it twenty-five or thirty miles. They might have stayed the night at Deer Lake, and Mr. Hamilton so expected; but when the train was gone, Joe, without discussion, got the canoe into the water and he stood grimly waiting. So Mr. Hamilton got in.

They slept that night beside the river, and at dawn went on. Joe carried around Little Falls, Mr. Hamilton helping as he could. But during that second day of sweating travel, Joe's frigid silence began somewhat to melt. By the time they reached their goal and had their gear ashore, things were, on the surface, as they had always been between these two; and Mr. Hamilton was humbly grateful for this much of forgiveness, and he called Joe to watch the salmon leaping in their efforts to breast the falls, and the two men applauded success and jeered failure as if these were human contestants whose antics they observed.

One great fish tried the barrier over and over, lifting his lumbering bulk out of water in clumsy leaps hopelessly inadequate. There were many failures, but none so abject as his. When, after supper, Joe launched the canoe for fishing, in the easier flow of water well below the falls, the men could see the silver glint of many scales, rasped loose by bruising ledges, drifting in the river's bold current, drifting, drifting toward the sea.

And that night it rained and rose the water and penned them in their tent. Fishing was impossible. They had no cooking fly. Joe cooked in the rain, and they ate in the rain, and for the rest of the day they sat huddled with their gear in the scant shelter the tent afforded. Their clothes and blankets were soggy, and for two days it rained with a mild continuing persistence that raised the river four feet and made a torrent of it. And thereafter, even when the rain ceased, clouds and fog persisted, while they waited for the waters to fall.

Their tempers suffered; yet on the surface a certain serenity was maintained.

Joe nursed his grudge, but did not air it; the other man read his mind and was angry at what he read, but would not broach the matter. Yet his tongue slipped once. While Joe was busy at the fire, Mr. Hamilton went to watch the jumping salmon; and, returning, said:

"The old big one is still trying it! Hardly strength enough to jump clear of the water now! You'd think he'd know he was too old for the job!"

And Joe loudly clattered the frying pan on the rocks of the fireplace, so that Mr. Hamilton realized too late that he had opened the wound anew. But he thought that by another morning the waters would have fallen sufficiently to allow them to fish, and matters must be better then.

126

In the morning the sun did shine; they had good sport with lusty grilse of five or six pounds, and a salmon or two, and their humors improved, and at the nooning Mr. Hamilton said:

"Joe, why don't you set up one of the other rods and we'll both fish?" They were not using the gaff, freeing the played salmon, saving only a few grilse for the pan. And Joe agreed. But when presently they were on the river again, Joe with that old seventeen-foot rod which he preferred, Mr. Hamilton with the lighter gear, Joe was frowning gloomily. This time, though, he spoke.

"I see a short rod in your case," he said dourly. "What's that for – trout?"

Mr. Hamilton, sitting in the bow, was grateful that Joe could not see his face, crimson with a guilty shame.

"Why, no, Joe," he confessed. "That's a dry-fly rod. Ten-and-a-half feet long. They say it will handle anything that swims."

He heard Joe's snort behind him. "Dry fly!"

"They're proved killers, Joe," Mr. Hamilton argued, "when the salmon wouldn't touch a wet!"

"Ten foot long!" Joe grunted.

Mr. Hamilton tried to laugh. "You darned old mossback!" he cried. "You acted the same about this rod the first year. Remember? You're as hard to move as a mule!"

Silence. Silence behind him like a heavy cloud, persisting, oppressive, crushing. He fished under the weight of it for a long hour. If Joe would only argue, say something, curse, roar, explode, then, as if by a thunder-shower on a sultry afternoon, the air might be cleared.

But Joe said nothing at all.

The situation was explosive; the detonator might have been anything. It happened to be a fly, a Jock Scott tied on a No. 4 hook. Mr. Hamilton, fishing with a Montreal, hooked a piece of heavy drift moving half submerged and broke his leader. He swung the rod back so the line came within Joe's reach for replacements, and Joe set to work.

But when the repairs were made, Mr. Hamilton looked at his fly and saw the Jock Scott there.

That fly, in his mood of the moment, irritated him out of all reason. Joe had advised a Jock Scott after lunch; Mr. Hamilton had insisted on the Montreal, and had since hooked and played and freed one salmon. He said: "Blast it, Joe, I don't want a Jock Scott! I want a Montreal!"

"Jock Scott's what we've always been using on the Humber on a sunny afternoon," said Joe inflexibly.

"Then it's time to try something else," said Mr. Hamilton, blind with wrath. "Every time you get hold of my leader you tie a Jock Scott onto it! You're a senile, stubborn jackass! The only way to get any sense into that granite head of yours is to crack it open with a canoe pole, and I'm a mind to do it!"

He twitched the Jock Scott off the leader and threw it over the side and swung his rod to Joe again.

"Put on a Montreal," he said curtly. "I'm sick of arguing with you!"

But for only answer he felt the canoe heave, and turned to see that Joe was taking the anchor in.

Mr. Hamilton was ashamed of his outburst and ashamed to say so. He said nothing.

Joe thrust the canoe ashore. He stepped out, not heeding the other man at all. With a stony countenance he collected his own few personal belongings – including the derby hat – and put them in the canoe.

Mr. Hamilton, during these proceedings, had sat on the shore without movement, not even watching. Joe finished, and he spoke at last.

"I'm going out," he said briefly. "You can suit yourself! Stay or go as you're mind!"

Frank's own words best fit the rest of the tale. "And that's how Joe Denny came to run the Little Falls," he explained. "He told me about it himself that winter. He said he was mad clear through.

"Mr. Hamilton, when Joe said that, hadn't any choice but to come along; so he went to taking down the rods, and Joe packed the tent and gear, neither one of them speaking. By four o'clock or so they were ready, and Joe pushed her off and Mr. Hamilton got in front and Joe in back.

"Joe told me he never left his seat till they got to Deer Lake."

Now, for downstream work in quick water, a sensible man uses his pole, not only to pick his course but also his speed, lest his craft, with too much headway, escape from his control and run headlong to destruction. I knew this, and I asked:

"You mean that he never used his pole?"

"Never touched it all the way," Frank assured me. "Run everything he came to. Mind you, the water was high and heavy and fast. Being high, it covered some of the rocks, but there were plenty left. Joe ran it all, and I never heard tell of any other man, drunk or sober, crazy or in his senses, that done it.

"But Joe did. He said he was so stubborn mad that he never thought of being careful at first at all. And then he knew he was being a fool, and that made him madder than ever. He kept expecting Mr. Hamilton to say something about being careful, and he had his mind all made up to tell the old man if he didn't like the ride he was getting, he could go ashore and walk!

"But Mr. Hamilton never spoke a word all the way. He sat in front, his back to Joe, looking straight ahead; and he filled his pipe whenever it was empty and smoked it steady and slow. Joe said there was times they went so fast the smoke came back past Mr. Hamilton's ears like a pair of reins on a trotting horse; but the puffs came steady and regular just the same.

"Along the first of it, Joe expected they'd both be in the water the next lick; and he said he didn't care if they was. They came near the top of the Little

128

Falls, and Joe was waiting for Mr. Hamilton to cry quits and want to go ashore, but the old man didn't. He just kept on smoking, as calm as if he was setting on the cabin porch down at Old Men's Pool. So Joe, mad at himself for being such a fool, swung her to hit the chute down the Little Falls.

"And about that time he remembered that Mr. Hamilton couldn't swim. Joe didn't mind being in the water any more than a salmon did, but Mr. Hamilton would have sunk like a stone. I tell you, any man starting to run the Little Falls, swimmer or no, he's got good cause to be afraid. But Mr. Hamilton never puffed his pipe any faster, nor turned his head, nor held on, nor even stiffened in his seat.

"They hit the chute and down they went, and Joe said, thinking that Mr. Hamilton couldn't swim, the sweat came out on him like a squeezed sponge. Halfway down you have to swing her hard. There's this great rock right in the way, and the river trying to pile you into it. Joe didn't know, after, whether he swung her with his paddle or the prayer he said; but next he knew, they were in the easier water below.

"So Joe looked at the back of Mr. Hamilton's head, and he loved that old man, and he told me he cried for as much as two miles of river, thinking what might have happened from his stubbornness and foolishness.

"And he took almighty care to hold her right side up from then on. But just the same, being proud of what he'd done, and kind of wanting to brag about it, the way a man will, he stuck to his paddle, never touched his pole. And by and by they was back to the landing.

"Joe stuck her nose ashore, and he was too weak to move. He just set there. But Mr. Hamilton stepped ashore and kind of stretched himself, being stiff from setting still so long. And he turned around to look at Joe, and he kind of grinned, and Joe stepped out into the water and came to land.

"Mr. Hamilton was the one to say what they both were thinking. Joe couldn't speak. His throat had kind of knotted up on him.

" 'Joe,' Mr. Hamilton says, 'we're a couple of fools! Old fools, too! Both of us ought to know better!' And he grinned, and he says: 'But, Joe, you were right about the Jock Scott. That would have been the better fly!'

"And he stuck out his hand, and Joe hung onto it. That was all he could make out to do."

Frank was silent; and I asked: "So they came back to the Old Men's Pool?"

"Yes," he said softly. "And everything was smooth as cream from then on till Mr. Hamilton went home. Not a hard word spoke on either side."

He concluded: "Mr. Hamilton died that winter, but Joe wouldn't rightly believe it when the word came. He claimed it wasn't true. He was all of seventy and his head was pretty old. You couldn't make him believe it. The pool filled up when the ice went out that spring, same as it is now; but Joe came down and got the cabin ready, case Mr. Hamilton did come.

"And Joe stayed at the cabin, and he'd be up at the railroad to meet every train, all that summer, looking for Mr. Hamilton. Next spring it was the same. He stayed down there in the cabin alone; but it was a hard walk up to the train, and that year he wouldn't always make it. If he didn't, and his boy Mat was the engineer, Mat would have the fireman whistle the running blow, so old Joe down't the cabin would hear, and know the train wasn't stopping, and not worry about meeting Mr. Hamilton, and rest easy in his mind.

"The other train crews took it up. Joe's been five-six years dead now, but it got to be a habit with them and they stick to it. Easing Joe Denny's mind so he'll rest easy. Yes, sir, every train that passes by still whistles the running blow for the Old Men's Pool!"

The Old Men's Pool is reprinted courtesy of Doug Mauldin, who reproduced The Happy End (1939) *as part of his limited-edition series, "The Fifty Greatest Books of Derrydale Press."*

130

MORTGAGE
ON A DOG

Vereen Bell was only 33 when he was killed in the 2nd Battle of the Philippines during WWII. As a result, many of his dog stories have gone virtually unnoticed, even though they rank among the best ever written. This late thirties' classic reflects the wonderful wit and lively style that hallmark all of his books, novellas and magazine articles of gundogs and the sporting life.

By Vereen Bell

ud Lee lay hiding underneath the elderberry bush chewing contentedly on a sweetgum stem when his small son came and said, "Pa! It ain't that little old fool from the bank this time. It's a big old fool with a revolver in his belt, and he's gittin' ready to load our stuff on his truck."

Jud stared incredulously. "If that bank has set the sheriff onto me just because I owe three years of rent," he said ominously, "I just be durn if I ain't goan git mad! They just keep worrying me and worrying me about that old money, and I ain't goan put up with it much longer."

The sheriff spoke to him pleasantly and the deputy nodded as he brought out a chair and put it in the truck.

"Sheriff," Jud said, "let's talk this over. If you put me out of here, my little family won't have nowheres to go at."

"You had the money after your dog won them trials, and you spent it, and the bank says for me to turn you out and that's all there is to it." He spoke to his deputy. "Keep the stuff coming, Alwin."

Jud watched his meager belongings being loaded. They were really going to throw him out.

From the interior the deputy called, "Sheriff, he's got a right nice bed in here, but there's a dog laying on it and he keeps growling at me when I try to git him off."

"Bring the bed on out, dog and all."

The deputy folded the mattress with Jud's bird dog, Fred, inside, and came stumbling out with it. He opened it up on the truck, and Fred looked around and then went back to sleep.

"Sheriff," Jud said, suddenly, "I've thought up sump'm. There's a doctor in town, and he's stuck on that durn dog yonder, and I bet I could git him to make a loan on Fred!"

The sheriff motioned to his deputy. "Just wait, Alwin." He said to Jud, "The bank said that I wasn't to listen to nothing you said, unless you happened to mention selling a valuable dog you had. They never spoke of mortgaging no dog, but if they git the money that's all they care about. Come on and we'll go to town. I'll go, and we'll take the dog."

The receptionist in Doctor Ingram's office told Jud that the doctor was in but busy.

Jud said, "Shuh, he'll drop whatever he's doing when he hears it's about my old dog, Fred." And without waiting, he pushed through the door to the doctor's office before the receptionist could get up to stop him.

The doctor was examining a woman patient when Jud burst in. The woman gave a horrified scream. The startled doctor pushed Jud outside and shut the door.

"You idiot, you shouldn't have come bursting in there like that!" the doctor said angrily.

"Shuh, Doc, don't worry none. Stuff like that don't embarrass me. Let me tell you my proposition."

"If you've got a proposition, tell it to me quickly."

Jud's face saddened. "Well, the sheriff's out at my place a-fixing to turn my little family out into the cold."

"That's exactly what he should do. Goodby."

"Wait. You've always had a hankering to buy my dog Fred."

The doctor's interest quickened. "You mean you're actually willing to sell Fred to save your farm?"

"Not exactly. I figured to mortgage him to you until another one them trials, and then I would win the money to pay you back."

The doctor's eyes gleamed briefly. "Jud, the only reason I would consider such a proposition is because it may end in my owning the dog. I warned you about that. Now there's an open trial at Spencer this weekend. I'll pay the bank sixty dollars – one year's rent, enough to stall them off for several months – and

132

I'll put up the forty-dollar entry fee at Spencer, and I'll give you thirty dollars for transportation and expenses. Miss Monroe, please go with Mr. Lee to my lawyer's office and have him draw up an airtight lien on his dog Fred for the sum of one hundred and thirty dollars. I'll keep the dog here until you get back. Remember, Jud, next week bring either a hundred and thirty dollars or *my* dog Fred."

With thirty dollars cash money in his pocket and the bird dog Fred at his heels, Jud had started to the bus station to learn the bus schedule when he passed a used-car lot. At once it occurred to him that, if he was going to be traveling here and there following field trials, it would really be better to have his own car to drive. He got into conversation with the salesman, and went from one car to another, and finally, in the absolute back of the lot, they came to a vehicle the salesman was willing to let go for a cash down payment of twenty-five dollars.

The car did run pretty good, for the shape it was in, and Jud drove around town a couple of times, with Fred holding his head out the back window and grinning into the breeze. When he stopped, Clem Frisby, who had come to town to get some new calendars, approached him.

"Well, Jud, you acting mighty biggity, now that you got a car. Passed me right by while ago without a lift of a finger."

"I swear I never seen you, Clem, er I'd a-shore retched out and wove to you. Me and my money-making dog is all set to go win a field trial. Git in and go. We'll be back Monday er so."

"I'd shore like to see old Fred outhunt them city dogs," Clem said, "but right here at the end of the physical year when the stores is giving out new calendars, I ought to stay on the job."

"Git in. You got enough calendars."

Clem hesitated another moment, and finally unloaded his armful of rolled-up calendars on the floor of the back seat and got in. "Okay," he said with an excited grin, "let 'er go."

pencer was a hundred and fifty miles away, and after a while the novelty of the ride began to wear off, and as night came Clem and Fred went to sleep. The car rocketed through the darkness, its one light blinking occasionally. For an hour the motor ran as smoothly as could be expected, and then suddenly began a rapid, hammering knock that grew in intensity until Clem roused up and Fred cocked his head inquiringly. Jud kept the accelerator pedal on the floor.

Finally Clem shouted, "Don't it sound to you like one them bearings is burnt out a little bit?"

"Yep. Sounds like it."

Clem went back to sleep. The knocking grew still louder. Clem woke up and said, "If that thing's going to keep up such-all a racket as that, let's stop and git it fixed."

The next town was fairly large. They were reluctant to slow down for fear the car wouldn't crank again, so they leaned out and yelled, "Where's a garage at?" but the few passers-by who were able to understand them above the clatter were too astonished to answer in time, so Clem said, "I'll hop out and get the inflammation and catch you coming round the block." Jud circled the block. Clem was waiting but missed him on the first round, and Jud had to circle him again.

Clem directed him to the garage, and as they drove in the whole night shift of mechanics came near and regarded the car interestedly.

"We want to git a bearing fixed, and we're in sort of a hurry," Jud said. "How much will it cost?"

"Can't tell, offhand," said the foreman. "Maybe you've busted a piston too. We'll take a look."

A half-hour later he said. "This repair job will cost you about fifteen dollars."

Jud said, "Fifteen dollars! You must think I'm made of money! Can't you fix up a bearing out of a piece of old shoe leather?"

"Not hardly, " he answered. "Might as well git it fixed. You can't run like that – the burnt-out bearing driving the piston will wear your crankshaft down, and then you'll really be into it."

"Tell you what," Jud said. "Just take the durned old piston plumb out."

"You can't do that. There's another piston has to operate in rhythm with it. They'll be out of balance and she'll go to pieces."

"Then take the other piston out, too," Jud instructed.

The garageman argued, but Jud insisted. So they took out two pistons, crammed cardboard into the empty cylinders to keep any stray raw gas from leaking into the crankcase, and the job was done. When time came to crank up, all the garage employees retreated to the other end. Clem stood down, too.

The motor started all right, and the four cylinders that had pistons fired fine; but there was a break in the roar when time came for the empty cylinders to fire. This caused the car to shake. Fred in the back, held his seat with difficulty, and his face took on an apprehensive look.

Jud cut the motor, and Fred, having momentary purchase for his feet, sprang through the window and ran to the other end of the garage, where he hid beneath a disabled car.

"You come here, sah!" Jud called. But Fred didn't come until Jud crawled underneath and got him.

Again he cranked up, and someone got in beside him, but the vibration of the car was such that his companion was just a blur.

"That you, Clem?" Jud shouted.

"Yep, That you, Jud?" Clem shouted.

"Yep."

Out on the road again, the tailpipe shook loose from the muffler so that part of the exhaust gas seeped up through the floorboards, and Fred presently sank to the seat in a grateful semicoma.

Jud said, "What's that clicking noise I keep hearing?"

"It's my false teeth hitting together," Clem complained. "I shore hate fer them to git all chipped up."

134

"Here," Jud said. "Just hold this old croaker sack between your teeth."

Clem bit down on the sack and it worked fine. The next thing that bothered him was the heat that threatened to scald his feet.

"Suppose she catches afire?" Clem shouted suddenly.

Jud thought for a moment, and then his face lit up. "She's insured, so the man says. Just before we git to Spencer, if she'd catch and burn up, it would be right nice. We'd be there, and git our money back too. Now if she catches, you grab your calendars, and I'll grab old Fred, and we'll git out and let 'er burn up."

"Reckon we hadn't ought to have a little fire drill?" Clem suggested. "I'd hate to forgit to save my calendars."

"Ain't a bad idea," Jud said. "After while, now, I'll make out she's afire, and we'll practice up."

"That's it, do it when I ain't expectant."

Presently Jud slammed on the brakes and shouted, "She's afire!" Clem grabbed his calendars, and Jud dragged out the torpid bird dog.

"We got it down, pat," Clem said with satisfaction. "What's the matter with Fred? He looks sorta sick."

"Just sulling," Jud said. "He'll be all right when he sees we're a-going bird hunting."

Just before dawn, with the croaker sack in his mouth straining Clem's snores, the car really did catch fire. Jud slammed on the brakes and cried, "Clem, she's afire shore enough!"

Clem stumbled out, still holding the sack between his teeth, Jud, dragging Fred out, didn't see that Clem had opened the hood, and in his half-sleep state was throwing sand on the blazing motor. The fire quickly smothered.

"Well, I'll just be durned," Jud said in disgust. "Look what you went and done. You act to me like you ain't never had nothing insured before!"

With Clem chewing apologetically on the sack, Jud cranked up angrily and they drove on.

The field trial assembly was waiting impatiently when Jud's car drove up, stopped and backfired, causing Judge Rice's horse to rear. The field-trial judge was angry even before that.

"Is that the post entry Dr. Ingram phoned in last night?" he asked Jud, when Fred staggered shakily out.

"Yep," Jud said. "His name is Fred and he's raring to go."

Judge Rice bit off his words. "So are we, Mr. Lee. We've been waiting here ten minutes. You're in the first brace. Next time, be here when you're supposed to."

Jud said to Clem, "He sounds like somebody with a guvment job."

The judges rode out to the front of the gallery, and the secretary of the club announced, "First brace, Wildwood Jack and Fred. Bring your dogs forward."

Wildwood Jack was eager, jumping about and straining in the grasp of his handler. Fred trotted alongside Jud with a fatuous grin on his face. When they were out front, the big judge glanced at his watch. He started to say, "Are you ready, gentlemen?"

Wildwood Jack broke away in quick jumps the instant of release. Fred strolled forward a few steps, then lay down and panted contentedly. The gallery, already impatient to get started, was forced to draw up to prevent running over Fred.

"Your dog," Judge Rice said elaborately, "doesn't quite show the drive we like to see in a class dog."

"Judge," Jud said worriedly, "somebody has tampered with that dog! Fred, you git going, sah!"

Fred wagged his tail briefly, and put his head on his legs.

"That dog ain't at hisself. He don't belong to lay there like that," Jud said, "and he don't belong to wag his tail."

Clem had gone back to the car, intending to follow in it as best he could, in company with the dog wagons and a spectator truck. Finally he got it cranked and underway. Fred, hearing the unmistakable racking noise of the motor, lifted his head in alarm. As the sound drew nearer, Fred got his feet up and started running.

With Fred on his way, Jud steered his horse to the rear of the gallery where Clem followed in the car.

"Something bad ails old Fred. Maybe I should have give him a through of medicine before we come," Jud said. "But it's too late now. Listen to me, Clem. If we can keep him out yonder in front, maybe he'll git back at hisself. He's took it into his head that he don't like our car, so if he tries to quit again, I'll raise up my head and you race the motor to beat all hell, so he can hear it."

Clem accepted this responsibility with pride. "We'll work in co-ornication and keep old Fred a-going," he said.

Wildwood Jack found birds. It was a small covey huddled in a hawthorne thicket, and when they burst out the other side, the dog was steady to wing and shot, and the gallery murmured in approval. Jack was sent away, and he raced along the fringe of the cornfield.

Fred had not been seen since the initial sprint which carried him over the hill and out of sight. On the right side of the course was a creek swamp, on the left beyond the broad and varying avenue of fields, a body of short-leaf pine woods. Jud began to wonder, worriedly, if Fred had taken it into his head to run away.

But presently, after galloping his horse hard, he found him. Fred was asleep in a patch of sunlight in the woods.

"I'm plumb disagusted at you," Jud said angrily. "Git up and go to work. Er do you want to do your hunting from now on with an old fool doctor that smells like sheep-dip?"

Fred made no effort to get going, but lay there looking up at Jud lazily. Presently, however, the gallery drew near. Jud moved his horse out into the clear and held up his hand to Clem. Quickly there came the racing and badly broken rhythm of the old car. Fred lifted his head in sudden alarm, and the next instant he sprang away and headed across the cornfield.

136

This second sprint cleared Fred's lungs somewhat of the gas, and instead of disappearing into the woods on the other side for another nap, he swung back out in front, far ahead of the gallery and gave the appearance of hunting. In fact, when Wildwood Jack found his third covey, Fred was in the vicinity and seeing his bracemate on birds, honored the point.

"Well, I'm glad to find out the old fool will back," Jud said. "First time another dog ever found a covey in front of him."

Mrs. Terrill, who owned the hunting preserve the trials were being run on, drew her frothing horse alongside Jud and said, "Is that really so, Mr. Lee?"

"It's the truth, ma'am, and you know the truth will go from here to heaven."

"I do hope your dog is feeling well," she said.

"No'm, he ain't." He leaned slightly toward her and whispered, "I'm thinking he's been messed with."

Her eyes opened wide in horror. "Why, the poor thing! How terrible!"

But Fred was doing better now. He was covering his ground nicely, and Jud figured that if he could get him on birds a couple of times he might have a chance to be called back in the second series, even though Wildwood Jack had him beat on finds. But whereas Fred was now willing to hunt, his nose was badly off, and was proved a few minutes later.

Fred was seen to strike scent near a gallberry clump, then to turn, draw a few steps and point in fine style. Jud shouted, "He's got 'em, Judge, shore'n hell," and they rode to the place.

Jud dismounted, and with his gun in hand walked toward the pointing dog. Just as he got there, however, a sow with eight little pigs, to Fred's astonishment, emerged from the gallery clump and with offended dignity, walked away.

"Did you ever see the beat of that?" Jud asked.

"I certainly did not," said Judge Rice coldly.

With ten minutes left to run, Jud became desperate. I'm shore about to lose my old dog to that doctor. Then Fred came in from a long swing out to one side, and just as he was about to pass the front of the gallery he wheeled and pointed. Every horse was drawn to a quick stop.

"Your dog is pointing straight at me," said Judge Rice.

"You must be standing sprang in the middle of the covey," Jud said. "Back up real easy like and maybe they won't flush."

The judge backed his horse, then drew him around to one side. But strangely, Fred slowly turned with the man, still pointing. The judge, perceiving this, moved all the way around the dog, and Fred kept moving with him, pointing.

"Lee," Judge Rice shouted, furiously, "your dog is pointing me."

"I'll be durn if he ain't! First a sow, and then you," Jud said. "Judge, you didn't eat quail for breakfast, did you?"

"No, I did not!" roared the judge. "Make that dog stop pointing me, Lee, and furthermore, don't ever run him in another field I'm judging, you understand?" He rode off.

After another brace had been put down and the gallery moved on, Clem and

Jud were sitting on the running board, with Fred tied to keep him from running away from the old car.

"Well, I guess I've lost my old dog sure enough," Jud said, and tears rose in his eyes.

"I ain't never seen him zibit so many idiocentricities," Clem said. "It turned out to be a pretty good deal fer that doctor."

Jud straightened. "Clem, listen here! When I went up to see that lawyer, that doctor made me leave the dog in his office! You know what he done? He give Fred a dost of some kind of pizen, to make him act like that so I couldn't win!"

Clem ejaculated, "I just be durn!"

At this moment portly Mrs. Terrill rode back. "I couldn't go away without telling you how sorry I am that you lost, Mr. Lee," she said. "But I'm sure you must be wrong when you say someone tampered with your dog."

"No, I ain't wrong," Jud shouted, "and I've done figured out the very scoun'l what done it."

That afternoon Mrs. Terrill's big car stopped in front of Doctor Ingram's building, and out got Jud and Clem and the dog Fred, and Mrs. Terrill, and an officer of the S.P.C.A. and a policeman. They went inside.

Doctor Ingram, in a bright herringbone suit, looked at the assembly in amazement.

Jud spoke. "First thing is to give you your old money back. Here she is, a hund'ed and thirty dollars. Now you ain't got no more mortgage on my dog."

"Congratulations!" the doctor said. "Fred must have won!"

"You ain't fooling nobody with that made-up friendship. This fat lady here give me the money and took over the mortgage. Fred never won that field trial and you know how come!"

"What on earth are you talking about?"

The S.P.C.A. officer said gently, "Let us handle this little matter from here, Mr. Lee."

The outraged protests of the doctor got pretty loud, so Jud and Clem slipped out the door for quieter surroundings.

"It just goes to show you," Jud said darkly, "that you can't tell who to trust in this world. I shore wouldn't a-thought it of that doctor."

"He shore turned out to be a wolf in cheap clothing," Clem said.

They walked on. Finally Jud said, "You know, Clem, I still think that judge had et quail for breakfast."

"Mortgage on a Dog" is from Brag Dog and Other Stories: The Best of Vereen Bell, *published by Wilderness Adventures, Inc.*

THE DAY THE DUCK HUNTERS DIED

Nothing escaped "the winds of hell" and the deadly, suffocating snows that swept across the Upper Midwest on that fateful day in 1940.

By Tom Davis

I t is easy to forget.

It is easy to forget that there was a time – not so very long ago, really – when there was no Gore-Tex, no Thinsulate, no neoprene, and no polypropylene. There was a time when outboard motors, far from the sleek and powerful marvels of today, were crude, cumbersome beasts, unreliable under the best of circumstances and all but useless under the worst. There was a time when there were no cell phones, no emergency beacons, no Flight for Life helicopters.

There was a time, too, when there were no weather satellites, no telemetry to provide data that could be plugged into sophisticated formulas and fed into supercomputers for timely forecasts. Indeed, that the weather could be predicted with *any* degree of accuracy then – November, 1940, to be precise – seems almost miraculous, meteorology in those days being one part science and two parts the divination of omens, signs and portents. Nothing brings this into starker relief than the fact that, a little over a year later, what appeared on radar to be a swarm of aircraft approaching the Hawaiian Islands was dismissed as some sort of malfunction by military officers who refused to trust this newfangled and unproven technology.

Of course, some things do not change with the passage of time, and one of these constants is the love of duck hunters for the kind of wet, raw, blustery, thoroughly miserable days that keep normal people indoors with the fireplace crackling and the teakettle whistling on the stove. And just as absence makes the heart grow fonder, the longer the duck hunter is made to wait for such a day, the hotter burns his pent-up desire to escape to the sloughs and bays and marshes, and there – decoys artfully set, blind brushed and grassed, dog expectant and quivering, call poised to be pressed to lips – scan the lowering skies for birds that ride the wind.

T he fall of 1940 had been a mild one in the Upper Midwest, an extended Indian Summer of warm temperatures and little rainfall. In other words, the duck hunting had been disappointing. Oh, there had been the usual "local" birds early in the season – teal, widgeon, shoveler, the odd mallard – but without any heavy weather to set the migration in motion, the great flocks of northern ducks were still in the prairie provinces of Canada, fattening up for the long flight south. Hunters throughout the region, from the Dakotas across to Wisconsin, from Minnesota down to southern Illinois, were on pins and needles, knowing that the change in the weather they so dearly wanted was overdue, that it could happen any day.

Finally, on Sunday, November 10, came a forecast that held promise. The outlook was for clouds, snow flurries and colder temperatures. Wildfowlers were ecstatic, and what made this good news even better was that Monday, November 11, was Armistice Day – the predecessor to Veterans Day and, for many people, a holiday. Although as holidays go it was a fairly somber one: The grinding effects of the Depression still lingered in the U. S., and in Europe, where just twenty-two years earlier the eponymous armistice had been signed, war raged once again.

Still, it's not much of a leap to suppose that the typical waterfowler of the Upper Midwest, upon hearing the forecast on the radio or reading it in the local newspaper, felt blessed – even jubilant. Other concerns were pushed aside; nothing mattered now but getting ready for tomorrow's hunt. Decoys, shell boxes, shotguns and calls were checked and re-checked; ditto for boats, motors, gas tanks and oars. Clothes were carefully laid out; sandwiches were made, wrapped in wax paper and refrigerated; thermos bottles were placed next to coffee percolators. The dog was given an extra bait of food, because in a few hours he was going to be one very busy retriever and would need all the energy and stamina he could muster.

The phone lines hummed as hunting partner called hunting partner, their voices crackling with excitement. They knew, with as much certainty as they knew anything, the ducks would be flying, and they aimed to be smack dab in the middle of them.

They got more than they bargained for.

I n his magisterial *Where The Sky Began: Land of the Tallgrass Prairie*, John Madson describes the genesis of a midwestern blizzard as a "tempestuous marriage" of cold, dry, polar air sweeping down from Canada and warm, moist, subtropical air welling up from the Gulf of Mexico. "Since its primary component is wind," Madson writes, "the classic blizzard is essentially a phenomenon of the open lands – particularly the plains and prairies, where the topography offers little resistance to moving air and the great storms can run almost unimpeded. There may be more snow in northern and eastern forest regions, and certainly as much cold. The difference between winter storms there and the classic prairie blizzard lies in the intensity of unbridled wind that plunges the chill factor to deadly lows, drives a blinding smother of snow during the actual storm, and continues as ground blizzards and white-outs long after snow has stopped falling. Depending on snowfall and wind, the storm may leave drifts three times as tall as a man and is usually followed by calm, silver-blue days of burning cold."

That, in a nutshell, describes the blizzard that screamed across the Upper Midwest on Monday, November 11, 1940, devastating everything it touched along the way. The winds blasted at a constant forty- to fifty-miles per hour, with gusts in excess of eighty. Over sixteen inches of snow fell in the Twin Cities, while more than twenty-six inches was recorded a few miles up the Mississippi River near St. Cloud. In LaCrosse, downstream on the Wisconsin side of the Mississippi, the barometric pressure sank to an all-time low. The temperature dropped thirty degrees – from above freezing to single digits – in two hours, and continued to plummet from there. Wind-chills were virtually off the charts.

Nothing escaped the storm's furious, relentless, indiscriminate wrath. Livestock perished by the hundreds of thousands. So many turkeys died in parts of Minnesota and Iowa that after the storm, farmers were selling whole "fresh frozen" birds for twenty-five cents apiece. The losses to wildlife, especially pheasants, were spectacular. Communications and power were disrupted across thousands of square miles, and transportation was brought to an absolute standstill. Every town and village close to a main road became a refuge as stranded travelers sought shelter from the storm. Countless people opened their homes to complete strangers, providing whatever they could offer in the way of board and room.

But for some there was no shelter, no refuge. Motorists stuck in snowdrifts on remote stretches of road were buried alive in their cars, their frozen bodies not exhumed for days. On Lake Michigan, the freighter *William B. Davock* was sheared in two by monstrous waves.

The ferocity of the storm was almost beyond human reckoning. There are accounts of farmers who, after checking on their livestock, literally could not find their way from the barn to the farmhouse. Disoriented, pummeled by the wind, with no visible landmarks to guide them and no sense of east, west, north or south, they wandered blindly through a roaring white hell. The lucky ones bumped into something recognizable and groped their way to safety. The unlucky ones didn't.

Nearly everyone who survived the storm remarked on how incredibly difficult it was just to *breathe*. The air was so laden with moisture that it seemed as thick as syrup. And even when you were able to draw a deep breath, the cold seared your lungs like a red-hot blade.

This is what thousands of duck hunters, with their wooden skiffs and their cranky outboards and their canvas coats, found themselves caught in. Most of the world knows the midwestern blizzard of November 11, 1940 as the Armistice Day Storm. To sportsmen, it's simply the day the duck hunters died.

No one really knows how many people lost their lives as a direct result of the Armistice Day Storm. Although *Time* put the death toll at 159, the actual figure was probably closer to 200 – and about half them were duck hunters. According to John Madson, eighty-five duck hunters perished in Minnesota, Wisconsin and Illinois alone. As he wrote in *Where The Sky Began*, "Caught by the storm with little warning, they drowned as they tried to reach land, or stayed in their duck blinds as waves tore them apart, or simply died of exposure that night on the river islands out of reach of help..."

If a storm causing as much destruction and loss of life occurred today, someone like Sebastian Junger or Jon Krakauer would write a best-selling book about it. But while it certainly made headlines – a spread in *Life* was entitled "Midwest Tempest Strews Death By Land And Lake" – America was preoccupied with other matters. After the dead were buried, the damage was cleared and the bereaved had ceased to mourn, life resumed more-or-less as usual. And the weather for the remainder of the winter of 1940-41 was largely unremarkable.

But no one who was there ever forgot it. Nor did their memories, like photos left too long in a shop window, pale with the passage of time. It was the persistence of these memories that, forty-five years after the event, prompted a Minnesota man named William Hull to track down and interview over 500 people who'd lived through the Armistice Day Storm. He then selected 167 of these accounts and assembled them into a book called, fittingly, *All Hell Broke Loose*.

Now in its eighteenth printing, it's replete with tales not only of close calls and narrow escapes, but of countless acts of charity, generosity, selflessness and heroism. (There are a number of humorous, Keillor-esque tales as well, such as the one entitled "Three Hours Digging Path to Outhouse.") Not a few of these stories were told by duck hunters. While the specifics may differ slightly – some recalled seemingly endless flocks of divers like redheads, bluebills and canvasbacks, while others remembered wave upon wave of mallards – they all agree that they had never seen the sky so filled with ducks. They agree, too, that there was nothing in the weather that morning to presage what was coming, that the storm was upon them almost before they knew what was happening, and that it was only by the grace of God that they survived when so many others did not.

Every sportsman who was there has his own wrinkle to add to the story. Cyril Looker of Fremont, Wisconsin – in the heart of the wildlife-rich Wolf River bottoms – recalls standing on the shore near a powerline cut and burning up two boxes of shells as the ducks poured into Partridge Lake. The kicker, notes the eighty-three-year-old

Looker, is that the birds – mallards and divers both – were flying *beneath* the wires.

The account that eclipses all the rest, though – and that has made the Armistice Day Storm vividly and chillingly real for generations of sportsmen ever since – is the one written by the great Gordon MacQuarrie. Indeed, it's entirely likely that if MacQuarrie, then the outdoors editor for the *Milwaukee Journal*, hadn't been on the scene, the event would be little more than a footnote in duck hunting history. While a lesser writer might have filed a competent and informative report, MacQuarrie penned a masterpiece.

His story, under the headline "Icy Death Rides Gale on Duck Hunt Trail," appeared on the front page of the *Journal* on Wednesday, November 13. It was filed from Winona, Minnesota, a Mississippi River town about ninety miles downstream from the Twin Cities. The river there is a sprawling, two-mile-wide wilderness of islands, oxbows and backwater sloughs, and Winona was the epicenter of the disaster: At least twenty duck hunters died within fifty miles of the city.

"The winds of hell were loose on the Mississippi Armistice day and night," wrote MacQuarrie.

"They came across the prairie, from the south and west, a mighty, freezing force. They charged down from the high river bluffs to the placid stream below and reached with deathly fingers for the life that beat beneath the canvas jackets of hundreds of duck hunters . . .

"The wind did it, the furious wind that pierced any clothing, that locked outboard engines in sheaths of ice, that froze on faces and hands and clothing, so that survivors crackled when they got to safety and said their prayers.

"Mother Nature caught hundreds of duck hunters on the Armistice holiday. She lured them out to the marshes with her fine, whooping wind, and when she got them there she froze them like muskrats in traps. She promised ducks in the wind. They came all right, but by that time the duck hunters were playing a bigger game with the wind, and their lives were the stake.

"By that time men along the Mississippi were drowning and freezing. The ducks came and men died. They died underneath upturned skiffs as the blast sought them out on boggy, unprotected islands; they died trying to light fires and jumping and sparring trying to keep warm; they died sitting in skiffs. They died standing in river water to their hips, awaiting help; they died trying to help each other. A hundred tales of heroism will be told, long after the funerals are over."

MacQuarrie told of Gerald Tarras, a strapping seventeen-year-old who'd gone hunting in the Mississippi bottoms that fateful day with his father, brother, a family friend and their black Lab. They set up mid-morning in a drizzling rain; by noon they were trapped by six-foot waves, waves that pounded like huge iron fists and hurled freezing spray that turned instantly to boilerplate ice. The men beat on one another to try to keep warm, but it was a losing battle. At about two a.m., the friend uttered one last moan and died in Gerald's arms. Gerald's brother held out until eleven in the morning, but after twenty-three hours of exposure he, too, succumbed.

Then, shortly after noon, a small plane flew over. Gerald waved, and the pilot signaled that help was on the way. Rescuers in the government tugboat *Throckmorton* arrived at 2:30 – half-an-hour too late to save Gerald's father. They found the boy crouched against a stump, holding his dog for warmth, fighting to remain conscious.

Max Conrad, the pilot who led rescuers to Gerald Tarras, was one of the true heroes of the Armistice Day Storm. Dozens of hunters would later acknowledge that they owed their lives to him. On Tuesday the 12th, with the wind still howling but the skies clear, he took off from his hangar in Winona to help find the hunters who hadn't come home. Flying a redoubtable Piper Cub – and fighting to make even twenty or thirty knots of airspeed against the brutal headwinds – he scanned the frozen margins of the Mississippi for the living, but often as not discovered the dead.

When he located survivors – they were frequently huddled in the lee of a skiff they'd propped up as a windbreak – Conrad would circle low, cut the engine for a moment, and holler "Hang on! Help is coming!" A few minutes later, he'd return and, like manna sent down from heaven, drop a canister filled with sandwiches, whiskey, dry matches and cigarettes. Conrad would then circle until the *Throckmorton* or one of the many other rescue boats that had deployed in search of survivors could get a fix on the spot. He kept flying until ten p.m. that night, and he was out again at dawn the following day.

There is no telling how many hunters died for the simple want of dry matches. But even that was no guarantee, as there was still the problem of finding dry fuel to burn. Many a prized Mason decoy went up in flames, and a group of seventeen hunters stranded on the same island took turns shooting down limbs for firewood until their ammunition ran out.

The Mississippi River was not the only place where duckboats became sepulchers, of course. Two hunters died on Wisconsin's Big Muskego Lake, barely twenty miles from downtown Milwaukee. One of these men was alone in his skiff, trapped by waves and ice. Toward the end, another party of hunters glimpsed him standing in his boat with his head tilted back, his arms stretched outwards, and his palms turned up. It was as if he were imploring God – or perhaps commending his soul to Him. While the other hunters, who themselves were fighting to survive, watched helplessly, the man slumped back into his skiff, leaned heavily against the gunwale, and went motionless.

His spirit, like the ducks that drew him out on that terrible day, had flown.

The author wishes to thank Howard Mead of Madison, Wisconsin, for his assistance in providing background research.

WHY WE HUNT

This privilege of hunting is about as fine a heritage as we have in America, and it needs to be passed on unsullied from father to son, on down for generations to come.

By Michael McIntosh

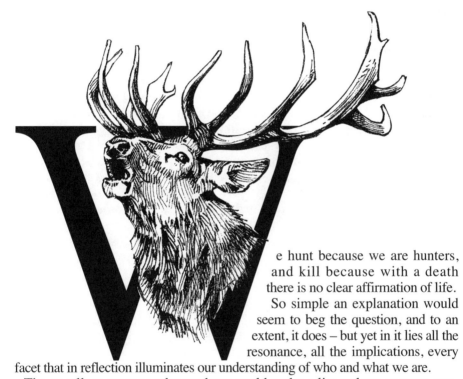

e hunt because we are hunters, and kill because with a death there is no clear affirmation of life. So simple an explanation would seem to beg the question, and to an extent, it does – but yet in it lies all the resonance, all the implications, every facet that in reflection illuminates our understanding of who and what we are.

The corollary reasons why we hunt could make a list as long as your arm. We hunt for the pleasures of companionship, to escape for a while the regimentation and stress of daily life. We hunt because we love to shoot, or enjoy the challenge of getting within close range of some wary, supremely capable game animal.

Good reasons, worthy reasons, valid reasons, certainly, but they all describe what we *get* from hunting, not ultimately *why* we do it. You can enjoy companionship by going to a baseball game or playing golf, relieve stress with a tennis racket or a canoe paddle, get all the shooting you want on a rifle

145

range or a clays course. You can conclude a successful stalk by pressing a shutter instead of a trigger.

But none of these is hunting, and thus we hunt, as if it provides something we can't reach in any other way. Which, of course, is true, and it lies deeply within ourselves.

A certain school of thought has it that *Homo sapiens* is the only reflective animal, the only organism that is truly self-aware. We may be, although I'm not entirely comfortable with the level of arrogance the position implies. But what's important is that we *do* have the gift, if you want to call it that, of self-awareness, and gifts are neither to be wasted nor abused.

To our credit, and despite the fact that some of our conclusions are certainly open to argument, we've been thinking about ourselves for a very long time. We reached something of a peak in this during the Middle Ages, when scholars came up with the notion of the Great Chain of Being in their attempt to perceive man's place and a scheme of order in a disorderly world, and though they didn't know it, their concept defined the nature of hunters for all time.

It being the Middle Ages, their main intent was to find a way of explaining how all things derive from God, even – or perhaps especially – those things that seemed particularly unChristian. All of Creation, the best thinkers concluded, is a chain, ascending link by link from inanimate nature to the deity, from stones to God. Plants grow from the stony earth, beasts are nourished by plants, man is nourished by beasts, man's spirit aspires to the level of angels, and so on.

Each component, moreover, is truly a link and owns something of its adjacent links. Stones are supremely durable; so are some plants, but plants have the advantage of life, though not mobility; beasts have life and mobility but not a spirit; man has life *and* mobility and a spirit; angels, although purely spiritual beings, may take on discrete form and in addition are able to perceive first-hand the nature of God.

It's a wonderfully integrated picture, and in its way, the Great Chain is a perfect conception of the nature of man. We are possessed of both angelic spirituality and animal passion, mediated by free will. This, as much as anything, is what the philosophers were struggling to understand and explain, and they did it by placing man at the very center, midway between inanimate nature and God, half angel and half animal. (Think about it for a moment, and it's clear that Freud didn't come up with the notion of Ego, Superego and Id all on his own hook.)

Now if you take away the medieval prejudice against the value of earthly things, if you grant every link intrinsic worth and don't get wound up in the sophistry of whether any link is somehow "better" than any other, then you've put your finger on what motivates a hunter.

146

We rejoice in that part of our nature where we are blood kin to quail and grouse and elk and elephant. Let a flock of geese wing low over a city park, and you can learn something by how the people there react. Some will give the birds a mere glance, others none at all. Yet others will stand transfixed, riveted on them, rapt and oblivious to everything else for as long as they're in sight. Those are the hunters, and what they're feeling is an urge to celebrate the exuberance of being alive by engaging other living things at the most elemental level.

The yearning to do so is as old as mankind. Once we killed our own food, first wild and then domestic, bled it, dressed it out and cut it up with our own hands, not in rancor but in reverence and gratitude that nature could supply a livelihood. Death was the natural counterpart to life, and both life and death had meaning because of it.

In a rural, agricultural environment, all the biological processes of life lie close to the surface. But through most of the twentieth century we have moved steadily away from nature. Now, urbanized and suburbanized for two or three or four generations, we have constructed artificial worlds and taken them as reality. Crowded together far removed from the natural world, infatuated with our accomplishments and anaesthetized by convenience, we're culturally content to think no further of an animal's life and death than is contained between a styrofoam tray and cellophane wrap and laid out in a supermarket display, where life and death have no meaning beyond its price per pound.

Some take this as evidence that medieval thinking was right, that an increasingly sterile existence somehow represents an improvement of our nature. Others feel it keenly as a loss, a void at some deep level and, in their longing to express the full range of our nature, are hunters.

One of my favorite pieces in my little art collection is a tiny, hand-colored linoleum-block print by Darla Smith, who is one of the finest living practitioners of that little-recognized medium. It shows a nude figure, probably but not necessarily male, in a wilderness landscape of trees and grass and sky, watching a flight of birds. He might be holding something in his hand – a stick, an arrow, a spear, it's hard to tell. Or he might be simply offering a salute to the birds. Hail, well, met. The integration among the elements is exquisite. Hunting was the farthest thing from the artist's mind when she carved it, but it explains hunting perfectly, right down to the title. She called it *Home*.

For us who are hunters, the need to engage nature firsthand is as powerful and as elemental as the need for food and comfort and sex. For us, engaging nature is to engage life itself.

I do not roust myself out of a warm bed in freezing darkness and struggle through mud, water and cold to watch sunrise over a duck marsh simply because I like the idea of it. I do not follow my dog – splendid, gentle predator that she is – mile after weary mile on foot, in sun or snow or pelting rain in search of something solely cerebral. Other men don't climb mountains, wander forests or tundra or grassland for the chance to train a rifle on a bighorn sheep or a whitetail or a caribou or a pronghorn merely because it's an intriguing thought.

We do it because of how it makes us *feel*. In the sting or solace of weather, in the fine agony of pitting leg muscles against elevation or distance, in the sweet misery of crouching in mud and water that's bare degrees from solid ice, in spending comfort against the stuff that nourishes our souls – in these do we find ourselves at last profoundly, exquisitely alive.

e hunt because we can, as an expression of the free will that binds together the duality of our nature, animal and angel. Somewhere in every human being resides a predator that has existed in us ever since we fully evolved the physical and mental capacity to pursue and subdue game. To some, the predatory spark is a fearsome thing, to be suppressed or sublimated or denied, deserving only of apology. Others recognize it as a worthy part of our nature that, when exercised as an act of will, becomes a celebration of our place in the natural world.

And to give life perspective and shape and meaning, there is death. One without the other denies the substance and the significance of both.

Read the editorial pages of any big-city newspaper and you'll soon come across the phrase "meaningless death," usually followed by some journalistic gnashing of teeth, leading to conclusions that seldom amount to more than disapproving resignation. It's as if we've created a civilization defined by random, mindless violence and don't have a clue how it happened or what to do about it.

In fact, it's the sign of a culture that has moralized and rationalized itself into near-paralysis, the result of having abrogated a shameful amount of personal moral fiber and self-reliance and individual responsibility, of having lost the ability to know the difference between reality and the fictions we create for entertainment.

In the process of contriving an artificial world and of losing touch with the realities of ourselves and nature, hunting has become in some quarters politically incorrect, to use one of the dopier catchphrases in current mint. To be a hunter these days is to earn the disapproval of a certain segment of what passes for a national conscience.

For my part, I can only respond to being deemed politically incorrect with another bit of late-twentieth century jargon: *Like I give a damn.*

I don't care about being politically correct. I care about being a decent man, about being loyal to those I love and to my own moral sensibility, and if

148

part of that sensibility finds its best expression in hunting, so be it. I don't need legislation or popular opinion or mass media to tell me what to think or how I should behave. To semi-quote John Madson, having my lifestyle impugned by some self-righteous bozo who doesn't know the first thing about how nature really works – or as John put it, doesn't know the difference between a Cooper's hawk and a fungo bat – is about like being run over by a baby buggy.

Actually, the farther our culture moves from any real understanding of nature, the more important hunting becomes on a personal level. The argument that we no longer need to hunt for subsistence is no argument at all. Of course we don't. We hunt for *meaning*.

Ask a hunter to define a meaningful death, and he'll describe something he loves – a pheasant or a moose or a goose, a wild turkey, a woodcock, a mule deer. The connection between love and death is the one key point that those who do not hunt can never fully understand. But the hunter does. He'll tell you that taking the life of a lovely animal, taking it cleanly and quickly and fairly and in a spirit of love, is an affirmation of both the animal's life and his own – because in that brief moment the animal and the hunter become one, in the certain knowledge that just as we share life, we will share death as well.

To hunt is to exercise the side of our nature that owns all the same needs and desires and instincts as do the animals we hunt. To hunt well, to hunt ethically, according to our best traditions, and with a profound respect for the game, is to exercise the other half, the angelic side, the side of us that looks for meaning and in the straightforward exercise of life well lived and death well brought, finds it.

To hunt is to be complete. To take into my hand the warm, limp, ineffably beautiful body of a bird my dog has pointed and that has just fallen to my gun is to feel at one with the whole scheme of life and death, to feel the humility and the comfort of having a place in something unimaginably greater than myself. And it is to know that one day I, too, will become part of the spirit that binds it all.

HORNED MOONS & SAVAGE SANTAS

SAVAGE SANTA

'Twas the night before Christmas in the old cabin, and the two trappers had just settled in when what to their wandering eyes should appear . . .

By Charles M. Russell

alking about Christmas," said Bedrock, as we smoked in his cabin after supper, an' the wind howled as it sometimes can on a blizzardy December night, "puts me in mind of one I spent in the '60s. Me an' a feller named Jake Mason, but better knowed as Beaver, is trappin' an' prospectin' on the head of the Porcupine. We've struck some placer, but she's too cold to work her. The snow's drove all the game out of the country, an' barrin' a few beans and some flour, we're plum out of grub, so we decide we'd better pull our freight before we're snowed in.

"The winter's been pretty open till then, but the day we start there's a storm breaks loose that skins everything I ever seed. It looks like the snow-maker's been holdin' back, an' turned the whole winter supply loose at once. Cold? Well, it would make a polar bear hunt cover.

"About noon it lets up enough so we can see our pack-hosses. We're joggin' along at a good gait, when old Baldy, our lead pack-hoss, stops an' swings 'round in the trail, bringin' the other three to a stand. His whinny causes me to raise my head, an' lookin' under my hat brim. I'm plenty surprised to see an old log shack not ten feet to the side of the trail.

" 'I guess we'd take that cayuse's advice,' says Beaver, pintin' to Baldy, who's got his ears straightened, lookin' at us as much as to say: 'What, am I packin' fer Pilgrims; or don't you know enough to get in out of the weather? It looks like you'd loosen these packs.' So, takin' Baldy's hunch, we unsaddle.

"This cabin's mighty ancient. It's been two rooms, but the ridge-pole on the rear one's rotted an' let the roof down. The door's wide open an' hangs on a wooden hinge. The animal smell I get on the inside tells me there ain't no humans lived there for many's the winter. The floor's strewn with pine cones an' a few scattered bones, showin' it's been the home of mountain-rats an' squirrels. Taking it all 'n all, it ain't no palace, but in this storm, it looks mighty snug, an' when we get a blaze started in the fireplace an' the beans goin', it's comfortable.

"The door to the back's open, an' by the light of the fire I can see the roof hangin' down V-shaped, leavin' quite a little space agin the wall. Once I had a notion of walkin' in an' prospectin' the place, but there's somethin' ghostly about it an' I change my mind.

"When we're rollin' in that night, Beaver asks me what day of the month it is.

" 'If I'm right on my dates,' says I, 'this is the evenin' the kids hang up their socks.'

" 'The hell it is,' says he. 'Well, here's one camp Santy'll probably overlook. We ain't got no socks nor no place to hang 'em, an' I don't think the old boy'd savvy our foot-rags.' That's the last I remember till I'm waked up along in the night by somethin' monkeyin' with the kettle.

"If it wasn't fer a snufflin' noise I could hear, I'd a-tuk it fer a trade-rat, but with this noise it's no guess with me, an' I call the turn all right, 'cause when I take a peek, there, humped between me an' the fire, is the most robust silvertip I ever see. In size, he resembles a load of hay. The fire's down low, but there's enough light to give me his outline. He's humped over, busy with the beans, sniffin' an' whinin' pleasant, like he enjoys 'em. I nudged Beaver easy, an' whispers: 'Santy Claus is here.'

"He don't need but one look. 'Yes,' says he, reachin' for his Henry, 'but he ain't brought nothin' but trouble, an' more'n a sock full of that. You couldn't crowd it into a wagon-box.'

"This whisperin' disturbs Mr. Bear, an' he straightens up till he near touches the ridge-pole. He looks eight feet tall. Am I scared? Well, I'd tell a man. By the feelin' runnin' up and down my back, if I had bristles I'd resemble a wild hog. The cold sweat's drippin' off my nose, an' I ain't got nothin' on me but sluice-ice.

"The bark of Beaver's Henry brings me out of this scare. The bear goes over, upsettin' a kettle of water, puttin' the fire out. If it wasn't for a stream of fire runnin' from Beaver's weapon, we'd be in plumb darkness. The bear's up agin, bellerin' an' bawlin', and comin' at us mighty warlike, and by the time I get my Sharp's workin', I'm near choked with smoke. It's the noisiest muss I was ever mixed up in. Between the smoke, the barkin' of the guns an' the bellerin' of the bear, it's like hell on a holiday.

"I'm gropin' for another ca'tridge when I hear the lock on Beaver's gun click, an' I know his magazine's dry. Lowerin' my hot gun, I listen. Everythin's quiet now. In the sudden stillness I can hear the drippin' of blood. It's the bear's life runnin' out.

" 'I guess it's all over,' says Beaver, kind of shaky. 'It was a short fight, but a fast one, an' hell was poppin' while she lasted.'

"When we get the fire lit, we take a look at the battle ground. There lays Mr. Bear in a ring of blood, with a hide so full of holes he wouldn't hold hay. I don't think there's a bullet went 'round him.

"This excitement wakens us so we don't sleep no more that night. We breakfast on bear meat. He's an old bear an' it's pretty stout, but a feller livin' on beans and bannocks straight for a couple of weeks don't kick much on flavor, an' we're at a stage where meat's meat.

"When it comes day, me an' Beaver goes lookin' over the bear's bedroom. You know, daylight drives away ha'nts, an' this room don't look near so ghostly as it did last night. After winnin' this fight, we're both mighty brave. The roof caved in with four or five feet of snow on, makes the rear room still dark, so lightin' a pitch-pine glow, we start explorin'.

"The first thing we bump into is the bear's bunk. There's a rusty pick layin' up against the wall, an' a gold-pan on the floor, showin' us that the human that lived there was a miner. On the other side of the shack we ran onto a pole bunk, with a weather-wrinkled buffalo robe an' some rotten blankets. The way the roof slants, we can't see into the bed, but by usin' an axe an' choppin' the legs off, we lower it to view. When Beaver raises the light, there's the frame-work of a man. He's layin' on his left side, like he's sleepin', an' looks like he cashed in easy. Across the bunk, under his head, is an old-fashioned cap-'n-ball rifle. On the bedpost hangs a powder horn an' pouch, with a belt an' skinnin' knife. These things tell us that this man's a pretty old-timer.

"Findin' the pick an' gold-pan causes us to look more careful for what he'd been diggin'. We explore the bunk from top to bottom, but nary a find. All day long we prospects. That evenin', when we're filling up on bear meat, beans and bannocks, Beaver says he's goin' to go through the bear's bunk; so, after we smoke, relightin' our torches, we start our search again.

"Sizin' up the bear's nest, we see he'd laid there quite a while. It looks like Mr. Silvertip, when the weather gets cold, starts huntin' a winter location for his long snooze. Runnin' onto this cabin, vacant, and lookin' like it's for rent, he jumps the claim an' would have been snoozin' there yet, but our fire warmin' up the place fools him. He thinks it's spring an' steps out to look at

the weather. On the way he strikes this breakfast of beans, an' they hold him till we object.

"We're lookin' over this nest when somethin' catches my eye on the edge of the waller. It's a hole, roofed over with willers.

" 'Well, I'll be damned. There's his cache,' says Beaver, whose eyes has follered mine. It don't take a minute to kick these willers loose, an' there lays a buckskin sack with five hundred dollars in dust in it.

" 'Old Santy Claus, out there,' says Beaver, pointin' to the bear through the door, 'didn't load our socks, but he brought plenty of meat an' showed us the cache, for we'd never a-found it if he hadn't raised the lid.'

"The day after Christmas we buried the bones, wrapped in one of our blankets, where we'd found the cache. It was the best we could do.

" 'I guess the dust's ours,' says Beaver. 'There's no papers to show who's his kin-folks.' So we splits the pile an' leaves him sleepin' in the tomb he built for himself."

From Trails Plowed Under *by Charles M. Russell, copyright 1927 by Doubleday, a division of Random House, Inc. Used by permission of Doubleday, a division of Random House, Inc.*

DUD GUIDES
A LADY

*When a crusty old salmon guide suddenly finds himself hired
out by an assertive young miss, things can go from bad to
worse at every bend of the river.*

By Arthur Macdougall

ome day," said Dan Nye, "git Dud Dean to tell you
'bout the time he guided a flapper down the East
Branch. But don't tell him that I put you wise.
Just break it easy-like. It'll be worth a thousand."
So one night, when we were camping at Foley Pond,
I broached the subject. I was comfortably arranged,
and Dud's pipe was going nicely.

"Let's see, Dud," I began, "didn't you guide a lady, or something, down
the East Branch one time?"

It was dark, but I could feel Dud's shrewd eyes turned on me.

"What d'yer mean by that, er sunthin'?"

I had got off on the wrong foot. "Why, why, you did, didn't you?"

A half-moment passed, then I heard Dud's inimitable chuckle.

"Maybe," he said, "I'll tell yer that adventure, if that's what ye're
fishin' fer. But git this straight: she was a lady. By time! I've had trouble
enough, settlin' that."

Then Dud went on with his story. Hereafter, Dud is speaking.

157

Let's see, time's draggin', an' you never did know enough to turn in. Wel-el, I'll begin it this way. That must of been the spring of 1913. Money warn't comin' in faster'n I c'ud use it, so I was pickin' up most any job that come my way. Erlong 'bout the fust of June, I got a crisp, short letter that said a friend had recommended me as a guide who knew the East Branch, some. An' w'ud I hire out to guide a party of one? It was signed, B.N. Turner.

Well, I read it over three-four times, an' showed it to Nancy. The letter was typewritten, by the way. Then I went down to Bingham station, an' got Pearl Woodward to fix me up a telegram sayin' the prop'sition looked all right to me. Next day, back comes an answer, tellin' me to be at Indian Pond, June fifth without fail.

"I hope Mr. Turner will be agreeable," says Nancy, when I was startin' out the day before the fifth, which w'ud be the fourth, like enough. By Jericho! If she'd known what I found out later, she w'ud have been real serious erbout *Mister* Turner bein' agreeable.

Wel-el, nothin' waits fer a man but trouble, as old Doc Brownin' useter say. I got everythin' fixed early the mornin' of the fifth. An' I had a nice, trappy little canoe I was real proud erbout. Of course I was feelin' purty good, becuz a party of one is easy guiding.

The train come in 'bout two o'clock. Fer a min-it, er so, nobody got off, but I see a colored feller, a-pilin' off a lot of duffle; so I sorta eased up in that direction.

Then off gits a woman, 'bout twenty-five, I'd say. Crotch! Come to think of it, she might be almost a grandmother, now. She had on long yeller britches, an' a green huntin' shirt. She was a sight – a sight, I mean! Upon my word, that colored feller blushed when he see me lookin' at the both of 'em. She gave him a bill. An' the conductor waved his hands. Thar we was, the flapper an' me, a-standin' all alone on Injun Pond platform. It warn't none of my business, as I see it, jist then, so I started to go over to the dam, where thar was some fellers workin' that I knew.

But she held up her hand. "Are you the guide, Dud Dean?" she asks me.

"Sometimes," I says.

"I am B.N. Turner."

Crotch, yer c'ud have used me fer lon-chinkin'.

"But I was expectin' a man," I says, becuz it seemed like some explanation was necessary. Then I went on to say, "Instead of a –"

She cut me off short, like a kid that was speakin' out of turn at a Christmas exercise.

"I can't see that the fact I am a woman makes any difference. My money is jist as good. An' you have been hired to guide me down the East Branch. This is the East branch, ain't it it?" she says, wavin' her hand at the river.

"It is," I says, "but it w'ud take us more'n the rest of this day to make The Forks."

She kinda screwed up her face at that, like I had wandered from the subject, an'

158

she c'udn't foller me. So I started in to clear up the situation, as Jim Perkins useter say, tellin' erbout some fight he'd jist got licked in.

"It 'ud mean campin' out two nights," I says.

"Oh," she says, sorta smilin'. I rec'lect that she was real purty, when she smiled, but that warn't often. Most of the time her face was like a starched shirt. "I brought my own tent," she says.

I had been lookin' at her baggage. It looked like a small circus outfit I once seen down to Bingham. So by way of bein' pleasant, I says to her, "Where's the wild animals?"

Wel-el, yer sh'ud have seen her scowl at me. "I find this banter silly," she snaps at me. "The question is: are you goin' to guide me down the East Branch, as you agreed, by wire, to do?"

"I am not," I says, an' I meant it. Why, gosh all-hemlock. It was the dumdest prop'sition fer them careful-goin' days. Ye've got to remember, Mak, that this was in 1913. Thar's a cool wind been blowin' sech foolishness out of the air since then, an' I must say the air smells cleaner to me.

"Why not?" she shot back at me, 'ith her eyes lookin' right through me. "Is it ag'inst the law to guide a decent woman down the Kennebec?"

"Not if her husband –" I begins.

"Bosh!" she says. "Jist becuz you live in the woods, don't think that thar's stumps on Broadway. Rot! An' tommy-rot!"

"Madam," I says, "speakin' of Broadway, didjer ever hear of the Straight an' Narrow Way?"

Wel-el, thar ain't no sense in draggin' that one. Between you an' me, I was young an' reckless in them days. So I stored most of her junk in the drivers' shack, an' we got inter my canoe. Fust off, she was bound to string up a nice little rod.

You know the East Branch. Thar's some mean water in it. Fer one place, thar's the Hullin' Machine, an' a dozen more slipp'ry places. I had to carry 'round some. Then we'd ease down inter some of them nice pools. About two 'clock that mornin' they had shut down the gates at Injun Pond, an' the pulpwood drive was away ahead of us. Conditions was ideal fer fishin'. Thar was a chance fer squaretails, salmon, an' what not, as Doc Brownin' useter say when he was called out in the middle of the night.

When it come to fishin' that woman had everthin' I ever see hooked by the ear. More'n once she dum near hooked one of mine. But in them days good fly-men warn't so common, an' I was purty good at dodgin'. A dozen times I had to yell at her, like the referee of a dog fight, to keep my canoe right side up. She was worse'n a monkey fer ballast.

An' mind yer, I never saw a better day fer fishin' on the East Branch. Thar was plenty of fish – plenty. Yer see a head of water slushes 'em out of Injun Pond.

Lots of 'em are Mooseheaders. It was strange that she c'udn't hook one. They'd roll up slow an' dignified. Then she'd fetch a squeal, an' a heave, yankin' the fly right out of their reach. I c'ud hear their teeth click.

Wel-el, along 'bout then she begun to drop some of her know-it-all an' own-it-all ways.

"Oh, darn," she says, "what shall I do?"

"Yer might stop yankin' your fly out of their reach," I says.

But that jist froze her up, an' she turned her back on me. I never see sech a person. It took me all the afternoon to figger out jist what ailed her.

Bineby, while we was loafin' through a purty stretch of water, a nice little salmon that 'ud go three pounds, maybe, lashed out at her fly. She done her best to yank it away from him, but warn't quick e-nough. He nailed that Jock Scott good an' tight. It s'prised her so, she dum near dropped her rod in the river. That's all that saved the rod at the start, I reckon.

Soon's she see her line a-swishin' through the water, she begin to pull back, but that didn't do no harm, becuz she never touched her line er reel. Gor-ry, but that salmon warn't long in headin' fer the next pool below us.

Anyone that knows me, knows that I ain't ever been able to take my fly fishin' like a drink of cold tea, an' I useter git real excited in them days.

"Git a hold on that line," I yells at her, an' at the same time I headed my canoe fer the rips.

That fish had some start on us, an' he was in the next pool when we got thar. Then the fun begun, but all that flapper c'ud do was to squeal an' pull back on her rod. Thar was somewhere near ten turns of line 'round the bow, an' hanged if thar was any tellin' where the rest of it was, although that girl looked like a bobbin half unwound.

It was jist at that stage of the confusion in general that the fish begin to stand right up on his hind legs. "Oo-oo-ooo," she squeals.

"Tarnation!" I busts out. "Give me that rod! D'yer hear?"

It has always been my intention to be a gentleman, wherever, an' whenever, but I guess I fergot that I had a lady aboard. I purty nigh upset the canoe, myself, a-reachin' fer that rod. Fust thing I knew, I had it in my hands. I'd a looked less foolish if I had known e-nough to let her finish what she'd begun. With all them turns, bowlines, hangman's knots, sheep-shanks, an' what not, I had erbout as much chance of landin' that salmon as a deacon at a Democratic rally.

He fetched one er two jumps, an' was gone. It took me half an hour to untangle that line. While I was workin' away on the line, I heard a funny noise an' looked up quick. By gum if that flapper warn't bawlin'. I felt meaner'n a rabbit 'ith fleas, but I c'udn't think of nothin' to say.

Someone oughter write a book fer all young guides to study. Thar ain't nothin' from fust aid to funeral services that they don't need to be ready fer. Wel-el, bineby she slowed down some, an' seemed to change. I think she must have seen the pity in my eyes, becuz she got madder'n a set-on bumble bee, an' says with a voice that was shaky, but mean, "Ye're discharged!"

I was so dumfounded, I jist set an' stared at her. It was the fust time anybudy had

160

ever tried to fire me.

"What?" I says.

"Don't you understand American?" she says, slow an' careful. "You are fired!"

I set out to laugh, but finally I says, gentle as I c'ud, "Now see here. I don't blame yer, Mrs. Turner. Naturally yer don't feel very good, but it's a long walk back to Injun Pond, an' I happen to be headed down river. Call it fired if yer want to, but I suggest that yer rid erlong 'ith me."

That woman had brains, of course. Fer a min-it, she sot an' looked at me, like I was the missin' link, an' turned what I had said over in her mind.

"Very well," says she, short, an' her voice under control ag'in.

I finished reelin' up her line; threw her rod in the bottom of the canoe; an' dug the paddle deep. As I remember, I had some fool idea of reachin' The Forks b'fore sunset, which w'ud have busted a mallard's record, an' then some.

K eep in the middle," I told her. "Don't throw your weight all on the one side. An' git your underpinnin' under yer."

Maybe that made her mad, I don't know. Anyway, jist as we hit the white water, an' I was diggin' to miss a nasty rock, she put her heft where it 'ud do the most good, from her point of view. All I c'ud remember, afterwards, was that I see the river comin' up inter my face, an' then it got dark, an' so still that I stopped hearin' anythin'.

The next I knew, I was layin' on some almighty hard-feelin' rocks. Fust off, I figgered that it was the bottom of the river, somewheres between where I'd gone down an' the Atlantic Ocean. But I put out my hands an' the rocks felt sorta dry. Then I begin to hear someone cryin'. "Can't be my funeral," thinks I, "becuz I can't smell no flowers."

Next I heard a voice, way off an' distant, sayin', "Are you dead, Mister Dean?"

I made out to answer, "No, marm, I don't think so, becuz I feel kinda chilly."

Yer see, I was gittin' some sense back. Fust thing I saw, when I opened my eyes, was a tree. It warn't much of a tree, but it had some sky behind it. So I set up. My head was sorer than a bobtailed pup. I s'pose likely I'd bumped it on the bottom of the river. Then I see her settin' thar – wet an' most of the starch gone out of her, by the looks.

"Where's the canoe?" I says.

"I hung onter that," she says. "It's d-d-down below here a little bit."

"Well," I says, "how'd I git here? Did I bounce here?"

"No-o-o."

I kinda felt all over myself an' got up on my feet. Thar didn't seem to be nothin' gone, an' I was all in one piece. Well, two an' two is four, most gen'rally. She'd pull me out, somehow. I took a squint at the sun, an' decided it was 'bout five. That gave us three hours, er so, of light. But we was in a pickle, jist the same. The grub I had brought along was in the bottom of the river.

We kept goin' till darkness had set in, an' then went ashore to fix up some sort of a camp. Nights git chilly 'long in June up in this country, 'specially if ye're damp. I had a knife, an' managed ter strip off some bark fer a lean-to roof. Then it came to me that my matches was all wet. Jumpin' hornpouts, talk erbout a gone feelin'.

I'm hanged, though, if that flapper, er flipper, didn't produce a dinky little watertight matchbox. I've never been 'ithout one since. In fact, the one I've carried fer years – no, never mind that. I got a nice fire goin', but we had nothin' to eat. Which was tough. I made two birch-bark cups, an' a bigger dish ter heat water in. Yer can do it, easy enough, if yer don't let the fire git up above the water line. It tasted hot an' comfortin'.

Then we sot down fer a long night. After a while she begun to talk.

"I s'pose that you consider me all kinds of a fool," she says

"No," I says, "I don't, but I wish yer w'ud tell me jist what your idea was in takin' this trip."

Wel-el, she jist wanted to git out an' see places like she had read erbout. That was all thar was to it. She was one of them females that had done too much thinkin' erbout the terrible injustices of a man-made world. One of them sort that think men w'ud still insist that their women wear veils, an' stay indoors, if they had their way. Never stoppin' to think that the days when women did wear veils an' stay indoors was the days when veils an' doors was purty essential. B.N. Turner, anyhow, had an ingrown idea that a woman was jist as good as any man, an' had set out to prove it. Which a min-it's reflection shows up to be a plumb foolish notion. I ain't never seen much real diff'rence 'tween a female an' a male. A mean woman's as mean as a mean man, an' a good woman is as good as a good man, if not better.

She told me that she didn't intend to give up her independence, jist becuz she was married to a man. That was the only real funny thing I see er heard durin' that trip. I've never noticed any of Nancy's independence oozin' away. We've shared an' shared alike. What we've got, we've got together. What we had to take on the jaw, as yer might say, we took together. If I wanted to go fishin', I went fishin' in spite of criticism. If Nancy wanted to go to a W.C.T.U. meetin', she went. An' I told B.N. Turner so. That seemed to interest her. She 'lowed that Nancy must be a woman with the modern point of view.

"Well," I says, "Nancy has always run her own affairs, 'ithout borrowin' my britches. An' that, young woman, is a text fer meditation."

Oh, I preached her a durn good sermon, if I do say so.

"If yer want to be a whale of a success, ye've got to work 'ith sech material as comes to hand," I says. "Wearin' yeller britches may be comfortable, an' sensible, but it don't fool nobudy – t'wouldn't if yer c'ud make your husband wear dresses. Most men ain't worth imitatin'. When women recognize that, they may git somewhere. Independence ain't a matter of yeller britches an' hard-boiled airs. Jist take dumpin' me in the Branch, which I don't blame yer fer doin'. To do that, yer had to dump yourself, an' your comforts. Strikes me," I says – Oh, well, I've fergotten jist what I did say after that. Never mind.

e set thar, an' shivered, an' dried out, fust in front, an' then in back. The fire got real warm, an' bineby I sorta dropped off to sleep. I dreamed that I saw Nancy comin' up the river in a canoe, an' she was lookin' fer me. After that I lay thar, kinda half awake an' half asleep.

Bineby B.N. Turner give me a shake.

"Wake up!" she whispers "Thar's a puppy, er some dog, tryin' to come in through the back of this lean-to."

I set up straight. Ye've heard a wood pig, out in the night, kinda cryin' an' pleadin', like he'd lost his soul mate. "Scat out of here!" I says, throwin' a stick.

An' the last thread of that mask she wore fell off her face. She had only sold herself on the idea that she was hard-boiled. She was jist a scared kid. Seems she'd been listenin' to that porcupine fer a long time. Thought it was a wolf, er sunthin'. Take almost any person an' put 'em out in the deep woods at night, an' the veneer of civilization's assurances falls off. The night has a voice of its own, an' it has done me a heap of good to listen.

Jist to git her mind back to normal, I told her what I knew 'bout porcupines, which, if I do say so, is a lot more'n the average woodsman, becuz I'm one of the few that has taken the trouble to notice them. Most folks call 'em stupid critters, an' let it go at that. They do a lot of aggravatin' damage, like chewin' camp floors an' doors. They damage an' kill some growin' trees. Our state paid a bounty on porcupines fer several years. I ain't sayin' the money was wasted. They do git purty numerous, by spells. But I do say that I c'ud have spent that money wiser . . . on house cats that have gone wild, an' half wild in the woods, fer instance. But never mind that. What I told B.N. Turner was erbout the amusin' tricks I'd seen porcupines do. Nobudy, nor no thing is as foolish as we're apt to assume.

Anyhow, I didn't sleep no more, an' I c'ud see that she appreciated it. So we got started down the river with the first light of mornin'. It's a nice ride down the East Branch. By crotch, it's beautiful! B.N. had washed in the river, afore we started, an' blamed if she didn't look kinda human-sweet, in the mornin' light. I drove the canoe fer all I c'ud. When we got down to The Forks, she asked me to find someone to take her right over to Moxie Station. Said that she c'udn't wait to git back home. Um . . . don't it beat all how I run on, when I git at a yarn?

I got Dan Nye to take her over to Moxie Station. When she left, out goes her hand.

"Good-by, Mr. Dean," she says, "ith sunshine in her face. "You'll never forget this trip, will you? Neither shall I. Thank you."

I put my canoe in the Kennebec, an' went along down the river to Bingham. An' I'll bet ye're wonderin' how I squared all this 'ith Nancy. I'll tell yer 'bout that. Somehow, I c'udn't make up my mind to tell her, though I've always practiced bein' open an' above. Yer see, folks was awful set, in them days, on what is called conventionalities. It was jist erbout as bad to ignore them as to bust the Ten Commandments wide open. So I made up my mind to keep the whole business to myself. An' I'd already sworn Dan Nye to keep his mouth shut.

When I got home, Nancy says, "Well, how'd yer like Mr. Turner?"

"Wel-el," I says, "he was kinda s'prisin' in some ways."

Right then I see Nancy was eyin' my clothes, which was wrinkled. Anybudy c'ud see that I'd been in the water all over. An' Nancy knew it hadn't rained none.

"I sh'ud say that he was surprising," she says. "Can't you go fishin' without fallin' in?"

"I c'ud, but –"

"I know all erbout it, Dudley Dean," she snaps out. "You poor spineless thing."

Crotch, I thought I was in a box, if she knew *all* erbout it.

"Well, Ma," I begins, but she w'udn't let me finish.

"How much did *he* pay you?"

"Who?" I says, kinda blank like.

"Who w'ud I mean, but this man, B.N. Turner?"

"Oh," I says, "twenty dollars."

Wel-el, that kinda salved Nancy.

"That," she admits, "is good pay for two days, if only you had backbone e-nough to leave liquor alone."

That smarted me some, becuz I ain't never messed 'round with booze, but if she wanted to think that I'd fallen into the river in that way, I decided it was all right.

Maybe, ye're wonderin' if Nancy ever did find out the difference. Wel-el . . . you know Nancy.

"Dud Guides A Lady" originally appeared in Arthur Macdougall's Dud Dean and His Country, *published by Coward-McCann, Inc. in 1946. It was later published by Countrysport Press in Macdougall's* Remembering Dud Dean.

KILLING A LION
WITH A KNIFE

*Beginning around the turn of the 20th century, Harry Wolhuter
served forty-four years as a ranger in South Africa's Kruger
National Park. His accomplishments were legion; his life a
legend. What follows is first a selection from the Foreword to
Wolhuter's memoirs, written by J. Stevenson-Hamilton, another
late warden at Kruger National Park, followed by Wolhuter's
amazing escape from a pair of hungry lions.*

By Harry Wolhuter

hen, in July 1902, I made my
debut in the Low-Veld as warden
of the newly reproclaimed Sabi
Game Reserve, I naturally looked
round anxiously for someone of local
experience who might serve me as
guide, philosopher and friend.

Every "old hand" whom I approached
said the same thing, "Try and get hold of Harry Wolhuter; he knows the
country better than anyone else.

When at last I was successful in making contact with him, I found that
Wolhuter's appearance and manner justified his reputation. Tall, spare but
powerfully built; purposeful, for all his quiet voice and unassuming manner,
he seemed emblematical of the best type of pioneer hunter.

All the years of close companionship and friendship that have since passed,
I have never ceased to regard the day of that first meeting as a red letter one
in my life. I suppose there can be few if any men in Africa possessing a

deeper knowledge and wider experience of bush lore in all its phases and in his prime, Harry Wolhuter held all the qualities requisite to give effect to that knowledge and experience; a powerful frame, an iron constitution; cool courage and quiet determination.

His unique exploit in killing, single-handed, and armed only with a knife, a full-grown male lion which had seized him, and was carrying him off, was in itself a feat rendering superfluous any further tributes to his rare courage and coolness; but it is worth remarking that in the many hazards – happily all safely surmounted – which he has since incurred in the course of his duties, his nerve has shown itself to be just as calm and steady as it was when he underwent that terrible experience.

Unfortunately, he never fully got over the injuries he then received. Nevertheless, right up to the date of his retirement in 1946, he was still taking chances with lions, and only a year or two before, he had even dispatched a badly injured one with a knife, "to save a cartridge!" – J. Stevenson-Hamilton.

I n August, 1903, I was returning from one of my usual patrols on the Olifants. On the second day after leaving camp my objective was a certain water-hole en route, at which I intended spending the night, but when we reached it, we found that the pool was dry. It was now about 4 p.m., and the only thing to be done was to push on to the next waterhole which was about twelve miles distant. Accompanying me were three police boys driving the donkeys which carried all my possessions, and three dogs; the latter all rough "Boer" dogs, very good on lions. I instructed the boys that I would ride ahead along the path to the next waterhole and they were to follow. I then started to go ahead along the trail, and of the dogs, "Bull" escorted me; the bitch "Fly" and a mongrel-terrier remaining with the boys.

Although it became dusk very soon I continued to ride along the path – as I had often travelled that route by night during the Boer War to avoid the heat of the summer sun. I gave no thought to lions, as I had never before encountered these animals in those parts. Most of the herbage had been recently burnt off, but here and there a patch of long grass remained. While riding through one of these isolated patches, I heard two animals jump up in the grass in front of me.

It was by now too dark to see, but I imagined that the animals in question were a pair of reedbuck, as this had always been a favorite locality for these antelope. I expected them to run across the path and disappear; but instead, and to my surprise, I heard a running rustle in the grass approaching me.

I was still riding quietly along when two forms loomed up within three or four yards, and these I now recognized as two lions, and their behavior was such that I had little doubt but that their intentions were to attack my horse. Although, of course, I had my rifle (without which I never moved in the veld), there was no time to shoot, and as I hastily pulled my horse around, I dug the spurs into his flanks in a frantic effort to urge him to his best speed to get away in time; but the approaching lion was already too close, and before the horse could get into its stride I felt a terrific impact behind me as the lion alighted on the horse's hindquarters.

hat happened next, of course, occupied only a few seconds, but I vividly recall the unpleasant sensation of expecting the crunch of the lion's jaws in my person. However, the terrified horse was bucking and plunging so violently that the lion was unable to maintain its hold, but it managed to knock me out of the saddle. Fortune is apt to act freakishly at all times, and it may seem a strange thing to suggest that it was fortunate for myself that I happened to fall almost on top of the second lion as he was running round in front of my horse, to get hold of it by the head. Had I fallen otherwise, however, it is probable that the lion would have grasped *me* by the head, and then this would assuredly never have been written! Actually, the eager brute gripped my right shoulder between its jaws and started to drag me away, and as it did so, I could hear the clatter of my horse's hooves over the stony ground as it raced away with the first lion in hot pursuit; itself in turn being chased by my dog, "Bull."

Meanwhile, the lion continued dragging me towards the neighboring Metsimetsi Spruit. I was dragged along on my back, being held by the right shoulder, and as the lion was walking over me his claws would sometimes rip wounds in my arms. I was wearing a pair of spurs with strong leather straps, and these acted as brakes, scoring deep furrows in the ground over which we travelled. When the "brakes" acted too efficiently, the lion would give an impatient jerk of his great head, which added excruciating pain to my shoulder, already deeply lacerated by the powerful teeth.

I certainly was in a position to disagree emphatically with Dr. Livingstone's theory, based on his own personal experience, that the resulting shock from the bite of a large carnivorous animal so numbs the nerves that it deadens all pain; for, in my own case, I was conscious of great physical agony; and in addition to this was the mental agony as to what the lion would presently do with me; whether he would kill me first or proceed to dine off me while I was still alive!

Of course, in those first few moments I was convinced that it was all over with me and that I had reached the end of my earthly career.

But then, as our painful progress still continued, it suddenly struck me that I might still have my sheath knife! I always carried this attached to my belt on the right side. Unfortunately, the knife did not fit too tightly in its sheath, and on two previous occasions when I had had a spill from my horse while galloping after game during the Boer War, it had fallen out. It seemed almost too much to expect that it could still be safely there after the recent rough episodes.

167

It took me some time to work my left hand round my back as the lion was dragging me over the ground, but eventually I reached the sheath, and, to my indescribable joy, the knife was still there! I secured it, and wondered where best first to stab the lion. It flashed through my mind that, many years ago, I had read in a magazine or newspaper that if you hit a cat on the nose he must sneeze before doing anything. This particular theory is, of course, incorrect; but at the time I seriously entertained the idea of attempting it, though on second thought I dismissed the notion, deciding that in any case he would just sneeze and pick me up again – this time perhaps in a more vital spot!

I decided finally to stick my knife into his heart, and so I began to feel very cautiously for his shoulder. The task was a difficult and complicated one because, gripped as I was, high up on the right shoulder, my head was pressed right up against the lion's mane, which exuded a strong lion smell (incidentally, he was purring very loudly, something after the fashion of a cat – only on a far louder scale – perhaps in pleasant anticipation of the meal he intended to have) and this necessitated my reaching with my left hand holding the knife across his chest so as to gain access to his left shoulder. Any bungling, in this manoeuvre, would arouse the lion, with instantly fatal results to myself!

However, I managed it successfully, and knowing where his heart was located, I struck him twice, in quick succession, with two back-handed strokes behind the left shoulder. The lion let out a furious roar, and I desperately struck him again; this time upwards into his throat. I think this third thrust severed the jugular vein, as the blood spurted out in a stream all over me. The lion released his hold and slunk off into the darkness. Later I measured the distance, and found that he had dragged me sixty yards. Incidentally, it transpired later that both first thrusts had reached the heart.

The scene, could anyone have witnessed it, must have been eerie in the extreme as, in the darkness, I staggered to my feet, not realizing how seriously I had wounded the lion whose long-drawn moans resounded nearby. I thought first to frighten him off with the human voice and shouted after him all the names I could think of, couched in the most lurid language. Suddenly I remembered the other lion that had chased my horse. It was more likely that it would fail to catch the horse, once the latter was at a full gallop, and then, what was more probable, it would return to its mate, and find me there, quite unarmed except for my knife – as of course my rifle had been flung into the long grass when I fell off my horse.

At first I thought of setting the grass alight to keep away the second lion; and, getting the match-box from my pocket, I gripped it in my teeth, as of course my right arm was quite useless, not only on account of the wound from the lion's teeth in my shoulder, but also because its claws had torn out some of the tendons about my wrist. I struck a match and put it to the grass, but as there was by now a heavy dew, the grass would not burn – fortunately, of course, as it turned out, else my rifle would have been burnt.

My next idea was to climb into a tree and thus to place myself beyond the lion's reach. There were several trees in the vicinity, but they all had long stems, and with my one arm I was unable to climb them. Presently, however, I located one with a fork near the ground, and after a great deal of trouble I managed to climb into it, reaching a bough some twelve feet from the ground, in which I sat.

I was now commencing to feel very shaky indeed, both as a result of the shock I had sustained, and loss of blood; and what clothes I had left covering me were saturated with blood, both my own and that of the lion, and the effect of the cold night air on the damp clothing considerably added to my discomfort, while my shoulder was still bleeding badly, I realized that I might faint from loss of blood, and fall off the bough on which I was sitting, so I removed my belt and somehow strapped myself to the tree. My thirst was terrible; and I would have offered much for a cup of water. One consoling reflection was that I knew my boys would find me as I was not far from the path.

Meanwhile, I could still occasionally hear the lion I had stabbed grunting and groaning in the darkness, somewhere close by; and presently, resounding eerily over the night air, I heard the long-drawn guttural death-rattle in his throat – and felt a trifle better then as I knew that I had killed him. My satisfaction was short-lived, however, as very soon afterwards approaching rustles in the grass heralded the arrival of the second lion which, as I had surmised, had failed to catch my horse. I heard it approach the spot where I had got to my feet and from there, following my blood-spoor all the time, it advanced to the tree in which I sat. Arriving at the base of the tree, it reared up against the trunk and seemed to be about to try to climb it. I was overcome with horror at this turn of affairs, as it appeared as if I had got away from one lion, only to be caught by the other. The tree which harbored me was quite easy to climb (had it not been so, I could never have worked my way up to my perch), and most certainly for a determined, hungry lion! In despair I shouted down at the straining brute, whose upward-turned eyes I could momentarily glimpse reflected in the starlight, and this seemed to cause him to hesitate.

Fortunately, just then my faithful dog "Bull" appeared on the scene. Never was I more grateful at the arrival of man or beast! He had evidently discovered that I was no longer on the horse, and was missing, and had come back to find me. I called to him, and encouraged him to go for the lion, which he did in right good heart, barking furiously at it and so distracting its attention that it made a short rush at the plucky dog, who managed to keep his distance.

And so this dreadful night passed on. The lion would leave the tree and I could hear him rustling about in the grass, and then he would return, and the faithful "Bull" would rush at him barking, and chase him off, and so on. Finally he seemed to lie up somewhere in the neighboring bush.

Some considerable time later, perhaps an hour, I heard a most welcome sound: the clatter of tin dishes rattling in a hamper on the head of one of my boys who was at last approaching along the path. In the stillness of the night, one can hear the least sound quite a long way off in the veld. I shouted to him to beware as there was a lion somewhere near.

He asked me what he ought to do and I told him to climb into a tree. I heard a rattling crash, and he dropped the hamper, and then silence for a while. I then asked him if he was up a tree, and whether it was a big one: to which he replied that it was not a tall tree, but that he had no wish to come down and search for a better one as he could already hear the lion rustling in the grass near him! He informed me that the other boys were not so far behind, and I then told him all that had happened – a recital of events, which, to judge by the tone of his comments, did little to reassure him of the pleasantness of his present situation!

After a time, which seemed ages, we heard the little pack of donkeys approaching along the path, and I shouted instructions to the boys to halt where they were, as there was a lion in the grass quite near, and to fire off a few shots to scare him. This they did, then as they approached to the tree in which I sat, I told them first of all to make a good fire, which did not take long to flare up, as some form of protection in case the lion returned; and then they assisted me down from the tree. It was a painful and laborious business, as I was very stiff and sore from my wounds, and I found the descent very much harder than the ascent.

The first question I asked my boys was whether they had any water in the calabash which they always carried with them. They replied that it was empty, and so the only thing for us to do was to set out for the next waterhole, which was about six miles farther ahead. Before leaving, they searched unsuccessfully for my rifle in the long grass. To arm myself I took one of the boys' assegais, and then, with the donkeys, we set forth. Before leaving the place we took some firebrands from the fire and threw them into the veld in the direction where the lion had disappeared; nonetheless, he followed us for a long way, and we could hear him now this side of the path, now that; but we had three dogs with us now, and they barked at him, successfully keeping him off.

At last we came to one of my old pickets of the Steinacker days where the huts were still standing. Here, formerly, there had always been a large pool of water, so I sent two of the boys with the canvas nosebag which was the only utensil we took for carrying water. My disappointment can be measured when they returned to report that the pool was dry, for you must remember that not a drop had passed my lips since the previous day.

170

I said that I must have water, or I would die, and told them to take a candle from among my baggage, place it in a broken bottle and with this rough lantern to go and search for water. They were two good natives, and off they set once more. They seemed to be away for hours, but when they did finally return, they had the nosebag half full of muddy fluid; and this they set on the ground in front of me. It was pretty filthy-looking stuff; still it was water; and I knelt down beside it and drank until I could drink no more – leaving just a little with which they could wash my wounds. They proved to be too awkward and clumsy over the latter job, however, and after a few minutes I could bear it no longer, and ordered the boys to desist. Actually the wounds received no dressing of any kind (I could not see the largest wound, which was on my back) until I reached Komatipoort – four days later!

I then told the boys to unroll the blankets so that I could lie down. My arm was so painful that I instructed them to strap it to one of the poles in the roof of the hut, thinking thereby to ease the pain, but it did no good, and afterwards I had it undone again. I need hardly add that there was no sleep for me that night, and next morning I was in a raging fever; and though I had walked six miles on the previous evening, I was now unable to walk – or even stand.

We remained over in the camp that day and I sent the boys back to skin the dead lion. I instructed them to return to the tree in which they had found me, follow my blood-spoor for a short distance when they came to the place where I had stabbed the lion, and then to follow its blood-spoor for a short distance when they would find its carcass. I could observe that they were a bit dubious about the reality of my having actually killed the lion (though they had politely refrained from hinting their skepticism) as it was an unheard of thing for a man to kill a lion with a knife.

All my orders were obeyed, and in due course they returned with the skin, skull, and some of the meat, and the heart to show me where I had pierced it with the knife. They also brought with them my horse which had later returned to the scene of the accident. It is strange that the horse should have returned, after the terrible fright it had sustained, but I put this down to the companionship between horse and man in the veld. The bridle was broken, but the saddle was intact; in fact, I am using the same saddle today, forty years later! The boys brought the horse to the door of my hut where I crawled to see him. He was badly clawed on the hindquarters, and we rubbed a little salt into the wound (I should have done the same to mine at the time) and this certainly seemed to stop septic poisoning setting in as a result of the lion's claws. The horse recovered completely, but, though it was a valuable animal – being salted – and a good shooting horse, he was of no further use to me afterwards as he remained so nervous that the sight of a mere buck in the veld was sufficient to make him attempt to bolt. I was obliged therefore, to part with him – much to my regret.

171

My boys told me that the best treatment for the wounds caused by the lion was to bathe them in the soup formed as a result of boiling its skull, but I remarked that though this treatment might prove effective with natives, it would not be suitable for a white man.

I knew that there were some native kraals not more than four miles away, so sent one boy off to commandeer assistance in order that I could be carried by *machila*, in relays of four bearers, to Komatipoort. Having collected the necessary number of natives, I instructed them how to make the *machila* with blankets, and early in the morning we set out on a five days march to Komati.

My wounds now became septic, I had fever, and was in great pain. I could, of course, eat nothing and took only water which I consumed in great quantities: two of the natives being occupied solely in carrying it in calabashes, which they replenished whenever we passed any. By the time we finally reached Komatipoort my arm and shoulder were swollen to enormous size, and were smelling so badly that I had to lie with my face turned the other way. On my arrival at Komati, Dr. Greeves attended me, but he had no morphia to deaden the pain which by now was excruciating. Next day my friend W. Dickson accompanied me by train to Barberton Hospital, where I received every care and attention.

I remained on my back for many weeks, and at one period the doctor despaired of my life. Once again, however, a sound constitution saw me through, and although I have never since had the full use of my right arm, I consider myself exceedingly fortunate in not having lost it altogether. As it is, I can still, with difficulty, lift it high enough to pull the trigger! After some months I was able to return to M'timba to continue my duties. I once again began to hunt lions; and as I had an old score to wipe out, I think I did so with interest! The chief souvenirs of my grim adventure, the skin of the lion, skull, and the knife concerned (the latter has never been used since) are preserved in my house, and they have all been photographed many times.

The faithful and plucky dog "Bull," who played a great part in preventing the other lion from climbing the tree and pulling me down, was eventually killed in combat with a baboon, though the baboon also died as a result of the fight. The old bitch "Fly," after presenting me with several good litters of puppies, was finally killed by a leopard. Each of them, in common with many other unrecorded dogs and horses – faithful and staunch companions of the men in the veld – played their part in the achievement of the present-day world famous Kruger National Park, and all of them deserve their small tribute.

Wolhuter's saga is reprinted here courtesy of Jim Rikhoff, the founder of The Amwell Press, which published the story in its 1990 book, Cats! Tales of Hunting Cheetah, Lion, Leopard, Cougar, Tiger & Jaguar.

KING OF THE MOUNTAIN

Smiling wide enough to break, he could hear his Dad's story in some perfect hunt camp of the future, how he would make some parts of it funny enough to die for, but always in the end, how he had made that perfect, impossible shot. But then, with the tearing whistle of the bullet, the story suddenly had a different ending.

By Pete Fromm

A ll through the long drive, Sean, my roommate for my first two months of college, kept sipping beer, telling me about deer hunting in Pennsylvania. He was so wound up about going hunting out here he couldn't quit babbling about tree stands and buckshot and fourteen-point bucks.

I began laughing, wondering if Pennsylvania was on the same planet as Montana, and when he reached for another beer, I did too.

Once we left the pavement he drove like crazy, and when I shouted, "That's the tent!" he had to stand on the brakes. Dust billowed over us as Dad slipped out the tent door, smiling and shaking his head. His hands were empty and I smiled back, feeling bad that we'd been the ones to start the drinking.

When we climbed out of the truck I introduced Dad and Sean. Dad said, "Ready to get after some of these big bucks?"

173

"Damn right!" Sean answered, as sure of himself as I'd guessed. He was the only guy I'd ever brought hunting.

We moved inside and stood around the stove, already glowing red. "We'd have helped set all this up, Dad," I said.

"I was starting to wonder if you'd even show." Dad pointed at Sean's beer. "Am I too late for happy hour?"

I looked away, but Sean said, "It's always happy hour," and Dad fished around in a grocery bag and lifted out one of his half-gallon bottles of bourbon.

Sean said, "Whatchya got there?"

Dad raised his eyebrows. "Can I mix you a little toddy?" That's what he calls whiskey mixed with anything.

Sean said, "Sure," and Dad glanced at me. I shook my head. "I might have a beer," and I walked out to Sean's truck for the cooler. It was chilly outside, a little breeze rattling through the dead cottonwood leaves.

Dad fixed dinner, telling stories while he and Sean pounded down toddies. They were having the time of their lives. I tried keeping up, but had to quit when my ears began to buzz. I don't like it to get even that far. Some of Dad's stories were awful funny though, and this was the only way they got out nowadays. When he told the one about the dog he'd trained to run alligators, and Sean just kept nodding like anything was possible, it was too much for me.

I rolled out my bag and they laughed and called me names, but I just pulled the bag over my head. A little while later I heard Sean puking out alongside the tent, followed by my dad's thunderous horselaugh, so different than the shy smile when he first met us. He bellowed, "Thought you were man enough to piss in the long grass, eh?" Sean groaned and I listened to Dad pick him up and get him to bed, laughing and joking the whole time. Like he was the greatest guy in the world.

In the morning, as I was tying my boots, Dad peeked from his cot and said, "Your friend looks pretty green around the gills."

I smiled, though it wasn't funny. "He sure does," I said.

Dad watched me a second, then sat up. "Think we should give the draws a try?"

"Whatever."

"Better wake up Sleeping Beauty then."

Sean only mumbled. Didn't even open his eyes. I'd planned on him and me hunting on our own if Dad got bad.

Dad and I went straight out from camp, each taking a side of a draw and keeping our eyes open for anything we might push out. Once I saw a doe and two fawns slip away in front of him, but I could see the wrinkle of ground that blocked them from his sight. I stayed quiet, watching them get away.

When we hit the bottom we met up and side-hilled, wondering if a whitetail might break out of the heavy stuff. But nothing did and when the next draw unfolded we started up it. This time Dad took the south face, slow-walking between the ponderosas. I had tougher going through the firs and scrub, but Dad was careful to match my speed.

We should've had a third guy at the top, closing off the escape route. Even if we didn't flush anything, I wished Sean was up there, watching my dad gliding up the steep parts, quiet and alert and careful, caring only about the hunting.

I was wondering what Sean's dad was like when Dad shot. I looked just in time to see a string of does boiling over the rim on his side of the draw. He was hot-footing forward and out in front of him I saw a doe on her side, not moving. "She's down!" I yelled, starting for the bottom before climbing back to Dad.

By the time I got there Dad had the guts out, all shiny against the dust-dry, flinty dirt. He's the quickest, cleanest gutter I've ever seen. He smiled and asked if I'd seen them.

"It was too thick. Did I kick them out?"

"Pretty as a picture."

We'd been out less than two hours and our breath still made clouds. He cut out the heart, careful to leave the sack around it so it wasn't all bloody. He doesn't like anything the way he likes the heart. Then he cracked the pelvis with his knife and flopped a leg at my head, so I had to catch it or get smacked, an old trick of his. He grinned. "Ready?"

"I guess," I said, and we started the short, hard drag to the crest. We took a blow there, sweating hard, deciding we'd leave the deer and walk back for the truck.

Sean was still inside the sun-hot tent, sweating and sleeping. Dad looked at him a second, then before I could say a word, he reached into the water bucket and pitched a handful into Sean's face.

Sean sputtered and squirmed, then sat up suddenly, eyes wild. I turned and walked out of the tent as Dad bellowed, "Roll on out, boy. I already got one down and clean."

Just before I turned the truck's key I heard Dad yell, "I plow deep while sluggards sleep!" his standard wake-up shout since I could remember.

Sean didn't come out until Dad and I were tying the deer up on the game pole. "It's a doe," he said, sounding scornful.

"So?" Dad asked, in the voice I'd learned meant trouble.

Maybe Sean could tell that much. He said, "It's a big one," and Dad said, "Damn right." A minute later he said, "You should've seen Chet push them out to me. Like clockwork," and I hoped maybe we'd passed the worst of it.

We ate a huge breakfast, my dad cooking like always, though I could tell he was running out of steam, the night chasing hard after him. When the food was heavy in our stomachs, he pushed some stuff from his cot

175

and spread out. "A little shut-eye, and we'll knock the stuffing out of them again this afternoon."

Sean had only pushed his breakfast around his plate. He was back in his sleeping bag in a heartbeat.

I looked at them, my dad fully dressed on top of his sleeping bag, his mouth already open, his breathing getting louder. All of a sudden it was too hot in the tent and I took my coffee outside. I looked around our little camp at the edge of the trees, looking so much like the camps I'd loved when I was a kid. The coffee in my stomach went all acidy. I pitched what was left in my cup, swinging it wide and listening to the crunch of the downed leaves it hit. Picking up my rifle from the picnic table, I walked away.

I didn't see a thing. I wasn't really even hunting, more just putting distance between us. When I finally gave up and came back there was still no sign of life from the tent. I sat in Dad's lawn chair and tried not to look at them sleeping. It was nearly three; time to be going again. I nudged Sean with my toe but he didn't move. I started to knock around some, on purpose, but neither one of them even fluttered an eyelid.

Finally I walked up to my dad's cot, bending close to look at him. His breath was terrible. I whispered, "I plow deep while sluggards sleep," wondering, if I ever had kids, if I'd be able to roust them out of bed with that friendly chant. I'd always looked forward to it when I was little.

Suddenly I grabbed my dad by the armholes of his hunting vest and shook him as hard as I could, yelling, "*I* plow deep! *I* do!" That's not at all what I meant to say, or even do, but I kept shaking until he sat up and pushed me away.

He stared at me, blinking, his hair sticking all over. "What's the matter?" he asked, shy and confused.

I looked at him a moment more, then said, "Nothing. We should get going if we're going to get anything tonight." He kept looking at me, so I walked out of the tent.

When they crawled out, Dad looked almost as rough as Sean and I felt bad about shaking him so hard. He dug in his pocket for his keys, and said, "Let's try the mountain."

"All right, but it's getting late."

"Plenty of time."

hile Dad got ready I told Sean about the mountain, things I'd told him before, at school. He said he was sorry he'd slept through half the day, but then he chuckled and said he still doubted he could walk very far. "Your old man can really put it away," he said.

"Yeah," I said, looking at the way the clouds raced along.

"That's great. If my old man ever caught me puking drunk, I'd be dead meat."

"It's great all right," I said.

Dad came out of the tent and fired up the truck, cradling a can of Coke between his legs. I scrunched in next to him and Sean rode shotgun. We were nearly to the mountain when Dad hit the ruts wrong and some of his Coke went flying and I was able to smell what was in the can. He was perking up by the time we piled out of the truck.

The mountain really wasn't anything but a big hill and we stood at its base a minute, working the stiffness out of our legs. Dad didn't even try to hide it when he took a bottle out of his toolbox and added some to his Coke. I wondered if he'd take his gun out. I wondered if he'd gone that far.

Usually Dad makes the plans, but when he started to say something about toddies I said, "You head straight off here, Sean, and round this edge. That puts you into a meadow. If you don't feel like walking, it's a good place to sit and wait."

Dad watched me take my rifle from the rack. The clouds had spread out some, straggly scraps of blue letting some sun through, and I pointed to the mountain's west face. "I'll go up there and work around. They might be up catching the last of the sun. I'll try to spook anything back to you, Sean. Or you can come with me if you want." I was talking too fast and I wondered if Sean could even understand me.

He smiled, looking up the hill. "I'll sit in the meadow."

Dad kept staring at me. "Aren't you going to tell me what to do?" he asked as soon as I started off.

I wanted to keep going, but I stopped and turned around. "OK," I said. "You stay here. We'll be back at dark." I started walking away again. "Have yourself a toddy," I said, plenty loud for him to hear. I was sweating before I even started the climb.

I paused when the truck was out of sight. I could see Sean about half a mile away, just about to the meadow, his orange vest a dot in all the murky green below the line of sunlight. I kept going up, the sun hardly hot enough to warm me, but nice to have all the same. It was a while before I saw the string of mule deer single-filing along the high, open face of the hill, easy to pick out in the sun.

They were out of range and heading toward the truck, not the meadow. I looked back to where Sean was sitting but I couldn't see him now. There was no way to turn these deer to him. It'd be a miracle getting to them myself. I felt bad, but I'd really thought I'd given him the best chance.

I dropped below the lip of hill I'd just crested and started running toward the truck. To keep the ridge between me and the deer, I gave up most of the elevation I'd gained, but I was still puffing hard by the time I reached a neck of trees where I could run up and hope to cut off the deer.

There wasn't any time to catch my breath so I started up the hill, darting from ponderosa to ponderosa. I tried keeping an eye out for the deer, but mostly had to watch the ground, so I wouldn't break my neck.

When the does started to cross the timber, not sixty yards above me, I was panting so hard I could barely hold my scope on a single animal. They ambled along, each going through the same clear spot. I tried to calm down and wait for a good shot. But suddenly, my gun still bouncing all over the place, the scope filled with huge antlers that instantly made everything harder. I only had a second and I tried to time the bounce of the crosshairs and aim into his boiler room. I let one fly.

By the time I had the scope back to my eye, there was nothing to see. I lowered the rifle and saw the last few deer disappear. They'd jumped the trail and started straight up the hill; typical muleys, going up a little way, then turning to see if anything's following.

I couldn't see into the patch of timber the buck had been about to enter, but I thought I heard something solid – a big thing falling all at once. I smiled, already not sure if I'd really heard it, or if it had really sounded like what I hoped it was. I started creeping forward, having to stop when I remembered I hadn't jacked in a second shell.

With my thumb ready to flip off the safety, I edged into the dark patch. I took a few steps, my heart going hard, but not from the uphill anymore. Then I saw him, down in the duff, some of it scraped up by his hooves. His antlers had hung up in the same mess of dirt and rock and long, old needles, so that while he was lying on his side, his head was twisted around, resting on his rack, looking straight up into the last of the sunlight. A steady wisp of steam drifted out of his open mouth.

I was trembling by the time I got to him. I'd shot bucks before, but nothing like this. I smiled and reached down to touch him. Dad wouldn't believe it even when he saw it. He'd had his best mounted when I was a kid. I'd spent years staring at it over the TV. This one looked like its big brother. He wouldn't believe his eyes.

I dragged him down out of the thicket and started the knife into him, hoping Dad would still be sober enough to tell stories about this one someday. I dumped the guts, keeping the heart in its own sack the way he'd taught me. I could already hear how the story would sound in some perfect hunt camp of the future, me sitting quiet while he made up all the details he'd missed by staying at the truck. It would seem like I knew everything and parts of it he'd make funny enough to die for, but in the end, no matter what else got added, I would always make that perfect, impossible shot.

I was smiling wide enough to break, more over how his stories would sound than over the deer. Then the gigantic rip of sound so close made me leap, and even as my mind was separating the blast from the tearing whistle of the bullet, I felt the sting of water in the corners of my eyes,

178

squeezed out by the force of the shot and the skipped beat of my own heart. I shouted, "I'm right here!" and started crawling for a huge ponderosa at the edge of the dark patch, still shouting, "I'm right here! I'm right here!"

After a few seconds I peeked around the tree and there on the knob of hill behind me was my dad, holding his rifle loose at his side, still pointed at me. He was a good fifty yards away, but I knew I'd never seen anything like that fear or shock on his face. I shouted, "I'm right here!" again, just because I couldn't make anything else come out of my mouth.

"Damn, you scared me," he said, in a big, relieved rush.

"I scared *you*?" I shouted.

"They're all over the hill above you," he said, starting to wipe that look off his face. "Get behind that tree and I'll take another shot. I missed."

He was bringing his rifle up and I hunkered behind the wide trunk of that pine. That same crashing tear sounded out, but it wasn't as big this time, knowing it was coming. I realized the first shot hadn't really been that close.

"Damn it," Dad shouted, laughing. "You scared me so bad I'm shaking like a leaf. Knock one of them down for me."

I poked my head around the tree to look at him and he was standing up, in full view of everything. The deer were long gone. I couldn't have knocked one down with a rocket.

"Don't shoot," I said, but he was already shouldering his rifle, coming down to me.

He was chuckling some, getting ready to laugh everything off. "You made me cut myself," I said.

His laugh got hold of him and he started singing. "I'm right here, I'm right here," in some weird falsetto.

That fast I could hear all the stories years from now; me bleating, "I'm right here," over and over again, digging my face into the ground and hugging trees; how I let the deer get away because I scared him so bad shouting like that. I heard every one of his stories about it, and I realized I was still holding the heart I'd cut out for him.

When he reached me he whistled and said, "My God, you shot the king of the mountain," and I said, "Don't say a word about it. Not one word. Not ever."

He looked at me and I knew he understood what I meant, and he knew he'd done everything wrong. But he just bent down to take a leg. I stepped in his way. "Don't even touch it," I said.

When he looked up, I thrust the heart at him. "Take this," I said. "I saved it for you."

"You want to drag it out, be my guest," he said, taking the heart. "But I owe you one from this morning, and I'd give you a hand."

179

"Damn right you owe me one," I said, not knowing myself exactly what I meant. I threw myself into dragging the deer down the mountain away from him. I shouted over to the meadow, where I still couldn't see a trace of Sean.

There was no answer for a moment, then a faint, "What?" drifted out of the bottom.

Dad didn't say a word.

"Give me a hand with this thing," I shouted. "I got the king of the whole damn mountain."

Pete Fromm wrote this version of "King of the Mountain" for Sporting Classics *prior to the publication of his popular book of the same title.*

THE LAST REUNION

They had come together on this final reunion as the last survivors of the Chesapeake Bay & Rod Society. They were passionate anglers, gentlemen who knew all about loyalty and tradition, and even the right way to die.

By James Tenuto

I can hear the young guides talking about us. Young bastards. My eyesight might not be what it was but there's nothing wrong with my hearing. I can hear a mouse piss on a cotton ball.

The guides, Luke and Matthew, are sitting in the great room, probably toasting their toes by the fire and knocking back a few cans of that over-rated Rocky Mountain brew. They're either too young or too ignorant to enjoy a real flyfisherman's libation. My doctor, another bastard, has restricted me to two drinks a day, with the unexpected result that I savor my couple of fingers of scotch in the traditional tin cup with a splash of ice cold branch water.

Luke's voice is antiseptic, sterile and devoid of any accent. He is the worst sort of Montanan, a former Californian. Matthew, on the other hand, has that nasal Western twang, passed down by generations of cowboys and small town bank presidents.

"I'm not saying those guys are old," said Luke, "but I heard one of them brag that he cut bait for Izaak Walton." That's not true, as I, for one, have never cut bait.

181

"But you hafta admit," Luke continued, "the old codgers can fish. Once the Admiral loosens up he has the prettiest casting technique I've ever seen." I grinned. I had been out with Luke that day and I made a sidearm cast under an overhanging willow branch. His eyes nearly popped out of his head.

"My dad says they've been coming here for years," Matthew said. I can remember his father. Hell, I remember his father as a young man! "Says they've been coming here every year since after the war."

"Wow, that's gotta be like twenty-something years," mused Luke.

"Not the Vietnam War," Matthew retorted, "World War II. We're talking fifty years, a half a century, man."

"How old are they anyway?"

My attention wanes. We're 92, the General and I, and Matthew's nearly right. Next year it will be fifty years since we started holding our reunions at the Double Dutch Ranch.

Originally we were ten, all members of the class of 1924 at the United States Naval Academy. We called ourselves the Chesapeake Bay Rod & Fly Society, and we kept our sanity during our Plebe Year by remembering trout streams we had fished, and telling each other the lies all fishermen tell. During our more collegial years at Uncle Sam's School for Wayward Boys on the Severn, we would fish as often as we could – streams in Pennsylvania or the Rapidan. Once we fished with President Herbert Hoover. He wrote the Superintendent reporting that we were all fine young men and destined to become great officers.

After we were commissioned, eight of us as ensigns in the Navy and two as second lieutenants in the Marine Corps, it became more difficult to get together. There were families, careers and then the war; these were not unimportant, mind you, but they were not flyfishing, either.

My ears cock like those of a good hunting dog's, drawn again to their conversation.

"Have you seen *the rod*?" asked Matthew.

"Sure. It's a beauty," replied Luke.

"What's the story?"

"I'm not a hundred percent sure," answered Luke. "I know that they bring it every year, but as far as I know, no one's ever fished with it."

"You wouldn't fish an antique rod like that. Some collector'd pay thousands for it."

"No, I think whichever one of them lives the longest gets the rod."

And if I'm the fortunate one, I intend to fish it. It's a Garrison split cane rod and it's been at the heart of our tontine. In July 1946, the seven of us who survived the war came to the Double Dutch Ranch for the first time. As I recall, we were plenty drunk. In those days there wasn't a sawbones alive who could have restricted any of that crowd to two fingers a day. We ceremoniously placed the empty bottles of scotch around the fire. The Sea Lawyer made the suggestion. Each would contribute a few dollars and he would buy the Garrison rod, a 1943 2 $^3/_4$-inch Hardy Sunbeam reel, and some silk line. In accordance with the time-honored traditions of tontines, to the last man alive would go the spoils. We entrusted the temporary possession of the outfit to the youngest in the group.

As the years, and then decades, passed, our numbers decreased. The Korean War claimed one, an aircraft accident another, heart attacks a couple of more, cancer the last. Now it was just the General and me.

The General is sleeping in the next bed. The man has an incredible capacity for sleep. He claims that he took a long nap when he was on the beach at Iwo Jima. Nothing bothers the General. He faces life with the equanimity common to those who have faced death on many occasions. We often used a jocular toast at our reunions before World War II: "To a bloody war and swift promotion." These became prophetic words, as most of us who survived did so at flag rank, with the General a general.

When we chided him on his ability to sleep anywhere, the General merely laughed. "The key to my success, gentlemen, I was the most rested field officer in the Marine Corps."

I, on the other hand, sleep very lightly, the result of many years of shipboard duty. I awake instantly alert. The better to hear young bastards.

"Whaddya say we find the bunkhouse and turn in?" asked Matthew. "We've gotta take the generics float-tubing tomorrow." He means geriatrics.

So finally I sleep.

I ate one of those indulgent breakfasts that you enjoy so much when you're away from home. I'm strictly a bran cereal and juice man at home, but if someone else obliges to slave over the stove I'm amenable to just about anything. Flapjacks, thick slices of home-cured bacon, fried eggs and coffee graced the table this morning. The Double Dutch maintains the facade of a working ranch. We all eat at a communal table, guides, sports, the few cowboys still remaining and Dutch Evans. Dutch Evans, the grandson of Old Dutch Evans, struts around in a cowboy hat. He evens wears the thing fishing, and it adds to his ridiculous appearance. He also wears a blue fishing vest. Blue! Makes him look like some kind of poofter. But that's what happens when something moves from the practical to the world of high fashion.

There's a young couple from Connecticut staying at the ranch. They're enrolled in the "Seven-Day Flyfishing Course," at $2,250 each, mind you. I overheard them while they practiced casting. He snapped flies off the leader with ferocious whip-like backcasts, swearing a blue streak. "Oh, Caldwell," she exhorted, "you must have patience, dear. After all, everyone is doing it." She has a reedy, annoying, grounds-for-divorce voice.

To go with her neon pink hat, she's wearing a pink vest, and at the breakfast table, too! Not that she carries a damn piece of gear, mind you, but she's got the color coordinated vest.

183

Frankly, there's only one color vest that's acceptable to my way of thinking. Tan. Period. Well, maybe green. Those Limeys make a good vest. The Sea Lawyer owned one. Once he fell into the river, and an hour later I noticed he still had a considerable amount of water in the back pocket. It appeared as if he had his own live well.

Luke gives me a gentle slap on the back. "Well, Admiral, you're stuck with me today. When you and the General are ready you can meet me out by the Hummer." They park the Hummer just under our window, and while I'm struggling with my waders – Neoprene 7mm, at my age you tend to get cold – I overhear Luke and Matthew.

"Thought I'd never say this, but thank God I've got the oldsters," Luke said. His voice was muffled by a wad of Redman shoved in his cheek, probably illegal in California. It makes him look like an axe murderer.

"She won't do a thing," complained Matthew, whose lot in life was the Connecticut couple. "I've got to make the cast, set the hook and then hand the rod over to her. I net the fish, remove the fly, release the fish, and then start the process all over again. Meanwhile, her husband is making another bird's nest that's like that old Gordon knot!"

I mentally correct Matthew, "Gordian knot," but I am pleased nonetheless for the classical reference.

"Been through a dozen leaders in three days. The knots are so hopeless I just clip the leader and tie a new one on. It'd help if he drew a sober breath."

"The wife, though, that's a two-man job guiding her. I have to walk her out into the stream with her grasping my arm like she was one of them detentes at a coming-in party."

"That's one thing I admire about the Admiral," Luke said. "He shakes me off if I try to help him. 'Young Mr. Luke,' he says, 'give me credit to know which water I can wade. If I can't wade it alone, I won't wade it at all.'

"Yesterday he goes in way downstream and works his way up a run, slower than a glacier, but on his own. He's got a #14 Royal Wulff on ..."

"Tied it on himself, I 'spect."

"Certainly. He can't see anything up close. Like a hawk at a distance, but nothing right in front of his face. I swear those cheaters he uses for close-in work double as microscopes. Anyway, he false-casts once and then drops the fly over a big brown. He twitches it once and smack, a major league take. He plays the fish quickly, waves off me and the net, and goes back to work on the run after he lands and releases the hefty brown.

"I went to check on the General, who was fishing below. A bit later the Admiral walks down to see how we're doing, and I asked him how he did. He holds up seven fingers and smiles."

I had heard enough. I roused the General, who was napping following that huge breakfast and the exertions of struggling with his waders, and we tottered to the Hummer.

The General didn't care much for the Hummer. Nor did he care much for modern warfare. "Goddamn thing has better appointments than my den," he observed. The General is possessed of a syrupy Southern voice, made even more rich by bourbon and cigars.

"This is the sportsman's edition, General!" explained Luke. "I'm sure the military version is bare bones."

"Leather interior, cellular phone, sportsman's edition, my ass. An open-air jeep with the windscreen down, a .50 cal strapped on the back, and chompin' on a cee-gar. That's war!"

We drove to a small, three- or four-acre lake teeming with rainbows and browns. Luke used the on-board air compressor to inflate three float tubes. He called them U-Boats, which raised my hackles, I can tell you. I spent the better part of two years trying to sink U-Boats, and now I was beholden to one to keep me afloat on some pint-sized lake."How's about we lunch right here?" Luke asked. "What's say we harvest a coupla three pan-sized 'bows?" "What's say you wander over to that field there and harvest some trout, son," spit the General. "I intend to catch a few in the lake and break their pretty necks."

Luke helped us launch and reminded us to keep our legs moving, even slowly. "You'll cramp up, otherwise," he explained. "But if you do, give me a holler and I'll tow you in."

I must admit that I had a wonderful time. There is a sense of weightless-ness that gives no end of relief to 92-year-old legs. Luke had the tubes inflated tight as a drum, we had only a slight, panting breeze to contend with, and we had little trouble negotiating the lake.

I tied on an elk hair caddis, rubbed it thoroughly with Mucilin, and made a short cast. An accommodating rainbow of reasonable proportions did me the honors. I played him quickly and before I could protest, Luke came over like a motorboat and netted the rainbow. "My God," I shouted, "if you took the net off that thing and replaced it with a paintbrush you could do ceilings."

"Admiral, it's tough landing fish in a tube," Luke offered by way of explanation.

"Luke, I'll land them myself with my own net, thank you."

We heard a bull roar from the General, who held aloft a pan-sized rainbow. "That's one!" he shouted, dispatching the fish quickly and placing it in an old wicker creel he had resting on his lap.

We fished for the better part of two hours before we set sail back to shore. Luke helped us climb out of the U-Boats and then went about preparing lunch. From the small refrigerator in the Hummer he took out a cucumber and tomato salad, with just enough onions to give one a touch of heartburn. He also removed a small propane stove and a black cast iron skillet. He melted about half-a-pound of butter in the skillet, and then cleaned and cooked the trout.

The General watched these preparations with avidity. "My God," he sighed,

185

"you could fry a turd in all that butter and it would probably taste just fine." The General had a problem with cholesterol, but he decided to ignore the admonitions of the medicos while on his annual fishing junket.

After he finished serving the trout, Luke strolled over to the Hummer and came back twirling a couple of tin cups. "Gentlemen," he announced, reaching into his backpack, "I know that Dutch is under orders to restrict your drinks to two a day, but I can hardly allow such a fine meal go without a touch of the old demon."

"By God, Luke," I said, "that's the most urbane speech you've ever made. You have my permission to splice the mainbrace."

"What's that mean?" queried Luke.

"It means pour, son," said the General.

After such a splendid repast and aided by a generous dollop of Glenfiddich, I expected the General to make haste to find himself a soft patch of ground and check his eyelids for light leaks. Instead, he became, uncharacteristically, I might add, quite lugubrious.

"Do you remember our last trip with the Commodore?" asked the General.

I did, a float trip a few years back. The Commodore's eyesight was so bad that the guide would call when to strike.

"Luke," the General continued, "the Commodore nearly made it into the *Guinness Book of World Records* under the category, 'Most Heart Attacks.' The sawbones over at Bethesda hooked him up to a heart monitor, he wore a clip over his index finger and he had this gadget that reported his pulse.

"Anyway, we were floating the river, Matthew's father, Thomas, was our guide. That man could handle a McKenzie boat, let me tell you. About an hour into the float the Commodore has a heart attack.

"Thomas gives him some nitroglycerin and tells him, 'You hang in there, Commodore, we're going to a take-out point about four miles downriver and we'll get you to the hospital.' The Commodore is still peaked and I'm sitting with him, describing the water as we pass. 'Oh, there's some fine holding water, Commodore' or 'I bet they're stacked up in that tailwater.'

"The Commodore rallies, he even has a little color in his cheeks. His voice is barely a croak, 'Thomas,' he says, 'do you think I can fish. Hell, if I'm gonna die, it might as well be fishing.'

"Thomas says that he can't see how that can hurt. He's still pulling at the oars of that McKenzie boat like Ben Hur and he's spotting fish and calling strikes for the Commodore. Meanwhile, I was watching the heart rate monitor. 'Whitefish on, Commodore,' Thomas would shout. Pulse 90. 'Rainbow on, Commodore!' Pulse 120. 'Brown on, Commodore! Pulse 150. Damnedest thing I ever saw."

It was quiet for a moment. "Did he die?"

"Yes," said the General, "but not until a few months later. He died watching a golf tournament on television."

There passed one of those embarrassing silences where no one knows exactly what to say, how to move the conversation, or what course of action to take. If you're standing you usually shuffle your feet or kick some dirt, sitting you stare at your hands. Frankly, the interminable silence was becoming, well, eternal.

We were saved by a trout, or rather, The Trout. A slap of water more like a beaver than a fish woke us from our reverie. Luke was on his feet in a second. "That's Grandpa and my guess is hoppers!" Luke told us that Grandpa was a rainbow trout of monstrous proportions. Though a wily creature, he had been landed a few times.

Luke helped us back into the float tubes and gave us a short tow and a small push. "I'll clean up and join you in a few minutes." He waded back to our lunch site. The General made his way, vigorously, mind you, over to where Luke had pointed out the lair of the legendary Grandpa. "There's an undercut bank and he just waits for hoppers or mice to fall in."

The General tied on a Dave's Hopper and he stripped about fifty feet of line using long, slow, elegant casts. I had my rod resting across the tube, content to watch my old friend. The General knew that he had only one cast, one chance at Grandpa. The line shot out and he placed the hopper right on the edge of the bank. He gave it one little twitch and the fly tumbled into the water.

What I saw next reminded me of old newsreels showing the submarine launch of a missile. Grandpa came out of the water in stages, building up speed until he was nearly clear of his element. As the big rainbow fell back into the water, the General set the hook.

"My God," he shouted, "he's as big as one of your old battlewagons, Admiral!" The battle was joined, two old warriors using all their strength and cunning. It would be a long battle, I could audit it occasionally, as I didn't want to make the General self-conscious. Flyfishing is not a spectator sport.

Luke was next to me in his float tube, grinning maniacally, his cheek swollen with that foul tobacco. "The General's in for the ride of his life," he said.

"Lord, I do believe he's towing me!" announced the General. Sure enough, his line was tight, he wasn't able to take any to the reel, and he was moving, towed by Grandpa.

I turned my U-Boat away from the General, and purposely started fishing. I asked Luke to stay close in case I needed his help in netting a fish, but I just wanted to keep him away from the General. I landed a fat rainbow who tailwalked and took me to the backing twice and I allowed Luke to feel useful. He netted the fish, removed the fly, and I even held the trout so he could snap a photograph.

"Aw," Luke moaned, "it looks like the General lost Grandpa." I looked over and saw the General, his rod down, his head lolling back. He was sleeping! I figured the meal and the excitement of hooking Grandpa had finally taken their toll. "Asleep in a float tube," I laughed. Luke and I agreed to let him rest. I continued to fish, the sun beginning its slow descent. I happily slipped into a rhythm of casting, covering a lot of water, raising a few fish, putting down others.

Luke suddenly asked me turn around and check the water at the far end of the lake. "What's that look like to you, Admiral?"

I saw the General's head was now tilted forward, his chin against his chest. I searched the water and saw the white streak. "I believe that's a fish belly, Luke, a damned big trout's belly."

I can hear the young guides talking about us. Their voices are hushed, almost reverent.

"So the Admiral says, 'It looks like a big fish belly.' Now I'm finning over there like a motorboat. The General hasn't moved an inch, you know, and when I get there I see that he's dead. Stone dead, already cooling off like. The Admiral comes floating up next to me.

" 'General,' he says, 'wake up, you old bastard.'

" 'He's passed,' I says. The Admiral blinks once, and then moves past me to the General's float tube. He takes the rod out of the General's hands…"

His left hand was on the reel, the right locked on the cigar-shaped cork of his rod, his index finger pressed down hard on the green flyline. Death's own drag. I reeled in Grandpa, a heavy, sluggish dead weight.

"Then he grabs Grandpa by the tail and tries to revive him. 'He hasn't been dead as long as the General,' he tells me. These are some hard men, let me tell you. Me, I was stunned, I just sat in my tube watching him.

" 'Luke, it's hopeless,' he says. 'They killed each other.' "

"Man, that's eerie," said Matthew.

"Damnedest thing I ever saw," said Luke. "Then there was the business of towing the General to the bank and getting him out of the float tube and into the Hummer. The Admiral takes down all the rods, collects the gear, and slips into the front passenger's seat."

Luke had laid the General in the backseat. He always was a sawed-off little fellow – we called him a "sandblower" at the Academy – and he'd shrunk a bit with age. He appeared to be very peaceful, resting really, in his waders, old shirt and even older vest. His hands were folded near his waist.

" 'I wish we could bury him in that get-up rather than his dress uniform,' says the Admiral. What a pair! Then he looks over at me," continued Luke, "and he says, 'You did a fine job today, Luke, the General would have been proud of you.' "

There was that uncomfortable silence again. Matthew was the man of the hour. "You know," he said, "I could get to enjoy this stuff."

Mind you, he's talking about a single malt scotch that costs as much as he makes in a day, with the tip.

"The Admiral said that it was on him. He said something about passing along some fine traditions. He said that we were good boys, just a bit young. And he said it was a beautiful death, said it was the way he wants to go."

"At 92," said Matthew, "how many seasons does he have left?"

I don't know. But whatever time I do have left on the stream I'll savor immensely. I'll be fishing a Garrison cane rod with a Hardy reel and landing trout on a silk line.

MAN, TIRED

He would have to keep it all to himself, forever, because people would say he was a fool or that he was crazy. But they'd be wrong, because he had won something that day, in the teeth of that terrible storm.

By Gordon MacQuarrie

He discovered he was tired when he put the magnum duck gun in the car and bumped his head on the suspended trunk door. He had never done that before. His reflexes were dull. Maybe the boss was right; the boss had said the circles under his eyes looked like upside-down rainbows.

The edge of the steel door had given him a good one. He did not feel it keenly. His nerves were not carrying the message. His head should have hurt, and probably did, but he didn't know it. Then he thought, "I'm studying myself detachedly, like a drunk."

Twelve months in town – not working; mostly worrying. Not working with his hands at all. He recalled a piece in the paper wherein a doctor explained how he was curing crazy people by giving them work for their hands to do.

Just twelve months in town. Up half the night and in bed half the morning. Campaigns, conferences – contacts and contracts and confusion. Then war – did everything twice as fierce. Out of these he was supposed to make sense.

Sometimes he had succeeded, at least enough so that the boss had said, "Joe, you get out of here. We can't afford to have both of us go nuts."

He got behind the wheel and counted the damage. The fat round duffel bag, the bigger one with the zipper, the brown drill sacks holding the decoys, the greasy Duluth packsack. When he started the motor, his fingers remained too long on the contact button. He would have to drive carefully. He turned the trip mileage back to 000. When it reached 390 he would be there. And when he arrived, he would first light a fire on the hearth . . .

The last fifty miles were the best part of the trip. He ate ham and eggs in a truckers' restaurant and began the last lap. The trees closed in across the blacktop. A flooded barrow-pit at the roadside showed ice at the edges. All the leaves were gone except the stubborn rusty ones on the scrub oaks. The spruces and pines were scowling darkly. The farms were poor and bleak.

Under a yellow corner light in a town barricaded with pulpwood he turned east off the blacktop. His tires ceased purring and swished in sand. Beyond the tiny town lay the river and the bridge. Crossing the bridge he remembered that the water under it came from his lake. It came twisting fifty miles down through the sand to make a river big enough for a bridge.

Beyond town the jackpine pressed in on the sand road. A horned owl floated over it, and a buck deer with ivory-tipped antlers stood and stared. Beyond the rich man's turn-in with its high, proud gate, he sought the faint trail through the jackpines. He went beyond it and had to back up to catch it. The jacks reached out with their fingertips and brushed the car. Some of them were down across the trail. He got out stiffly and swung them parallel to the ruts in order to pass. Toward the end of the road he just drove over them. He was so tired.

Over the hill beyond the last turn was the place – yellow cedar logs with a gentle roof, and in the last light of day the leaden lake beyond. A big doe got up from her bed in front of the cabin stoop and ambled away.

The flat-filed key opened the door. Inside there was the warm mustiness of cedar. He lit a kerosene lamp and struck a match to paper on the hearth, and the chimney roared. Nothing was changed. His snowshoes were crossed on the farther wall. There was the X-legged table with the blue oilcloth. He heaped the fire, and then flopped on the davenport and immediately fell into a heavy sleep.

In the morning the fire was out, and his car lights were burning. He had got up in the night and found two heavy blankets, but he did not recall doing it. He felt better!

It was astonishing to feel better in the morning. He unloaded the car and made breakfast on the ancient range with the nickel-plated oven door. Making toast, he laughed aloud. It was ridiculous how little it took to make a man happy.

190

The day was mellow. October's dusty shafts warmed him as he went to the woodpile. He lit a pipe and drew hard upon it as he unlocked the shed, and his fingers closed around the hickory helve of an ax.

The splitting wood was weather-seasoned Norway chunks. It worked beautifully. Chickadees came to feed on the liberated grubs. A chipmunk scuttled by. The man sweated; he sweated for the first time in months. When he wiped his forehead with the cuff of his flannel shirt, it felt fine and itchy.

He piled the pinkish Norway chunks by the fireplace. The room was warming. A blue jay screamed. He fell asleep. He fell asleep like a beaten dog, thinking.

The sun was touching the trees to the west when he awoke. To the east the lake was crimson from reflected light. There was a bit of breeze from the northwest. He had slept sixteen hours out of twenty-two. He washed and shaved, and when it was near dark he went to the tiny boathouse and dragged out the skiff.

He clamped on the motor, tried it, dumped decoys in and brought gun and shell box from the cabin. The far shore beyond the water was faintly aglow. A bunch of bluebill ducks cut the center of the lake, heading for the south bay. He might meet them there in the morning.

He sang through the dish washing. After shaking the oatmeal pan on the stove to prevent the bottom from burning, he opened the window in the bedroom and set the tiny alarm clock, remembering to lay it face down so that it would run. He figured he might not be able to sleep because he had slept so much. He went out like a light.

When the alarm tore loose, there was snow on his pillow. It had drifted through the screened porch to his window. It seemed impossible; the moon had been climbing up when he went to bed. Yet there it was. He slammed the window and dressed, shivering.

The place was like an icebox. Over the ridgepole the wind was crying. He felt like cheering. The bluebills would be in. They had come smashing south in late October from Lake Superior and from Minnesota and from the vast, far reaches of the Canadian provinces. He lit the range and fireplace, and put on two suits of underwear.

The old outboard acted badly at first, but finally it caught. He skirted the point shoal instinctively in the dark, and the wind caught him fair. It hurled the little boat forward in leaps and bounds, hammering his back and coming so hard that it blew spume past the racing craft. With motor cut, it knifed through sawgrass, and he felt the prow grate on sand. Tactics were automatic now. Two hundred yards down the shelved beach was the end of a blunt point thrusting into the wide shallow south end of the lake. Off to his right from the point lay the Hole in the Wall, a quarter-mile reach of water lying against the larger bay like a remora on a shark. It provided maneuvering room for incoming ducks.

He spread the decoys. The boat tossed, and he was continually rowing back into the wind for position. Sometimes an anchor rope fouled over a decoy head, and he would have a time getting close enough to fix it. He counted the stool in the growing light – forty of them in the shape of a lopsided horseshoe. The longer side thrusting far out into the bay downwind, and a half-dozen in the quieter waters beside the blunt point. They were sleepers, confidence men spread to convince suspicious birds that the place was safe enough for bluebills to brave the dangers of the near shore.

No one had built a blind on the point. This pleased him. It made him feel that the place was still his very own. He hacked off Norway pine and scrub oak boughs for a blind. The wind was so strong that he had to stick them deep in the sand. Tomorrow he would bring a shovel and dig a little pit for his feet to dangle in. It would be more comfortable.

Light came hard and gray beyond the cutover across the bay. Good enough. Let sunny days come after; this was a duck day. If just a few bluebills came like they used to when he had hunted here with his father thirty years ago! They used to make two dives at the decoys and then try to sit among them. They used to come in strings and echelons that embroidered the horizon. They used to –.

Four slashed in, storm-battered, and as they hovered in the wind, he killed two cleanly. It was a fifteen-minute battle to retrieve them with the light boat. They were bluebills, fat as pigs, fresh from northern marshlands. Maybe they had never seen a man before.

He plucked them in the blind, letting the wind carry off the down. Thirty came in, their dark legs braking the wind. While he battled the wind to retrieve three more, a flock of powerful flyers zoomed over the decoys – canvasbacks, of course. No other bird with white on its back could buck wind at that speed.

A pair of redheads came, and he collected them methodically, and again the ones with white came over. He picked the drakes by their brighter backs. It was good to feel them in a man's hand – bull-neck canvasbacks. He forgot that he had removed his gloves and was trampling them into the snow in the bottom of the blind.

He forgot that the blind did not cover him well. He forgot everything but the enchantment of waterfowl in the storm. Sweat stood on his face.

A hundred Canadas honked over in the storm – too far. A flock of chickadees loitered for a minute in the woods at his back, and a burly Canada jay sat in the blind cover with bold, staring eyes.

The soft skin of his hands had broken into blisters from the oars. His face burned, and he laughed when he discovered his trampled gloves in the snow. He drank hot coffee, not because he felt a need for it, but because it gave him something to do between flocks. He remembered other days. He prayed a little. He was grateful.

The storm built up. He knew what was happening to the north and west. Traffic was being stopped on the prairies. Canada's winter wheat was snow-covered, and Lake Superior's a devil's playground.

By pick-up time the bay was tossing so hard that the coontail tips were showing in the trough. He drank the last of the coffee and buttoned his hunting coat at the neck. Lifting the decoys was a nightmare. It took almost an hour in the lashing lake. When he finished, his hands were burning red.

He squinted through the storm on the way home. The snow was thicker. It was a good one, all right. He'd have to carry in extra armfuls of birch for the fireplace. The motor throbbed evenly. Faintly at his left he caught glimpses of the shore fifty yards distant and steered by it. He skirted the long point widely. A bad time to shear a pin.

Around the long point the wind was at its strongest. The ducks in the boat bottom were snow-covered, and when the motor went dead he was thinking how good the cabin would feel. The motor stopped and the boat went sidewise. He looked for the gas can. It was missing. No time now for anything but instinct. He flung himself forward on top of the ducks, and let the boat ride in the trough until he got the oars into their locks, then he sat up and rowed.

In five minutes his blistered hands were bleeding. He kicked a loose decoy overboard to determine his speed. It was a half-mile to his beach, and he was making that much an hour.

There was no time to remove his hunting jacket. The wind would have caught him. His breath came rapidly, and he felt a queer taste in his mouth, and he remembered when he ran the quarter-mile in college. He kept rowing. His eyes saw black spots in a field of boiling gold. He knew he was fighting for his life.

It was a good feeling. It felt like the time he beat that fellow Hargrove in the quarter and ran the last fifty yards without remembering it. The boat touched shore, but the wind was so heavy that when he stopped rowing it was pushed out again. He stepped overboard in the shallow water, dragged up the boat, and then fainted.

When he came around, the taste was stronger in his mouth, and his lungs ached. He pulled the boat up, threw out the anchor and walked up the hill.

The morning fire still showed coals. He heaped on fuel and stared at the growing blaze. He would have to be careful and never tell anyone. He would have to keep it to himself forever, because people would say he was crazy. They would not understand that he had won something.

That was it. He had achieved something with his hands and his body. Of course, he had been a fool to let the tank go dry in that buster. But he had made it. He looked out of the window toward the lake. He could not even see the boat on the shore. The fireplace roared, and he drank strong green tea, scalding hot.

The incident on the lake swept by him like a cigarette tossed overboard from a boat. No, he would never tell. No need to mention it. They'd think he was trying to be heroic or was just a fool. And they'd be wrong. It had done him good.

Tomorrow the ducks would fly again. They would loiter until freeze-up in the coontail-littered bay. There were ten of them in the kitchen. When he had time, he'd walk over and give half of them to Andy at the Corners.

Tomorrow he would fill the motor tank again and go. Tomorrow he would not forget to fetch a shovel to dig a pit for his feet to hang over. Tomorrow the little alarm clock that only ran face down would summon him in the dark, and he would be off.

This version of "Man, Tired" is from Last Stories of the Old Duck Hunters, *a collection of MacQuarrie's stories from the 1930s and '40s, published by Willow Creek Press.*

THE GIFT

*It was a very special Christmas gift . . . the only present that was
everything one person had to give. A holiday remembrance by
one of America's most beloved outdoor writers.*

By Gene Hill

hope most of you can remember a Christmas made
special because a certain longing was satisfied in an
unforgettable way – something more than a present, more
than a surprise.

I've always been partial to stories about kids seeing odd-
shaped packages under the tree and knowing, just *knowing*
that Grandpa or Dad had finally come through with the old
20 gauge or fly rod or a puppy, usually unwrapped. At that moment, I don't
remember ever seeing any such parcel under the tree with my name on it. I
do recall getting a Flexible Flyer which was very much wanted but not all
that much of a surprise. I don't recall any kid of that era being truly surprised
by a Christmas package. The barns and various sheds and the house were
under such strict surveillance that if a new field mouse moved in we knew
about it, much less a bicycle or a fly rod or a shotgun.

Back in Depression times when the average American factory worker
earned less than $1,000 a year, and the average farmer less than that, presents
for small boys tended to fall into the "What does he need?" category.

195

Luckily, "need" could sometimes stretch to cover No. 1 Blake & Lamb traps, a pocket knife or new rubber boots; it might even stretch as far as an adventure book about Africa or the Far North or the mysterious ocean, if you had any reputation as a "reader."

Our Christmas Days seemed noisier then. The kitchen was over-stuffed with ladies cooking too much food. The men argued about horses and guns and dogs, and the kid wrestled around underfoot until they were shooed outside to do chores or play games. The farm dog had been waiting for them on the porch since dawn.

The normal procedure in our house was that no present could be fooled with until Christmas morning. No jigging of any boxes under the tree (we did, of course). We were given one present to open after supper on Christmas Eve – just one and no second guessing. We usually had a rough idea of what was in the box; at worst it wasn't more risky than picking out a piece of chocolate and hoping it wasn't filled with jelly. What we didn't want to get stuck with was a piece of clothing. Chances were it would be handmade and we would have to try it on. The workmanship would be praised.

And we would act surprised, in spite of the fact that we were frequently measured all summer and fall by the local seamstresses and knitters, who hoped their guesses on rate of growth had been correct and that the garment could be let out, if it lasted long enough.

hen it was my turn on this particular long-ago Christmas Eve, I pointed to a box that had just arrived with a favorite aunt who seemed to be especially fond of me. The fact that she rarely saw me may have influenced this relationship. She was capable of real surprises. Once, against my family's advice, she gave me a BB gun. Another time she gave me a doughboy's helmet from World War I. I knew which package was from her and I was about to open it when my father took it away and handed me another one. "I think you'll like this one," he said. In a box far too large to afford the smallest clue, wrapped in several old copies of *Fur, Fish & Game*, was my much-wanted flashlight!

A flashlight may not seem very exciting unless you grew up in a house that was lit by kerosene lanterns, with toilet facilities located a considerable distance away from the house. The flashlight allowed you to read in bed when you were supposed to be asleep gathering your strength for chores. And, you could put the lighted end in your mouth, sneak into your little brother's room late at night, and scare him witless! Somehow, having a flashlight changed your life a little in those days. Kids who had flashlights were no longer supposed to be afraid of the dark; you were growing up, however slowly.

Before I got my flashlight, my father wouldn't take me coon hunting. Of course, I was too small to keep up with the men. It must have hurt my father to keep saying *no* when it was obvious that to be permitted to tag along was one of the things I wanted most in the world to do. On the nights when the men hunted, I would lie awake with my head on the sill of the open window, straining to hear old Red barking, but I never did.

"You're not big enough to have a flashlight," my father would tell me. It must have seemed a softer thing to say to a boy than to remind him endlessly that he was too big to carry and too little to go it alone. But that was over now. I was finally big enough. My father's excuse no longer worked.

I ran out of the house without remembering to say "Thank you," and stood on the lawn shining the topmost branches of the maple tree. Red, no doubt excited by the light, let out long rolling moans from his kennel run. My father came out and we agreed that the flashlight was perfect – perhaps the best one he'd ever seen. Red started a low chopping bark. "He thinks we've taken over his job," Pop said. Then, after a minute or two of silence, he said: "Why don't you go get your boots and coat and put Red in the car?"

I knew the field like the back of my hand from fetching water to the haying crew, but the mystery of the strange shadows cast by the full moon through the fingers of the drifting fog was compelling. We stood there listening to the ghost voices of owls while Red sorted through pungent footsteps of possums and skunks. We waited in silence, wondering if I was really big enough to be coon hunting, and if so, should I no longer hold my father's hand.

My father swung me up on his back when Red started barking treed. I clung like a monkey with one hand, holding my flashlight ready with the other in case my father needed to see where he was going. Red quieted down when we reached the tree and Pop and I both shined our lights from branch to branch. My light found one golden dot and then another. The coon was peering down from a dark hollow near the top. My father told me to stay where I was and then he left. If I had any thoughts about being left there alone with Red, I kept them to myself. I didn't ask where he was going, either. Men don't bother each other with trivial questions.

My father came back carrying a ladder he'd borrowed from a nearby farm. He leaned the ladder against the tree, climbed up, peered into the hole, and then called down for me to join him. When I reached the top of the ladder, he held me up so I could shine my light into the hollow. There were two pairs of eyes. "It's a mother and her baby," I said. And that's all I dared say, knowing full well that a good part of our income came from my father's trapping and coon hunting. But he knew what I had said.

I turned off my flashlight, put it in my pocket and waited until my father knelt and I swung my legs around his neck. He picked up the ladder with one hand and walked back to the Model A. My flashlight lit the way.

While I waited for Pop to return the ladder, I showed Rod my flashlight and promised him that this was just the first of many hunts. Red fell asleep, but I kept my light on, just in case.

When Pop came back, I climbed up on his lap and worked the choke on the Model A for him. We drove home, my hands under his on the steering wheel.

Memories accumulate under the weight of added Christmas Eves. But every time that night comes, I go off by myself for a while and remember the smell of the night air and the echo of Red's voice in the dark. I look at the tree brooding over the ribboned boxes and remember with a terrible yearning that I was fortunate enough to have been given, once in my life, a present that was everything one person had to give . . . a present so incredible that it had to be wrapped in a full moon.

Reprinted with permission of Cathy Hill.

NOTHING TO DO
FOR THREE WEEKS

*He was a pine knot millionaire – hunting partridge on the
tote roads and ducks on the lake, catching big crappies and
trout in the rivers, gathering blueberries for food and pine
knots for the fire, all work fit for a king.*

By Gordon MacQuarrie

I left long before daylight, alone but not lonely. Sunday-morning stillness filled the big city. It was so quiet that I heard the whistle of duck wings as I unlocked the car door. They would be ducks leaving Lake Michigan. A fine sound, that, early of a morning. Wild ducks flying above the tall apartments and the sprawling factories in the dark, and below them people still asleep, who knew not that these wild kindred were up and about early for their breakfast.

The wingbeats I chose to accept as a good omen. And why not? Three weeks of doing what I wished to do lay before me. It was the best time, the beginning of the last week in October. In the partridge woods I would pluck at the sleeve of reluctant Indian summer, and from a duck blind four hundred miles to the north I would watch winter make its first dash south on a northwest wind.

I drove through sleeping Milwaukee. I thought how fine it would be if, throughout the year, the season would hang on dead center, as it often does in Wisconsin in late October and early November. Then one may expect a little of everything – a bit of summer, a time of falling leaves, and finally that initial climatic threat of winter to quicken the heart of a duck hunter, namely me.

199

To be sure, these are mere hunter's dreams of perpetual paradise. But we all do it. And, anyway, isn't it fine to go on that early start, the car carefully packed, the day all to yourself to do with as you choose?

On the highway I had eyes for my own brethren of the varnished stock, the dead-grass skiff, the far-going boots. Cars with hunting-capped men and cars with dimly outlined retrievers in backseats flashed by me. I had agreed with myself not to go fast. The day was too fine to mar with haste. Every minute of it was to be tasted and enjoyed, and remembered for another, duller day. Twenty miles out of the big city a hunter with two beagles set off across a field toward a wood. For the next ten miles I was with him in the cover beyond the farmhouse and up the hill.

Most of that still, sunny Sunday I went past farms and through cities, and over the hills and down into the valleys, and when I hit the fire-lane road out of Loretta-Draper I was getting along on my way. This is superb country for deer and partridge, but I did not see many of the latter; this was a year of the few, not the many. Where one of the branches of the surging Chippewa crosses the road I stopped and flushed mallards out of tall grass. On Clam Lake, at the end of the fire lane, there was an appropriate knot of bluebills.

The sun was selling nothing but pure gold when I rolled up and down the hills of the Namakagon Lake country. Thence up the blacktop from Cable to the turnoff at Drummond, and from there straight west through those tremendous stands of jackpine. Then I broke the rule of the day. I hurried a little. I wanted to use the daylight. I turned in at the mailboxes and went along the back road to the nameless turn-in – so crooked and therefore charming.

Old Sun was still shining on the top logs of the cabin. The yard was afloat with scrub oak leaves, for a wind to blow them off into the lake must be a good one. Usually it just skims the ridgepole and goes its way. Inside the cabin was the familiar smell of native Wisconsin white cedar logs. I lit the fireplace and then unloaded the car. It was near dark when all the gear was in, and I pondered the virtues of broiled ham steak and baking powder biscuits to go with it.

I was home, all right. I have another home, said to be much nicer. But this is the talk of persons who like cities and, in some cases, actually fear the woods.

There is no feeling like that first wave of affection which sweeps in when a man comes to a house and knows it is home. The logs, the beams, the popple kindling snapping under the maple logs in the fireplace. It was after dark when I had eaten the ham and the hot biscuits, these last dunked in maple syrup from a grove just three miles across the lake as the crow flies and ten miles by road.

When a man is alone, he gets things done. So many men alone in the brush get along with themselves because it takes most of their time to do for themselves. No dallying over division of labor, no hesitancy at tackling a job.

There is much to be said in behalf of the solitary way of fishing and hunting. It lets people get acquainted with themselves. Do not feel sorry for the man on

200

his own. If he is one who plunges into all sorts of work, if he does not dawdle, if he does not dwell upon his aloneness, he will get many things done and have a fine time doing them.

After the dishes I put in some licks at puttering. Fifty very-well-cared-for decoys for diving ducks and mallards came out of their brown sacks and stood anchor-cord inspection. They had been made decent with touchup paint months before. A couple of 12-gauge guns got a pat or two with an oily rag. The contents of two shell boxes were sorted and segregated. Isn't it curious how shells get mixed up? I use nothing but 12-gauge shells. Riding herd on more than one gauge would, I fear, baffle me completely.

I love to tinker with gear. It's almost as much fun as using it. Shipshape is the phrase. And it has got to be done continuously, otherwise order will be replaced by disorder, and possibly mild-to-acute chaos.

There is a school which holds that the hunting man with the rickety gun and the out-at-elbows jacket gets the game. Those who say this are fools or mountebanks. One missing top button on a hunting jacket can make a man miserable on a cold, windy day. The only use for a rickety shotgun is to blow somebody to hell and gone.

I dragged a skiff down the hill to the beach, screwed the motor to it, loaded in the decoys and did not forget to toss in an ax for making a blind and an old shell box for a seat. I also inspected the light and found it good. It was not duck weather, but out there in the dark an occasional bluebill skirled.

I went back up the hill and brought in fireplace wood. I was glad it was not cold enough to start the space heater. Some of those maple chunks from my woodpile came from the same sugar bush across the lake that supplied the hot biscuit syrup. It's nice to feel at home in such a country.

How would you like to hole up in a country where you could choose, as you fell asleep, between duck hunting and partridge hunting, between smallmouths on a good river like the St. Croix or trout on another good one like the Brule, or between muskie fishing on the Chippewa flowage or cisco dipping in the dark for the fun of it? Or, if the mood came over you, just a spell of trampling around on deer trails with a hand ax and a gunnysack, knocking highly flammable pine knots out of trees that have lain on the ground for seventy years? I've had good times in this country doing nothing more adventurous than filling a pail with blueberries or a couple of pails with wild cranberries.

If you have read thus far and have gathered that this fellow MacQuarrie is a pretty cozy fellow for himself in the bush, you are positively correct. Before I left on this trip the boss, himself a product of this same part of Wisconsin and jealous as hell of my three-week hunting debauch, allowed, "Nothing to do for three weeks, eh?" Him I know good. He'd have given quite a bit to be going along.

Nothing to do for three weeks! He knows better. He's been there, and busier than a one-armed paperhanger.

Around bedtime I found a seam rip in a favorite pair of thick doeskin gloves. Sewing it up, I felt like Robinson Crusoe, but Rob never had it that good. In the Old

Duck Hunters we have a philosophy: When you go to the bush, you go there to smooth it, and not to rough it.

And so to bed under the watchful presence of the little alarm clock that has run faithfully for twenty years, but only when it is laid on its face. One red blanket was enough. There was an owl hooting, maybe two wrangling. You can never be sure where an owl is, or how far away, or how many. The fireplace wheezed and made settling noises. Almost asleep, I made up my mind to omit the ducks until some weather got made up. Tomorrow I'd hit the tote roads for partridge. Those partridge took some doing. In the low years they never disappear completely, but they require some tall walking, and singles are the common thing.

No hunting jacket on that clear, warm day. Not even a sleeveless game carrier. Just shells in the pockets, a fat ham sandwich and Bailey Sweet apples stuck into odd corners. My game carrier was a cord with which to tie birds to my belt. The best way to do it is to forget the cord is there until it is needed; otherwise the Almighty may see you with that cord in your greediness and decide you are tempting Providence and show you nary a feather all the day long.

B y early afternoon I had walked up seven birds and killed two, pretty good for me. Walking back to the cabin, I sort of uncoiled. You can sure get wound up walking up partridge. I uncoiled some more out on the lake that afternoon building three blinds, in just the right places for expected winds.

This first day was also the time of the great pine-knot strike. I came upon them not far from a thoroughfare emptying the lake, beside rotted logs of lumbering days. Those logs had been left there by rearing crews after the lake level had been dropped to fill the river. It often happens. Then the rivermen don't bother to roll stranded logs into the water when it's hard work.

You cannot shoot a pine knot, or eat it, but it is a lovely thing and makes a fire that will burn the bottom out of a stove if you are not careful. Burning pine knots smell as fine as the South's pungent lightwood. Once I gave an artist a sack of pine knots and he refused to burn them and rubbed and polished them into wondrous birdlike forms, and many called them art. Me, I just pick them up and burn them.

Until you have your woodshed awash with pine knots, you have not ever been really rich. By that evening I had made seven two-mile round trips with the boat and I estimated I had almost two tons of pine knots. In even the very best pine-knot country, such as this was, this is a tremendous haul for one day; in fact, I felt vulgarly rich. To top it off, I dug up two husky boom chains, discovered only because a link or two appeared above ground. They are mementos of the logging days. One of those chains was partly buried in the roots of a white birch some fifty years old.

No one had to sing lullabies to me that second night. The next day I drove eighteen miles to the quaggy edge of the Totogatic flowage and killed four woodcock. Nobody up there hunts them much. Some people living right on the flowage asked me what they were.

An evening rite each day was to listen to weather reports on the radio. I was

202

impatient for the duck blind, but this was Indian summer and I used it up, every bit of it. I used every day for what it was best suited. Can anyone do better?

The third day I drove thirty-five miles to the lower Douglas County Brule and tried for one big rainbow, with, of course, salmon eggs and a Colorado spinner. I never got a strike, but I love that river. That night, on Island Lake, eight miles from my place, Louis Eschrich and I dip-netted some eating ciscoes near the shore, where they had moved in at dark to spawn among roots of drowned jack pines.

There is immense satisfaction in being busy. Around the cabin there were incessant chores that please the hands and rest the brain. Idiot work, my wife calls it. I cannot get enough of it. Perhaps I should have been a day laborer. I split maple and Norway pine chunks for the fireplace and kitchen range. This is work fit for any king. You see the piles grow, and indeed the man who splits his own wood warms himself twice.

On Thursday along came Tony Burmek, Hayward guide. He had a grand idea. The big crappies were biting in deep water on the Chippewa flowage. There'd be nothing to it. No, we wouldn't bother fishing muskies, just get twenty-five of those crappies apiece. Nary a crappie touched our minnows, and after several hours I gave up, but not Tony. He put me on an island where I tossed out half-a-dozen black-duck decoys and shot three mallards.

When I scooted back northward that night, the roadside trees were tossing. First good wind of the week. Instead of going down with the sun, Old Wind had risen, and it was from the right quarter, northwest. The radio confirmed it, said there'd be snow flurries. Going to bed that windy night, I detected another dividend of doing nothing – some slack in the waistline of my pants. You ever get that fit feeling as your belly shrinks and your hands get callused?

By rising time of Friday morning the weatherman was a merchant of proven mendacity. The upper pines were lashing and roaring. This was the day! In that northwest blast the best blind was a mile run with the outboard. Only after I had left the protecting high hill did I realize the full strength of the wind. Following waves came over the transom.

Before full light I had forty bluebill and canvasback decoys tossing off a stubby point and eleven black-duck blocks anchored in the lee of the point. I had lost the twelfth black-duck booster somewhere, and a good thing. We of the Old Duck Hunters have a superstition that any decoy spread should add up to an odd number.

Plenty of ducks moved. I had the entire lake to myself, but that is not unusual in the Far North. Hours passed and nothing moved in. I remained long after I knew they were not going to decoy. All they had in mind was sheltered water.

Next time you get into a big blow like that, watch them head for the lee shore. This morning many of them were flying north, facing the wind. I think they can spot lee shores easier that way, and certainly they can land in such waters easily. In the early afternoon, when I picked up, the north shore of my lake – seldom used by ducks because it lacks food – held hundreds of divers.

203

Sure, I could have redeployed those blocks and got some shooting. But it wasn't that urgent. The morning had told me that they were in, and there was a day called tomorrow to be savored. No use to live it up all at once.

Because I had become a pine-knot millionaire, I did not start the big space heater that night. It's really living when you can afford to heat a 20-by-30-foot living room, a kitchen and a bedroom with a fireplace full of pine knots.

The wind died in the night and by morning it was smitten-cold. What wind persisted was still northwest. I shoved off the loaded boat. Maybe by now those newcomers had rested. Maybe they'd move to feed. Same blind, same old familiar tactics, but this time it took twice as long to make the spread because the decoy cords were frozen.

A band of bluebills came slashing toward me. How fine and brave they are, flying in their tight little formations! They skirted the edge of the decoys, swung off, came back again and circled in back of me, then skidded in, landing gear down. It was so simple to take two. A single drake mallard investigated the big black cork duck decoys and found out what they were. A little color in the bag looks nice.

I was watching a dozen divers, redheads maybe, when a slower flight movement caught my eye. Coming dead in were eleven geese, blues, I knew at once. I don't know whatever became of those redheads. Geese are an extra dividend on this lake. Blues fly over it by the thousands, but it is not goose-hunting country. I like to think those eleven big black cork decoys caught their fancy this time. At twenty-five yards the No. 6s were more than enough. Two of the geese made a fine weight in the hand, and geese are always big guys when one has had his eyes geared for ducks.

The cold water stung my hands as I picked up. Why does a numb, cold finger seem to hurt so much if you bang it accidentally? The mittens felt good. I got back to my beach in time for the prudent duck hunter's greatest solace, a second breakfast. But first I stood on the lakeshore for a bit and watched the ducks, mostly divers, bluebills predominating, some redheads and enough regal canvasback to make tomorrow promise new interest. The storm had really brought them down from Canada. I was lucky. Two more weeks with nothing to do.

Nothing to do, you say? Where'd I get those rough and callused hands? The windburned face? The slack in my pants? Two more weeks of it . . . Surely, I was among the most favored of all mankind. Where could there possibly be a world as fine as this?

I walked up the hill, a pine-knot millionaire, for that breakfast.

"Nothing to do for Three Weeks" is from Old Duck Hunters and Other Drivel, *1988. It is reprinted courtesy of Willow Creek Press.*

VENGEANCE

Enraged by the pain deep within his chest, the old bull bunched his muscles and charged up the trail, his horns plowing through the brush and shaking the trees. There was not much time and he had to reach the hated voices.

By Terry Wieland

ount Longido is an ancient volcano that rises 3,000 feet from the Masai plain in northern Tanzania. Long extinct and eroded to a stump, it is dwarfed by its close neighbors, Mount Meru and Mount Kilimanjaro. Longido is now little more than a high crater encircled by steep, rocky hills. The crater is several miles across and grown over with trees. The name comes from the Masai *Ol Donyo Ngito*. Ngi is a type of black rock found on the mountain, and for centuries the Masai have climbed Longido to sharpen their spears and *simis* on the dark rocks. A few Masai live up in the crater, growing plots of maize in small clearings and grazing their cattle on the surrounding hills. The only way up from the plain is along a winding trail though the jungle.

The highest remaining point of Mount Longido is a sheer rock pinnacle like the prow of a ship. It is usually obscured by clouds, and on the higher slopes

205

the thick brush turns to rainforest. From the upper reaches you can see all the way to the border post at Namanga, twenty miles north, and into Kenya as far as Amboseli National Park.

Our camp was on the southern slope facing Kilimanjaro across the Ngasarami Plain. There was a large Masai settlement nearby, and the village of Longido with its one dusty street, its police post and two one-room saloons, the vatican City Bar and the Lion. The Lion was the more upscale of the two. It had a door.

Rumor had it that high on Mount Longido lurked a few Cape buffalo bulls, too old to breed, too cantankerous to associate with, living out their lives alone. A few people had been up there and seen tracks, that was all. But they were big tracks. I had hunted Cape buffalo waist deep in swamp water and dry as dust in sand and thornbush. Why not on a mountaintop?

We left camp early in the morning, Jerry Henderson, Duff Gifford and me, with a cook, a tracker, a skinner and a game scout. We found the trail and started to climb, and reached the crater shortly before noon with the sun blazing overhead. The Masai gave us tea and cobs of scorched maize. Two young *morani*, clad in brilliant crimson and carrying spears, short swords and clubs, agreed to come with us up the mountain. They reappeared moments later dressed in gym shorts but still armed to the teeth, and their lean, athletes' bodies swung easily up the mountain.

By late afternoon we were at the base of the pinnacle and the Masai huts were just dots far below in the crater. With darkness came the rain. We shivered and dozed through the night and awoke to find ourselves wrapped in thick mountain mist.

Our retainers huddled around the campfire, soaked and miserable. We could see no more than twenty feet in any direction. There was little to do except shiver and wait for the sun to burn off the fog.

"Let's take a walk out onto the rock face," Duff said. "When the clouds blow away, we'll be able to see down into the crater."

Duff and Jerry and I left on our own, carrying only rifles and binoculars. Our staff was happy to stay by the fire. That was our first lucky break that morning – the first of many.

The slopes of Mount Longido are cut by dozens of ravines carved by centuries of torrential rains. Some are so deep they could be called canyons, others are just *dongas*, but all are overgrown with vegetation and jumbled with boulders.

We found a rocky promontory and settled down, each watching a different valley. It was like being high up in an enormous stadium – or would have been but for the thick, shifting fog. We shivered and waited. A sporadic wind began to blow. The clouds came and went, clearing one minute, enveloping us the next.

It was during one of these brief clear moments that I happened to catch sight of a grey-black object disappearing into some brush on a far hillside. Just a quick glimpse, and then the fog rolled back in.

"Duff, I saw one," I said, almost but not quite sure I really had. Maybe all I had seen was a rock. But when the fog drifted away again, there was no grey rock right there. It must have been a buffalo. He had shown himself in a clearing for a split second at the precise moment a window had opened in the fog, and I just happened to have my binoculars trained on the spot. And that was lucky break number two.

We sat and willed the fog to clear. By now, it was 9:30; the sun was well up and the rising wind made short work of what was left of the clouds. The slopes and the crater were all in plain sight, and for half-an-hour we studied the hillside across the valley. For Duff and Jerry, I pinpointed as best I could where I thought I had seen the buffalo disappear.

There was the bare face of a large boulder just to the right of the spot. That was the only real landmark in the hodgepodge of brush. As the minutes passed, I became less and less sure. Had I really seen a buffalo? Had I really seen *anything?*

"What'd you see, exactly?"

"Just the back end, and just for a second."

"Which way was he moving?" Duff is from Zimbabwe, and his Rhodesian voice was clipped and military as he gathered information, but he seemed to have no doubts.

"Along the hillside, from left to right. About halfway up."

Half-an-hour went by. By that time, I was almost convinced I had been hallucinating. When the buffalo did not reappear, Jerry wandered back to watch the other valley.

"I've got an idea," I said to Duff. "Let's have Jerry stay here to spot for us, and you and I go down and look for him."

Duff grinned. "Sounds good to me," he said, and softly went to get Jerry.

"We'll cross straight over to the hillside and use the tree as a start line," Duff told him, pointing to a bare-trunked acacia that rose taller than the others. "When we get there, we'll work straight along toward the big boulder on the right.

"If you see us get off course in that thick stuff, signal. Or if you see the buffalo . . ."

Jerry nodded a quick assent, gave me a clap on the shoulder, and a soft Texan "Good luck." Then we dropped down the steep hillside with Duff leading. Almost immediately we came upon a scraped-out hollow. The musky urine smell of buffalo hung in the air, and we found hoofprints the size of dinner plates.

"Well, we know there's one here," Duff whispered. "Big old boy, too."

We continued down along one of the bull's established trails. There was a warthog skull under a bush and, a few feet away, one of its ivory tusks, slightly rodent-chewed. I put it in my pocket for luck, and that, I think, was break number three.

cross a creekbed and climbing again. Now, we could look back and see Jerry perched high on the rock, watching us. Through the binoculars, he gave a thumb's up. We were on course, and almost immediately found the bare-trunked tree. A clearing stretched along the slope in front of us, and at the far end I could just make out the big rock face. Break number four.

It was approaching 10:30. The sun was high and the air had warmed. I was sweating in my goosedown shirt. Worse, it was noisy, catching on every thorn and twig. I tore it off and stuffed it into my belt.

Duff, in shorts and khaki vest, moved through the brush like a leopard, and his cropped hair and muscled shoulders in front of me reinforced the image. We were edging along the clearing now, a few feet apart, communicating by signs and instinct as if we had hunted together for years.

He was watching for tracks and I was looking past his shoulder when the bull stuck his head out of the bushes about 150 yards in front of us, right beside the boulder. I hissed and pointed. We froze. The buffalo had not seen us. He swung his head from side to side, and the boss of his horns was so big it made his horns look stubby, but they were not. His boss was heavy and black and met on the top of his skull without a gap. He was, indeed, a big old boy.

The bull looked around, then slowly withdrew into his sanctuary.

We breathed again and melted into the thick brush out of sight.

"He's big, he's wide," Duff whispered. "You want him?"

"I sure do."

We crawled along inside the screen of brush until we came up against a large rock, then crept back up to the clearing. We found ourselves on the edge of a deep *donga* jammed with a jungle of scrub. On that other side, sixty yards away, was the rock face where we had seen the bull. This was as close as we were going to get.

"Can you shoot from here?"

I nodded, found a clear spot to sit down, jacked the scope up to four power and wrapped the sling around my arm. Just as I leaned forward the big buffalo came out again, right on cue. He seemed to be going somewhere. I put the crosshair on his shoulder and squeezed.

As the .458 bucked up into my face, the bull hunched and roared and dashed down into the *donga*, deep into the thickest of the thick brush.

"Shoot again," Duff yelled, but there was no time and then the bull was out of sight. We could hear him, moving around down in the donga a few yards away. Then the rustling stopped and all we heard was his breathing, heavy and rasping.

We stood together on the lip of the *donga*, looking down into the undergrowth. I replaced the spent cartridge in the magazine of the Model 70 and turned the scope down to one. Then we waited.

208

"He's hard hit," Duff said. "He blew blood out of his mouth as soon as you shot. Hear him"

From the brush, the sound of heavy panting came to us. He was no more than fifteen yards away, maybe less.

"Hear him? Can you hear him? He's *kuisha*," Duff said. "Finished. that was a good shot, bwana. You got him in the lungs. We'll give him ten minutes, see what happens."

We stood side by side, trying to pierce the brush with our eyes, listening to the harsh breathing, waiting for the long, drawn bellow that would signal the end.

But the only sound from the *donga* was the rough grating of each painful breath, in and out, in and out, in and out.

The old bull had lived alone on the mountainside for many years. There was a small herd of younger buffalo up there too, cows and calves and bulls, maybe a dozen in all, but they wanted nothing to do with him and they avoided his valley. He bedded on a slope overlooking the crater and each day visited the creek that bubbled down the mountain, then up and along his favorite hillside, browsing as he made his way toward his own special place.

There was a boulder there, and some thick acacias, and in the shadow of the boulder it was cool for him to doze through the heat of the day. To one side was a donga, and a narrow trail that led down into up and out of it. He crossed though the donga each day. Although the brush looked impenetrable, with his four-foot horns he could force his way through.

On this day, as the clouds cleared (cleared as they did almost every day up here, away from the plain, away from the big buffalo herds), he sensed there was something wrong. He caught a whiff of something – smoke, perhaps – but there was no smoke on the mountain; the Masai stayed down in the crater and the smoke from their fires rarely drifted this far up.

But there was something, something; once or twice he emerged to look along his backtrail before retreating into his hideaway. Finally, he decided he would climb the hill to a better vantage point. As he came out he caught it again, not leopard, not Masai; a scent he had smelled only once or twice before in his long life, and just as he quickened his pace he was slammed in the ribs and a tremendous roar slapped his head and a cough was forced out of his lungs by the impact of the bullet and blood sprayed from his mouth.

Involuntarily he bucked and sprang. His trail was at his feet, the familiar trail down into the donga, and he let it carry him into the friendly gloom. Once there, he paused. His head was reverberating from the crash of the rifle and he could feel his breathing becoming heavy as a huge vise tightened on his chest.

From above came the sound of voices and his rage began to build as his lung filled up with blood.

The bottom of the donga *was a tunnel through the vegetation, scoured clean of brush when the heavy rains came. The old bull slowly walked a few yards up the creekbed, then turned and lay down facing high earth banks, and over his head a roof of solid vegetation. They would have to come down the trail. He fixed his eyes on it, six feet away. Now let them come.*

And there he waited as blood spurted out the bullet hole, his heart pumping out a bit of his life with each beat. Each breath came a little shorter and the pool of bright red blood under his muzzle spread wider, and his rage grew inside him like a spreading fire. He heard them whisper "Kuisha. . ." Not just yet. And heard them say "give him ten minutes . . ." Yes. Ten minutes. He was old and he was mortally wounded but he was not dead yet.

The old bull fixed his gaze on the trail and concentrated on drawing each breath, one by one, in and out, in and out.

The minutes ticked by. Three, four . . . seven, eight. Duff and I waited on the bank. Only the wounded buffalo's rasping breath broke the silence on the mountainside.

"I know you want to see . . ." Duff whispered

"Not me, bwana," I answered. "I can wait here forever."

"When you hear him bellow . . ." he began, and we heard rustling in the *donga.*

The Cape buffalo watched as the pool of blood grew and he felt himself growing weaker. Ten minutes. We weren't coming. Not much time left now. He heaved himself to his feet and a gout of blood poured from his mouth.

The bull could have eased silently down the donga *and died, off by himself. But he did not want to go quietly. He wanted to take those voices with him. And since they would not come to him . . .*

He bunched his muscles and sprang, charging up the trail. His horns plowed through the brush and shook the trees. He could not see us yet, but he was coming hard. There was not much time and he had to reach the hated voices.

He's moving, get ready!" Duff yelled. We saw the brush trembling and his hooves rocked the hillside, but we could not see the bull. Not yet. He was only yards away and moving fast, but where would he come crashing out? We couldn't see a damned thing.

And then a black shaped burst from the bushes five yards down and to my right. "Shoot!"

210

I tried to get the scope on him, but all I could see was black. I fired, hoping to catch a shoulder, worked the bolt and Duff and I fired together.

As we did, the bull turned his head toward us. His murderous expression said, "Oh, there you are!" and his body followed his head around. I was between Duff and the buffalo, and the buffalo was on top of me and all I could see was the expanse of horn and the massive muscles of his shoulders working as he pounded in.

No time to shoulder the gun now – just point and shoot and hope for the best. I shoved the .458 in his face and fired as I jumped back, and the bull dropped like a stone with a bullet in his brain, four feet from the muzzle of the rifle.

"Shoot him again!" Duff shouted, "In the neck!"

"With pleasure," said I, weakly, and planted my last round just behind his skull.

Duff and I looked at each other and said, "We're alive . . .!" as a faint Texan victory yell drifted down to us from the high hilltop where Jerry Henderson had watched the whole affair.

We were alive, and that was the luckiest break of all.

e gave the meat to our Masai guides, and they brought the skull and cape down the mountain for us the next day. It took three hours to skin him out. They built a fire, and as the skinner worked, we roasted chunks of Cape buffalo over the flames, carving off bites with our belt knives and tossing the remains to the Masai dogs.

The meat was tough, but juicy and rich tasting. Duff and I ate sparingly and chewed long. If you are what you eat, we were one mean bunch of bastards when we came down off that mountain.

Then the reaction set in. For two days I did little except stay in camp, sometimes talking, but mostly just off by myself. I set up a camp chair in the shade where I could catch the breeze through the day and look out across the plain to the smoke rising off the slopes of Kilimanjaro. I had a well-worn copy of Hemingway that has traveled with me around the world, and it was then I discovered that there are circumstances when you cannot read, so mostly I sat and stared at Kilimanjaro in the distance, or rose and walked to the edge of our camp and looked back up the slopes of Mount Longido.

Jerry Henderson has killed nineteen Cape buffalo over the years, and Duff Gifford several hundred at least. The big bull on Mount Longido was my third, so I am not exactly new to the game – and of course, I had read the stories and heard the tales.

In the first split-second when my buffalo burst from the bushes, I thought he was the most wonderful creature that ever lived, and when he dropped at my feet with a bullet in his brain and his eyes still open and fixed upon me, at that moment I knew a thousand times more about Cape buffalo than I had even minutes before.

OLD GLORY'S TROUT

Occasionally a man is given something he never really earns or deserves. How he responds can be the truest measure of his heart.

By Howard T. Walden

n the morning of a fateful day, Tom Garrison took the special-delivery letter from the boy who had bicycled and walked it all the way to the March Brown Club from the post office at Stony Forks. Before opening it, Tom looked at Professor Kent and me, who were getting into our waders. His glance had a lift of anticipation.

"It's from Doc Hatch," he said. The mere announcement, if you knew Doctor Hatch, founder, chief sustaining member and perennial renewer of jaded morales among the March Browns, was enough to spark your interest in the immediate course of events. For Hatch was not the man to write a special-delivery letter to tell you his wife's peonies were budding.

Tom opened it and read: "Englishman I met in El Alamein during the war – by name Brigadier General Edgerton H. Blake-Carrington – is in town looking for peace and not finding it. I'm sending him up to play with you guys. He has some fishing stuff but I haven't had time to see it. Putting him on Number 3 for the Forks on Wednesday. Meet him, one of you, and drive him in. A man of good will – and he damn near turned Rommel back from Alamein all by himself."

213

"Brigadier General Edgerton H. Blake-Carrington." The Professor intoned the syllables. "The name itself sounds like an artillery barrage. Wonder what the H stands for."

Tom knew a little about the General. "As it happened," he said, "he was Colonel of a British Eighth Army tank regiment in North Africa when Hatch met him. The word 'met' is hardly just. Hatch was over there with some other medicos on a government-sponsored look-see to find out about war wounds. At the time things were tough – Rommel had the British backed damn near to Alexandria. The then Colonel B-C was brought in with a leg torn up by shrapnel, the wounds full of sand and crank-case oil and whatnot. The British, who had discovered penicillin, didn't have any. Doc Hatch did. And Hatch considered B-C important to victory. Also, he liked B-C."

Tom fluttered the letter in his hand. "You can see by this that B-C didn't die."

"The Doc picks up the damnedest people," Professor Kent said, threading his line through the guides. "On Wednesday, his letter says. That's today. And Number 3 is due at Stony Forks at seven thirty, yes?"

"Yes," Tom said. "This very evening."

The professor said he would meet B-C. Poor Hatch, someone had to look after his global waifs. Never a season went by but what the Doctor found his refugee from the world's brashness and sent or brought him to our sanctuary on the Big Stony.

"The March Brown Protective Aid Society," Tom muttered to himself. He was knotting on a small Iron Blue Dun. "Why can't we have a little privacy now and then?"

"Somehow they never can fish worth a damn," the Professor said.

"That's why Hatch brings 'em up here," Tom observed. "By comparison, with them his own fishing looks almost professional."

This eminent surgeon, Hatch, though his enthusiasm for fishing knows no superior, is not notable for outsize trout, or indeed for trout. In his earlier seasons he committed every angling sin in the book, some so incredibly grotesque that, according to Tom, no one but Doctor Hatch could have committed them. The Compleat Tangler, Tom had named him, as I said on another page.

But this story concerns Doctor Hatch in a vicarious and absentee fashion. This time he was away, he hadn't fished with us for nearly a week, and only his ambassador from overseas was there to stand figuratively in his waders.

This is a story, first, of a trout, a kind of rebel among brown trout, who hit my marabou streamer early that very afternoon. That proved him an individualist, for brown trout of this one's dimensions are supposed to attack marabous and other minnow imitators only at night. Most browns have been, I think, regimented: they surface-feed when they're supposed to surface-feed, nymph when they're supposed to nymph. A dreary conformity has fastened upon the once unpredictable tribe of *Salmo trutta* or *fario*.

Just now they were supposed to be doing nothing. They had had word from their fuehrer about a disengaging action. But this heretic was able to defy all official edicts; maybe, indeed, he was the fuehrer himself. For by my poor standards he was a big brown. I saw his head, his dorsal fin, his tail, all at once, at the end of a thirty-foot cast. His head was bigger than your fist if you're not a longshoreman or Joe Louis. His dorsal fin was a forearm's length astern of that.

Tom and the Professor, wise fishermen, had gone in an hour before. My dark Hendrickson and others hadn't drawn a rise in an hour. There was streamside heat and a sabbath stillness and slack water devoid of insects or the bulges of feeding trout.

At this point a consultation of the manuals would have divulged a lure but would have revealed nothing about the pleasure of retiring from the stream at such a time.

Fifty yards upstream was the modest clubhouse of the March Browns; downstream were a thousand yards of the Big Stony which I could fish without poaching on the next fellow's water. I had those two alternatives to cope with, and the former was not without its casual enchantments. Our house has a screened porch with rocking chairs, overlooking the stream. Already I thought I could hear the creak of the rockers and the tinkle of ice in glasses . . . And yet, maybe I should try a few of those thousand downstream yards, with wet flies or nymphs or something, before going in.

I found myself taking off the Hendrickson or whatever it was. Somewhere I had read that a small Black Gnat, wet, would draw 'em in the slack motionless hours. Okay, maybe those disciplined browns had had word from their chief of staff about small Black Gnats.

I'll never know. Something else in the box caught my eye. Under a felt flap attached to the lid lay that siren of a marabou, that blonde witch whom I fancy as a potential retriever of days which are duds. Her white semblance of chastity is beguiling in sentimental or desperate moods.

She was on as quickly as you can hum the first bar of the Lorelei. She was on too quickly, in fact, for I didn't even pause to change my 3X leader for one stout enough to hold the kind of prospect who might be interested. A grave error, of course. I knew it but I let it slide. Roll-casting the marabou across the lower reach of the Club Pool would be what it had usually been, a nice exercise in tactics, nothing more.

A sunken log lay against the far bank, thirty feet from where I stood in midstream. On the first business cast after getting her wet, the marabou came down over the log, the current had her at once and I started the little jerky retrieve, keeping her close under the surface and watching her swim, tracing the shimmering silvery course –

At first, when I saw it, I didn't believe it. There was a split second of incredulity, of downright denial of the whole affair. That fish coming out from under the log was too big for anyone to believe. I saw him whole – his head and his open jaws, his topline, dorsal fin and upper tail. He assaulted the marabou in

215

a single and savage thrust amid a great surface swirl of water.

I struck – after the moment of disbelief had passed and realization had seeped bright and hot into all this make-believe fancy. I felt an immovable resistance for an instant, and then the break and the weightless emptiness, and looked over my shoulder to see my line and part of my leader written all destitute on the surface upstream. The ripples were spreading away from the scene of the crime; otherwise I could have believed I had dreamed it all.

Back at the house, five minutes later, my story was accorded an almost militant indifference.

"Pour yourself a drink," Tom said. "How big d'you say he was?"

"I have my ideas of course, but you wouldn't subscribe to them."

Tom yawned and made small circular motions with his glass, tinkling the ice around. "Well, *about* how big?"

"Twenty-five inches. A minimum guarantee of two feet. And heavy."

They were unimpressed. "Supposed he had been twenty-eight inches," the Professor remarked. "It's tougher to lose a twenty-eight-inch fish than a twenty-five-incher, any day. You're not so badly off."

"Your lot could be worse," Tom echoed. "You might be unemployed, with twelve kids. Cheer up, my friend."

You would think that a subject so devoid of fascination as my hypothetical fish would be dropped. There were other things to talk about, certainly – the labor situation and the Democratic primaries and the probable rise in agricultural purchasing power. But one or two desultory attempts to switch the talk onto some such vital topic got nowhere at all.

"Probably seventeen inches," the Professor said after a while, as if talking to himself.

"What's seventeen inches?" I inquired.

"Oh, er, your fish."

"Listen, you damn cynics –"

"I assume you're going back after him," Tom said, "after he has had time to quiet down."

I said that I was, tonight, and if anyone messed around the Club Pool before then –

Tom drummed his fingernails on the arm of the rocker and addressed the Professor in a resigned voice. "Here we are up here on a respite with this – this extremist. Expenses, fun, responsibilities, pleasures – all are split three for one. If I hook a dollar bill with my fly each of you gets 33 cents of it. But now we run up against what may be a fair fish and –"

They shamed me out of it with their innuendos, feints and oblique sorties around my poorly defended flanks. I surrendered the rights to that fish to each of them; one hour apiece on the Club Pool before I should again try it myself, they

216

to toss for choice of time, and the same hour-apiece sequence to continue, with rest periods between, until the fish or our patience expired.

The Professor won the toss for the privilege of opening the offensive. Mindful of his mission in Stony Forks he chose the hour of six to seven P.M. Then he would meet the General and return to camp with him about eight o'clock.

Tom allowed that he should be on hand when the General arrived, so he chose the hour of nine to ten. That left me with a late-afternoon hour (too soon) or a midnightish one (too dark). I opted for tomorrow's dawn. If I had pricked that trout badly, the longer rest would be helpful.

Fishing with his usual precision the Professor drew a goose egg in his evening hour and departed to meet General Blake-Carrington at Stony Forks.

T om and I had supper and at eight o'clock the Professor drove in with the General. The Professor introduced us and when no one was looking he winked at me solemnly. Doctor Hatch's North African find was an upright and formidable soldier, a giant of a man who seemed at first glance imbued with the physical attributes of the tanks he had shepherded across Libya's and Egypt's sands. His face was the color of a desert sunset. If you thought of his wounds at all, you could judge when he walked that the repair of the leg was complete. Hatch had run the show when they had put the odd pieces of that leg together. This job, you had heard from Tom via the esoteric world of medicine, and you knew it now in your own terms, was one of Hatch's best. You wondered how the hands which had managed that piece of surgery could so bungle a dry-fly cast. And you loved the Doctor a little more for that bungling which was so specially his.

General Blake-Carrington smiled down at us, put out his great hand and disarmed at once the vast formidability of his presence. He protested his utter lack of trout-fishing knowledge, but conceded that the sport might be jolly. He had brought up what he called a "hybrid and possibly quite wrong" outfit and hoped to try it in the morning. Would we look over his gear later, when he had unpacked, and advise him on the fundamentals of fishing?

I accompanied Tom to the stream for his postponed hour, to kibitz his operations from the bank and to give the General time to get settled. Halfway through his allotted time Tom took a twelve-inch rainbow who danced all over the Club Pool in the course of the fight, so disrupting that placid stretch that Tom finished out his period in the long riffle upstream. "Anyway," he said, "how do we know he'll stay where he was?"

Well, how did we? That shallow run above the Club Pool is a place for a big brown to feed in the hours of dusk or dark. And maybe dawn.

Maybe dawn . . . I thought about it as we walked back to the club. British people, I have heard, are early risers. British literature is full of dew and dawn mists and the cock's shrill clarion. It would be just like General Blake-Carrington . . .

217

The Professor met us outside in the firefly-studded dark. "Wait till you see his stuff," he said.

"Nice?" Tom inquired.

"His surf rod's a beauty," the Professor said, and I remembered his wink when he was taking the General's gear out of the car.

General B-C was well settled, except for his fishing things, when we entered. Smoking a large pipe before the fire, he was surrounded and besieged by a mess of the strangest oddments of fishing equipment ever seen on the Big Stony's banks. British understatement had been implicit in the General's recent appraisal of his tackle. "Hybrid and possibly quite wrong" was no fit way to describe the awful heterogeneity of gear to which he introduced us. A hybrid is a blue-blooded aristocrat compared with the many-sired rabble which the good Briton offered for our inspection. Saltwater rods were married to freshwater reels and these were wound with yards of Cuttyhunk. A four-ounce pyramid sinker and a #12 Parmacheene Belle kept company as the terminal gear of one rig; at the end of another yardage of stout seagoing string a nine-foot tapered leader was attached to a three-way swivel. Neatly arranged on the mantelpiece was a goodly complement of surf squids, cork floats, #20 nymphs, more sinkers and a bottle of dry-fly oil.

"Where's your swordfish pulpit, General?" Tom asked.

The General admitted that he had seldom, if ever, fished before. "This paraphernalia," he explained, "was loaned to me by a number of friends –"

"Friends?" I echoed.

" – of diverse fishing habits. Some are saltwater fellows, others seem to like frogging about in ponds. I took whatever was offered. Last night in my flat I tried to put bits of it together. It does appear, now, that some of my rigs are ill-conceived, indeed perhaps quite unworkable on these waters."

"Quite," the Professor agreed. "Do you mind if we unhook 'em and fix up a good one for you?"

The General seemed profoundly relieved to place himself and all his borrowed angling goods unreservedly in our hands. In an hour we had unscrambled the ill-mated pairs and set up the best fly-fishing assembly that could be effected with the stock at hand. Two simple rigs on level leaders: one a wet-fly combination of Cahill dropper and Coachman tail, the other a plain Mickey Finn. Some dry flies and tapered leaders we let alone, fearing to get the General over his depth on his first try.

Tom suggested a worm if the fly rigs proved troublesome. We gave the General a few hooks and advised him on handling a big fish and other tenets of the lore. Also, we told him of the lunker we had marked down in the Club Pool and the details of our campaign.

Though no fisherman, the General was instinctively sound in his perceptions. "It's as serious as that, eh?" he said. "Of course I'll keep off this pool then."

I hurried to invite him to fish any and all of our water, feeling a little awkward at his show of deference. He wouldn't take that trout in a century but the chance of his disturbing the fish concerned me.

218

I overstayed the alarm in the morning, and to save time decided to forego the bacon and eggs. A pot of coffee, half full, was on the stove, apparently left from last night though I didn't remember it. I heated it, gulped a cupful and went to the tail of the Club Pool as the dark thinned and the first birds became vocal. The sort of morning I wanted was easing in out of the night – windless and warm and full of a gray mist that didn't augur rain but was just part of the dawn trappings. Already, as I rigged up, three fish of twelve inches or so were rising within casting range. It was a temptation to go after them, to rig light and fine with a small gold-ribbed Hare's Ear. But the presence of these lesser fish was of course a fair sign of the absence of the greater one.

I thought again of the shallow run above the Club Pool. In that lower part of it which I could see from here, no break was apparent anywhere on its surface. It might be just the place and the time. I tied on the best 1X leader I had and started up there. The lure could wait. Maybe I'd see him show or gather otherwise some inkling of what he might be up to.

The Big Stony curves above the top of the Club Pool and as I walked along more of it became visible to me. I had covered part of the distance when something caught my eye a hundred yards up river.

A man, a tall, rubber-booted, tweeded and curve-stem-pipe man stood knee-deep in the stream, slowly reeling in line to his dangerously bent rod. It was, I saw, the Briton, the Carrington, that Blake. He had been up ahead of me; had neatly made breakfast while I slept, and left the coffee for me.

A tremendous slow surge on the surface, forty feet below the General, showed momentarily the flanks and fanlike tail of a great trout. I hurried toward him along the stones of the bank.

That fish was done; the General, somehow, had licked him many minutes before, there in the predawn darkness. The level leader had so far held. But the job wasn't over. There was still the yard-by-yard operation of bringing him home, and the landing. I thought of the final exhausted surge that has won many a big trout its freedom, and at the same time I noticed that the General had no net. Fortunately, mine was big, bigger than I almost ever need.

"Easy," I said. "Lower your rod a little."

"He's played out, quite, poor fellow," the General observed casually. "An absurdly long tussle, really."

"They're never safe until they're on dry land. Get him into this quiet water and I'll net him for you."

"Net him?"

"Of course. There's no good beach here – and even if there were . . ." I prayed for that leader, and it held. "That's it – a little more. Easy." A great heavy fish, as long as an axe handle and with spots as big as nickels, he was resisting still with his last strength. The net went under him from down-current, came up and lifted him clear.

With the sudden slack line the General's hook and the remains of a gob of

219

worms came free. "I tried the flies at first," he explained, "but they became desperately tangled in the shrubbery."

Well up on the bank I put the trout down and stood feasting my reverent eyes on his heroic dimensions. The General seemed delighted with his success. Then I saw something in the corner of that great mouth. "It's him," I said.

"Eh? Who?" General Blake-Carrington was comfortable about ignoring my grammatical slip.

"The trout we told you about last night. Look." Working gently I extracted my marabou streamer from the trout's lip. "He hit that yesterday."

"Oh, he is really yours, then."

"Like hell he's mine. I lost him, you got him."

And as I released the marabou I saw something else, or what was left of it, deeper in the big jaw. Another lure, a bucktail about the size of my marabou but it wasn't like anything any of us used. It had red, white and blue wisps of deer hair still clinging to the long hook shank. It had been there for days, I judged. Some poacher's bucktail no doubt, a badly tied job. To extract it would be a major operation so I snipped the hook. The General asked to see it and when I handed it to him he regarded it closely, for a long moment.

"I say," he said, "he really won't live much longer. Don't you think, before he expires, we'd better put him back?"

"Back?" It was a sudden and unforeseen turn of affairs. The General had felt pretty good about that fish. "God, General, you're sporting," I observed.

"Sporting? How, sir?"

"You've seldom fished and maybe you don't know. But in this country, and I guess in yours, it's sporting to put a trout that size back in the stream. Not only sporting but maybe foolish. They're terrific predators on smaller trout."

"I see," he said slowly. "Well, he has earned his freedom. He fought me to a standstill for twenty minutes before you came with the net. And he's dying. Are we sportsmen, eh – you and I? And as to his predations, well, we perpetrate ours too, I dare say."

Of all fish, this was one I didn't want to see lost. There were those two unbelievers, asleep back there in the club. But the General was challenging me now. And I'd have to answer him quickly. There was a dying labor in the great gills, and a slow alternate expansion and contraction of the fins.

"Look, General," I pleaded, "you've seen haddock that large in stores. They're fish – so much a pound. But a stream-caught trout this size isn't a fish, it's a miracle. This one you have here – I'd give my right arm for. Oh hell, never mind. He's the prize of a lifetime, that's all. And he's yours. I'll knife him now for you –"

"I don't want him," the General said, very simply.

I was annoyed a little at the futility of trying to persuade this rock of a Briton. "What's the real pitch on this?" I asked. "Are you giving him up because you think he's rightfully our fish – because of what we told you last night?"

He didn't answer at once and, when he did, his reply seemed evasive and hesitant. "It is rightfully your fish," he said. "You chaps run the show up here, have your scheduled campaigns all nicely arranged. Your hearts are set on this fellow. And I'm just a visiting amateur – I didn't angle for him as you would."

He didn't sound convincing. Few more if any such fish were in the Big Stony but some good ones were left and General Blake-Carrington thought we were fishermen enough to take them. There was another reason but for the life I couldn't track it down. Maybe, like some other soldiers who have killed men in war, this one wouldn't kill game or fish for sport. There were such men. But I considered that a moment and decided it was no good.

I took out the thirty-inch tape I brazenly carry and laid it along the trout's length from tip of the lower jaw to the center of the tail. "Twenty-six and a quarter inches," I announced.

I would extract whatever thin juice of moral triumph might be left in the core of defeat. "General," I said, "before we put him back, do you swear that you will bear witness that this is the true and exact length of this brown trout, to any and every one who may question us on same, particularly those two skeptics in yonder cabin?"

He avoided my direct look for a second, then he turned to me squarely. "No," he said, "not to any and every one – not to your two friends. I am going to ask – and I must insist on this – that you never tell Hatch I caught this fish. Don't let him ever know, directly or indirectly.

"Okay. But why?"

"It might – it might hurt his pride. A swashbuckling fellow, this Hatch, but under it is something fine and vulnerable. I, for one, wouldn't hurt that thing."

I thought I saw a light.

"Doc Hatch really saved your life, didn't he?" I asked.

The General answered quietly: "He did, sir. And with anyone else in the world on that job I'd be a helpless cripple today, if alive – at all. Anyone else in the world, I say . . . Hatch was lucky, indeed, that he didn't lose his own life while mending me."

I looked at him inquiringly. The Doctor had never intimated this to any of us.

"The hospital tent, if you could call it that, was under heavy fire. Two orderlies, helping Hatch, were killed."

I asked, after a moment, "Did he ever indicate, if I'm not too inquisitive, that never in all his fishing life has he caught a really distinguished trout?"

"I gathered that, yes. But look here, Doctor Hatch has had a distinguished trout *hooked* – and very nearly landed."

"So?" The single word must have asked where, when, how, everything.

"Indeed. Last week when he was up here with you fellows. A distinguished trout, sir, by your own admission." He pointed to the fish at our feet. "That trout," he went on, "was very nearly Doctor Hatch's fish. On this –" He held up the remnants of the red-white-and-blue bucktail. "Hatch tied this himself, called it 'Old Glory.' Ever see it before this morning?"

"Never." I could only look, very blankly, at General Blake-Carrington.

"Exactly. Hatch is like that. His queer pride, you see. You chaps would have ribbed him. Same way with the fish – if he had told you of his half hour's battle, and of losing the fish at the end, you wouldn't have believed *that*, he thought."

I still couldn't find any clear words to offer the General.

"But he told *me*, for I'm a worse blunderer than Hatch himself. He needed an audience and I was a safe one, what? But if he knew that with all my vast incompetence *I* had caught this big one that he lost . . . Let's save Old Glory's trout for Hatch. A sort of reverse lend-lease, eh? Maybe Hatch will hook him again. Or one of you chaps, in your scheduled periods. Any of that would be all right. But for *me* to take him – no."

I looked down at the trout again. There was still time but not much. "All right," I said. "Wet both your hands in the stream, gather up your fish and wade out there with him. Don't drop him in; ease him in very gently."

He did as he was told. I stood beside him as he lowered the huge trout into the stream. The fish hung in the current for a moment as if unaware of its freedom, then the tail and the fins moved and the great form faded slowly downstream.

The General watched the V-ripple spread out. "I've seen an almost spent torpedo make the same show," he said.

He looked at me and smiled a half-embarrassed little smile, like a boy. I could see that he felt much better about the whole thing, not with any smug pride, but in a way that was private and warm. He had been in a spot, as I see it now. He could have let me find my own reasons for his decision to release his fish. It might have been easier that way. But B-C had taken a decent course without letting Hatch down. If his simple loyalty was without logic, so are many of the profound convictions of men. It had truth, as the dark reasoning of the heart knows truth.

Wait till I see Hatch, I was thinking, who sends his agents, his foreign spies, to find his fish and save them for him . . . Then I remembered I'd committed myself to secrecy for all time. And suddenly I knew that if ever I should land that trout I'd release it. The Doctor just *might* hook it again.

"I'm sorry about *you*, sir," the General said, as if reading my thought. "Could we go up to my room and have a drink to that fish – and to our bitter little secret?"

"Old Glory's Trout" is from The Last Pool, *published by Crown Publishers in 1972.*

222

THE PURSUIT OF PETER BELLISE

He had come to this dark and lonely world to fulfill the dream of another. But now, as the ring of gaunt and hungry wolves pressed closer and closer, the other man's dream had become his worst nightmare.

By Robert W. Murphy

he half-breed, Peter Bellise, beached the canoe, stepped out, and pulled it up on the shore. He was a stocky man, barrel-chested and muscled like a bull, but graceful; his swarthy, pleasant face was a little thin because he had just returned from a hard month in the back country laying out a new trapline. He started up the hill toward the log buildings of the Hudson's Bay Company with the woodsman's short, quick stride, and the pack of wolfish dogs belonging to the Indians camped about rushed down to snarl at him. He stooped for a stone and threw it without breaking his stride; there was a yelp, and the pack, recognizing an experienced man, promptly lost interest in him.

In the fragrant dimness of the store, the factor, Duncan MacDonald, was patiently waiting on an indecisive squaw. Bellise leaned against the opposite counter and drew a deep breath to savor the smells of the place: the smoke-tanned leather; the black rope tobacco; sweetgrass from the muskegs made into baskets; bacon, coffee; the freshness of new ash canoe paddles and the

223

faint fragrance of maple sugar. These things were good to him; he closed his eyes, took another deep breath and held it, and when he opened his eyes again, the squaw had made her decision and was going out the door.

MacDonald came across the store, tall and rangy in the gloom. "Hello, Bellise," he said. His words had a faint burr to them, for he was a Highland man. "You got my message, I take it. It means a trip, and you'd be wanting a few days' rest first."

"Sure," Bellise said. "I rest four-five days, mebbe. I have long trip, I eat little. Game, she is ver' scarce."

"Ay," MacDonald said. "It will be a bad winter, I reckon, with the rabbits low." He was silent for a moment and looked at Bellise with a faint smile, for Bellise was a good and trustworthy man. "It's a letter from Morton, in the States. Morton wants his gyrfalcons. He's come back from the war."

"So," Bellise said. He had forgotten Andrew Morton and the airplane Morton had sent for him on MacDonald's recommendation four years before. In that airplane he had flown high above the earth for uncounted miles, into a fabulous world that was like a strange dream even now. He had spent a month in a place called Long Island, with a man who trained hawks for Morton. Under this man's instruction he had learned to handle hawks himself – to catch them, take care of them, fly them at game. It had been an interesting thing, even more strange than the world in which he found himself for a time. Morton's peregrine falcons had captured his hunter's imagination with their terrible and breathtaking plunges from the upper air upon their quarry; their look of wild freedom, even when they were on their blocks, leashed and earth-bound, had found an echo in his freedom-loving spirit. "I want you to learn this," Morton had said, "because you are to go up around Hudson Bay and bring some of these out." He showed Bellise a mounted gyrfalcon; it was larger than a peregrine, the largest of the falcons. "They're better fliers than the peregrines, Bellise; they're big enough to handle anything. Nobody's had any gyrfalcons for a long time. They'll never make it alive if you don't learn all you can here."

Bellise had learned well; he would have gone north two weeks after the plane had brought him home, if the war hadn't broken out. Thinking back on it, he still couldn't understand why Morton had gone into such an elaborate affair, why Morton would spend more money on hawks in a year than would have maintained him, Bellise, in great splendor for a lifetime.

"Me, I do not know why he does this," he said to MacDonald, bringing his thoughts back to the present again. "The hawks, they have the great beauty when they fly, yes. But he does not need meat, and a gun kills more."

"Havers!" MacDonald said. "It's a sport. They don't trap foxes; they get horses and a great pack of dogs and chase them all over creation." They looked at each other for a moment, a little bemused by the outlandish vagaries of rich men, and more than a little scandalized by the enormous expense of these vagaries. "You'll go?" MacDonald asked finally.

224

"I go, me," Bellise said. "I take dog team, hein?"

"Ay," MacDonald said. "I'll send an Injun to the telegraph. He said to do that. He's going to send a bush flier here to pick you up and take you north."

"Bien," Bellise said. He was silent for a moment; the recollection came to him of the fenced fields, the multitude of No Trespass signs and the lack of freedom, the two men he had knocked down because they tried to tell him where he couldn't walk. He rubbed his cheek and glanced at MacDonald. "Me, I do not think they will live with M'sieu Morton, these hawks."

"Eh?" MacDonald said. He had caught a faint note of regret in Bellise's tone, and it puzzled him. No breed or Indian, in his experience, had ever indicated sympathy for any bird or beast before. "Don't you want to do it?"

"Is ver' warm there," Bellise said, avoiding a direct answer. He shrugged. "The hawks," he said, "they have the great beauty when they fly." He looked at MacDonald as though he were a little ashamed of himself.

The last few hours of the trip they flew above snowstorms, and the bleak shore was snow-covered when the pilot, Burnside, made his landing and brought the plane into a little flat beach. They got the dogs off first, and then the three boxes of pigeons and the sledge.

"So pigeons was what they have in those boxes," Burnside said. "Well, now I've seen everything, even a man taking pigeons to the North Pole. Maybe you'll be sending one of them with a message to MacDonald when you want to come home."

"No," Bellise said. "Two weeks you come back. I meet you here."

"Okay," Burnside said. "You and the pigeons meet me here. You be here, though. The weather won't get any better from now on. It'll probably be so bad I won't be able to stick around."

Bellise nodded; they finished unloading the plane, and Burnside started the motor. He let the plane drift out a little way, waved, turned into the wind, and gunned the motor. The plane went down the bay in a cloud of flying spray, took off, and quickly vanished toward the south.

When it was out of sight, Bellise pitched the tent, fed the dogs and straightened up the camp. He put the pigeon boxes on the lee side of the tent, to keep most of the wind off them, started the alcohol stove, and cooked his supper. The bleak landscape and the farther bare rocky headlands of the shore darkened rapidly as he ate; it was very dark when he had finished. He smoked a pipe by the light of the gasoline lantern, relaxed, contented and comfortable. It began to snow again, and he knocked out his pipe, extinguished the lantern and crawled into his sleeping bag. For a time the dark and lonely world was held by silence, disturbed only by the whisper of the snow on the sides of the tent. Then, far off, a wolf howled. Another answered it, and was in turn answered by the wailing, melancholy howl of a third. Bellise stirred in his sleeping bag. He grunted at the sounds; they

225

indicated that the wolves, finding the hunting difficult, were drawing together into a pack. Hungry wolves would dare far more in a pack than they would dare singly or in pairs, and the wolves of this place had not had enough experience with man and his firearms to maintain their proper distance.

The snow had stopped falling by morning, and Bellise began flying his pigeons. He let half of them out, and stood by, waving a shirt to keep them from returning to their box. They flew well, wheeling and darting in their formations against the pale sky; if there had been a gyrfalcon within miles, it would have come and pitched among them like a thunderbolt, but no gyrfalcon appeared. After half an hour, Bellise let the pigeons return, shut them up and fed them. He was a little disappointed, but not too much; most of the ducks and shorebirds had gone, and there was little to hold hawks near the bay.

In the afternoon he hitched up the dog team and took a box of pigeons several miles up the shore, to the highest headland in the vicinity, and let them out. From the height upon which he stood, the world was even more lonely and inimical than from the camp – a world of leaden water, barren, rocky shore, and broken country white with snow and seemingly empty of life. He was used to loneliness, but not of this sort. He could see too much and too far; he liked better the forests where he ran traplines, which were as empty of man, but had a still and somber friendliness.

The pigeons mounted high above him, their wings flashing as they swung between him and the declining sun. They seemed to accentuate the loneliness of the land, and as he watched them the thought came to him that it was a foolish thing to take a hawk, grown in the cold, sweeping vastness of the country, into the soft land of little fields of the south. The leashed peregrines, birds of more settled lands, always seemed to be longing for the wide sky; it would be worse for gyrfalcons. His mind played about this thought for a while, and presently he shrugged, let the pigeons come in, and went back to camp.

That night the wolves came closer. They gathered about a thousand yards away and awoke him with their howling. He got out of the sleeping bag with a curse, picked up the rifle, and went outside. It was cold and clear, the stars glittered frostily; the dogs, growling, had gathered close to the tent, and they crowded around him. He cursed them in the same tone he had used for the wolves, and fired a shot toward the howling. The night swallowed the sound, and the wolves immediately fell silent. He stood listening for a moment to a quiet that seemed to stretch to the ends of the earth, and went back into the tent again.

The next morning he broke camp and started inland. He traveled for three days, flying the pigeons morning and afternoon, without seeing a gyrfalcon. More snow fell; it nearly covered the low scrub now, and because the country was flat, broken only by gullies and occasional high points of land that looked pretty much alike, he began to get the feeling that no matter how long he walked, he was always in the same place.

He was a little disappointed by the scarcity of hawks, and the wolves had begun to irritate him. Ordinarily, he had a great contempt for wolves, or at least for the timber wolves he knew. They kept out of the way or, at most, howled once or twice from a distant vantage point, and went on. These, which he decided were white wolves from farther north, driven down by hunger, didn't go away. They hung on, shadowing him, and every night they seemed to come a bit closer. The dogs were in great fear of them; always underfoot, snarling into the dark. Bellise's sleep was broken into; he began trying to bushwhack them during the day, staking the dogs out and hiding among the gullies and hummocks, but with no success.

In the middle of the fourth night he was awakened by a hysterical and bloodcurdling uproar around the tent. He got out of the sleeping bag, grabbed the rifle and ran out. There was a thin moon; the dogs crowded around him, and stumbling about he saw a great white beast, with its head high, running off with a dog nearly as big as itself in its jaws. It wasn't more than fifteen yards away, and rapidly vanishing into the gloom. He shot. The wolf dropped the dog and fell, rolled over, then got up on its forelegs and dragged itself swiftly out of sight. A few seconds later he heard the rest of them finish it.

The next morning he started on a wide circle that would take him back toward the bay. It had been six days since Burnside had left him, and he estimated that it would take him six or seven more to get back. He had lost one dog, and thought it possible that he would lose one or two more, which would slow him down, but he was sure that the killing of the wolf the night before would make the rest of them more cautious for a time.

The day was uneventful until after noon, when three ptarmigan flushed forty or fifty yards in front of him. He was idly watching them fly off when he chanced to glance above them, into the sky. He stopped in midstride, staring; for high in the blue he saw a tiny dot dropping. It hurtled down with such tremendous speed that he had difficulty following it; its velocity through the air made a sound like tearing silk, and Bellise's skin crawled as he watched. It hit the leading ptarmigan; there was a crash like the report of a gun, and an explosion of feathers. The ptarmigan rolled over and fell; the gyrfalcon swung up, paused for an instant, and swooped. It picked the ptarmigan from the snow and carried it to a rocky knoll about a mile away.

It had been the most spectacular stoop Bellise had ever seen, a terrible thing, much higher and harder than any made by Morton's peregrines. It had brought his heart into his throat, and he knew now why Morton, as a falconer, wanted a gyrfalcon or two. He let out the breath he had unconsciously been holding, and decided to camp where he stood. He unharnessed the dogs, pitched the tent, and began to straighten out the gear he would use in the morning.

The gyrfalcon had slept on a high shelf running across the precipitous face of the rocky knoll, and awoke with the first faint gleam of light. She was a big, sleek bird with the hooked beak, large dark eyes, and needle-sharp talons of all falcons, immaculately white on her crown and upper back and tail, with a few dark lines on the sides of her head; her wing and upper tail coverts and lower back were barred with arrow-shaped spots of blackish brown.

She had eaten late, and not being hungry, she was still for several hours; her stillness was far from being an inattentive one. She was never inattentive. On that eminence above the plain, with her superlative vision, she would instantly have seen anything that moved within an immense area. She was out of sight of Bellise, having gone over the top of the knoll with the ptarmigan the afternoon before to get out of the wind, and the rock hid him.

The mounting sun warmed her; she stared at it with fierce eyes and spread her wings a little to take in its warmth. Presently she felt the beginning of hunger, not pressing, but pleasant; she shook herself again, walked to the edge of the shelf, and jumped into the air. The warmed, rising currents took her, and her long narrow wings beat upon them. They flowed around her like water, firm and sustaining, but shifty enough to make the managing of them a keen wild pleasure. She went straight away from the knoll for several miles, rising slowly higher, until she found a great updraft. She swung into this; it took her up several thousand feet without effort. The earth sank away and curved off to the far horizons, white and empty, and she hung with her wings still and her head to the wind.

It was then that she saw, far away, the pigeons wheeling about. Hunger stabbed her, and she started for them at tremendous speed. As she crossed high above the knoll, the pigeons caught sight of her and hesitated in their swinging. She was above them a few seconds later; she selected one, rolled over, and giving a few swift wingbeats, started straight down like a meteor. The pigeons were fleeing when she started her stoop. They flashed down to their box sitting in the snow; the last one managed to hurl itself through the door three feet in front of the hawk, which swooped up to hang above the box, puzzled.

As she hung there, another pigeon appeared from beneath a mound of snow, struggling as though it were being pulled by a cord across the ground. The gyrfalcon dropped on it; it moved another two or three feet, and then the bow net banged over them. The gyrfalcon screamed with rage, rolled over on her back, and took the net in her talons, but it was thin and bodiless, and she could not hurt it. She was caught.

Fifty yards away, Bellise threw up the white canvas under which he had been hiding, and stood up. He held tightly the cord attached to the pigeon and the cord attached to the net, and ran up. Working quickly, he disentangled the gyrfalcon, slipped a leather hood over her head, and put her into a woolen sock. She was blinded and bound, and so shocked that she didn't struggle any more. Her freedom was ended.

As soon as Bellise got back to the tent, he put leather straps – jesses – on the gyrfalcon's legs and began to man her. This was a procedure as old as falconry, and had been standardized for centuries. It consisted of carrying her, hooded, on his fist for hours at a time, keeping her awake, stroking her with a short stick and talking to her; in this way her wildness was slowly overcome and she was made accustomed to man. She didn't take kindly to it. Although she couldn't see, she wanted her freedom desperately; she jumped off innumerable times, flapped about and hung head down; and innumerable times he replaced her gently and patiently. He made supper and fed the dogs, carrying her, then decided to carry her all night. He pulled the sleeping bag to the door of the tent, laid the rifle handy, and wrapped himself up.

It wasn't so bad for the first four or five hours; the gyrfalcon jumped off his fist frequently and kept him occupied. After midnight, however, although she was still ready to hiss and bite at the stroking stick, she began to tire. The gyrfalcon's head fell forward occasionally, and Bellise rolled his fist to wake her, but that was all he had to do. A pale aurora began to play; the long, ghostly beams marched with majestic silence across the sky.

In the immense and brooding silence, Bellise, robbed of sleep by the wolves, began to nod. His arm dropped, and the struggling bird awoke him; he got a block, put her on it, and nodded again. He dreamed of the gyrfalcon: the hooked beak no more cruel than the land that nourished it, the dark, hooded stare and the fierce will that flung it a thousand feet down through the cold and empty air. In his dream the bird screamed defiance at him, the screaming grew louder, and he awoke to find the wolves in camp again.

The snarling confusion swirled close around him in the aurora's pale light, almost across his feet. The gyrfalcon was flapping wildly at the end of its leash, and his plight seemed so desperate to his startled and half-awake senses that he didn't act coolly. He caught up the rifle and emptied it among the great leaping white forms; the shots crashed against the night. Almost instantly the dogs were about him and the wolves gone. A dead dog and a dead wolf were lying in the torn snow, and Bellise ran into the tent for the cartridge box.

He couldn't find it. He switched on the hanging flashlight and frantically turned everything upside down in his search, but it wasn't there. He enforced deliberateness on himself and searched again, panting. But it was gone; he had lost it somewhere, in packing or unpacking, or on the trail. He knew that he would never find it, and cold sweat came out all over him.

He straightened up slowly and walked to the entrance of the tent. The aurora was dying out, and as he watched darkness cover the land again, calmness came to him. He estimated his chances, and knew them to be poor, but far from hopeless; he had got out of situations before that had seemed as desperate. All he had to do was get to the shore of the bay and hold on until Burnside came – and Burnside would be early rather than late.

He looked at the dogs. There were three left instead of the four he expected; the wolves had apparently carried one off; and of the three, one was going to be dead by morning. He brought them all into the tent, unhooded the gyrfalcon in the dark and left it on its block, and got into his sleeping bag. Before he went to sleep he made what plans he could.

He awoke before it was light. The gyrfalcon hissed at him and fought him, but he hooded her, and after carrying her for a time, finally got her to eat a little. He knew he should use the time spent on her to better advantage, but the time he spent on her was partly for Morton, who had paid his money to have her brought out in good shape, and partly a gesture, a defiance, belonging to the exhilaration he had felt the night before; he was determined to take her out, cost what it might. Then he carefully selected the things he intended to leave – things that added to his comfort, but were not necessary, such as the tent. He killed most of the pigeons, and so got rid of one of the boxes; dead pigeons were easier to carry, and would keep as well frozen.

The injured dog had died during the night, and because the two that were left could make little progress, he pulled with them. It was awkward work on snowshoes, and to complicate it, he carried the gyrfalcon on his fist most of the time. This cut into his traveling badly, for she continued to jump off despite the hood, to try, although unable to see, to regain her freedom. He knew exactly how much time and effort it would cost him to continue to carry her, but kept on with it. After he had camped and eaten, he carried her long after dark; she struggled as much as on the first evening. There should have been a slight indication that she was resigning herself, but there was none.

The wolves left him alone that night, but early in the afternoon of the next day, for the first time, he saw two of them. They came out from behind a hill at their deceptive, sliding gait, paused and stood watching him, just within rifle range. It was as though they suspected he couldn't shoot at them and were trying him out. He stopped and waved the useless rifle at them, but they didn't move.

After watching them for a time, he put the rifle back on the sled, and for the rest of the afternoon stopped frequently to dig stunted trees and bushes out of the snow and chop them up. He piled the sled with firewood, until he had enough to keep a fire going all night. He camped early that night, and built a small fire as soon as it began to grow dark. A thin sickle moon climbed the sky; he ate and fed the dogs and carried the gyrfalcon, but she still showed no signs of growing calmer.

The night wore on; he was awakened to replenish the fire by the gyrfalcon jumping from his fist or an increased snarling from the dogs as the wolves drew in a little closer. When he threw on more wood, he could see their eyes shifting and vanishing as they drew back, then gleam faintly farther away. He didn't get much sleep, and was not much rested in the morning.

That day the wolves didn't bother to conceal themselves as they followed him. They had grown much bolder. They trailed him openly, following two hundred yards or so behind the sled. There were nine of them left, great powerful brutes so thin that they looked like perambulating skeletons covered with fur, and he was a little dismayed when he first counted them. He would have felt confident of being able to cope with two or three with the ax if they rushed him during the night; he could do nothing against nine.

He built two fires that night and stayed between them. The wolves came closer; they were no longer vague shapes in the dim light of the crescent moon, but close at hand, dreadfully thin and patient creatures regarding him wistfully, outlined by the glow of the fire. He hardly slept at all.

By noon the next day even his great strength began to break. There were moments when he fell asleep pulling on the sled, and awoke to the gyrfalcon's flapping wings and the snarls of the dogs, standing still, confused and with the faceless white land heaving around him and the wolves moving in. Everything became detached and a little distant, like events in a grim and improbable dream. He lost track of time; he moved like an automaton; he cut more wood and built more fires. He surrounded himself with fires; at one time he thrust a flaming branch into the muzzle of a wolf that had got to within arm's length of him, and laughed at the smell of burning hair and the animal's yelp as it plunged about, cooling its mouth in the snow.

Then, suddenly, he was rational again. It was day; fire surrounded him, and wolves surrounded the fire. He was on a height of land, and far off he could see the dull waters of the bay. It seemed an impossible distance, a mirage on the horizon. He stood up, and the circle about him stirred; the wolves stood up, yawned and stretched. He stepped over the fire; the nearest wolf slashed at him; the circle surged forward. He dodged back of the fire again, and with flailing arms threw embers and blazing brands among them until he forced them back.

One dog had vanished, and he had not even seen it go; it had been forced beyond the fire, torn to pieces and devoured in the moment his back was turned. He built up the fire again with desperate haste, and knew that he would never get beyond it and that soon the wood would be gone. He would never get to the bay. He turned and saw the gyrfalcon on its block close behind him, and picked it up. It hissed and struck at him, and jumped from his fist. It was as wild as it had always been; the carrying and handling he had given it, which would have manned any other falcon he had ever known, had made no impression on it whatever. It wasn't stupidity that made the bird continue to batter itself hopelessly about, but the complete and essential wildness of its spirit, its unyielding determination to be free.

He wondered for a moment whether he could ever have tamed it, and it pleased him to know that he wouldn't have the chance. For he had tried his best to take Morton the bird he had paid for, and his honor was satisfied; it could be free now, as he realized he had always wanted it to be free. He cast it, cut off the jesses, took off the hood, and threw it into the air. The long wings beat strongly and took it away from him into the sky.

He watched it diminish and fade from sight. Then he replenished the fire and stared for a time at the waiting wolves. Presently he began to nod. He was too deeply asleep to hear the airplane that roared over him and landed on its skis not far away, too deeply asleep to hear the shots or see the wolves go off or recognize Burnside and the other man. He swayed between them as they held him up, gaunt, singed, and smelling strongly of smoke, half awake and mumbling.

"Just as well we didn't wait for my motor to get fixed," Burnside said, and grunted as he got a tighter hold on Bellise. "Come on, sport, wake up. This man came all the way here just to see your pigeons. Where are all the hawks?"

"The hawk," Bellise mumbled. "The hawk, she fly away."

PATSY & THE PRINCESS

First published in the September 1935 issue of Field & Stream, *this is one of Archibald Rutledge's best-known stories of bird dogs and bird hunting.*

By Archibald Rutledge

he daughter of Carolina Frank is a princess by right. I became Patsy's owner when she was only four weeks old, and she already showed her blue blood and all it means in a pointer pup. Sensitive, patrician and affectionate, she was not happy unless she could curl up in my lap by day and sleep on my bed at night.

She was high-strung to a degree. When she first barked, the sound of her own voice almost scared her to death. One day she retrieved an old tin can and brought it up the front steps, and the noise it made when it got away from her made her tremble. Most pointers have a very businesslike temperament, but Patsy was as gentle as a setter. You know, some dogs are ladies and gentlemen; and some just aren't.

While she was still so young that weeds would throw her down and briers were impassable barriers, I used to teach her to trail by shooting a starling and dragging it around the yard, turning her loose on the scent. At seven weeks of age she was broken to my .410 gun, was trailing and was pointing staunchly.

Her behavior with rabbits puzzled and amused me not a little. Apparently she considered them legitimate playmates; and when one fled at her approach, she would stand and gaze after it with a most woebegone expression, as if she felt that her little comrade had deserted her. On the scent of birds of all kinds she displayed a stern demeanor, as if she had discovered her mission in life. But she wanted to romp with rabbits, and they wouldn't play the game.

It has never seemed to me necessary to take a bird dog into the wilds to train him. Most of the work can be done right at home; and the sooner it is started, the better. Of all qualities in a bird-dog pup, give me nose. By careful and intelligent handling, almost anything can be done with a young bird dog that has a good nose. Affection and gentleness on the part of the trainer count far more than any harsh measures yet devised. If your pup has an indifferent nose, he will never amount to much in the field, even with blood, looks and pedigree in his favor.

Establishing oneself in a dog's confidence is the foundation of training. For example, if a man ever lures a dog to him affectionately and then beats him, that dog's trust will be shaken forever. I never whipped Patsy for anything. It took a little patience to teach her that stockings, old shoes and rugs are not meant to be lugged into obscure corners of the house and there chewed up, but I knew she was only a baby, and she learned quickly.

No man would knock the block off his year-old baby for pouring a cup of milk on the living room floor, but many a man will nearly kill a puppy for some little infraction of domestic manners. Start them very young, and treat them gently and fairly. They like square shooters just as well as men do. A bird dog is just like a boy; let him run wild for the first part of his life, and you establish chances against his ever settling down to reliable behavior.

P atsy was two months old when the season for upland game opened in Pennsylvania. Now, you know how hot it is when you possess a puppy of that age at such a time. You think: "He can't possibly give me any sport this year. This child could never take it. Perhaps later I may take him out a few times, and next year he will be a real dog. I may send him to a trainer, or to some friend in the South, where the season lasts until March. It's hardly right to take this babe into the woods."

Such thoughts might have been mine had Patsy not been so different. As the first day approached, and my activity with guns, shells, alarm clock and hints of what things a hunter likes for lunch apprised my wife of the coming of the Great Day, I made my revolutionary

234

decision. I would not only take Patsy out, but I would take her into the big mountains, after the prince of American game birds – none other than the ruffed grouse, the mountain pheasant, the partridge of New England – *Bonasa umbellus* himself.

On this first of November I arose at my usual heathenish hour. I carried Patsy downstairs to the kitchen. It was to be her first early start! I laid her in a corner, and then busied myself with getting breakfast. Soon I saw that she had gone fast asleep again! With night still huge and ominous outside, Patsy looked pathetically innocent and little, and I felt somewhat like a brute over this matter of risking her in the wilderness. But my heart was hardened, and I took her with me.

On the fifteen-mile drive up Path Valley, she lay fast asleep beside me, content to go anywhere if she could be with me. To a dog, a man is either a god or a devil. I have a notion that if we'd act more like gods toward our dogs we'd get a lot further with them. I am no authority on gods and have no personal interviews to report, but my understanding is that they are kindly and tolerant, especially toward their inferiors; whereas devils are full of anger, hatred, malice and all other kinds of rascality. Certainly every puppy begins by conceiving his master to be a god; it is that master's business never to do anything to make that dog change his mind.

I stopped my car in a lane leading from the highway into the mountains. Patsy snored contentedly. Under the circumstances I felt like the Dutchman who, seeing his beagle hound running a skunk across an open field, exclaimed, "What chanst for me to get sport today already yet?"

The day promised to be mild and still. A filmy haze lay over mountain and valley. I heard a red fox give his rasping bark. A horned owl weirdly intoned his eerie notes. Over the mountains, day came all pink and pearly. It was time to start.

I took a drink of hot tea, then gave Patsy a snifter of the same, and we started; this is, I started up the lane, carrying my grouse dog under my arm. By the time we got into the brush on the lower benches of the mountain, there was light enough to shoot. I set my puppy down, and together we began the invasion of some of my old grouse haunts – pine thickets, old orchards, laurel glens, deserted pastures where smothers of grapevine cover stone walls, abandoned mountain fields where grow the sumac and the wild rose and the greenbriers, on the fruits of all of which grouse delight to feed.

As my preliminary training of Patsy had included encouraging her to range out, in the twilight of the dawn I was happy to see her keeping about thirty yards ahead of me, a white fairy in those dusky solitudes. A light frost was beginning to melt, making conditions ideal for Patsy to pick up a trail.

fter some fifteen minutes we came to a gentle slope, on the incline of which was a pile of dead pine brush. While thirty yards away from this my little princess hesitated; then she drew to a dead point. A damp air was breathing from the pine-tops toward her. What did she have? There are plenty of quail in these coverts, but my mind told me that she had a grouse; and it was the first one she had ever winded. If she had hunted grouse for ten years, she could not have acted more perfectly.

Easing around until I got behind her, and scanning the country ahead to calculate just where his lordly majesty would go when flushed, I walked in carefully. When I came to Patsy, she did not break point, but she did look up at me, as if saying "I've got something; I only hope it's what you want."

Passing her, I walked slowly up toward the brush-pile. Three grouse hurtled out, each choosing a different direction. I have always found it a most difficult thing to make a double on grouse when several get up together. When I try it, I usually miss all of them. One of these was perceptibly larger than the other two; an old cock he was, and when he thundered up he headed for his mountain home. As he bore to the left, I had to lead him; I also shot above him.

By good chance, this old cock got in the way of my shot, closed his wings and pitched downward with great velocity. I called Patsy. But at the sound of the gun she did not break point! No sir; there she was planted. Walking back, I patted and praised her; then I picked her up and carried her to where her first grouse lay. She tried to retrieve him for me, but he was too big. Stumblingly she dragged him toward me.

All this called for some special demonstration on my part; so I sat down, took my baby in my lap, stroked her sensitive head, and otherwise gave her to understand that she was behaving like a champion. She kept sniffling delightedly at the big bird, and I knew that from that day forth I was to have a grouse-minded dog.

andering a little higher into the hills, we came to a rivulet gushing along among mossy rocks. Here were kalmias and great thickets of greenbriers under the oaks and hemlocks. Patsy, who had now traveled about a mile, was showing signs of getting tired. Several times I stopped for a few minutes to rest her. Coming to a dense patch of laurel, I sent Patsy in for a scout. I could see the open woods on all sides of this thicket, and kept watching for my dog to come out. But no dog.

"It must be a point," thought I, sidling ahead through the dense greenery.

236

All was silence. I didn't want to call for fear of flushing something out of range. I had a sudden apprehension about a rattlesnake. This is bad country for snakes, though they are rarely abroad after the first frosts. Besides, if a snake strikes a dog, the dog always gives notice by a sharp yelp. No sound had come from Patsy. I was puzzled, and was greatly relieved when I saw her standing with both forepaws on an old dead chestnut log. She was almost hidden by the over-arching laurels.

At first I thought she had come to the log and, finding it too much for her, was waiting for me to help her over. But then I caught in her eyes that dreamy look dear to every lover of a bird dog: she was fast on point. I walked in carefully. When I got to Patsy, I stopped to stroke her head and stepped over the log. Nothing happened. Well, I thought, an old dog is often fooled; what can you expect from a youngster?

A little circling among the bushes brought me no results. I returned to Patsy. "Lady," I said, 'scuse me, but you're a liar."

Still the elf held her stand.

"Now, ain't that sumpin?" I muttered, and began to glance around for a land turtle, the scent of which will sometimes mislead even a champion bird dog. But nary a turtle.

I picked Patsy up, and to my surprise she was as stiff as a little statue! Her whole body seemed to resent my interfering with her business. The dream-light never left her eyes. I set her down, and she continued to point, only this time she took two steps to the left and she seemed intent upon the log.

Just then I heard a slight movement in the dry leaves in the shelter of the old chestnut log. In another second, two grouse tore away from the side of the log, where they had been all along, as Patsy had so faithfully been trying to tell me. They went down the mountain. At fifty yards, as they hurtled into a smother of hemlocks, I shot rather blindly, and could see no result except a single small feather drifting idly downward.

"If I had done half as well as you did," I told Patsy, "we'd have all we are allowed in Pennsylvania in one day."

With no faith that I had done anything. I came to the place where my dead grouse should have lain. As I expected, there was no sign of it. Here was a perfect shambles of logs and limbs, the debris of a lumbering operation. I had a hard time getting along, and it was much worse for Patsy. Just as I was on the point of carrying her out of this hopeless thicket, she came to a stand. As she was under a deep tangle, I laid down my gun and literally had to crawl to get to her. Two feet in front of her nose, wedged under a log, was my grouse! When he had struck the ground, he had had life enough left to dash to hiding, but he was now dead. I retrieved him and my baby champion.

"It's the limit," I said, meaning both kinds, and, picking up my gun, started back for the car.

Patsy is but one of many bird-dog puppies that I have started very early. If this can be done normally and gently, it's the thing to do. Of course, I have been fortunate in living on the outskirts of a village, and quail nest right by my house. But many fundamentals can be taught a puppy without actual access to live game birds. Most of the books about training bird dogs have a good deal to do with reclaiming vagabonds and reforming criminals. But if you will get a puppy of patrician blood, make him love you, and start him on his career while he is still toddling, most of the difficulties that come with the breaking of a year-old, senseless, half-wild dog will never appear.

A bird dog has a real mission in life. Make this clear to him during the first three or four months of his life, and the chances are that, instead of having to show him further how to hunt, from then on he will be teaching you the finer points of the game.

"Patsy and the Princess" is from Bird Dog Days, Wingshooting Ways, *edited by Jim Casada.*

WILD

Just when you think a hunt couldn't possibly get more dangerous and exciting, something really wild comes along.

By John Whinery

he dogs barked. Then, one appeared upside down above the shoulder-high grass, tossed into the air by the enraged buffalo. Next came another cur, flipped end over end.

The four mongrel dogs with all ribs showing belonged to the five pygmy trackers who with my French professional guide, Rudy Lubin, made up the team. We had followed buffalo tracks since early morning in the three-tier rainforest – a canopy thirty stories high over lower trees over brushy, viny, thorny thickets. All of it under clouds hanging low in thick, moist air.

In Cameroon, we were one or two degrees north of the equator. I sweated profusely in the hot, wet place with sticking and scratching foliage so thick the pygmies used sharp machetes to clear the way. We had found the forest buffalo, which grow to 800 pounds, and are said to be as bad about charging as their Cape cousins.

A cleft in the forest canopy allowed the tall grass where the mongrel

239

dogs found the buffalo and attacked. Size differential made no difference. They knew their job and it meant food. There was no statuesque stand with tail-high point; these dogs would bite from all sides, holding for the hunter. We'd followed three buffs. One remained as we came close to see it. Between its horns, on its forehead, a dog flailed the air. The buffalo turned to face us. The dog fell off.

The pygmies ran. Rudy and I stood perfectly still as I slid the safety off. The buffalo glared. Body size and horn boss showed it to be a cow. A dog nipped at her heel. She turned, then backed away . . . from five yards. The jungle quickly hid us.

We stood, rifles leveled, for minutes . . . long minutes, listening. She didn't come. We didn't go for her. Although either sex was legal, we hadn't come to shoot a female.

While we walked out, tendrils of mist still hung in the morning sky. Then rain, too warm to refresh, fell steadily. Earlier, my glasses had fogged. Useless, I took them off and adjusted my scope to compensate. Somehow the dogs, all four of them, found us at the truck. They appeared beat-up. One limped, but none bled.

Following the pygmy trackers was a wonderful experience. They showed the very essence of the hunt, pure hunting – *primeval*. Our lead man would stop to listen with his left leg posed in the air. Focused! At first thought by white men to be sub-human, the small people have shown otherwise. They have become bilingual – French and their own language. They have a sense of humor and have superbly adapted to their difficult environment. Their curs, working close, are better trained than most of the dogs I've hunted with.

Probably unchanged since prehistory, the jungles of Cameroon are hard to believe. They both thrill and scare. Seeing barked tree roots beginning twenty feet up and strutting out to buttress the gigantic trunks; seeing three- and four-foot-long monitor lizards darting and big elephant-felled trees convinces one of his smallness. And the sea of leaves, through which we often moved, sharply shorted our view. Only our knowledge and gear evidenced civilization. In such a primordial place, one's survival instincts surface. The hunt here requires discipline and will. It's not for the faint-hearted.

A former logging camp now served us. We got there from town after eight hours on a single-track road – open in the river washes, otherwise walled by thicket and forest. Rough-cut planks on a pair of tree trunks laid across the streams supported the pickup, but two bridges looked so "iffy" we chose to walk across.

240

The morning after the dog-tumbling, we seven men plus dogs again rode the old Toyota pickup down narrow logging roads, sometimes just traces . . . the jungle too vast and too thick to hike. The pygmies' eyes didn't miss a track and when they judged it recent, we followed. We would hunt whatever animal had left fresh tracks. In the previous two weeks we'd found bongo, Peter's duiker, blue duiker, sitatunga and Red River hog, which looks like a cross between a feral pig and a javelina.

Soon we came upon fresh buffalo spoor so easy to read that even I could track them through the tall grass. There were several animals, one they judged huge – Cape buffalo size.

We followed along a river for about a mile, then the animals headed into the forest on a trail. Rudy walked ahead of me, our trackers to the side and ahead a bit. I remembered the experience Bill Matney, another hunter at the camp, had the day before when suddenly a buffalo appeared coming on fast. The buff was young, he thought, but still big.

"I was totally surprised and transfixed, with my eyes and mind glued on him," Bill had related. "I didn't move. Instinctively, I held my rifle across in front of me. He ran over me. Then, after twenty yards or so, he decided the forest was the place to be and he ran back up the trail. I felt a fool; somehow I didn't get hurt, only scratches from the fall."

A hundred yards into the forest the tracks went left. We entered thick underbrush and I again offered my rifle to Dieudonné, the largest pygmy, to ease my travel, but he shook his had and said, "*Tien, Patrone. Il est pres d'ici,*" (Take it boss. He's quite near.). He pointed to mud scraped from an animal high on some sharp-edged elephant grass. Between my fingers it was almost liquid. We were not far behind.

Quietly as possible we worked our way through the forest for fifteen minutes. The stillness was as immense as the trees. Then, a dog yipped, a tentative yip. Another barked and the dogs closed in for another gang fight and tumble. Maybe not too smart, these mongrel dogs had much spirit of combat. A buffalo made a loud, low grunt. The trackers urged me forward and I tried to ignore the thorns that stuck and vines that held.

Just fifteen or twenty yards ahead, the dogs and buffalo mixed it up. Barks, grunts and some yelps, which said the dogs were being hooked or hit. Another wild, close encounter. Rudy and I hurried – it was like running under water.

A shrill scream stopped us. It came from our right. Total quiet followed for about five seconds. No one moved. Then, more angry, high-pitched screams from both our left and right.

Rudy turned. "Gorillas," he said.

To the screaming, the barking, and buffalo grunting came the rapid *tat, tat, tat* of a big male's knuckles beating his chest. And he bellowed, deep and heavy. All of it was loud, close but hidden. The pygmies vanished. Rudy and I stood alone in the soggy forest, absorbing the powerful sounds of rage, fear and anger.

The buffalo had led us between a family group of gorillas and their peripherally stationed guard. Then, added to the ferocious noise came roars – abruptly beginning and ending roars, like a horn honking.

The enveloping leaves blocked our view – and theirs. Foliage hanging so still contrasted sharply with the cacophony of screams, grunts, roars, barks and chest poundings . . . stillness amidst chaos. Made it seem louder. Then, motion in the stillness, perhaps ten yards left, hip high. A blur of black arm, big nose and big eyes showed. It screamed. It feigned a charge – just a step or two – and was gone.

It wasn't terror or even fear that I felt. It was intense awareness. Every sense, every pore and nerve red-lined. I glanced questioningly at Rudy. He put his finger to his lip. Of course we'd not run. There was nothing for us to do. Too many animals, only two rifles. The sounds overwhelmed. I thought, *never again would I hear such a ruckus.* I also heard my heart pounding in my ears.

The fight seemed to be moving away to our left and as the distance grew, a little relaxation came. Then, one of the dogs let out a wild howl. It must have been grabbed, thrown or swatted hard by a gorilla. That may have motivated the other dogs to quit. One came to us and then two more seeking cover. We wished them away or that they could have brought the big buffalo. But apparently he was gone and gorillas were not for dogs to fight.

Continuing their honks, screams – which reminded me of shouted obscenities – and the chest beating, the gorillas moved away. The danger passed. Our small friends reappeared and acted with bravado that those darned gorillas had ruined our hunt (their meat).

Walking out, I had mixed feelings: exhilaration from experiencing the primitive world, and sadness the hunt was over. I had no more time. But a trophy would not be needed for me to remember. That fierceness – so close! – will be in my memory as long as I have one.

There was no killing of buffalo, but the hunting, "the chase," was genuine, good and exciting beyond fantasy.

Now, remembering, knowing those buffalo and their friends the gorillas who saved them that day are still there, *wild*, in that fantastic, humid, dense rainforest gives pleasure . . . and perspective to my life.

242

THE ROAD TO TINKHAMTOWN

The almost overwhelming choice of our readers as "the best outdoor story ever written," Corey Ford's original handwritten manuscript has never appeared in any book – until now.

By Corey Ford

he road was long, but he knew where he was going. He would follow the old road through the swamp and up over the ridge and down to a deep ravine, and cross the sagging timbers of the bridge, and on the other side would be the place called Tinkhamtown. He was going back to Tinkhamtown.

He walked slowly, for his legs were dragging, and he had not been walking for a long time. He had not walked for almost a year, and his flanks had shriveled and wasted away from lying in bed so long; he could fit his fingers around his thigh. Doc Towle had said he would never walk again, but that was Doc for you, always on the pessimistic side. Why, here he was walking quite easily, once he had started. The strength was coming back into his legs, and he did not have to stop for breath so often. He tried jogging a few steps, just to show he could, but he slowed again because he had a long way to go.

It was hard to make out the old road, choked with young alders and drifted over with matted leaves, and he shut his eyes so he could see it

243

better. He could always see it whenever he shut his eyes. Yes, here was the beaver dam on the right, just as he remembered it, and the flooded stretch where he had to wade, picking his way from hummock to hummock while the dog splashed unconcernedly in front of him. The water had been over his boot-tops in one place, and sure enough as he waded it now, his left boot filled with water again, the same warm, squidgy feeling. Everything was the way it had been that afternoon. Nothing had changed. Here was the blowdown across the road that he had clambered over and here on a knoll was the clump of thornapples where Cider had put up a grouse – he remembered the sodden road as the grouse thundered out, and the easy shot that he missed – they had not taken time to go after it. Cider had wanted to look for it, but he had whistled him back. They were looking for Tinkhamtown.

Everything was the way he remembered. There was a fork in the road, and he halted and felt in the pocket of his hunting coat and took out the map he had drawn twenty years ago. He had copied it from a chart he found in the Town Hall, rolled up in a cardboard cylinder covered with dust. He used to study the old survey charts; sometimes they showed where a farming community had flourished once, and around the abandoned pastures and under the apple trees, grown up to pine, the grouse would be feeding undisturbed. Some of his best grouse-covers had been located that way.

The chart had crackled with age as he unrolled it; the date was 1857. It was the sector between Kearsarge and Cardigan Mountains, a wasteland of slash and second-growth timber without habitation today, but evidently it had supported a number of families before the Civil War. A road was marked on the map, dotted with X's for homesteads and the names of the owners were lettered beside them: Nason, J. Tinkham, Libbey, Allard, R. Tinkham. Half the names were Tinkham. In the center of the map – the paper was so yellow he could barely make it out – was the word "Tinkhamtown."

He had copied the chart carefully, noting where the road turned off at the base of Kearsage and ran north and then northeast and crossed a brook that was not even named on the chart; and early the next morning he and Cider had set out together to find the place. They could not drive very far in the jeep, because washouts had gutted the roadbed and laid bare the ledges and boulders, like a streambed. He had stuffed the sketch in his hunting-coat pocket, and hung his shotgun over his forearm and started walking, the old setter trotting ahead of him, with the bell on his collar tinkling. It was an old-fashioned sleighbell, and it had a thin silvery note that echoed through the woods like peepers in the spring; he could follow the sound in the thickest cover, and when it stopped, he would go to where he heard it last and Cider would be on point. After Cider's death, he had put the bell away. He'd never had another dog.

It was silent in the woods without the bell, and the way was longer than he remembered. He should have come to the big hill by now. Maybe he'd taken the wrong turn back at the fork. He thrust a hand into his hunting-coat; the sketch he had drawn was still in the pocket. He sat down on a flat rock to get his bearings, and then he realized, with a surge of excitement, that he had stopped for lunch on this very rock ten years ago. Here was the waxed paper from his sandwich, tucked in a crevice, and here was the hollow in the leaves where Cider had stretched out beside him, the dog's soft muzzle flattened on his thighs. He looked up, and through the trees he could see the hill.

He rose and started walking again, carrying his shotgun. He had left the gun standing in its rack in the kitchen when he had been taken to the state hospital, but now it was hooked over his arm by the trigger guard; he could feel the solid heft of it. The woods were more dense as he climbed, but here and there a shaft of sunlight slanted through the trees. "And the forests ancient as the hills," he thought, "enfolding sunny spots of greenery." Funny that should come back to him now; he hadn't read it since he was a boy. Other things were coming back to him, the smell of the dank leaves and the sweetfern and frosted apples, the sharp contrast of sun and the cold November shade, the stillness before snow. He walked faster, feeling the excitement swell within him.

He had walked all that morning, stopping now and then to study the map and take his bearings from the sun, and the road had led them down a long hill and at the bottom was the brook he had seen on the chart, a deep ravine spanned by a wooden bridge. Cider had trotted across the bridge, and he had followed more cautiously, avoiding the loose planks and walking the solid struts with his shotgun held out to balance himself; and that was how he found Tinkhamtown.

On the other side of the brook was a clearing, he remembered, and the remains of a stone wall, and a cellar-hole where a farmhouse had stood. Cider had moved in a long cast around the edge of the clearing, his bell tinkling faintly, and he had paused a moment beside the foundations, wondering about the people who had lived here a century ago. Had they ever come back to Tinkhamtown? And then suddenly, the bell had stopped, and he had hurried across the clearing. An apple tree was growing in a corner of the stone wall, and under the tree Cider had halted at point. He could see it all now: the warm October sunlight, the ground strewn with freshly pecked apples, the dog standing immobile with one foreleg drawn up, his back level and his tail a white plume.

Only his flanks quivered a little, and a string of slobber dangled from his jowls. "Steady, boy," he murmured as he moved up behind him, "I'm coming."

He paused on the crest of the hill, straining his ears for the faint mutter of the stream below him, but he could not hear it because of the voices. He wished they would stop talking, so he could hear the stream. Someone was saying his name over and over. Someone said, "What is it, Frank?" and he opened his eyes. Doc Towle was standing at the foot of the bed, whispering to the new nurse, Mrs. Simmons or something; she'd only been here a few days, but Doc thought it would take some of the burden off his wife. He turned his head on the pillow, and looked up at his wife's face, bent over him. "What did you say, Frank?" she asked, and her face was worried. Why, there was nothing to be worried about. He wanted to tell her where he was going, but when he moved his lips no sound came. "What?" she asked, bending her head lower. "I don't hear you." He couldn't make the words any clearer, and she straightened and said to Doc Towle: "It sounded something like Tinkhamtown."

Tinkhamtown?" Doc shook his head. "Never heard him mention any place by that name."

He smiled to himself.

Of course he'd never mentioned it to Doc. There are some things you don't mention even to an old hunting companion like Doc. Things like a secret grouse cover you didn't mention to anyone, not even to as close a friend as Doc was. No, he and Cider were the only ones who knew. They had found it together, that long ago afternoon, and it was their secret. "This is our secret cover," he had told Cider that afternoon, as he lay sprawled under the tree with the grouse beside him and the dog's muzzle flattened on his thigh. "Just you and me." He had never told anybody else about Tinkhamtown, and he had never gone back after Cider died.

"Better let him rest," he heard Doc tell his wife. It was funny to hear them talking, and not be able to make them hear him. "Call me if there's any change."

The old road lay ahead of him, dappled with sunshine. He could smell the dank leaves, and feel the chill of the shadows under the hemlocks; it was more real than the pain in his legs. Sometimes it was hard to tell what was real and what was something he remembered. Sometimes at night he would hear Cider panting on the floor beside his bed, his toenails scratching as he chased a bird in a dream, but when the nurse turned on the light the room would be empty. And then when it was dark he would hear the panting and scratching again.

Once he asked Doc point blank about his legs. "Will they ever get

246

better?" He and Doc had grown up in town together; they knew each other too well to lie. Doc had shifted his big frame in the chair beside the bed, and got out his pipe and fumbled with it, and looked at him. "No, I'm afraid not," he replied slowly, "I'm afraid there's nothing to do." Nothing to do but lie here and wait till it's over. Nothing to do but lie here like this, and be waited on, and be a burden to everybody. He had a little insurance, and his son in California sent what he could to help, but now with the added expense of a nurse and all. . . . "Tell me, Doc," he whispered, for his voice wasn't as strong these days, "what happens when it's over?" And Doc put away the needle and fumbled with the catch of his black bag and said he supposed that you went on to someplace else called the Hereafter. But he shook his head; he always argued with Doc. "No," he told him, "it isn't someplace else. It's someplace you've been where you want to be again, someplace you were happiest." Doc didn't understand, and he couldn't explain it any better. He knew what he meant, but the shot was taking effect and he was tired. The pain had been worse lately, and Doc had started giving him shots with a needle so he could sleep. But he didn't really sleep, because the memories kept coming back to him, or maybe he kept going back to the memories.

He was tired now, and his legs ached a little as he started down the hill toward the stream. He could not see the road; it was too dark under the trees to see the sketch he had drawn. The trunks of all the trees were swollen with moss, and blowdowns blocked his way and he had to circle around their upended roots, black and misshapen. He had no idea which way Tinkhamtown was, and he was frightened. He floundered into a pile of slash, feeling the branches tear at his legs as his boots sank in, and he did not have the strength to get through it and he had to back out again, up the hill. He did not know where he was going any more.

He listened for the stream, but all he could hear was his wife, her breath catching now and then in a dry sob. She wanted him to come back, and Doc wanted him to, and there was the big house. If he left the house alone, it would fall in with the snow and cottonwoods would grow in the cellar-hole. There were all the other doubts, but most of all there was the fear. He was afraid of the darkness and being alone, and not knowing the way. He had lost the way. Maybe he should turn back. It was late, but maybe, he could find the way back.

He paused on the crest of the hill, straining his ears for the faint mutter of the stream below him, but he could not hear it because of the voices. He wished they would stop talking, so he could hear the stream. Someone was saying his name over and over. They had come to the stream – he shut his eyes so he could see it again – and Cider had trotted across the bridge. He had followed more cautiously, avoiding the loose planks and walking on a beam, with his shotgun held out to balance himself. On the other side the road rose sharply to a level clearing and he paused beside the split-stone foundation of a house. The fallen timbers were rotting under a tangle of briars and burdock, and in the empty cellar hole the cottonwoods grew higher than the house had been. His toe encountered a broken china cup and the rusted rims of a wagon wheel buried in the grass. Beside the granite doorsill was a lilac bush planted by the woman of the family to bring a touch of beauty to their home. Perhaps her husband had chided her for wasting time on such useless things, with as much work to be done. But all the work had come to nothing. The fruits of their work had disappeared, and still the lilac bloomed each spring, defying the encroaching forest, as though to prove that beauty is the only thing that lasts.

On the other side of the clearing were the sills of the barn, and behind it a crumbling stone wall around the orchard. He thought of the men sweating to clear the fields and pile the rocks into walls to hold their cattle. Why had they gone away from Tinkhamtown, leaving their walls to crumble and their buildings to collapse under the January snows? Had they ever come back to Tinkhamtown? Or were they still here, watching him unseen, living in a past that was more real than the present. He stumbled over a block of granite, hidden by briars, part of the sill of the old barn. Once it had been a tight barn, warm with cattle steaming in their stalls and sweet with the barn odor of manure and hay and leather harness. He liked to think of the barn the way it was; it was more real than this bare foundation and the emptiness inside. He'd always felt that way about the past. Doc used to argue that what's over is over, but he would insist Doc was wrong. Everything is the way it was, he'd tell Doc. The present always changes, but the past is always the way it was. You leave it, and go on to the present, but it is still there, waiting for you to come back to it.

He had been so wrapped up in his thoughts that he had not realized Cider's bell had stopped. He hurried across the clearing, holding his gun ready. In a corner of the stone wall an ancient apple tree had covered the ground with red fruit, and beneath it Cider was standing motionless. The white fan of his tail was lifted a little, his neck stretched forward, and one foreleg was cocked. His flanks were trembling, and a thin skein of drool hung from his jowls. The dog did not move as he approached, but he could see the brown eyes roll back until their whites showed, waiting for him. His throat grew tight, the way it always did when Cider was on point, and he swallowed hard. "Steady, boy," he whispered, "I'm coming."

248

He opened his eyes. His wife was standing beside his bed and his son was standing near her. He looked at his son. Why had he come all the way from California, he worried? He tried to speak, but there was no sound. "I think his lips moved just now. He's trying to whisper something," his wife's voice said. "I don't think he knows you," his wife said to his son. Maybe he didn't know him. Never had, really. He had never been close to his wife or his son. He did not open his eyes, because he was watching for the grouse to fly as he walked past Cider, but he knew Doc Towle was looking at him. "He's sleeping," Doc said after a moment. Maybe you better get some sleep yourself. A chair creaked, and he heard Doc's heavy footsteps cross the room. "Call me if there's any change," Doc said, and closed the door, and in the silence he could hear his wife sobbing beside him, her dress rustling regularly as she breathed. How could he tell her he wouldn't be alone? But he wasn't alone, not with Cider. He had closed off the other rooms and slept on a cot in the kitchen with the old dog curled on the floor by the stove, his claws scratching the linoleum as he chased a bird in a dream. He wasn't alone when he heard that. They were always together. There was a closeness between them that he did not feel for anyone else, his wife, his son, or even Doc. They could talk without words, and they could always find each other in the woods. He was lost without him. Cider was the kindest person he had ever known.

They never hunted together after Tinkhamtown. Cider had acted tired, walking back to the car that afternoon, and several times he sat down on the trail, panting hard. He had to carry him in his arms the last hundred yards to the jeep. It was hard to think he was gone.

And then he heard it, echoing through the air, a sound like peepers in the spring, the high silvery note of a bell. He started running toward it, following it down the hill. The pain was gone from his legs; it had never been there. He hurdled blowdowns, he leapt over fallen trunks, he put one fingertip on a pile of slash and floated over it like a bird. The sound filled his ears, louder than a thousand churchbells ringing, louder than all the heavenly choirs in the sky, as loud as the pounding of his heart. His eyes were blurred with tears, but he did not need to see. The fear was gone; he was not alone. He knew the way now. He knew where he was going.

He paused at the stream just for a moment. He heard men's voices. They were his hunting partners, Jim, Mac, Dan, Woodie. And oh, what a day it was for sure, closeness and understanding and happiness, the little intimate things, the private jokes. He wanted to tell them he was happy; if they only knew how happy he was. He opened his eyes, but he could not see the room any more. Everything else was bright with sunshine, but the room was dark.

249

The bell stopped, and he closed his eyes and looked across the stream. The other side was basked in gold bright sunshine, and he could see the road rising steeply through the clearing in the woods, and the apple tree in a corner of the stone wall. Cider was standing motionless, the white fan of his tail lifted a little, his neck craned forward, one foreleg cocked. The whites of his eyes showed as he looked back, waiting for him.

"Steady," he called, "steady, boy." He started across the bridge. "I'm coming."

Published with permission of Dartmouth College and Laurie Morrow.

THE TROLL

Had it all been a dream or had he somehow crossed into another world, a world filled wth wonders he'd not fathomed before.

By Michael McIntosh

orey Hawkins slowed his Rover and then stopped alongside a run that looked promising. He was a mile upstream from the old bridge. The water here was glossy and gliding, hinting at some depth in a stream frequently punctuated by riffles. It was a cool day, and though not yet late afternoon, the surface was occasionally pocked with rise-forms.

He opened the Rover's hatch, pulled on his waders, laced his felt-soled shoes and uncased his 4-weight rod. He mounted the little reel, stripped off some line, and strung up. The tippet looked a bit scuffed, so he clipped it off and tied on a length of new 5X. He could change later to 4X if the fish proved of much size. Selecting a No. 12 Adams, he tied it on and felt a satisfying little pop as the Pitzen knot settled.

He eased out into the water, checking behind to ensure room for his backcast – which wasn't much as the stream was scarcely twice the width of the road alongside. Stripping out enough line to reach the near edge of the pool, he made a couple of false-casts and laid the Adams gently onto the water. The current wasn't especially strong and didn't belly the line much, so he only needed to mend once before the fly reached the end of its tether and swung toward the shallows. A smooth pickup, one false cast; this time he laid the fly a little farther upstream and let it drift lightly down.

By the time he'd paid out enough line to reach the center, three fish had risen to the Adams but none had taken it. Corey Hawkins stripped in his line, false-cast a few times on just the length of the leader, pinched the fly in a Kleenex, and put on a drop of floatant.

After two more fruitless rises, he was drifting the Adams at the far edge when a fish finally took it. The rod said it wasn't a big fish, so he simply stripped it in. It was a six-inch brown trout, barely hooked in its lower lip. Corey Hawkins dunked his hand, cradled the fish, eased out the barbless hook, and gently laid it back into the water. It flitted away like a minnow.

For the next hour or more, he moved downstream, fishing a succession of riffles and pools, raising few fish. The two he caught were no larger than the first. No wonder there isn't anyone else on the stream, he thought and decided to give it up at the bridge, now within sight just downstream.

As he approached the bridge, Corey caught a whiff of the stench of rotting flesh. Right under the span, he noticed a pile of fish heads at the edge of the bank, a pile the size of a sleeping Labrador. They were trout heads, big ones all, wriggling with maggots and surrounded by a cloud of greenbottle flies. The smell was dreadful.

His mind started sifting questions: *Where did these fish come from? How did they get here? Raccoons? Otters? What?*

A deep, gurgling sound broke in. It sounded like someone clearing his throat from inside a toilet. Corey looked up to see a figure standing halfway down the embankment, shrouded in the shadows of the bridge.

"Fishin'?" the figure growled.

"Yes," Corey said.

"Gettin' any?"

"Uh, not really."

The figure descended the embankment and into the light. It was squat and toadlike and walked with a waddling gait. The face was vaguely human, horribly contorted. One eye was where an eyebrow ought to be, the other low as a cheekbone. The nose was bulbous and bumpy. The ears were nearly at the top of the head, which showed a few scraggly hairs sprouting from a scrofulous scalp. The whole visage was a landscape of warts and lumps.

Corey glanced upward. In the gloom where the embankment and bridge abutment met he could just make out a small table and a chair. The memory of a childhood story flashed in his mind.

"Are you a . . . troll?" he asked tentatively.

"Yep. Sure as hell am."

"And you live here, under the bridge?"

252

"Well where the hell do you think I'm spoze to live?" the troll said gruffly with a wet-sounding sniff.

"Just wondered," Corey said. He looked down at the pile of fish heads. "Where did these come from?"

The troll looked at Corey as if being questioned by an imbecile. "I caught 'em," he said.

"In this stream?"

"For Chrissake!" the troll snarled. "Ya think I drive out to the Henry's Fork or the Battenkill or wherethehellever? Course I caught 'em in this stream!"

"Just wondering," Corey said. "From what I've seen today, I wouldn't guess there was one fish that size here, much less this many."

"You wonder about a hell of a lot, don't you? Plenty of big fish in this stream. You just have to know where to look and how to fish 'em." The troll peered at Corey, who couldn't decide which of the misaligned eyes he should look into.

"So you ain't caught shit. What're you usin'?"

Corey held up his rod with the Adams clipped to a guide.

The troll snorted loudly, splatting a gobbet of snot on the hand he was waving in disgust. "You think a big fish is gonna take that little pussy thing? Are you out here to catch fish or just drown worms?"

Corey drew himself up. "I fish dry flies," he said stiffly. "I don't fish with worms."

"Figure of speech," the troll said. "I been watchin' you. You know how to fish. You're just doin' it the wrong way with the wrong thing. I can tell you how to catch some trout."

"I'm Corey Hawkins," Corey said, not extending a hand and hoping the troll wouldn't, either. "I'm a stockbroker, and I love fishing. I'll be very grateful for anything you can teach me."

"Whatever," the troll said. "C'mon." He started trudging up the embankment. Corey followed, looking from side to side as the gloom under the bridge deepened. At the top he saw that the table he'd noticed earlier was actually a nicely set-up fly-tying bench – vise, bobbins, scissors, assorted tools and a single candle providing light. Next to it stood a No. 3 galvanized washtub about three-quarters full of what appeared to be the same pattern of fly. He didn't recognize them, but they looked impossibly ugly.

"Siddown," the troll said, dropping into the single chair behind the bench. Corey looked around and then perched on the rim of the washtub.

"Do many fishermen come by here?" he asked?.

"Yeah, quite a few. Most of 'em just wade on under the bridge and don't notice me. And I don't say nothin' unless I see somebody that looks like he knows what the hell he's doin'. Then sometimes I go down and talk to 'em. Met some interesting guys that way. Fella name of Zern came through . . . oh, years ago. We musta set on the bank half a day. He was a funny sumbitch; had more stories than you could shake a stick at.

"Nother fella by the name of Teesdale came by one time. We talked a long while, too. He was another funny sumbitch. I thought at first we might be related

253

somehow, 'cause he looked a lot like a gnome, but it turned out he wasn't. He sure as hell knew how to fish, though. When I gave him one my flies, he cleaned up on this stream, fished way past dark 'cause he knew that's when the big browns come out. Even came by later to tell me how he'd hooked a muskrat by mistake. Laughed so damn hard I almost fell in the river.

"Mostly, anybody that stops gets a free fly, and they always seem to come back for more."

Corey glanced behind him, into the tub. "You sell these?"

"Hell, yes. Even a troll needs a little money now and then. I don't pick up a fat goddam paycheck at the end of the month, y'know. Sumpm 'bout these flies just seems to get them big browns all wound up. Messed with 'em for years till I came up with the right pattern. Take a look."

Corey reached into the tub and pulled out a fly. He couldn't have said what it was meant to imitate, except perhaps a caterpillar badly in need of a haircut. "Is this all you tie?"

"Yep," the troll said. "All I need."

"How do you do it?"

"Well," the troll said, leaning back in his chair, "the tail is some kinda soft feather, and the body is dubbed billy-goat ruff. I dye it with my own special formula." He leaned over and hawked a glob of black phlegm onto the ground. "The hackle is just about any dark-colored feather I can find. Crow, mostly. You tie?"

"Yes," Corey[a] said, "I tie my own dries."

"Know how to palmer a hackle?"

"Of course." Corey opened his box and held out a fly. The troll took it in a gnarled hand tipped with filthy, jagged fingernails.

"Sheeit," he said. "This thing looks like it was hit by Arnold Palmer. You may know how to wind a hackle, but you sure as hell don't know how to wrap one."

Corey stiffened. "Then perhaps you'd show me."

"Fat chance," the troll said. "But you can have that one."

"What do you call this?" Corey asked, peering at the monstrosity from every angle.

"Woolly Booger. Dunno why," the troll said, ramming a forefinger an inch into his nose and rummaging around. "Just sompm that came to me."

"Well, how do you fish it?"

"Now that I'll tell you," the troll said, examining the prize just dredged from his nostril. "Drop it within a foot of the opposite bank, let it hang a few seconds, and then strip it back. How fast or slow depends on the fish. Some things you gotta figure out for yourself, one day to the next.

"One other thing I'll tell ya'. Change out that piddly-ass tippet you got. Put on sumpm heavier. If you wanna catch big fish, you better have some big tackle. Now go on. I'm busy." The troll turned to the half-completed fly in his vise and began winding thread.

Corey turned to go and noticed a fly rod leaning against a piling. "May I look at this?" The troll grunted.

It was an ancient-looking bamboo with almost no varnish left. It had taken a set in three directions, but even so it had a feel that seemed to come alive with only the slightest flex of the wrist. Looking closer in the dim light, Corey saw the word Payne written on the butt. He set it down and without another word turned down the embankment toward the river. At the water's edge, he called back. "Where do I fish?"

"Downstream," the troll rumbled. "Just fish the way I told you and you'll find 'em."

"You might consider giving this fly a different name, something with a little more dignity."

"I don't give a shit what you call it," the troll said. "Hell, call it Buggery if you want to, long as it works. Now get outta here."

A long riffle reached below the bridge. Corey walked the bank to the tail, changed his tippet, and tied on the troll's fly. It looked to be a No. 8, its point wickedly barbed. He flattened the barb with his pliers.

Wading out, he picked a spot on the opposite bank just where the riffle fell into deeper water. Three or four false-casts paid out enough line, and he laid the fly about eighteen inches from the water's edge. He guessed at about a two-foot strip and started pulling. The fly wallowed sluggishly at the surface for a few feet and then sank. When the butt of his leader appeared, he picked it up, aimed for a spot just a few feet down from the first, and let out a bit more line.

This time the fly landed about eight inches from the bank with a faint p–lop. On the second strip the rod bucked and bent. This was no six-inch fish. By the time Corey got to his reel the fish was charging downstream. He gave it some headway, palming the spool, then started to apply pressure. The fish turned and tugged. Corey held as much tension as he dared and from there fought it solely off the reel, gaining line as he could, giving some back when he feared for his tippet.

The battle lasted nearly five minutes. When he felt the fish's resistance flagging, he reeled it in and reached for the landing net hanging at his back. Rod held high in one hand, only the leader showing beyond the tip, he slid the net under the fish and gazed in wonder at a magnificent brown trout possibly two feet long, its spots glowing like neon in the slanting sunlight. He unhooked it delicately and lowered it back to the water. He let it lie in the net for a minute or so, until it righted itself and swam out through the hoop.

Corey Hawkins fished until nearly dark, moving slowly downstream. The drama played out eight more times. None of the fish were quite as large as the first, but even the smallest was surely no less than eighteen inches.

One more cast, he thought, feeling euphoric. By then he had the distance down and laid the sodden, ugly thing right under the grass of the opposite bank. He was just reaching to the first guide when the little rod bent almost double and the reel nearly whined as line spun off. He hit the spool with the heel of his hand, felt a moment's hesitation, and then the sudden, sickening slack as the tippet broke.

orey Hawkins waded back and climbed the bank to the road. Walking along in the dusk, he wondered if he'd had a dream or somehow crossed into another world – trolls and Woolly Boogers and big fish – things his experience had not fathomed before.

He stopped at the bridge, walked out a few feet and called down, "Are you there?"

"Yeah," the troll growled. "Do any good?" The voice sounded hollow, as if from a distance.

"I caught nine big fish and then lost my fly to the last one." He heard a raspy, fading chuckle.

Corey climbed down from the road and looked under the bridge. No bench, chair, candle, nor washtub, and no troll. No scuffs in the gravel or dust, only a few forlorn weeds seeming to say that nothing nor no one had been there in ages.

He cast about, looking for what, he could not say. Just as the sun showed a final peek above the western hills, a single ray shone under the bridge and lit a flat stone on the ground. On it lay a fly, its black body wound in a crow's feather. Corey Hawkins picked it up and held it gently, like an offering.

Author's Note: *The concept of this story came from conversations I had with Bill Headrick, whose mind and sense of humor run in the same sort of meanders as mine. We took some pretty wild swings at ideas for the plot, but in the end decided on a fairly straightforward tale about the meeting of two worlds, both valid and with a common purpose. Bill contributed much, both in concept and detail, and as always, I'm grateful for his perspectives.*

As a secondary theme, we thought to explore the origin of one of the world's great flies. If it seems fanciful, it is – but remember, a lot of dry-fly guys think the Woolly Bugger was invented by a troll, anyway.

SOMETHING SPECIAL

Sometimes the most treasured gifts of all are the most commonplace things – things like music and fish and a father's love.

By Peter Wood

ast year my Dad died. Old age. He was 89. Since then I've wanted to do something special for him, in tribute – like write a novel or a musical. He was a songwriter, perhaps best known for his songs *Till Then* and *Shoo-Fly Pie* and *Apple Pan Dowdy*. He also wrote for the *Captain Kangaroo* children's television show.

He used to be Guy Bonar Wood. But now he's evolved into something else: a memory, a melody someone hums or perhaps a monarch butterfly that lights upon my knee.

Recently, Zoe, my five-year-old daughter, tried to figure out Grandpa.

"If Grandpa is dead, does he still have bones?"

"No, I don't think so," I smiled. "Grandpa doesn't need bones anymore."

"Does he have skin?" she asked.

"No. In heaven, he doesn't need skin, either."

"What's heaven like?" she asked, tilting her head.

My mind was humbled for an explanation. I took a deep breath.

"Well, heaven is like . . . home," I said.

"And that's where Grandpa is?"

"Yes."

"How do you know?" she quizzed.

"Well, I . . ." I hesitated and looked into her big brown eyes.

She looked past my ear, into the silent blue sky. Here we stood on earth, a father and daughter, trying to unsnarl the mystery of Grandpa's death.

The following morning, Zoe and I stepped into a small boat. We were going flounder fishing in Shinnecock Bay – just like I had done with my father thirty years ago. I remember Dad's big gnarled hands steering the boat, his curly white chest hair and his large nose. His fatherly smile.

Dad usually found a spot in the middle of the bay, toward the right. When he was fairly sure, he'd cut the motor, drop the anchor and we'd start fishing. We didn't need to talk. To him, speech was an inferior form of silence. Within our boat there was always a simple peace and warmth as the tide softly lapped against the bow. He and I would just sit and fish quietly, the tempo of our hearts beating together.

Dad was an unusual man. All of my friends' fathers started out young as artists and ended up old as businessmen. But not Dad. He always wandered into the darkness of his mind. That's where his music was – and sadness. Sometimes he would whistle a tune, light and airy; at other times, he would hum a melody, sweet and soft. There always seemed to be an underlying sadness inside him. Perhaps it was because as a young boy growing up in Manchester, England, he only met his own father once, for twenty minutes, at a park bench.

Music was the fruit of my father's sadness. Sometimes he preferred the music within himself to the discordance of the real world – but he was never detached or distant from me. My fishing memories breathe within my heart. Fishing with my father was a wonderful spoonful of happiness.

I looked at little Zoe and felt a deep sadness. She would never get to know my father and never hear him whistle a tune, light and airy, or hum a melody sweet and soft. Her grandpa will be an old, dusty CD collection on the shelf.

I had found our spot in the middle of the bay, toward the right. I dropped anchor, got our fishing gear squared away, baited her hook with a silver killie and plunked her drop-line in. The number-5 sinker thumped bottom, about fifteen feet down.

We sat fishing, listening to the rhythm of the waves hitting the boat. After about five minutes, Zoe said, "Say something."

"Why?"

"Because you're too quiet."

"You know, when I was your age, Grandpa always took me fishing here."

"Did you catch any fish?" she asked, holding her drop-line in her tiny hands.

"Oh, yes. Flounder – in this very spot. Grandpa once told me that it's best to fish with your best friend."

"Why?" she asked.

258

I looked out at the sun-speckled water. "Because when you're sitting with your best friend you don't feel the need to talk too much."

Just then. Zoe's line bobbed down violently.

"You got something!" I chimed.

Zoe's eyes widened. The silent, intimate tug of a fish made her explode with laughter and delight.

"Pull him in!" I instructed, as I watched her awkwardly pull up her line.

I saw a happy five-year-old boy fishing with his father once more.

"Daddy! Daddy! Look!" A head slowly emerged from the water. It was brownish-gray, floppy and flat.

"A flounder!"

We pulled him in, but the fish wiggled out of her hands and splashed back into the water.

Zoe shrieked.

"I want him back!" she cried. She collapsed into my arms, sobbing. I held her close.

"It's okay, Zoe," I said. "He's back home now."

"It's not fair," she said, sobbing. "He's mine. I want him back."

"I know. I know," I said. "I miss him, too."

After an hour, we motored home as the seagulls arabesqued in the bright blue sky. I noticed Zoe quietly staring up at the hairy white clouds as she sniffed the fish on her hands. The fishy smell still lingered on her palms, between her fingers and on the webs. "He's still on my hands," she said, sadly. It appeared like she might start crying again so I began to whistle a tune, light and airy.

"That's Grandpa's song," she smiled.

"Yes."

"Shoo Fly Pie and Apple Pan Dowdy," she sang, "make your eyes light up, your tummy say howdy . . ."

"That's right!" I beamed.

"Can Grandpa hear me singing his song?" she asked, still sniffing the flounder on her fingers.

"Yes," I said.

"How do you know?" she quizzed.

"Well . . ." I responded, "Grandpa is . . ." I groped for an answer, but, as usual, there was a hush from my brain. "Grandpa is . . . *everywhere!*" I finally spat.

"Well, I don't think he can hear us. If he doesn't have bones or skin, he can't have ears."

"Well," I said, wondering if what I was about to say to her was thin thought or thinktwists or mental gymnastics or plain hokum. But she was looking at me intently, so I cut the motor and said, "Zoe, I think Grandpa is still here."

"Where?"

"Well, it's like this – your daddy's fish, that you're still smelling on your hands, is still here."

"No, he's not."

"Yes, he is. You even said so yourself. He's still on my hands, you said." Her face looked puzzled.

"Grandpa is still here, too," I continued.

"Where?" she asked, her voice rising an octave.

"Well, just like you can't see your daddy fish anymore, you can't see Grandpa anymore, either. But we can still hear him."

"How?"

"Well, Grandpa is now his music. We can't *see* music, but we can *hear* music. That means a little bit of Grandpa is still here. Grandpa *is* music."

"Grandpa is music?"

I nodded. "So, now we *sing* Grandpa." I smiled.

Her face scrunched up with confusion. "We *sing* Grandpa?"

"Yes."

Utterly baffled with my explanation, Zoe fiddled with the drop-line, which was becoming more and more tangled, in her lap. She watched the seagulls swoop and dance in the blue sky. "Okay," she said, "so I can still *hear* Grandpa, but I can't see him anymore. Right?"

"That's right," I nodded.

"Because he doesn't have any more bones," she clarified.

"Or skin," I added.

I started up the motor and we headed home. We listened to the Shinnecock Bay music – the gulls, the water leaping against our boat, the wind kissing our faces and the tempo of our hearts beating together.

That evening, after my wife had given Zoe her bath and had tucked her in bed, I tiptoed into her room. I heard tiny snores. She was lying on her stomach, as usual, holding her two favorite stuffed animals – a large white unicorn in one arm and a small pink unicorn with rainbow hair in the other. I sat down on the bed beside her. "I love you," I whispered. I had always hoped these words somehow slid up into her ears and nestled into her brain. "You're so smart," I whispered. "And so pretty and so happy." I hoped I was helping her build a strong mental foundation, a sturdy self-esteem and a solid emotional security.

These three traits, like three slippery fish, tend to elude us.

I looked through the darkness of the bedroom walls – Powerpuff Girls posters, butterfly stickers, her vertical growth chart and the framed photo of a smiling grandfather cradling a two-year-old Zoe . . . *Dad, I wish you could see her swinging on the monkey bars. And she's learning the doggy-paddle in swim class on Wednesday nights. And I wish you could see how well she's drawing. You'd be so proud . . .*

260

Suddenly, as if awakened, Zoe shifted on her back. Was I talking? Was I having a private dialogue with someone? But her beautiful eyes remained closed and her tiny snores resumed. I looked into her pretty face and I knew that I wanted to give her as many spoonfuls of happiness as my sad father had given to me. I bent down to kiss her hand and when I did, a daddy flounder smell slid up into my nostrils.

When my Dad died I wanted to do something special for him, like write a novel or musical. Then I looked down at Zoe, and I thought maybe I'm already doing something special.

I closed the door softly, humming.

THE LEGEND OF
BWANA COTTAR

*The first American-born professional hunter in Africa,
Charles Cottar would survive three leopard maulings and
near-fatal attacks by elephant and buffalo to found the
First Family of Safari.*

By Brian Herne

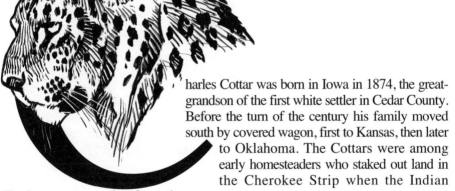

harles Cottar was born in Iowa in 1874, the great-grandson of the first white settler in Cedar County. Before the turn of the century his family moved south by covered wagon, first to Kansas, then later to Oklahoma. The Cottars were among early homesteaders who staked out land in the Cherokee Strip when the Indian Territory was opened up for settlement.

Charles modeled his early life after that of his trailblazing heroes, Daniel Boone and Davy Crockett, wearing his hair long in frontier fashion and hunting wild game with an old-fashioned musket. He soon grew to stand a brawny six-foot-four. His insatiable wanderlust, combined with his fast draw and dead aim, led him to Texas where he served a spell as a two-gun sheriff. Several years later he moved back to Oklahoma where he married and settled down for awhile, though his maverick thirst for adventure remained unquenched. In 1910 Cottar pulled up stakes and set off on a solitary mid-life pilgrimage to Darkest Africa. At the start of that fateful journey, none would have guessed that Charles Cottar was destined to gain fame as the first

263

American-born white hunter in East Africa, and that his name would be indelibly etched in the annals of safari lore.

The spark that fired Cottar's imagination and propelled him out of his own country and onto the shores of a primitive wilderness rose out of the blaze of publicity that heralded Teddy Roosevelt's 1909-10 hunting expedition in Africa. As newspapers around the globe trumpeted the myriad mysteries of Africa, Cottar vowed to see the land of King Solomon for himself. By the time Roosevelt's cavalcade had reached the white rhino country along Uganda's Nile Valley on the last leg of a thirteen-month trip, Charles Cottar had packed his guns and was on the high seas, steaming toward the tropical green waters of the Indian Ocean.

Cottar's voyage ended at the old Arab port of Mombasa, gateway to British East Africa where he boarded a railway carriage that would carry him 320 miles inland to the territory's capital. At Nairobi the Oklahoma plainsman found himself in a dusty settlement where men still packed pistols, wore Stetsons and traveled by horseback or rickshaw. Among its powerful attractions for Cottar, Africa's frontier town had one feature which surpassed all others: it was smack in the middle of a sportsman's paradise. Lions strolled the back streets, while Cape buffalo wallowed in papyrus swamps near the celebrated Norfolk Hotel, and elephant often plundered vegetable gardens. From almost any place in the town countless wildebeest, Coke's hartebeest, zebra, Thomson's and Grant's gazelle, eland, wart hog and ostrich could be seen on the surrounding plains.

In Cottar's day there was no requirement that a white hunter accompany a visitor on safari. The only condition was that a basic game license be purchased. Lion and leopard were considered "vermin" and could be hunted by anyone prepared to gamble his life. Graveyard headstones bearing epitaphs such as "killed by a lion" or "killed by a buffalo" bore ample testimony to the bloody deaths suffered by greenhorns who tangled with the Big Five on their own. Yet danger was a magnet to Charles Cottar, and instead of a white hunter, he cut expenses by hiring an African *neapara* (headman). The old *neaparas* were invaluable characters who had once marched at the head of slaving caravans or guided famous explorers to the interior. They kept the safari porters in line if need be, often with the strong-armed aid of a *kiboko*, a stiff whip made of hippo hide. But *neaparas* shared one failing: they were not hunters, and knew little about the habits of game, stalking or judging trophies. These tasks were left to gunbearers who came from specialized hunting tribes, such as the WaKamba.

At Nairobi railway station Cottar and his thirty African porters, along with three riding mules, a half-dozen pack donkeys, tents, chop boxes, kerosene lanterns, skinning knives, trophy salt, medical supplies, bedding, machetes and axes were loaded on boxcars of a slow goods train bound for a station called Kijabe. As the train rumbled to the edge of the Great Rift Valley at 6,500 feet, Cottar was stunned at the enormity of the panorama far below. Two extinct volcanoes studded the valley floor, surrounded by golden grasslands carved with dry streambeds lined with thickets of yellow-barked acacia. In the distance a blue haze of mountains beckoned.

Charles and his men followed a hand-drawn map supplied by Leslie Tarlton, the Australian white hunter who had outfitted his safari. Their route led to the freshwater lake at Naivasha, then beyond to a string of shallow soda lakes where every variety of bird and mammal could be found. On the grassy plains of Masailand, Cottar hunted rhino, then spoored buffalo in brushy gorges at Hell's Gate. Charles marched to the 6,000-foot Laikipia Plateau, home to huge herds of game. As his safari edged around the forested slopes of the Aberdare mountains, Charles knew his search was over, and he had found the big game hunter's Holy Grail.

Back in Nairobi Bwana Cottar, as he was now known, heard tales of giant tuskers deep in the rain forests of the Belgian Congo. The Congo was irresistible to hard-bitten adventurers who hankered to hunt for excitement and profit, without the bothersome expense of game licenses. On the west bank of the Nile at a place called Lado, a wedge of land was the center of a territorial dispute between the Belgians and British. The poachers seized upon the dispute to operate in Lado, poaching ivory from under the noses of the Belgians, secure in the knowledge the British would ignore their shenanigans.

Poaching in the Congo was dangerous work, and several hunters died there. Frequent dust-ups with vigilant Belgian patrols sometimes ended in deaths or arrests. A famous poacher named Billy Pickering was killed by an elephant that tore his head off and then trampled his body to pulp. Another poacher by the name of Broom was shot dead by authorities. Belgian Askaris had once wounded the greatest ivory hunter of all, Walter D. M. "Karamoja" Bell, as he sat in a canoe midstream in the Nile. Ironically, Bell was one of the few hunters in the Congo who was legitimate, having taken the trouble to buy licenses. The Askaris paid a price for their temerity, for Bell returned fire with his 7mm rifle.

In the Congo's great Ituri forest, a region not much better known today than in Cottar's time, Charles made friends with the Efe pygmies. They alerted him to Belgian patrols and showed him how to hunt at close range in the thickest jungle. With their skillful help Cottar accumulated a sizable grubstake of ivory. But elephants and Belgian *Askaris* were only part of the risk. Charles left the Congo with deadly *spirillum* tick fever. Comatose, he was carried by his native bearers over 400 miles to the shores of Lake Victoria, and then 200 miles by train to Nairobi. He survived this extraordinary journey and recovered, but the effects of the disease remained with him to the end of his days. His life was saved only by the endurance and tenacity of his African safari crew.

For the next few years Cottar traveled back and forth between Africa and the United Sates. In 1915 he packed up his wife and nine children and left

Oklahoma for good. A few miles northwest of Nairobi, Charles carved out a new homestead where he built a tropical bungalow-style house. The comfortable home was built on stilts, using wood and corrugated iron sheeting.

After the first World War, Charles founded his now famous Cottar's Safari Service. He returned often to hunt the game-filled plains of Masailand, and took to referring to the entire region as "Cottar Country." Those who entered his self-proclaimed territory did so at their own risk. His eldest daughter, Evelyn, recalled that he once "shot a few holes into the roof of a car that came into *his* country. They left in a hurry!"

Although Bwana Cottar was among the first to import Ford cars to Kenya, he favored riding mules for hunting. Charles built frames on his safari trucks and covered them with mosquito netting in order to transport his prized mules into big game areas. To reach certain parts of Cottar Country, it was necessary to leapfrog perilous "fly belts" inhabited by fierce tsetse flies whose bites were lethal to domestic stock, and sometimes to humans.

One day while hunting with a Winchester .30-06 for meat, Bwana came upon a leopard feeding on a guinea fowl. Cottar fired at the cat, but before he could reload the leopard swarmed all over him, biting him savagely on the shoulders and face. With his great strength, Cottar used his rifle as a stave to throw off the cat. To his amazement the leopard lay dead where it fell, having succumbed to his bullet. It would be the lightest of three leopard maulings he would experience.

Sometime later Cottar spotted another leopard in open country, and this time he ran it down on horseback. He lassoed the winded beast around the neck, then dismounted and hobbled its hind legs. Leaving the leopard to recuperate, he went to get his motion picture camera. Charles instructed his wife Anita to crank the film and his young son Mike to stand guard. Bwana planned to star in the first real-life action movie of a man tussling with a leopard.

As the camera rolled and Charles boldly advanced, the great cat, still hobbled, made a powerful lunge. Cottar swung up his rifle, but the snarling feline knocked him to the ground before he could shoot. Charles wrestled with the leopard and then fired a fatal shot. In those few short moments the cat had done great damage. Doctors told Cottar he had blood poisoning, and insisted on amputating his leg to save his life. He refused, and to everyone's surprise but his own, Bwana recovered. Anita never lived down the fact that the movie was out of focus and useless.

During his years as a white hunter, Charles and two of his sons offered unprecedented international hunts that began in Africa and ended in India or Indochina. He saw no difficulty in shipping his gunbearers and crews, along with safari vehicles and tentage, to the Far East. He once arrived at the foot of a nearly impassable mountain range in India. Cottar dismantled his cars and had them carried up the escarpments on the backs of elephants, then reassembled them on a plateau, ready for the hunt. These logistical exercises boggle the mind. Considering the great distances and modes of travel at that time, it was an unparalleled accomplishment in outfitting.

266

Over his long career, Bwana's fiery vitality and great strength saved him more than a few times in serious entanglements with dangerous game. Cottar's bullet once failed to stop the charge of a bull elephant in a thorny rendezvous. The enraged tusker grabbed Cottar and threw him into some brush, then unaccountably broke off the attack. Bwana escaped with a few broken ribs. Another time a buffalo knocked him down and gored him. Bwana lay on his back in the dust, while the buffalo shoveled him along the ground with its horns, trying to finish him off. Cottar got one foot on each side of the bull's neck and bracing his legs, he let the animal push him around until he could lever another shell into his .405 Winchester.

Although Cottar later suffered a stroke that partly paralyzed his left side, he continued to hunt with incredible energy for another twenty years. He also endured regular bouts of blackwater fever, an advanced and often deadly form of malaria. Doctors warned him that blackwater would kill him. Cottar ignored their warnings, convinced his end would come not from disease, but in the jaws of a lion. Elephant, buffalo and leopard had tried to kill him, and they had failed. He had not been horned by a rhino, but he dismissed old *faru* as being too ugly and too stupid to kill him. Although he had shot more than fifty lions, he was certain that one day a tawny cat would spring upon him from ambush when he least expected it. Bwana feared nothing on earth, yet he believed his days would end in a flurry of fang and claw, and he would die in writhing agony beneath the equatorial sun. Down the dangerous safari road, Cottar's gloomy prediction turned out to be off the mark, but not by much.

During the monsoon rainy seasons in Africa, Bwana often returned to America to promote his safaris. In 1940 it seemed the Gods had smiled when he landed a rich contract for a lecture tour across the U.S. Cottar needed spectacular film for his tour, and with his eldest son Bud, he headed for Barakitabu (Difficult Road) in Masailand to set up *campi* at their favorite spot beside a shallow stream-crossing.

One morning as they hunted the green foothills of the Loita Range, they surprised an old rhino, which immediately charged. Bud fired, wounding the beast which veered away into the dense brush. As his son pursued the rhino, Charles waited behind in the glade. All of a sudden the screech of tick birds pierced the stillness. Knowing the birds' cries signaled the presence of a rhino or buffalo, Charles quickly unshouldered his heavy wooden tripod. The brush crackled like gunfire as an angry rhino tore out of the thorns looking for trouble. It paused briefly, its head held high, its long horns tilted like lances at Bwana's mid-section. Charles kept his eye to the viewfinder and cranked away. As he rolled off the film, the rhino charged, boiling through the dust. It was exactly the kind of dramatic footage he so badly needed.

Charles figured he would film until the last one-hundredth of a second, then throw up his big .405 Winchester and drop the beast with a solid bullet in the brain. In worst case he could jump aside as the clumsy *faru* brushed past in his blind charge. When the thundering beast was on him, Cottar fired at point-blank range. The bullet struck muscle and bone, but the long horn now near the ground before the moment of impact, scooped upwards, ripping Bwana's thigh. The rhino's two-ton impact knocked the big

267

man down, just as *faru* fell mortally wounded across Cottar's legs. Yet the battering rhino had failed to loosen Bwana's grip on his rifle. Pinned down by the great thrashing body, Cottar rammed his rifle into the rhino and fired several more rounds.

Bud heard the gunshots and sprinted back to his father. He saw where the horn had opened Bwana's leg and passed through an artery. Bud fashioned a tourniquet to staunch the blood pumping from his father's thigh. Bwana's sun-shot eyes calmly gazed at a spiral of vultures with wings razoring the air, their shadows swooping doom over his tanned face. Cottar impatiently motioned toward the gunbearers who were tying a tarpaulin to shade him.

Mortally wounded, Charles commanded, "Tell them to stop. It's no use. I'm done for. Roll it back."

As he lay on Masailand's baked black-cotton soil, he fixed his blue eyes on the sky above Cottar Country. One hour later the 66-year-old hunter had bled to death.

On a Sunday afternoon Bwana's many friends paid their last respects at Nairobi's Forest Cemetery. His loyal African safari crews were there, too, and none had dry eyes. The *kali* old hunter had gone to meet his God Ngai on the frozen jagged peak of Mount Kenya.

L ong after his death, Charles Cottar's legend lives on in the safari world. The dynasty he founded is now in its fifth generation. His eldest son Pat ("Bud") followed in his father's footsteps, accompanying the Duke and Duchess of York as well as renowned wildlife photographers Martin and Osa Johnson, on their early safaris in Kenya. His middle son Mike was thought by colleagues and clients to be the finest hunter of his time. Among his noted clients was Woolworth Donahue, American dimestore heir. In July 1941, during a safari on the western Serengeti plains, Mike was charged by a buffalo which he shot at close range. In an incident which paralleled the death of Bwana Charles, the momentum of the wounded buffalo carried it forward, and it fell on Mike. The talented hunter died soon afterwards of a ruptured spleen. Ted, the youngest son, left Africa to live in California, but occasionally returned to hunt throughout the 1950s.

In turn, Mike Cottar's only son, Glen, became a white hunter in 1956 during the glorious heyday of safari. For the next forty years he pioneered expeditions into remote reaches of East Africa, Botswana, Zaire and Sudan. With his wife Pat, he developed tented photographic camps in some of the finest big game country. Glen died in 1996. Today, his only son, 36-year-old Calvin Cottar, maintains the fine traditions of Africa's First Family of Safari. His firm, Cottar's Safari Service, is named after that of his famous great-grandfather.

WINDIGO MOON

*Day after perilous day he pursued the magnificent ram,
enduring the cold and the loneliness and the icy peaks, gripped
by an obsession that bordered on madness.*

By Robert W. Murphy

t was a beautiful habitat group of white mountain sheep. As you
stood before the big case with its front of curving glass, the rocks
and peaks and sky seemed to come out of the case and surround
you, making you forget you were in a museum, making you
think you were in the northern Rockies with the stones under
your moccasins and the keen air in your lungs. You forgot
that the ram with his great curving horns and the two ewes
and their lambs had been killed and brought from that far-distant place and
mounted; for they seemed alive and breathing, the ram alert, the ewes poised for
flight to some narrow rock ledge in the background. It was as though you had
come around a corner upon them, nearer than any man had ever come before; in
the instant before they went away, leaping from rock to rock with the wonderful
split-second daring and coordination of their kind, you saw them grayish white
against the dark rock, their light golden eyes startled and their muscles tense.

"It's handsome, Jeff," I said. "It's as handsome as any group I've ever seen."

"We've worked hard on it," he said. "We're pretty proud of it. I wanted you to
see it before it was opened to the public tomorrow."

269

"The ram," I said, "hasn't the best head I've ever seen, but he's good. He's better than most."

"There was a bigger one," he said. "The biggest one there is, maybe."

Something in his voice made me look at him: The tall, lean-muscled man with gray eyes and a keen and decisive face who had shot them all, who had been a tireless, skillful hunter once and had given it up now and put his guns away. He was holding an empty cartridge in one hand, rolling it about in his fingers; apparently he had taken it from his pocket, as though he carried it all the time.

"You missed him?" I asked.

"No," he said. "No. It was a strange thing. That was when I stopped shooting. You aren't in a hurry, are you?"

He wanted to talk about it. "No," I said.

I went back again (he said) after I got the group. The ram didn't satisfy me, but he was the best I could get on the first trip. The weather closed in on us; the river started to freeze, and when that happens you have to get out quickly if you want to get out at all. For a time after I got back I didn't think of returning. The Yukon Territory is a long way off and it costs a lot of money to go there; I wasn't getting any younger, and sheep hunting is about the hardest work in the world. But after the ram was mounted he looked smaller than ever; and as I worked at my desk here during the winter and spring I caught myself wanting to see those mountains again. They were aloof and lonely, with that cool cleanness of line that satisfied something within me and can be found only in the northern wilderness. The upshot of it was that I offered to stand half the cost out of my own pocket and bring back a ram that would make the group the best in the world. The museum accepted this, and I made my arrangements.

I'd hunted in the Glenlyon Mountains the first time, above the juncture of the Pelly and the Macmillan, and intended to go there again. There was a Canadian Mounted Police patrol boat going up the Pelly in the middle of August; the time was a little late, but I decided to take the boat rather than paddle and track a canoe. I engaged the French Canadian Louis Dufour, who had been with me on the first trip, and met him in Selkirk the day before the police boat sailed. He was a good man; barrel-chested and squat and strong as a horse, a willing and good-natured fellow, always ready to show his fine teeth in a flashing grin. He showed them when we shook hands. "By gar," he said, "me, I lak for you to come back. Dis tam we get de big one, eh?"

I agreed with this; a big one was what I wanted. We decided to spend the night on the boat, and after supper I fell into conversation with Corporal James, who was in charge of her, about sheep. We sat on the deck until pretty late – there were only a few hours of dark twilight at that time of year – and he let me do most of the talking until bedtime. When he got up he said, "There's been a number of rumors about a ram as big as a house back in the Pelly Mountains, up around the head of the Lapie River."

Louis, who hadn't said much, stirred in his chair at this. "Is bad," he said.

"Damn bad. We no go dere, I t'ink."

The corporal grinned. "There are a lot of rumors about that, too," he said. "Rumors of bad luck. Only two men have ever been back there. One of them was killed by a slide, and the other got out, but he lost a leg. Both of them hunted that ram."

"Sure," Louis said. "Dey no hunt him, dey no get hurt. M'sieu Jeff, I lak de bighorns, but I no lak dis one. No, by gar!"

His tone had an unusual vehemence in it, a sort of superstitious fervor. I was surprised, for I'd never suspected him of believing in the powers of darkness. I was interested too . "What do you think, Corporal?" I asked.

"I don't know what to think," he said. "I take very little stock in the native devils, but this one might have something in it. It's had such universal acceptance that no one will go back there. The country's very difficult and practically unknown. Taking it all in all, I'd stay out of it."

"Sure," Louis said. "Dis ram, he too big maybe, he lak a windigo, le bon Dieu want he should stay, eh? We go same place lak last year, we have good camp, no trouble."

"That's it," the corporal said, and for an instant looked like a shamed small boy. "I don't believe in it, but I'd rather be safe than sorry. There's something queer about the place."

I hadn't expected him to say that. He'd started off in a rather joking tone, but it hadn't taken him long to change; and while he was changing I was making up my mind to go there. Maybe it was the rumor of a big ram, or maybe it was scientific curiosity; bad luck's a thing I've always doubted. It comes from sloppy preparation or economy in the wrong places or sheer laziness – something of the sort.

"We'll go there," I said.

Louis said, "Ah, Seigneur!"

"If it's too much for you," I said, "I'll let you off."

He looked hurt. "No," he said. "I go. But I don' lak him, me."

The corporal knocked out his pipe "I'm sorry I spoke about it," he said. "I wish you'd reconsider. It'll be a few days before we get to the Glenlyons, and you can think it over."

With that he went to bed, but every night thereafter he tried to talk me out of the notion. I had no intention of being talked out of it. We steamed on, dodging sandbars and riffles and sunken logs; we passed the mouth of the Macmillan and went into the Pelly, passed our camping place of the year before; the wide valley of the Pelly went by, the tall spruces and the poplars already taking their autumn colors. It grew wilder; we saw old beaver cuttings and once a family of Indians catching salmon, but little game. The corporal fell silent; back from the river the lofty, rounded ranges hung in the sky, and a sort of subdued excitement began to build up in me. When we came to the mouth of the Lapie they let us off, cached a canoe for our return trip, and we made up our packs.

271

"You'd better camp close to the Pelly," the corporal said.

"No," I said. "We'll go up the Lapie as far as we can. I want to get to timber line, on the inside range."

"Well," he said, "I wish you luck. I wish you'd stay where we could see you on the return trip. I'm sorry you didn't think better of it and stay in the Glenlyons."

We shook hands; he stood on the rear deck, and I could see his scarlet jacket for a long time.

Our camp was in the most beautiful spot I've ever seen. It was close to the creek in a grove of huge spruces; the creek with its cascades roared past it, and the magnificent mountains hung over it on all sides. The interior range was different from the mountains as seen from the river. It wasn't rounded; it was high and savage, carved into canyons and precipices. The peaks spired up to seven thousand feet, bleak and rough, some with snow on them, as untouched as they were on the last day of creation.

The ridges were connected above timber line, and that made it fine sheep country; for sheep ranged the open peaks even in winter, when other animals are driven into hibernation or to the timber lower down. They may come down to the mountain meadows to feed, but they always sleep high up. They are the true dwellers of the peaks; neither winter nor enemies can drive them off their range; eagles are the only living things that get above them. I was sure we would find them above us, and as soon as we got a semblance of order in camp we started out.

We climbed for nearly four hours, fighting our way up through the dwarf willow to the rocks, then clawing up the rocks to the summits. Once we saw a bunch of white dots several miles away, but the binoculars showed them to be ewes and lambs. We went on. The wind got colder; we left everything behind except an occasional flock of ptarmigan and the marmots that scuttled about and whistled at us. Far below, the valleys spread out, the darkness of spruce broken by the deep carmine of huckleberry and the gold of poplar; all around a bewildering sea of summits stretched to the horizon. It was the loneliest place imaginable, and one of the most beautiful – inhumanly, coldly, abstractly beautiful. A light haze began to gather on the more distant peaks, and Louis murmured that we should be getting back. We weren't far from the crest then, and I agreed to go back after we reached it and searched the other slope.

We made the summit and crossed it. The side of the mountain fell almost straight down for two thousand feet, but I hardly noticed that then; for on a shelf about one hundred and fifty yards below us, looking off to the left, was standing the most magnificent ram I've ever seen. I

272

know all the record heads; I know them to a quarter of an inch; they were nothing compared to his. I heard Louis gasp, and then the ram looked up at us. Standing outlined against the wild and distant escarpments across the valley, with a head such as no man has ever taken, he was like the ideal type of his species, perfect and unbelievable. I swung the rifle up, and as the sights settled a little behind his shoulder something stabbed me – a fierce unwillingness, a confusion of mind. It was extraordinary. I wanted him, and yet my brain refused to function. It was as though some unknown influence had paralyzed it; but my finger, trained by years of shooting, tightened on the trigger. As I pulled it a younger ram I hadn't seen scrambled up in front of the old one. It was too late to hold fire then; I heard the bullet smack into him and saw him go down as the old one took a short leap and vanished over the edge of the shelf.

Neither of us could move for an instant; then we started for the shelf. Rocks clattered around us, and I had to leave my rifle behind. We reached the shelf and I dug my toes and fingers into the rock; the drop in front of me brought my heart up against my teeth. I looked over, expecting to see the ram still falling, far below, but it was moving across the sheer rock, swift and sure. I might have gone back and got the rifle, but I never thought of it; I stared at the ram going across the rim of that gulf of air until he made a shoulder and leaped from sight.

I got my back against the rear wall of the shelf; my belly was tight and cold, and when I looked at Louis he was crossing himself. His swarthy face glistened with sweat, and his eyes had fear in them.

"Ah!" he said. "Ah, Seigneur! Dat one, bullets don' hit him, he walk down a cliff for flies. Now we go, now we see him, we go from dis place." He was really pleading with me. "M'sieu Jeff, you no can kill him. Please, we go, we go quick! Somet'ing happen sure, we go before!"

There was a faint echo of his superstitious fervor along my own nerves, for there had been an air of unreality about both the old ram and his escape. Now that the ram was gone, I wanted it more than ever; but it was really a strange thing that had happened to me, the paralysis of my mind that had been like a warning, that fixed my purpose. Bad luck! I'd come to that place to find out about bad luck, to prove there was no such thing, and I didn't intend to leave until I had proved it.

"No," I said, "we'll stay. We'll stay until we get him. I'll come up alone and sleep on the ridges, and you can keep camp." Louis was looking at me as though I was already a dead man; I pointed to the young ram lying on the other side of the shelf. "Do you think we can get him down the way he is," I asked, "or had we better skin him?"

He shook his head slightly. "Sure," he said, in a subdued tone. "You help, maybe we carry him lak he is."

The ram I'd killed was bigger than the one the museum had; it's the one in the case now; I spent the next day hanging him in a standing, life-like attitude from poles, photographing him for the taxidermists, and preparing his skin. The morning after that I started out. The nights were getting longer, and it wasn't quite broad daylight at five. I carried as little as possible – my caribou-skin robe to sleep in, a little bacon, tea, chocolate, biscuits, a frying pan, tin cup and alcohol burner in my rucksack. I was determined to stay on the ridges four or five days, avoiding the time lost in climbing up and down to camp. There had been a heavy frost when I woke, and I'd begun to worry about the weather. I didn't want to be frozen out before I got another chance at the ram, and time was precious. It wasn't the usual method of hunting sheep – where you climb to the summits and move about until a good head comes into stalking distance. This was a hunt for one particular sheep in a veritable haystack of peaks, an infinitely more difficult business.

I told Louis to watch the ridges, and if he didn't see me on the fifth day to come up. He nodded somberly, and four hours later I was on the crests. From the topography of the country and the way the ram had taken, I judged his probable direction and started into the range, away from the creek. I had to stay out of sight and off the skyline, do a lot of crag work on sharply inclined and slippery rock, and it was hard and dangerous going.

In much big-game hunting you are after an animal that can fight back. Sheep don't fight back, but their range fights for them; not for a moment when cornered, but all the time. You spend hours crossing rock faces, hanging over half a mile of empty air; you work and sweat and strain your muscles to exhaustion to make a certain key rock, and when you make it, you find it's loose and can't be used. You're in a vertical world, and the whole vast wilderness, like a frozen dark sea with patches of snow and green mountain meadows, stretches below. It is magnificent; in its wild and savage loneliness it seems to belong only to you; but beneath this, it seems to be perpetually watching and waiting for you to make a slight misstep, a slight miscalculation. Its aloof hostility slowly comes a little closer to you; it gets into the back of your mind; at the end of four days, with the loneliness, the toil, and the diet I had, it's possible I got to talking to myself a little.

I'd seen sheep, plenty of them, but not the old ram. I could have got several very large heads. But a thing all sportsmen know, a thing almost like a madness, had hold of me – and augmenting it was the determination to put an end to that silly business about bad luck.

I kept on. On the morning of the fifth day I woke up in the little canyon where I'd slept, feeling cold and stiff and a little dizzy, but with a strange, subdued excitement. It was as though something had been promised me while I slept, a sort of surety I'd see the ram that day. I cooked a little bacon and made tea, and set out. I'd made a great circle, and an hour later I was above camp; I trained my binoculars on it and made out Louis standing by the fire, apparently watching me with the other pair of binoculars. I waved my arms; he made some sort of gesture and I went on, up over the crest.

The morning had dawned rather cloudy; as I continued into the mountains a heavy overcast swallowed the sun, and the wind began to moan around the crags. Snow came after a while; it whipped around me, blotting out the distant peaks. It was very cold, and the footing grew more precarious. I should have given up and gone down to camp, but my excitement was stronger than ever. I was sure of seeing the old ram; I fought my way along for an hour more, made another summit, and crossing to the other side descended a little and got into the lee of a shoulder springing from a sharp slope of loose rock that the wind had blown bare. It was snowing so hard I couldn't see the valley; after I'd stood there for a few minutes it stopped, and looking down, I could see, over a clump of boulders, the dark curve of a pair of horns.

I knew them at once; there wasn't another pair in the world like them; and I knew if I could get to the other side of the shoulder the ram would be in sight. I couldn't climb over the shoulder; it went up sheer, but with luck I could get around the base. I dropped my pack, slung the rifle on my back, and, after a half-hour's ticklish work, raised my head and saw the old ram three hundred yards below, watching the valley. There was another short flurry of snow. I was afraid more was coming and that it would make him move.

I hurried too much, and that place wasn't made for hurry. As I raised the rifle my foot dislodged a rock and I fell down. There was a swift, gathering roar, a heavy blow on my head, and I didn't know anything more until I slowly became conscious of Louis' blurred face and the choking fire of brandy in my throat. He knew I needed food and rest; after watching me go over the crest he'd come up from camp to try to talk some sense into me.

I spent three days in camp, mostly sleeping and being fed by Louis, nursing my battered head and watching the Canada jays and red squirrels trying to steal bits of meat from the frying pan when Louis turned his back. I should have enjoyed it – the calm, the roar of the stream, the surrounding spruces spiring into the sky, the wild peaks rosy in the mornings and evenings, jagged and black against the aurora at night – but I didn't. The nights were growing increasingly colder, the leaves were falling faster; the time when the entire land would be locked tight by winter came nearer every hour.

I was nervous and impatient; I had to hurry; but while my enforced rest dragged by, a strange thing happened to me. I caught myself thinking sympathetically about the ram. I'd never done that before. I'd always looked on game with cool objectivity, as something to outwit and kill; in spite of myself, I began to see the ram's side of it. I'd seen him only once during the five-day hunt, but how many times had he seen me? Had he gradually become aware that I was after him like an implacable shadow, a being with a cool and calculating brain and a far-reaching rifle, a being who awoke in his heart a fear that grew and ran along his nerves like a sickness, filling his range, his hours of feeding and travel and rest, with terror?

This kind of thing made me devilish uncomfortable. Once or twice I was on the edge of chucking the whole thing, but I didn't. He had a wonderful head, and he was bad luck. He – or my haste – had almost done me in once; because of that I couldn't rest, couldn't chuck it up, until I'd taken the dare, proved it out – without haste the next time. On the third evening, when I told Louis I'd be going again in the morning, he dropped the frying pan and stood staring at me with a shocked and incredulous expression.

"Dis tam," he said finally, "he no work, I t'ink. He tired, he finish."

"Who's finished?" I asked.

He didn't reply, but walked across to the lean-to, brought back my ground-squirrel-skin jacket, and turned up the back of the collar; he'd sewed to it a Miraculous Medal of the Blessed Virgin, such as Catholics wear to protect them from harm; he'd got it from some mission post in the past. "He finish, sure," he said, and took the jacket and hung it up. His bearing during the rest of the evening was considerate, subdued, and gloomy. He'd given me up; when I left the next morning, he climbed a mile or so with me, shook hands, and stood expressionlessly watching me out of sight.

There was more snow on the summits now, and the days were shorter. There was an urgent need for haste, but haste was too dangerous. I knew a part of the ram's range and tried to guess the rest of it, to define it and cover it carefully and coolly. It was killing work, under a constant tension. The peaks, often above the mist and seeming to float upon it, appeared to draw in a little, to stalk me as I stalked the ram. The rubbish about bad luck was harder to laugh at up there, surrounded by that frozen grandeur.

I didn't laugh much. I saved my breath for more pressing matters, for I thought the hunt would be a long one and I'd need all the breath I could get; but on the second day, in a snow field, I came on some tracks that could have been left only by the old ram. He was going higher, retreating to the highest peak in the vicinity, and I knew it would be extremely difficult to get a shot at him. I redoubled my caution and my labor; I didn't know how far ahead he was, but I started my stalk right there. I kept out of sight and went circuitously, which, in that country, meant constant crag work. By sundown I'd started up the peak; I stopped awhile in a little chimney to make some tea, and waited for the moon to come up. It was cold – that thin, penetrating, high-altitude cold that comes when the sun goes down. My teeth chattered with it, and with excitement, for I'd decided to go on after moonrise, to take advantage of the semidarkness to get near him, and that was terribly dangerous.

When the moon came up, I started. Everything was changed and incalculable; shadows became rocks, and rocks turned into thin air; mist made precipices where there were none, and level ground out of precipices. I was within an inch of being a dead man twenty times that night, and will remember the rest of my life crossing on my belly a knife-edge a quarter of a mile long and no wider than a kitchen table, as slippery as glass. The sides fell straight down into gulfs of mist and blackness, and the peaks reared up all around, washed by moonlight, pale violet, glittering with snow, sometimes almost impalpable, but always waiting.

But I did it. Just before the moon went down I made out on a ledge the pale blur that was the ram. There was enough light to be fairly sure of him with the binoculars. He was a little beyond the crest, and dawn was coming; he'd probably move with it, and there wasn't time to get around the crest. I had to go over it. It was an almost perpendicular climb above a slope with no apparent bottom, and I hesitated a long time before I tackled it; finally I slipped off my pack and started up. My moccasins wouldn't hold and I kicked them off. The projecting bits of rock grew scarcer as I ascended; finally one of them slipped with me, but I managed to hook another with my knee and hang there. The sky was paling rapidly, and the cold light spilled over the world; as I hung there sweating I looked down and saw the steely dark glint of a lake that must have been three thousand feet below. I knew I wasn't good for much more, but in the strengthening light I could see how near I was to the top. There was nothing for it but a scramble, a last desperate muscular effort, so I scrambled. I gave it all I had left in me, caught a rock at the top, and was over. The loose rock went down with a diminishing rattle that seemed to last forever, and for a moment I lay on the top, too exhausted to move; then I saw the ram, hearing the falling rock, come to his feet.

He stood with his head up and his hoofs bunched against the jagged background and the pale colors of dawn, as unbelievable as he had been the first time I saw him; then the rifle went off. It went off with a roar, a shattering crash that echoed and reechoed in that silent place; no rifle on earth had ever made so much noise before. I had shot without being aware of shooting, without the conscious thought necessary to do it. It was a reflex, an uncontrollable thing, an indication that in my subconscious I was afraid of the ram, maybe. I couldn't possibly have hit him, in that light and without aiming. He didn't drop; he didn't move for an instant; then he simply vanished around the shoulder of the ledge. It was only then I realized he couldn't go up or down; the ledge thrust out of the smooth side of the mountain like a shelf. To get off it he would have to come toward me, and unless the formation of the cliff face changed beyond the shoulder, I had him trapped.

I didn't think then, any more than I'd thought when I shot at him. I was beyond thinking; after the long hunt, the cold and the loneliness and the night, I must have been a little mad. I went after him. I scrambled over the rocks like a lunatic and out onto the ledge. It was only three or four feet wide and hung over the valley, a horrible drop, but I didn't think about that either. I went along it and around the shoulder; and there, not twenty feet from me, the old ram stood with his back to the wall.

277

I didn't know what I'd expected, or whether I'd expected anything, but such close quarters stopped me dead. Sheep are shy creatures, but so are mice; and even a cornered mouse will fight like a fiend. That ram could have lowered his head, made one leap, and tumbled me into the gulf below. Maybe if I'd moved, if I'd reached for the trigger or brought up the rifle, he'd have done it – maybe not. I don't know and I never shall.

I stood there staring at him, and suddenly I realized fully what had been trying to impress itself upon me all along, what had affected my nerves and confused me and given rise to legends: That here, in this ram, was the ideal member of the species, the ultimate perfection that all evolution strives for, the impossibility you talk about and search for and never believe in. I couldn't shoot him. After hounding him down at the risk of my life, I couldn't do it. There would never be another one like him; he didn't belong in a damned museum, for people who wouldn't know perfection if they saw it to stare at; he belonged among these bleak and aloof and precipitous peaks until he died or a misstep dropped him down among the crags for the eagles to finish.

We both stood there without moving as the seconds stretched out. A little sense began to trickle back into me, and with it came the awareness of the valley far below, the tiny dark spruces, the meadows still holding their autumn color, the empty air . . . The old ram gathered himself. His muscles tensed, he seemed to squat a little, and the next instant he leaped over my head, landed near the edge of the shoulder, leaped again, and vanished around the corner. It sounded as though he was going over the crest.

When I'd crawled off the ledge onto solid rock, I sat for half an hour, until my heart stopped pounding. I knew then I'd never kill anything again. I was through; the encounter had cured me. Presently the thought came to me that I should preserve, as a memento, the last cartridge I'd ever take out of a gun. I pulled the bolt and ejected it. It had been fired.

It was the one I'd fired from the crest, and in my crazy haste to get to the ledge I'd left it in the chamber. I must say my skin crawled as I stared at that bit of brass. It had been lying in the chamber empty and spent, and I had a shockingly clear mental picture of what would have happened if I'd moved to fire it, breaking the hypnotic immobility that held both of us, to chance knocking the ram down before he could charge.

It was a long way to the valley from that ledge. There would have been a little time to recall the other two men who had hunted the old ram, and the corporal who took more stock in the native devils than he cared to admit. A little time, but not much.

Originally titled "There Was a Bigger One," this chapter from The Phantom Setter and Other Stories *is reprinted by permission of Harold Ober Associates Incorporated. Copyright ©1966 by Robert Murphy.*

THE GOVERNOR'S TROUT

Sean and Patrick had chanced upon the secret to catching the Governor's huge Loch Levens trout – the pride of all his possessions. And this very night, beneath a star-filled sky, would be the perfect time to pull off their daring exploit. Right under the Governor's very nose.

By Todd Tanner

ean Michael McCabe was exactly thirty-seven years old on the day his life changed forever. As it was his birthday, and as the little one-bedroom house was empty – Molly having gone off the day before to help her widowed sister, whose youngest had the cough and whose oldest the flu – Sean decided a stop at the pub might be just the thing for a thirsty man finished with his day's duties.

So instead of turning right he turned left, and left rather than right, and in no time at all he found himself seated in front of the bar at The Industrious Rabbit; the exact same Industrious Rabbit where the legendary Seamus Linehan, on a dare and a bet, had downed ten pints at lunch and then held his water till the Rabbit's smoky old Grandfather chimed midnight. They still – Sean included – speak of Seamus' feat fifty-two years later and, one and all, toast "Let it run, man, let it run!" each night when the hands stand straight up and Grandfather tolls twelve.

Now Sean, who's a man of moderation and known far and wide as the most level-headed in the county, had finished off perhaps a drop more than his usual when down to his right sat Patrick O'Rourke. And Patrick, who's a hound, a poacher and a scallywag when he's not in worse trouble, looked over at the four empty mugs on the bar (The Rabbit, as most of the county's fine establishments, makes a practice of not collecting "Retired Generals" on a man's birthday, so that his friends might know when he's had enough and send him off home to bed) and said, "Ho, Sean, I've got two presents for you on this great day of your birth. First, Michael the Barkeep will pull you a pint and it's on me, as we've always been fast friends. And second, I have the answer to that quintessential question of your very own existence. I'm prepared, in full and intimate detail, to explain how we're going to catch the Governor's trout."

And with that, Sean and Patrick put there heads together and lowered their voices, so no one could hear what was said, or even who said it.

ow the Governor's trout, as you well know, are the envy of every fisherman in the county, and quite a few outside the limits. They're of the Loch Leven strain, and grow to great size and, as the saying goes, "They're smarter than the brightest from Darby." The Governor himself, an acknowledged champion of the long rod, has spent fully one-half his life fishing his trout, and most of the remainder thinking over them, and yet he's only caught a handful and those were little ones, shorter than your arm.

Of course, his lack of success is small wonder when you note that the Governor's stream is slow and shallow, and it rises from the ground on one end of his great meadow and sinks back into the earth on the other, and the trout won't eat during the day.

"And why should they?" you might ask, as they're all nasty browns – known for their nefarious nighttime habits – and near impervious to the feathered tomfoolery plied by the Governor and his distinguished guests.

So that very night, at the stroke of Linehan's hour – "Let it run, man, let it run!" – here come two shadows skulking by the Warden's cottage, and one of the shadows belongs to Patrick O'Rourke and the other to our friend Sean. And Sean had his bamboo tucked inside its tube, and his reel in his pocket, and Patrick had his poacher's creel, and together they were dressed for the hunt.

"We'll have to be quiet, Sean," said Patrick, "or we'll have the Warden on us for sure."

Sean, being a sensible sort, said nothing.

The Governor's meadow is a fine meadow, indeed, and would be even if the Governor's stream didn't wander right through the middle of it. The grass is thick and lush – just the kind of place your cows would hope to spend a week or two – and it's dotted with small seeps that filter down to the streambed and add their volume to the slow-moving flow.

Of particular import to our story, this very meadow is (and, as far back as anyone can remember, always has been) perfect habitat for that most preferred of all nocturnal Loch Leven brown trout foods. And it's not Juneflies, or caddis, or grassjumpers, in case you've hazarded a guess. As evidenced by the noisome feeding that greeted Sean and Patrick as they neared the water, and the tiny lights flashing all around, the Governor's trout absolutely adore that most princely member of the insect kingdom.

The ever-succulent firefly.

Now Sean was well aware of this fact, as indeed were most of the county's brotherhood of the angle, for the secret feeding habits of the Governor's trout had long been exposed. Yet our friend had no recourse for, as everyone knows, an imitation of the fly that lights up the night sky doesn't exist. Indeed, the Governor himself had puzzled and worried away many an hour on just this problem, and spent time researching batteries and flylines that carry electric currents and other such solutions, but none had proved their success in the field. His field, that is, and that's the only one we're concerned with.

"Here it is!" said Patrick, as they sat down on the bank, and he reached into his creel and pulled out a small leather bag tied off with a bit of twine. "Do you have that dark green beetle birthed from stag's hair and the wool from a ram's stones?"

Sean nodded "yes" and held the tiny fraud up in his callused palm.

"Then this is your treasure, Sean, the one and only answer to the singularly reclusive nighttime habits of the Governor's much-coveted trout, and you and I are the only ones who know the mysterious properties of this fair elixir, or that it even exists. And tonight, with your skill and my alchemy, we'll pluck the Governor's Loch Levens, the pride of his possessions, from under his very nose."

And with those words, and not one more, Patrick opened his pouch.

Out came tumbling his stash, his stuff, the moist, crumbled remnants of luminescent lichen that he'd found down some dank shaft in the ground. For, you see, Patrick the Poacher knew every bolt hole and spelunker's hideaway in the country, and in one cave, dark and deep, he'd turned off his lamp as the constable's shouts neared, but instead of black there was light, the faint living glow of rare elf moss, and an idea hatched in his quite nimble mind. He gathered a handful of moss, popped it in his bag, and once the sounds of pursuit diminished, was off quick as you please.

So Sean rubbed his fly in the glowing clump of Patrick's hoard, and then ever-so-softly tucked one over the Governor's stream. The luminous fluff settled down nicely, and floated on the surface like a single star against the vast night sky. But only for a moment, though, because one of the Governor's trout lunged from below and snapped it right up.

The trout who attached himself to Sean's line was not yet full grown, being no larger than a small dog, but he comported himself with style, and it was all Sean could do to hold on for dear life. And when Mr. Loch Leven ran downstream, Sean had to follow; and when he ran upstream, Sean had to follow there, too. Once he slipped and fell, and said unkind words that we won't repeat, and once he stepped in a muckrat hole and said something worse. All in all, though, Sean fought a good fight, and after barely half an hour he slid the Governor's trout up on the bank.

And then a strong hand clapped him on the shoulder but, oddly enough, it wasn't Patrick's hand.

"Well, well, Sean Michael McCabe," said the Governor's Warden, Tom Daugherty. "That was a memorable sight, and nicely done. I've seen some fine stream-work in my day, indeed I have, but this night's the finest. It's a pity we'll have to go before the Governor on the morrow."

He tried this way, and tried that, but nothing Sean said could break the famous Daugherty resolve, and off they went to spend the night in the Warden's cottage. And it wasn't until later that Sean realized Patrick had slipped out like a mouse, and gotten clean away.

S o in the morn they went up to the estate house, and found the Governor at the pool practicing his roll cast. And the Governor was none too happy, and more than a little out of sorts when he learned that Sean had been poaching on his stream, and things were looking grim indeed for Sean Michael McCabe.

"And as final evidence of Sean's trespass, your Honour," finished up Warden Daugherty, addressing none other than the esteemed Governor himself who, in tweed cap, knickers and woolen vest – and his trout rod clasped firm in hand – appeared to be of the sternest, most unsympathetic sort, "I have here, in my very own possession, the ill-gotten proceeds of last night's felonious incursion." And Tom Daugherty reached into his burlap sack and hauled out by the tail a leg-long brown of some twenty and four pounds.

"My God, man!" bellowed the Governor. "You've poached my Prince Rupert! Do you know the penalty for snagging a trout of his stature? Out of my very own stream! It's six months in the county house with a pick and shovel for you!"

"Begging your Honour's pardon," broke in Tom, "but Sean didn't snag the Prince. Unlikely as it seems, he hooked your esteemed Rupert with a dry fly, and in the prescribed gentlemanly manner. He's a poacher, sir, and he deserves what he gets, but he's also a top-water man and I'll vouch that he's not sullied your stream with trebles nor nymphs."

"Astounding," said the Governor, "simply astounding." And after taking a minute or two to light his pipe, he sat down on the grass, his long legs folded like a newborn foal's, and motioned for Sean to sit beside him.

"I've been after this particular fish for years, Sean," the Governor mused, "and though I'm accounted a fair hand with a rod, he's done naught but laugh and offer me the fin. Yet you caught my Prince, an absolute scoundrel of a Loch Leven, with a dry fly. Hmmm, it seems that you and I will need to discuss a few things before we can resolve this matter properly . . ."

Neither Sean, nor Tom Daugherty, nor even the Governor himself, ever spoke one word of the conversation that came after. A nimble mind, though, can add two plus two plus two, and if you put them all together – a Warden with a sudden interest in spelunking, and a large, anonymous order for stag's hair and ram's wool at the local fly shoppe, and a new full-time gillie (who, for reasons never fully explained, received permission to fish the Governor's stream every other Tuesday) – well, I think you're beginning to see the picture.

And when Sean next saw Patrick the Poacher at the Industrious Rabbit three Saturdays after, he walked up and said, "Patrick, you rotten old scalawag, the next one's on me."

ROGUE MALE

How did the hero of Tsavo become the villain in East Africa's most enduring scandal? The true story behind Hemingway's Francis Macomber.

By Kenneth Cameron

he great elephant rounded a clump of acacia and swung toward the two hunters. Drying blood made dark stains down its wrinkled shoulder and neck, but despite its wounds, the big animal moved deceptively fast with that ambling gait that makes you misjudge its speed.

"Wait," the African veteran whispered.

The elephant rushed toward them – then abruptly it stopped, backed several steps. Its ears came forward, moving like fans, listening for them. Hot, tiny eyes were red with hatred. It came again with a rush, only a couple of strides, backed away, rushed again.

The trunk went straight up, and the big male elephant screamed.

"Shoot!" the veteran cried, knowing the charge was coming now.

But the other man only stood there. His eyes were fixed on this thing that wanted to kill him; his mouth was a little open, foolish looking. He was holding a London-made double .450 express rifle, and as the elephant opened its mouth and screamed, he could have raised it and put a bullet up through the mouth and into the brain – but he did not.

283

"For God's sake, shoot!"

But the amateur hunter could only stand there. He was trembling.

The veteran raised his own gun. It was the wrong gun for the task – an old military Martini-Henry carbine in .577/.450, its load behind the heavy ball hardly better than a shotgun's. But it was all he had. His face contorted with contempt for this man who stood transfixed beside him, he raised his gun and fired, then worked the breech to reload. The elephant recoiled a step as that ponderous bullet struck, and it screamed and recovered and came on. A gunbearer, trying to dodge the charging elephant, almost fell under it. The veteran shot again, the whole world coming down to that dark, dusty mass of flesh. The Martini-Henry boomed like a kettledrum; the elephant bellowed and turned away from the bitter smoke and the noise and passed them, so close the man could feel the breeze from its rush. As the beast went by, it reached for the gunbearer with its trunk, to rip him and trample him, but only knocked the cap off his head. It crashed into the acacias and disappeared, leaving behind it an incredible roar that hovered in the hot, thick air before dying into an absolute silence.

The man with the Martini-Henry felt his heart thud and turned over. His knees were weak, and he could feel sweat starting under his arms. He glanced at the amateur, still clutching his express rifle, staring at the spot where the elephant had disappeared.

"Why don't you go wait with your wife," the veteran said. "I'll take care of the elephant. Alone."

He didn't wait for an answer. With a signal to one of the gunbearers, he walked into the acacias after the animal, and the black man in the ragged European clothes followed.

There would have been nothing for the man with the express rifle to say, anyway. It was all too complicated by then, most of all by his wife, and the affair he knew she was having with the veteran hunter, here in the godforsaken bush.

The husband handed his rifle blindly to a gunbearer. He took a step and staggered, and sweat broke out all over him.

Thirty-six hours later he lay dead, his head burst apart by a bullet.

And his wife and the other man went on with the safari.

This real sequence of events happened in East Africa. In March, 1908. Twenty-six years later, the dean of professional hunters, Philip Percival, told the story – minus the real names – to Ernest Hemingway, who turned it into one of the classic short stories about Africa, *The Short Happy Life of Francis Macomber.* Twelve years after that, it was made into a motion picture called *The Macomber Affair,* starring Gregory Peck as the veteran hunter, Robert Pearson as the husband, and a stunning Joan

Bennett as the wife Hemingway called a bitch. Except for its tacked-on and silly ending, it was the best movie Hollywood ever made from a Hemingway source.

Yet, when the movie was made, the identities of the real-life figures were kept secret. Ironically, the man whom Peck portrayed was actually living in Los Angeles when the movie was released.

Who was the veteran hunter? And who was the woman who, in Hemingway's version, put the bullet into the back of her husband's head? And was the husband the "nice jerk" in Hemingway's story, or was he the angry coward so brilliantly played by Preston? Or was he the "English lord" of the gossip that still goes around?

Sometimes, fact is not only stranger than fiction, but a lot more interesting. In this case the veteran, the red-faced Wilson of Hemingway's story, the man played by the handsome Peck, was and still is famous for another of East Africa's greatest big-game feats. The book he wrote about is still in print and is a hunting classic.

This man was John Henry Patterson. The book was *The Man-Eaters of Tsavo*, the tale of the man who saved the Uganda Railway from man-killing lions in 1898.

So how did this hero, a best-selling author, become involved in a scandal that generated the ugliest of campfire gossip? And how did he lose his East African career, and his reputation, because of it?

A great deal of nonsense has been written about John Henry Patterson – some of it by Patterson himself, who was a master of personal disinformation – so that his legend has come totally unstuck from his reality. In the legend, he is a well-to-do gentleman, an educated man (public school and Sandhurst, the British West Point), and above all, a "sportsman." He is always Lieutenant Colonel Patterson, and that rank is always assumed to have been earned by his steady climb from his commissioning after Sandhurst. The legend assumes that he was a military engineer, thus explaining his working on the Uganda Railway long enough to kill the lions before dashing off to volunteer for the Boer War.

In reality, Patterson was none of these things. He was not wealthy; he was not a Sandhurst graduate; he was not a British Army lieutenant colonel (not until World War I, at any rate); and he was not what the British then called a gentleman.

In fact, John Henry Patterson enlisted in the British Army as a private at Dublin in 1885. Until then, he had been a groom in somebody's stable. He later gave so many versions of his birth date and place that it is impossible to pin them down, but he was probably 16 or so in 1885, an emaciated Irish kid with a first-rate mind, incredible courage and no future.

285

The Army became his mother and father – and his school. In 1886 he shipped for India, where he spent the next eight years with the Third Dragoon Guards. All the education he ever got was in the Army – the first and second class certificates of education, Lower Standard Hindustani, the sub-engineer's certificate. (Sorry – no Sandhurst.) He rose to the rank of sergeant and moved to the "unattached list," meaning that he served a civilian Indian department (railways) while remaining in the military. In 1897 he left the Army and signed on with the Uganda Railway as a junior assistant engineer, thus making his appointment with the lions and fame at Tsavo.

There is no question that he killed the lions, or that he did so heroically, if fairly stupidly. (He knew nothing about lion hunting and had virtually no help – he should have been killed.)

He left the railway in a fit of pique, forfeiting the cost of his passage both out and back, and returned to London to find himself in 1899 with a wife, no job and no prospects. He asked for his railway job back and was refused.

Then the Boer War crooked its finger at him.

Somehow – we shall never know *how* – Patterson got himself a commission in the gentlemanly Yeomanry. (Rather like an upper-class version of our National Guard, it became the Imperial Yeomanry when it served outside Britain. The Initials I.Y. were said by regulars to stand for "I Yield," although this was certainly not true in Patterson's case.) He must by then have talked like a gent and dressed like a gent; well, if it talks like one and walks like one . . . Anyway, in eighteen months he rose from lieutenant to acting lieutenant-colonel of Yeomanry (not of the British Army), had his own command, and was awarded the D.S.O. for heroism. (You have to smile at the image of this former sergeant of dragoons leading a cavalry regiment made up of gentleman riders.) After the war ended he was an honorary lieutenant-colonel, with the permanent rank of captain, later major.

And then the legend began. From this point, Patterson reinvented his past to match the man he had become. Ireland faded further and further away in a romantic mist (he once gave his birthplace as London); his parentage took on more gloss (his death certificate lists his father's occupation as "general"); and through his friends in the Yeomanry, he rose to a new position. This included, in 1907, his appointment as the Senior Game Ranger (warden) of the East Africa Protectorate – more or less modern Kenya.

In 1908, after only a couple of months in his new position in Africa (barely long enough to make some enemies, including the lieutenant-governor and the man he had replaced as head of the Game Department, Blayney Percival), Patterson organized a big safari to go into the unexplored country 300 miles north of Nairobi. His mission was to lay out a new eastern boundary for the Northern Game Reserve, which at that time filled most of modern Kenya's northern region. The area was inhospitable, mostly semi-desert; the route to it was lined by tribes still hostile to the British; and just to the north lay Abyssinia, home to large bands of heavily armed and quite ruthless raiders.

So Patterson invited two London friends to go along.

One of them was a woman.

James Audley Blyth was the younger son of Lord Blyth, one of the heirs to the Gilbey liquor fortune. Young Blyth had been an officer in Patterson's peacetime Yeomanry outfit, a Boer War veteran, and a passionate horse breeder.

Ethel Jane Brunner Blyth was the daughter of Sir John Tomlinson Brunner, a self-made millionaire and a staunch financial supporter of the Liberal Party, then in power. Ethel (Effie) Jane was in her late 20s, wealthy in her own right, willful, handsome if not beautiful.

The Blyths had one child, which they left in England. They no doubt seemed a happy enough aristocratic couple, however, there was a worm in the rose, one that Patterson did not apparently know about. James was an alcoholic. Perhaps this East African safari was meant to dry him out (he had reportedly been hospitalized with d.t.'s not long before.) Perhaps it signaled an attempt to repair damage done to his marriage by his drinking. Whatever the goal, the safari became a recipe for disaster.

They set out from Nairobi in February, 1908. Patterson led on a gorgeous white Arabian, Abdullah, followed by his old dog, Lurcher. The Blyths were horse people and also rode. (One of the affinities between Patterson and Ellie Blyth was their love of horses – his, of course, began when he was a groom. Another affinity was Ellie's money, which she had and Patterson almost certainly desired.) They went north, then west to avoid the hostile areas, hunting a little as they went. James wrote a letter home, describing the terror of tracking a lion in grass higher than his head, moving with the safety off the double rifle, not knowing where the animal was.

Ellie Blyth was the star of the safari. She turned out to be a brilliant shot who had no trouble handling a .450 express. The Samburu warriors, those gorgeous "butterflies" as the Masai call them, who prize carefully done hair, were stunned by Effie's long brown braids and eagerly touched her hair. Effie, wearing breeches like a man (most women in East Africa still hunted in skirts), rode and shot and dazzled.

And then James Audley Blyth got sick. First, he injured a foot; it healed over, abscessed, burst. He had to be carried on a litter. Effie and Patterson rode on ahead – together. James would get better for a day or two and totter around, even riding now and again, and then he would sweat and shake, and they would have to carry him again. He probably got malaria at some point, his alcohol-weakened immune system staggered under the twin blows of the abscess and disease.

287

The safari had by then turned east and north and reached the Ewaso Nyiro River. Patterson led them along the river to Neumann's Camp (about where Samburu Lodge is now), where the elephant hunter Alfred Neumann had had his base until his suicide two years before. There, Effie got sick and the dog Lurcher died. Patterson, in the dumps, tended both of the Blyths – in their tent or in his own (who knows, perhaps he dreamed of a different arrangement).

Effie improved, and they went on. Twice, they discussed the Blyths', or at least James', going back. But now they were so far away from any European contact that it was impossible to send the sick Englishman, who spoke no African languages, off by himself. Patterson may, in fact, have tried to make Blyth go back, leaving himself alone with Effie, surviving accounts are ambiguous on the point. The upshot was that all three of them went on, with an inevitable result.

Their rendezvous with tragedy was a place called Laisamis. It still has that name, a broad, gently rising flat surrounded by some shops and one-story buildings, in a rocky desert with a sand *lugga* trickling by and an Italian mission not far away. In 1908 there were no buildings and no missionaries, only some pools of water in the *lugga* and the great nowhere all around.

Two days before they reached Laisamis, they met the elephant. Patterson later said it was a rogue, a male made dangerous by isolation from the herd. James was riding that day, feeling a little better.

The three Europeans got down from their horses. Patterson told Effie to shoot, that it was her elephant – one of the few species she hadn't shot so far. She hit the bull twice with the .450, and it thundered into the bush. The two men went after it on foot while Effie stayed with the horses and the safari – a curious bit of sexism, as she would have been a far better companion in a tough situation than the sick Blyth. But by this time, a rivalry based on class and money and military rank may have developed between the two men, and Blyth may well have known he was now competing for his own wife. So he took the express rifle and set out.

And then they met the elephant and Patterson hit it twice with his Martini-Henry and then sent Blyth back to camp and went after the elephant alone. The next hour was perilous confusion as Patterson tracked the elephant, while the elephant tracked the safari. The natives told Effie that Patterson had been killed by the bull. Patterson was told Effie had been killed, and when he at last caught up with the beast, it was anticlimatically dead from its wounds.

The only real victim of the elephant was Patterson's prized Arabian. In one of its charges, the bull had put a tusk through the horse's vitals.

That night, the two men had a shouting argument, which Effie mediated. The ostensible subject was, apparently, the elephant's tusks. Patterson evidently wanted one as repayment for Abdullah. The real subject, not spoken, was nearer the heart and the lions.

But they patched it over and went on to Laisamis, where Blyth went out hunting and collapsed. Delirious and unable to stand, he was put to bed in his tent.

Effie spent that night – her first – in Patterson's tent.

In the morning Patterson exchanged a few civil words with James Blyth and then went to the center of the camp to oversee the loading. (There is no dispute on where he was.) Effie Blyth got up, dressed and crossed from Patterson's tent to her husband's.

And then conflicting testimony, gossip and speculation take over. Two things happened for sure, but people differ about which happened first. Effie screamed, and a gun went off. She may have actually been in the doorway. And she may have exchanged a few words with her husband.

Then Effie ran from the tent, and Patterson and his headman and the porters rushed to it, and they found James Audley Blyth with a gaping wound in his head, and a .450 revolver. Later, in Nairobi, the porters all testified that the wound was in the back of Blyth's head, and the gun was in his hand. Patterson, however, first testified that the wound was in the temple, and both he and headman Mwenyakai bin Diwani – who seems to have been the first inside the tent – testified that Patterson picked up the gun and handed it to the headman.

At which point somebody must have put it back in Blyth's hand, because that was where the porters saw it, with the muzzle in the dying man's mouth – unless they somehow saw it the instant before Patterson handed it to the headman. Or perhaps Patterson or Mwenyakai put it back into Blyth's hand so the porters could see the way it had been. At any rate, it seems impossible that a dozen or so porters all saw precisely the same thing and reported it in precisely the same words after only a second or two of looking. Far more likely – hence their use of the same words later – was their being made to see, with somebody (Patterson?) standing there and saying, "See? The point (the word they all used) is in his mouth and his thumb is on the trigger."

At Patterson's direction, they burned all of James Audley Blyth's clothes and papers, and they buried him in an intentionally shallow grave.

And Patterson took the safari on north, sharing his tent with Effie for the six weeks it took them to get up to Marsabit and back to Nairobi.

The ensuing scandal stunned Patterson and appalled Effie Blyth. Both left Nairobi after the most cursory of testimony, but they found no haven in London. Communications were good between the Protectorate and England, because many colonists had friends and relatives back home. By the summer Patterson was being accused in private of adultery and murder, with an official accusation of theft of government funds thrown in by the Nairobi administration (with good justification, it appears). The inquest (extra-legal, conducted by a Nairobi magistrate for lack of anybody else) gathered such testimony as it could, but there was no exhumation of the body, no visit to Laisamis, no forensic examination. Ironically, the Northern Game Reserve was outside normal jurisdictions, so there wasn't a legal mechanism for doing police work anyway.

An official verdict of suicide was issued; nonetheless, by the following year, as powerful a person as Winston Churchill was alleged to have said that he knew Patterson was guilty of theft, adultery and murder (Churchill, under-secretary of the Colonial Office when Patterson was appointed, had made an East African trip just before the event and had friends there).

Despite public exoneration in the House of Lords in 1909, Patterson had to resign his position, and he never went back to East Africa. Fate touched him again, however, when he took charge of the Jewish Transport Corps at Gallipoli. At this command he led the Jewish Legion in Palestine in 1918-19, which resulted in his enshrinement as a hero in modern Israel where his medals and uniforms are now in a museum.

Effie's wealthy father had engineered a complete cover-up on her part in both the affair and the death, a whitewash so complete that Lord Crewe, then the colonial secretary, wrote to an acquaintance that he had endangered his immortal soul by lying. (It was Crewe who had to assure the House that no crimes had been committed.) Papa Brunner cut a deal that had Patterson resigning and shutting up about Effie's role in exchange for the official exoneration.

Despite what the legend and the gossip later said, Patterson and Effie did not marry. Patterson was an ambitious man, certainly not above dreaming of being Effie's second husband, a millionaire's son-in-law. But it never happened. They did not run away together, as some people have reported since. They probably did not even see each other after 1909.

But in East Africa, the story survived, so vigorously that in 1934, professional hunter Philip Percival sat one night by the fire with an American client and told the moustached writer the story. And it clicked with Ernest Hemingway's ideas of courage and fidelity, and the tricky interplay between men and women.

Now, Phil Percival was the brother of Blayney, the man who lost his job as head of the game department to Patterson. He had good reason to despise Patterson. So it would not be surprising if his version made Patterson the villain. Yet, that is not the way Hemingway wrote it; quite the contrary. His Wilson, the professional hunter, is the terse arbiter of courage and male morality. Based on Bror Blixen and Phil Percival himself, he is a model Hemingway man. And in making the husband the victim of a gun fired by his wife, Hemingway may have picked up something suggested by Percival – that it was Effie, not Patterson, who shot James Audley Blyth. To do so, however, Percival would have had to be privy either to the official inquest records (not impossible, as the Nairobi government was as porous as a burlap sack) or to gossip from the safari porters themselves. At any rate, Phil Percival passed on the story in a version that allowed Hemingway to make

Phil's brother's old enemy the moral center.

As to what really happened in those few seconds in the tent at Laisamis, only three people could have known: Effie Blyth, Patterson and the headman Mwenyakai – and they never told. Did Ethel Jane Brunner Blyth step into her husband's tent, raise a revolver, and shoot the sleeping man in the back of the head? Or did she walk in to find him feverish and raving, a gun in his hand, accusations spilling from a mouth that he himself stopped with the pistol barrel and the shot?

We shall never know. One tantalizing fact persists: A year after the public whitewash, Patterson still had a sword to dangle over Papa Brunner's head, one that caused Lord Crewe to refer to him as "dangerous" and ultimately to warn him off. This threat could have been merely the facts of his and Effie's affair. Or it could have been a fact that only Patterson and Mwenyakai knew – the location of the pistol when they entered the tent.

The Irish groom, the honorary lieutenant-colonel, the hero of Tsavo, died in Los Angeles in 1947, taking his threats and secrets with him.

The Story Continues . . .

Patterson's killing of the infamous lions is told in The Man-Eaters of Tsavo *(1907). His very biased version of the events surrounding Blyth's death are in his book,* The Lure of Nyika *(1909). The story has been told in other versions than Hemingway's including Francis Brett Young's novel,* Woodsmoke *(1924), and J.A. Hunter's* Hunter *(1952), where Hunter made the connection with the Hemingway short story but named no names.*

The killing of the lions was the basis of the movie Bwana Devil *(1953). A version of Patterson's work on the Uganda Railway inspired the 1959 film,* Killers of Kilimanjaro.

The existing records of the actual events surrounding the Patterson-Blyth safari are scattered through a number of archives, including Britain's Public Records Office, half a dozen British universities, and the Library of Congress in Washington, D.C.

291

HORNED MOONS & SAVAGE SANTAS

A WINDY DAY

*On the days when the wind sounded a beckoning note, he
walked the upland fields to gather the harvest of November,
promises lost to the memory of yesterday.*

By Bob Cappelletti

t was a cold day, lonely and gray, its only pulse a blustery wind
that cut with ease through the thin November clouds. It randomly
lit the open field with streaking fingers of nervous light and
moved the fallow rye in corduroy waves that bounced along the
tree line to the creek bottom at its far edge. There, the old mill
house sagged in abandonment, far removed from a time when it
was busy and disconnected, like most things with purpose.
So many days ago.

I sipped my second cup of coffee slowly, and stared through the windshield,
dancing in the rye, back to another time.

I'd worked through two hot summers there, earning book money for school,
dragging sacks of meal over endless floorboards to the trolleys that ran to the
loading dock. The mill grist would hang in the summer heat like a hangover,
invasive, relentless, coating every hidden fold so that your skin seemed to crack
when you smiled, as if that act was repugnant to the responsibility that held you
there. The mill creek taught me the meaning of salvation, and like a habitual
sinner I was christened anew in its cool waters each day after the whistle blew.

293

Jeb nuzzled softly at my leg, impatient to be on with it, but I wanted to linger here a minute more. So many days.

Don't forget your gloves, son. It's a lot warmer in the truck than it is out there."

"Think we'll see birds, Dad?"

"The wind is awful hard on them, Joe. They'd rather run than fly. But don't worry, we'll roust those lazy old birds." We both laughed as I tickled his ribs. "Why, we've gotten one little lazy rooster up already. They'll fly . . . scout's honor."

He'd wanted to sleep, wanted to gather the last bit of warmth and innocence that can only be gotten from a child's bed. Even the smell of eggs and bacon frying on the big griddle hadn't budged him. Finally, I'd sent our big black Lab up to Joe's room, and soon the musical jingle of his collar trinkets was followed by the sound of little feet racing across the room. Joe had eaten quickly, and the three of us climbed into the truck and were soon riding in the darkness in silence, save the scratchy hum of tires on the oil and chip laid down by the county road gang last summer and the dog's steady, edgy panting from the floorboards at his feet.

Joe had just stared ahead, beyond the road to another place. I'd seen that same look on his face while waiting for his first ride on a school bus, and I knew he was working over the possibilities of the day, of his first time with the .410 that had been mine when I was working possibilities of my own. We finally came to the field at the edge of town as the morning light crested the horizon at our back, illuminating the frost-covered contours of the valley in a hoary brilliance that hurt to look at.

"Dad, why is it Saturday?"

"I don't rightly know son. I hadn't really ever thought about it. I suppose because yesterday was Friday."

A sudden gust buffeted the truck, and with it that low, soft siren song of the wind playing in the cracks died to nothing. As all memories do.

I took a last sip of coffee. It was time to walk. I always let the dog choose the way. Nose down and softly grunting, he worked the field in his typical journeyman fashion; wide sweep twenty yards to the left, cut back again to the right, stop, nose to the wind, move on. We crossed the stream and worked low into the bottom, paying particular attention to the thick tangles of locust snag and prickly briar. There, on the border of the creek, we'd taken holdover ringnecks from the neighboring gun club, jolted to the moment as they burst cackling from the weeds that bordered the warehouse ruins, hell-bent for the far side. But the day was proving desolate on many fronts.

I leaned on the back wall of the mill, by the low crook in the foundation ruins, exposed to grade on the creek side as high as the wild lilacs that had once grown there. On clear days the low November sun would bore into the mass of bluestone and mortar, providing a warmth so deep that it always made moving from that spot an act of great faith. Yet it was a lonely place, a place where seemingly even the wind was forbidden, and in the stillness and solitude, the dreams of a lifetime were visited upon the moment and all that you wished you'd said came flooding back, yet lay mute for the remembering.

It hadn't always been so. It had been a place of many words, where laughter floated like the flowered scent of soft spring evenings, and promises were carved into the future like the set of initials in the old cedar clapboards, now weathered and care-worn. It had been a mistake from the onset, but the proprieties had been observed. When Joe was three, she'd left behind the good china and a note saying that she was setting out to find what had not been mine to give.

Every year on Joe's birthday, a card arrived, each with a different postmark. Some were humorous, some were not, and I fancied that each somehow bore witness to the changing landscape of her personal drama, yet in the end I suppose it still came down to need. I dreamt once that I saw her through a storefront window as she judged her reflection in the hat department mirror, and it wasn't until she smiled that the vulnerability in her returned, and once again we were at this place where our love had lit fragile upon the lilac branches. But the dream fell, and I awoke as cold as the numbing mist now rising from the creek.

C'mon pop, can't stay here forever. I'm like to freeze.

I don't know why we always have to stop here anyway. I know you worked here as a kid and all, but the dog's got it covered. There's nothing here."

"I suppose. Least not any more. I guess it's time to throw out a few decoys."

"Now you're talking. Boy, I sure hope I have a son who'll keep me on track when my train slows down. And haul the gear."

"How about giving your old man a hand up? And we'll see who's on track when we get to Hansen's. Those greenheads should be just about done with the corn, and they'll be looking to light somewhere. If you can shoot as good as you talk, you might even come close to your old man!"

"No closer than we've always been, Pop."

"Ha! A teenager who gets up on time to go hunting is worth something, I suppose."

"Hey, as long as you get up, me and the dog will be there."

"Scout's honor?"

"Scout's honor, Pop."

Jeb and I made our way out of the bottom and crossed the low border wall into the rolling meadows of the Swede's farm. He'd passed several years before, and his family had chosen to tenant it out the first few years, but now the third son was making a go of it. As a boy, he had been his father's most faithful companion, and there wasn't a time that I visited this place that I did not find them together, working in silence, on those endless farm chores that are the very thing of it. He'd gone away to the war, and lived to tell. But he never did. It seemed like something had changed, for there was a perpetual sadness in his eyes and he shuffled like he'd already gone old in the joints.

I wondered at the purpose of it, for the boy never possessed that singular love of the land that binds a soul to it forever and sustains it through the hard times sure to come. Yet I still held hope for his labors, a selfish prayer for these fields, that I might have more time within them. For in the uniform rows and soft green grass there is a promise to the future, the simple assurance of order and continuity, so comforting to those of us for whom there is more behind than ahead.

We crested the little hummock that rolled slowly to the last rise before the swale, and went down the hill to the pond beyond the withered stands of silage. It was our private spot, a spot so good that you were always a little cautious when you got there, sneaking glances over your shoulder like spotting newcomers in Sunday pews. We would sit there once again, on apple crates amid the bulrushes, scanning the horizon until our eyes played tricks, silent hours passing easy like soft rain, awaiting the wings as they whistle-cut through the air, cupping to a soft chuckle. Yes, the sounds always come back.

You've been silent long enough, dad."
"That's what you do when you hunt."
"We've gotta talk about it sometime."
"I just don't know why you're poking the hornets nest."
"You're the one who taught me about what's right."
"Well I just wish I was as sure 'bout this as you are, son, but I'll be damned if I am. It doesn't seem so clear-cut this time out. Joe, bad news has a way of finding you all by itself. You go about your life, you work and you pray, you do right by all those you love, and still things got their own way. And they'll jump up and sting you on their own. And then you cry. No need to tempt it, son."
"Dad, it's done. I leave for basic training in a week."
"Like I said, what's there to talk about?"
"Nothing I guess. You just keep my crate warm. I'll be back, scout's honor."

The dog and I sat silently as the day played out, taking two greenheads and a teal, and though the birds weren't like they used to be, it didn't matter. It was enough just being in the fields, remembering the way of things, of what was and what would never be. Two Canada geese swung low off the far side and banked into a smooth glide across the mirrored pond, but I could never raise a gun to any pair. I had once heard the haunting wail of a lone mate, returning to the last known spot where they had been in tandem, calling, pleading for its one love. The dog shook in anticipation, but held fast.

"Not this time, Jeb. Hold . . . hold . . . easy . . . "

The geese picked up in a sudden burst of wings and water, honking in defiance as the Swede's son came running over the hill, lumbering over the low wall in his clumsy knee boots, getting tangled up with the dog who had run out in greeting and they both almost falling in the mud. As was his custom, he had come to survey those in his field, and satisfied, waved and left us to the remains of both this, and that particular day.

Hey Billy. What's got you so rumbled up?"

"Figured you and the dog would be here. Mr. Carston called . . . says to stop by the post office on your way home. Says it's real important."

No, there was too much here; it was time to move. I heeled up the dog and we walked, skirting the little pond, within the rolling swales, the gun cracked over my shoulder in official resignation. The return trip seemed to take longer, for the day had warmed slightly and as the wind eased back to a soft murmur within the trees, a velvet mist began to fall, and the air filled with the rising smell of the soil.

We paused at the old mill and once again I could feel the soft curve of her back, and the way my arm had fit in it so perfectly as we sat there, awash in the promise of our future, long before the loss, long before the knowledge that nothing is promised, least of all tomorrow.

As the Swede's son had promised, news awaited my return. One glimpse at the envelope, and I knew what it held for me, knew it as if it was a stone carried every day since birth. The government only seeks you out with bad news, and sends telegrams for the unbearable. Joe would be coming home, but our time together was done. He was buried on the last day of November, a day much like this one when we would have been working possibilities in the rye, on a day that should have been one of many more.

The years have kept patiently at their task, little daily concessions that diminish what once was the sum. Our black lab Buster is no more. He'd gone gray in the snout long before he stopped pacing the hallway by the door to Joe's room, and finally seemed content to lie in his cedar pillow by the back door, just waiting. His collar and tags hang by the mantel, and now Jeb waits by the back door.

There has been some comfort in the mounting dusk, but there are times, terrifying times, when I cannot remember the details, those vagrant parts of the soul which distinguish memory from dream. So I go to the fields, and on the days when the sun is low and the wind whistles through the cracks, I can recall what his voice sounded like, and the way his eyes crinkled when he smiled, and the feel of my hand in his hair, and once again there is an abundance of promise, if only in the moments we spent together that are now the harvest of my life.

I open the door to the truck and follow Jeb to our field. It is time to walk.

HIGH PERIL ON POLYCHROME MOUNTAIN

It was his last sheep hunt on the great mountain, and for two bone-chilling days he pursued the rams unrelentingly, from dawn to dark, scaling precipitous cliffs, inching across narrow ledges and sliding down icy slopes. An amazing adventure by one of our greatest hunters and naturalists.

By Charles Sheldon

arch 9. While climbing the mountains the past few days I had been uncomfortable because of warmer weather. It was a delight therefore to start out in the snapping cold, with the accompanying feeling of exhilaration. Several foxes had been running about and I noticed that one pair had kept together, ranging the lower slopes, always on the run. They were probably hunting ptarmigan. A large wolverine had eaten the poisoned bait and signs on the snow indicated that it had been very sick, yet it had gone upward toward Polychrome Mountain. I followed its trail and was disappointed to lose it among some bare areas high among the canyoned slopes.

Two bands of ewes were near when I descended, quickly frightening them. Going up the bar a couple of miles, I saw five rams – three with splendid heads – quite low near the saddle of Divide Mountain. They were in a position where they could easily have been stalked, but as neither of the coveted pair was among

299

them I kept on. The day was perfect, clear and calm, and the mountains were white and glistening in the bright sunlight – none of the fresh snow having yet been swept off. High on the slopes of the limestone mountain the two rams were seen, though too far off for me to distinguish their horns. Crossing to the west side of the bar I hastened forward, finding that they were the pair I was seeking, and in a position entirely favorable for a stalk, although so high that a long time would be necessary to accomplish it. Hurrying on for another mile I passed up a canyon and began a long dangerous climb. After three hours I had circled the slope to a point near the place where the rams had last been seen feeding.

The place was entirely in view but no rams were there. Working slowly around the craggy precipitous slope until satisfied that they had departed, I sat down to think the matter over. Suddenly two sheep appeared on the bar directly below me and my glasses revealed the pair I was stalking. They were soon joined by a yearling ram. The large ram with the close spiral led, the other two following and watching alertly in all directions. They stopped across the bar at the foot of Polychrome Mountain and began to feed. I was in plain sight high on the slope, but dared not move and had to remain for two hours, until they started upward on the rough slopes, giving me a chance to descend without alarming them. It was a long way and by the time I reached the bar it was too late to attempt to find them, then hidden high among the crags. So they would not see me, I waited until dark before starting back to the tent. It had been fascinating to sit high on the mountain on this fine clear day and watch the various bands of sheep. Conies [pikas] were abundant also, and their constant bleating had been the only sound breaking the silence of the mountain world.

Day after day while trying to approach these two rams my desire to get them had increased. Great care had been taken to keep my presence concealed from them and from the other sheep near by, yet now that they had crossed Polychrome Mountain it was doubtful whether they could again be found. I had not previously seen this wide-horned ram and thought that probably he belonged to a band occupying a feeding area well back in the rough jumble of mountains between Polychrome and the East Fork of the Toklat – a section I had not attempted to investigate. Like all the sheep, he and his companion were now working back to the feeding grounds they had occupied for seven months.

My snowshoe trail was well beaten for most of the way back, but hastening along in the dark, it was three hours before the camp was reached. There were now about eleven hours of daylight in which rifle sights could be seen.

March 10. The hunt for the two rams continued during another perfect day, without breeze or clouds, and the snowshoes creaked and squeaked as I sped along, exhilarated by the sharp cold air. From a point three miles up the Upper East Branch, the glasses revealed a band of sheep on the mountainside near the limestone peak, where I had attempted to stalk the rams the day before. Recognizing the possibility that they might have recrossed the bar to join these sheep, I thought it wise to take no chances and therefore tramped the mile across the bar in order to approach the area under cover of the slopes and at the same time keep watch of Polychrome Mountain. I had not gone a mile before the pair of rams were seen quietly feeding near the crest of the mountain, where they had last been seen the day before, and in a spot splendidly located for a favorable stalk. Recrossing the bar and advancing a couple of miles, I turned diagonally up the lower slope, leaving my snowshoes at the foot of the bluffs.

After putting on the creepers and pulling the straps extra tight, I began the ascent through great snowdrifts where it was most exhausting to force a way, and then up over icy slopes to the top of the bluffs. I remembered that when I had reached this spot in summer the continual chatter of ground squirrels filled the air, while now only the occasional bleat of a cony broke the stillness. I had gone but a short distance along the level top of the bluffs when the two rams walked out in plain sight on the farther brink of a canyon, and after looking about for a few moments, started upward, stopping now and then to crop a mouthful of food. I lay motionless on my side watching them. They kept ascending and finally walked faster, with a steady gait, and passed over the crest. I knew they had started for other ranges and that my only chance to get them was to continue following as long as daylight lasted. It was then noon and I rested while eating a good-sized piece of bread, at the same time watching the ewe bands high on the slopes across the bar. Although at that hour the temperature was about 10 below zero, the sun seemed to pour down delightful warmth.

I attacked the steep mountainside and worked upward, now struggling through a canyon, now through snow and broken rock until near the top, where the shale rose almost sheer for twenty feet with a perpendicular rimrock six feet high forming the crest. When studying the ascent from below no better spot had appeared, yet here I paused some time before attempting it. Then, with my rifle on my back and digging the ends of the creepers in the shale while holding on as best I could with gloved hands, I crawled up to the rock and found it loose and disintegrating.

I had taken two steps up by jamming the toes of the creepers between protruding pebbles and holding on with bare hands, and was placing my third foothold when the pebble on which my creeper was resting fell, and the stone I was grasping above began to loosen. The slope fell so precipitously for a thousand feet that I could not jump back without falling and dashing downward. After a moment of fearful suspense I managed to change my handhold, and by a scramble, succeeded in getting a good grip on the rim, where I held firmly as the rocks under my feet gave way. Drawing my body up, with elbows over the rim, I lifted myself up, swung one knee on the edge, and was soon on top. The sense of serious danger had been so strong and the exertion so great that I rested awhile to recover.

I walked to the point where the rams had disappeared and saw sections of their trail on the snow, passing over spur after spur toward the ranges that flank the divide of the East Fork of the Toklat. I followed their tracks, now and then pausing to view new areas of rough mountains – the silence unbroken save by the bleats of the conies. The canyons were deep, some more than a thousand feet. Passing over one spur and descending a deep canyon, I climbed over another spur as high as the mountain crest; and so kept toiling up and down, often losing the trail on the bare spaces and consuming time in regaining it.

After tramping over three spurs I could see the trail ahead crossing a very rough country and leading to a basin at the source of a tributary of the East Fork. Three more canyons and spurs were passed before I reached the crest of a mountain leading out at right angles from the main range. Then I saw the two rams three-quarters of a mile below, quietly feeding near the bottom of a basin, where the ground appeared checkered from the holes they had made in pawing away the snow. They were in a splendid place for a stalk, and my eagerness was intense as I dropped back below the crest and descended diagonally over the crusted snowbanks to the bottom of a canyon, where I slid rapidly downward to a point opposite them. Then began an ascent of three hundred feet on hard crust, where it was impossible to avoid making a noise. Pausing below the crest, with rifle ready but fearful that the rams, now within easy shot, had heard my footsteps, I crept forward and slowly arose. What was my dismay to behold them out of range on the crest of a lower ridge and taking a course back toward Polychrome Mountain!

There was nothing to do but take up the trail and again follow it. The rams were steadily traveling, keeping well ahead, always out of sight. Up over a mountain I climbed and then down, up again and through rough canyons, passing three high spurs and coming to the brink of a vast basin with walls almost perpendicular, separating the last spur from Polychrome Mountain. The rams had descended into it and had gone directly up the icy rock of the other side – how, I can never know. I saw them just below the crest, nearly opposite me. They stood in sharp outline against a golden sky, and going down on the other side, passed out of sight.

In order to reach the mountain I had to travel a long distance on the crest of the spur, broken by sharp crags and spired peaks. The sheep trail wound around on dangerous slopes, yet I was able to keep on it. Nearer the mountain the surface was less broken and here a large band of sheep had entered the trail, probably two days before. I was surprised to see a wolverine track following it – made apparently just after the sheep had passed. It is not improbable that the animal was following and hunting the sheep.

I reached the crest of Polychrome Mountain three miles north of where I had earlier ascended it, and half a mile south of the point where the rams had disappeared. Pushing along on the narrow rim, broken by fantastic pinnacles, I picked up the trail of the rams and cautiously followed to a peak rising from the crest, which I ascended and peered over. There, about three hundred and fifty yards ahead, was another sharp peak on the summit of which stood both rams, looking directly at me. Their alert attitude indicated clearly that they had seen me; they knew I was following them. The sight was impressive, but I was deeply disappointed at the thought that my long hunt would probably end in failure. They quickly turned and went below the peak. I followed, still going as cautiously and noiselessly as possible, and mounted the peak they had been standing on. They were watching from another peak about the same distance ahead, both looking at me as my head rose inch by inch into the line of vision. After a moment they turned and disappeared. The peak they were on was near the north end of the mountain and was the culmination of a great buttress that jutted well out from the crest, from which high cliffs on three sides fell away to precipitous slopes below. I realized at once that the rams might reach parts of the cliffs inaccessible to man and hide there, safe from sight or approach.

ith renewed hope however I went forward, cautiously climbing the peak, and found that their tracks were not visible either in the snow beyond, or anywhere below. It was evident that they were hiding on the cliffs; and after a short inspection I concluded they were on the north side. But finding no approach on that side, I turned and carefully inspected the south side. At first I tried to work forward near the crest, but was blocked by a smooth wall. Then, a little lower down, another possible route was attempted. It was very cold, my hands were numb, the sun had been down for a long time and darkness was at hand. Step by step I worked along the cliff, finding footholds or handholds among loose and doubtful rocks, with a perpendicular wall falling two hundred feet below me. With forced disregard of the danger of returning in darkness, I kept on till within twenty feet of the end, where the other side could be seen. I was making some noise when I reached it and before looking over paused to compose myself. It was too dark to see through the peep sight of the rifle, so I put up the open sight. The silence was complete; the slopes below were indistinct; the mountain crests were shadowy forms in the vast space leading to Denali – the great summit alone illumined by the sun.

Creeping upward and pushing my rifle forward, I slowly raised my head. There, only a hundred feet along the cliff and thirty feet below the top, were the two rams. They were lying side by side on a rock shelf jutting out from the wall, their breasts at the very edge, more than a hundred feet of sheer space below. They had heard me and both were looking at me as my eyes reached the line of sight.

The picture of these wild rams left an impression that will ever remain. My rifle quickly covered the nearest ram – the one with the close spiral – and as the report echoed and re-echoed, he stretched out convulsed, while the other sprang to his feet. Before he could run I fired again and he also dropped, but slowly rose again. At another shot he fell over the edge at the exact instant the other did; both shooting down through the air together, bouncing as they struck the slope below, and continuing downward for *three thousand feet* – their course marked by the snow that was tossed up like patches of vapor.

There was no time to rest, smoke my pipe, or enjoy the landscape, for though in a state of highly wrought exhilaration I instantly realized the seriousness of the situation – caught in the dark on the side of a cliff, with the cold of night rapidly increasing. I started back for a few feet in a very faint light, hoping to find some spot where I could sit, and if necessary remain all night. My squirrel-skin parka in the rucksack might possibly prevent me from freezing. I did find a spot, a very small one, and after putting on the parka, took my position. When my body was warm I began to feel for loose rocks, with the idea of placing them below me so that in case of being overcome with sleep, I would not slide downward, but could not find any. After a while the sky in the east began to brighten, then moonlight touched some of the rocks on the crest, reviving hope that later it might light the cliff sufficiently for me to leave. An hour passed, a fine half-moon rose in the clear sky, the snowfields were illumined between the black shadowy spaces, and light shone directly on the cliff.

My legs and feet were cold, but after stamping to start the circulation, and with rifle slung on my back, I moved step by step, often securing footholds in the dark spaces by feeling, and gradually arrived at a place I did not believe it possible to cross in the faint light. But a few feet below was a rift in the cliff lighted by the moon and showing a snow slope descending at a very sharp incline.

After some hesitation I let myself down and found a hard crust. Unslinging the rifle and using it to make footholes in the hard snow, I worked down to the bed of the canyon. Now that I was in the snow my relief was intense, for I knew that if necessary I could make a snow house and probably keep from freezing. The canyon about a hundred feet below was walled on both sides, and working my way through the narrow space I found the snow sloping smoothly almost to the foot of the mountain. Still holding the rifle as a brake, I sat down and slid rapidly, in a short time reaching a gentle slope close to the spot where the tumbling rams had landed. The joy and relief of that moonlight slide through the steep canyon, after the experiences of that day, can never be repeated.

At the spot where I had stopped was a smooth path in the snow, apparently made by some object sliding from the side of the canyon, Going up the opposite side I found the rams, their horns uninjured, the snow matted in their coats and glistening under the moon. Returning, I had not gone more than twenty feet down the smooth incline when I came upon a large male wolverine, frozen stiff. He was the one that had taken my poisoned bait the day before. After crossing the slope for two miles and just before reaching the cliffs a thousand feet above, he had died and rolled down.

I was too elated to mind the tramp of two miles to recover my snowshoes, or the longer tramp back to the tent, where the cheer of tea, food and warmth awaited me. That was my last hunt for sheep in the northern wilderness. The heads of these two rams now hang on my walls, constantly reminding me of the experiences of that day.

"High Peril on Polychrome Mountain" is from Charles Sheldon's Wilderness of Denali, *originally published in 1930 by Charles Scribner's Sons and reprinted in 2000 by The Derrydale Press.*

CHRISTMAS FOR TWO

He had set out into the swirling snow and biting wind to gather the family's traditional holiday dinner. But what he brought back was much more than a few ducks.

By Edmund Ware Smith

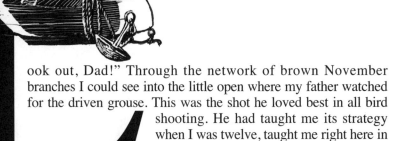

ook out, Dad!" Through the network of brown November branches I could see into the little open where my father watched for the driven grouse. This was the shot he loved best in all bird shooting. He had taught me its strategy when I was twelve, taught me right here in the old Atkinson cover.

He stood alert and calm, feet close together, gun forward in position of easy readiness, his left hand well out under the barrels. Then he saw the bird, and the gun moved in that clean, smooth swing for which he was noted. But this time, part way through the motion, there was a jerk of uncertain coordination. He fired twice, and kept turning away from me as he followed the bird's flight. He had missed again!

Stiffly, as though his legs hurt, he walked to an old apple tree and leaned against it. I scrambled over the stone wall and broke through the blackberry briars that separated us. Dad smiled. He opened his gun and removed the smoking shells – but he did not reload.

"It's my legs, Jimmy. They're tired – dead tired. They ache."

"But, Dad –"

The wind stirred a lock of silver-white hair that curled below his hatbrim: "Don't get excited. It's nothing but what most old fellows get. It's rheumatism."

This tall, fine-eyed man to whom I belonged; who had taught me grouse and wildfowl shooting; who had held my wrist while I caught my first trout; who had taught me to *walk*; this man – my father – was suddenly gone old before me, white-haired, sunken cheeked, and seventy! "Why – Dad!"

He leaned heavily on a low limb, taking the weight off his legs. "Hush-hush, now. It's nothing at all."

I had to help him home. He wouldn't go the shortcut – afraid someone would see him leaning on me, or see the muscles of his face drawn taut with pain. We went by Blanchard's wood road and up Hickory Lane along the marshes. The only person we saw was one of the Tibido children, a hungry, tousle-headed urchin of seven – barefooted, the first of November!

Dad never let on he had seen the child until I got him home and into his chair. Then he said: "I'm afraid we won't be able to do much for the Tibidos this Christmas."

Already Dad had begun to think of that!

I can remember as many as thirty of us around the long dinner table: Grandfather always carved the game which Dad and my older brothers had shot for the occasion. Grandfather would say: "Henry (that's Dad), is this knife as sharp as you can get it?" Dad would say "Yes, sir," but grandfather would pick up the steel and whet away for five minutes while our mouths watered. "There now, I guess we're ready," he'd finally remark, and plunge the knife into the breast of the roast goose or black duck, peering critically at the issuing juices to determine if the bird was properly done. Invariably it was. So grandfather would part his whiskers with practiced accuracy and say: "A-h-h-h!" and of course the womenfolk would all congratulate one another on their cooking.

Cranberry sauce, four vegetables, a sideboard creaking under its burden of assorted pies, cakes, fruits – and cider pitchers.

At Christmas dinner, the pièce de résistance was game – traditionally shot by members of the Osborn family. But the real ceremony, the welding of the Christmas spirit, came on Christmas Eve. That was Mother's. Every year she went down to the Tibido's shanty laden with baskets of food, the rest of us following with presents for the children. The Tibido children worshipped Mother. She gave because she loved to give, and they knew it.

After supper, at home, we sang *Hark, the Herald Angels*, *Holy Night* and *Little Town of Bethlehem* – accompanied by Uncle Alden on the melodeon. Then we gathered by the fire while Mother read Dickens' *A Christmas Carol* aloud. That was the final rite, and it seemed to bind us all inseparably.

She read by candlelight, and by the glow from the fire – tipping the book just a trifle to catch its light. Invariably she began with the same words, spoken in the same reverent voice: "Well, children – this is *A Christmas Carol*, by Charles Dickens." Mother had read that moving masterpiece each Christmas since I was old enough to listen. I think I could recite it all from memory.

Firelight! Marley's ghost rattling its chains while children listened in wide-eyed wonder. Once Uncle Alden went to sleep and snored. And once grandfather became so enraged over Scrooge's stinginess that he rose from his chair, thumping with his cane, and growling through his whiskers, "I'll pound that fellow to a pulp!" Nearly everyone was moist-eyed with sympathy for Bob Cratchit and Tiny Tim. You would see a handkerchief whisking upward now and then. On the rug, as close to the fire as they could get, slept our three foxhounds – Moby, Belle and Trailer. They twitched, concerned only with their dreams of primitive triumphs.

Most of all, I remember the expression in my father's eyes. This was his day of days. I can only guess at his deep, inarticulate happiness. Under those smoky, hand-hewn beams his family had grown, branched and matured. Devotion to its meaning, and gratitude for its unity and goodness, overflowed his heart and shone from the depths of his eyes. The Christmas Eve reunion was, I think, a reward for his renowned generosity.

Then, bit by bit, the reward diminished. First the War, and my two brothers lost. My sisters married and moved away. One by one the rooms were vacated, rooms from which for generations we had watched the seasons ebb and flow. Then Mother died – and this was to be our first Christmas without her.

The Tibido urchin had reminded Dad too abruptly of this. I could almost feel the hurt of his thoughts: the Osborn tradition washed up. Nothing left but an album full of tintypes, a basket of last year's tree decorations and a sheaf of newspaper clippings describing the liquidation of the Osborn cordage business. One of those clippings said: *Henry Osborn to settle one hundred cents on the dollar*. Dad did. He *would*. It left him almost nothing.

"No," I said to him now, "guess we can't help the Tibidos this year." Impetuously, I added: "Why don't you sell the old place? It's too big for us – now."

He looked at me with a slow far-away smile. The tiny wrinkles gathered at the corners of his eyes. "No, we can fill it Jimmy."

For days I could hear his voice saying that. Then the sound dimmed in the harsh practical clatter of my young and struggling business. By the 23rd of December I had forgotten what Dad said. I shouldn't have, for it was evidence of the strange hope within him. On the night of the 23rd I bought a dressed turkey from the market, and subsequently worked late in my office over a stack of bungled invoices. I bought that turkey because a submerged intuition hinted that Christmas dinner of wild game – for Dad and me, alone – would be like salting a wound. I went home late, feeling pretty grim.

In the inky dark of the front hall I stumbled over something, and switched on the light. There, arranged with patience and precision, was my duck hunting outfit. Not a detail was lacking, because it was laid out by an old master. Two dozen black duck decoys, tarred lines neatly wound and tied, anchor weights in perfect shape; hat, gunning coat, sweater, boots and gloves; Uncle Alden's historic old double gun; a box of chilled sixes; my duck call; a water bottle and box of sandwiches; row locks and oars – everything. On the table was the boathouse key and under the key a note:

"Be sure to hunt down all cripples. Lead 'em plenty.

"Don't use the duck call too much. Set out at Brick Oven Creek – and bring home the Osborn Christmas dinner! Good luck and good night. Your father."

Oh, time-honored advice – and between its matter-of-fact lines, my father's hunger to carry on a tradition through me! It wrung my heart. The first thing I did was to hide that turkey in the cold shed. If Brick Oven Creek failed to produce, I could always re-discover the turkey. But my prayers to the red gods were for black duck.

M orning on the marsh: A thin arm of red reached down the East, a shaft in a lead-gray sky. Gulls wheeled in, a warning from the open sea. Crows pitched and tumbled in the gusts. The ragged waves followed fast upon each other, and all of them bared their teeth in the salt wind which stung my eyelids.

Ghostly to be sitting there in the old blind at the mouth of Brick Oven! Forty years ago Dad's two brothers had built it of cedar stakes, wire and marsh thatch. Here, with the very gun I hugged across my chest, Uncle Alden had brought down three geese. Uncle Jim, for whom I was named, had rowed home from this blind with a mixed bag about which, after thirty years, the natives still speak. I had shot my first duck from this very set-out, father beside me to temper my ten-year-old excitement.

Abruptly now, through the swirling snowflakes, five blacks whipped down, their feet braced and wings set to the wind for landing. They nearly caught me reminiscing, but I dropped the farthest one and that gave me time to swing onto the nearest one as he flared. I doubled.

By the time I had pulled the grab from the mud flat and launched the skiff, the downed birds had vanished. Wind and snow made a bad business of retrieving. I ought to get a spaniel. When I located the birds, I was about half lost. I knew the wind direction, but had to guess at the angle back to the creek mouth. It was blind rowing, the snow thick and stinging. I never felt more lonely in my life, but I got back to my blind, bringing the foundation of the Osborn Christmas dinner. Two fat redlegs – northern blacks, down from the sub-arctic.

I cannot explain the scarcity of ducks that day of traditional duck hunters' weather – wind, cold, snow. Perhaps the birds had taken refuge in the fresh water ponds, inland. Once I started up, trembling to the call of wild geese, a big flock lost in the whirlpools of the sky. But I never saw them, and their weird, forlorn honking grew inaudible as they searched for haven.

At two o'clock, as the abnormally high tide started to ebb, I got another chance. Low to the water, a redleg came racing straight down the creek, the gale on his beam. My first barrel was ten feet over him. The second connected while the bird was almost stationary, beating back against the wind.

My last chance was the one which got me into trouble. A pair whistled over from behind me – just luck that I saw them at all. I got one of them by remembering to hold well under. The bird crumpled, but from then on the snow swallowed it. I merely guessed as to where it struck the water. Four birds, past three o'clock, and getting dark fast. Marking the direction of the fallen bird, I hastily took in the set, tossed the blocks into the skiff, and shoved off.

I rowed steadily for ten minutes, counting myself lucky to find the bird. Then, in my mind, I fumbled for the direction home, and I felt as if I were the last man on earth. I couldn't see thirty yards in any direction, and the weird curlicues in the water overside told of a raging tide rip. That, added to ten minutes hard rowing and a northeast gale – all moving in the same direction – had me bewildered on the matter of distance. I guessed myself over a mile from the Brick Oven blind and pulled cross-tide for shore. I figured to make land between Martin's Slough and the Town Bridge and pulled for an hour until it was black dark. You couldn't tell whether you were two yards or two miles from shore.

I stopped rowing and listened, but I could hear nothing above the wind. It was like being marooned on a cloud at midnight, and on every hand I felt the turbulence of the sky. I was properly scared when, suddenly, an oar touched bottom, and an instant later the boat beached violently.

I didn't have the faintest notion where I was, and this taught me something about being lost. You can plant your feet on ground you've trod since boyhood – and you won't recognize it! I saw a light, and after hauling up the skiff, picked up my four birds and headed toward it uncertainly. I was pretty well fagged, dazed by the wind, my face like chilled putty. I actually knocked on the door of that lighted house before I recognized it – the Tibido's poverty-stricken home! I was two miles off course!

From inside an excited child's voice cried out at my knock, her irony all unwitting: "It's Santy Claus! Santy Claus! Oh, mother! Open the door quick!"

Mrs. Tibido opened the door and I stumbled into the close warmth of the little kitchen. For speaking purposes my lips were useless, but I managed a gum-rubber smile for the circle of rapt expectant faces, young and old. Mrs. Tibido wiped her hands on her apron, and offered me one of them. I took the thin fingers in mine.

"We knew you'd come!" she said, happily, "All day the children have been expecting you, Mr. Jimmy."

"Merry Christmas," I mumbled.

That rather broke the ice, and the children rallied around tugging at me and begging me to come and see their Christmas tree. It would have cut you like a rusty knife! A spruce bush stuck in a cracked flower pot with white grocer's twine doing double duty as tinsel and snow. I shook some real snow off my hat onto the "tree." It glistened briefly, and the children's eyes danced.

You know what I did, of course. It was an impulse, I suppose – but it was a Christmas impulse. Anyone would have done the same thing. And it *did* add its mite toward perpetuating a tradition that mankind holds sacred – I mean the Christmas tradition. I left the four black ducks behind, and went my weary way homeward! The Tibidos totaled seven, counting their mauled kitten. The four ducks would assure them all of plenty. And Dad and I could have the turkey I had hidden in the cold shed. It was a fine plump turkey, and even though it wasn't bagged by one of the two remaining Osborns, it would taste good to them. I made a rather bad job of whistling through chapped lips.

Dad was out somewhere when I got home, so I took a hot shower and gradually came back to life. I shaved and dressed and got downstairs just as Dad came in the front door. He was leaning heavily on his cane, but the eagerness in his eyes was jovially apparent. He wanted to know all about my duck hunt.

"Come on," he insisted. "Out with it!"

I described each detail, each bird, the look and feel and smell of the marsh. I told him of getting lost in the storm. He was thirsty for every last drop of description. He sat gazing into the fire, his lips wrinkling with his own reminiscences. "Good!" he said, quietly. "It's good for a man to come face to face with the elements. It gives him respect for them, and for himself. Let's see the ducks."

I had been so long expecting that demand, that when the words actually came, I almost dodged. Just how could I explain the missing ducks, the even graver matter of the forbidden turkey in the cold shed – in the face of my father's intense eagerness?

"Well, Dad," I started, haltingly, "I bought a turkey yesterday. But when I got home late last night to find you had laid out my shooting gear, I knew you'd rather it was black ducks – for old time's sake, shot by an Osborn. So I hid the turkey, Dad – like a thief hiding loot. Then, tonight, when I saw the Tibidos, and the kids' Christmas tree, something got hold of me. I – I thought of Mother, and you, and other Christmases, and they all lumped together inside of me. But – anyway, we've got that turkey, Dad."

It was a solemn moment for me, that Christmas Eve.

So when father started to chuckle, then burst abruptly into laughter, I was a little confused and disturbed. But I think he divested himself of fifteen years during that laugh, the first truly good one I had heard from him since

Mother's death. It came right from the deep part of him.

He got his cane, and, still chuckling, went to the sideboard for the decanter and two small glasses. He filled the glasses and handed me one, lifting his own to his lips: "Here's to our Christmas, and to the Tibido's Christmas. They've got the ducks – *and* the turkey! God bless them, every one!"

"What turkey?" I asked, stupidly.

"*The* turkey! I was rummaging in the cold shed this morning, and found it. I've just come from the Tibido's now. I gave it to them!"

"But they wouldn't take *both*," I cried, half angrily.

"Of course they wouldn't. They didn't know. And I didn't know you gave them the ducks – not until after I'd given them the basket. I had wrapped the turkey so they couldn't tell what it was, just as Mother always did."

"Oh, Dad! If Mother were only here to share this with us!" I said, and I could have bitten out my tongue! Dad just nodded. He was thinking, too, that it was the sort of thing she'd appreciate.

That Christmas Eve had a kind of solemn splendor to it. Father and I were happy in a strange, moving way. The evening had a rare quality which makes your heart glad, and makes your throat hurt, too. Mine was glad when Dad said: "We'll have ham and eggs for Christmas dinner. In this instance, finer even than turkey or black duck!" And my throat hurt when, after lighting the candles, he sat in Mother's chair by the fire; when he reached up and took the book from the wall cupboard; when he opened it, leaning just a trifle to catch the light; when he looked up once at the emptiness of the great room, at the smoky hand-hewn beams, and at the memories that dwelt forever in those shadows. My throat hurt unbearably when he looked into the fire, and began: "Well, children – Jimmy – this is *A Christmas Carol*, by Charles Dickens . . ."

"Christmas for Two" originally appeared in Edmund Ware Smith's A Tomato Can Chronicle, *1937. Reproduced courtesy Derrydale Press, Lanham, Maryland.*

ACKNOWLEDGEMENTS

The publisher wishes to thank the following Sporting Classics *readers, staffers and senior editors who helped to select the stories for this anthology. They include: Jim Casada, Larry Chesney, Tom Davis, Mike Gaddis, Ken Kirkeby, Albert Mull, Ryan Stalvey and Todd Tanner. A special thanks to Minnesota artist and longtime friend Dan Metz for his superb black-and-white drawings, for our cover and throughout this book.*
– Chuck Wechsler, publisher